THE STAR WARS LIBRARY
PUBLISHED BY DEL REY BOOKS

STAR WARS: THE ESSENTIAL GUIDE TO DROIDS
STAR WARS: THE ESSENTIAL GUIDE TO ALIEN SPECIES
STAR WARS: THE ESSENTIAL GUIDE TO PLANETS AND MOONS
STAR WARS: THE NEW ESSENTIAL CHRONOLOGY
STAR WARS: THE NEW ESSENTIAL GUIDE TO CHARACTERS
STAR WARS: THE NEW ESSENTIAL GUIDE TO VEHICLES AND VESSELS
STAR WARS: THE NEW ESSENTIAL GUIDE TO WEAPONS AND TECHNOLOGY

STAR WARS ENCYCLOPEDIA
A GUIDE TO THE STAR WARS UNIVERSE
STAR WARS: DIPLOMATIC CORPS ENTRANCE EXAM
STAR WARS: GALACTIC PHRASE BOOK AND TRAVEL GUIDE
I'D JUST AS SOON KISS A WOOKIEE: THE QUOTABLE STAR WARS
THE SECRETS OF STAR WARS: SHADOWS OF THE EMPIRE

THE ART OF STAR WARS: A NEW HOPE
THE ART OF STAR WARS: THE EMPIRE STRIKES BACK
THE ART OF STAR WARS: RETURN OF THE JEDI
THE ART OF STAR WARS: EPISODE I: THE PHANTOM MENACE
THE ART OF STAR WARS: EPISODE II: ATTACK OF THE CLONES
THE ART OF STAR WARS: EPISODE III: REVENGE OF THE SITH

SCRIPT FACSIMILE: STAR WARS: A NEW HOPE
SCRIPT FACSIMILE: STAR WARS: THE EMPIRE STRIKES BACK
SCRIPT FACSIMILE: STAR WARS: RETURN OF THE JEDI
SCRIPT FACSIMILE: STAR WARS: EPISODE I: THE PHANTOM MENACE

STAR WARS: THE ANNOTATED SCREENPLAYS
ILLUSTRATED SCREENPLAY: STAR WARS: A NEW HOPE
ILLUSTRATED SCREENPLAY: STAR WARS: THE EMPIRE STRIKES BACK
ILLUSTRATED SCREENPLAY: STAR WARS: RETURN OF THE JEDI
ILLUSTRATED SCREENPLAY: STAR WARS: EPISODE I: THE PHANTOM MENACE

THE MAKING OF STAR WARS: EPISODE I: THE PHANTOM MENACE
MYTHMAKING: BEHIND THE SCENES OF STAR WARS: EPISODE II: ATTACK OF THE CLONES
THE MAKING OF STAR WARS: EPISODE III: REVENGE OF THE SITH

STAR WARS

The New Essential Chronology

STAR WARS®

The New Essential Chronology

TEXT BY DANIEL WALLACE
(WITH KEVIN J. ANDERSON)

ILLUSTRATIONS BY
MARK CHIARELLO
TOMMY LEE EDWARDS
JOHN VAN FLEET

LUCAS BOOKS

DEL REY

BALLANTINE BOOKS
NEW YORK

A Del Rey Books Trade Paperback Original

Published in the United States by Del Rey Books, an imprint of
The Random House Publishing Group, a division of Random
House, Inc., New York.

Library of Congress Cataloging-in-Publication Data

Wallace, Daniel.
Star wars : the new essential chronology / text by Daniel
Wallace ; illustrations by Mark Chiarello, John Van Fleet, and
Tommy Lee Edwards.
p. cm. — (The Star wars library)
ISBN 0-345-49053-3 (alk. paper)
1. Star Wars films—Chronology. I. Title. II. Series.
PN1995.9.S695W37 2005
791.43'75—dc22   2005041325

Printed in the United States of America on acid-free paper

www.starwars.com
www.delreybooks.com

2 4 6 8 9 7 5 3

Frontispiece art by Tommy Lee Edwards
Galaxy map created by Ian Fullwood

Interior design by Michaelis/Carpelis Design Associates Inc.

DANIEL WALLACE
To Grant

JOHN VAN FLEET
To Grace and Mae

TOMMY LEE EDWARDS
This one's for Iain Morris

MARK CHIARELLO
To John Van Fleet, my brother

Author's Acknowledgments

This book would not have been possible without the input and inspiration provided by others. Thanks to Steve Saffel, Keith Clayton, Erich Schoeneweiss, Colette Russen, Sylvain Michaelis, and Colleen Lindsay at Del Rey; Amy Gary, Jonathan Rinzler, Sue Rostoni, Leland Chee, and Pablo Hidalgo at Lucasfilm; Tommy Lee Edwards, Mark Chiarello, John Van Fleet, and Ian Fullwood for their amazing illustrations; and Jim Luceno, Haden Blackman, Abel Peña, Enrique Guerro, Jason Fry, Christopher McElroy, Michael Potts, and Bob Vitas for their advice and for the Star Wars resources they have written.

Finally, thanks to George Lucas for creating this universe, and for ending the movie saga in style with Revenge of the Sith. Lucas's imagination provided the backdrop for the other authors whose work is summarized in this volume, demonstrating that the *Star Wars* storytelling galaxy is a dynamic and welcoming place.

CONTENTS

Introduction to Students of History

History survives only if it is recorded. This was true when Palpatine's Empire purged thousands of years of records from the galactic archives, and it is even more important today, in the wake of the Yuuzhan Vong invasion that saw the destruction of the great library of Obroa-skai. More than ever, it is vital that historians assemble a formal account for future generations.

Fortunately, new data caches have been uncovered since the HoloNet rel ease of the first edition of this chronicle. Holes have been plugged and gaps filled in as untold information on the Clone Wars, the extermination of the Jedi, and the nature of the ancient Republic has come to light. Often we have interviewed surviving eyewitnesses to history to gain a personal perspective on galactic events. And, of course, the recent events of the Yuuzhan Vong war and its aftermath have been recorded while the wounds are still fresh.

The resulting chronicle covers more than thirty millennia of history, from the Rakatan Infinite Empire to the rise of the Jedi Knights; from the Sith War to the Clone Wars; from the death of the Republic to the birth of the new Jedi order.

In this, the thirty-sixth year since the destruction of the first Death Star that marks our calendar's zero point, it is even more apparent that we study the rich and glorious tradition of our past, and also remember the many dark mistakes. We must learn from both.

Voren Na'al, Archivist Emeritus
Historical Council, Galactic Federation of Free Alliances

A NOTE ON DATING CONVENTIONS

The years in this document are marked according to the new standard convention, which uses the Battle of Yavin as its zero point. This event, which saw the destruction of the first Death Star and the dawning of a new hope for the people of the galaxy, represents the symbolic beginning of our current society. Events that precede this event are indicated B.B.Y., while those after are noted as A.B.Y.

For an extensive list of historical resources visit www.starwars.com.

STAR WARS

The New Essential Chronology

PART ONE

Tales of the Ancient Republic

FORMATION OF THE REPUBLIC

THE PRE-REPUBLIC ERA
CIRCA 100,000–25,000 B.B.Y

Before its transformation into the Empire, the Old Republic stood for twenty-five thousand years. Its citizens liked to entertain the illusion that theirs was the only such civilization that had ever existed, but archaeologists have confirmed that this is certainly not true. Few details of the great powers of the pre-Republic era have survived, but what is known about the rise and fall of these societies provides us with the object lesson that no culture lives forever.

One of the earliest and most potent cultures can be identified only by the colossal objects it left behind. At some point that cannot be positively identified, these mysterious Architects created the Corellian Star system, tractoring its five planets into place around the star Corell, using the repulsorlift engine Centerpoint Station. The Architects may also have been responsible for the Maw, an unlikely cluster of black holes located near Kessel, and are believed to have frightened the advanced Sharu people of the Rafa system into adopting a forced culture of primitivism. The Architects populated the planets of the Corellian system with Dralls and Selonians, as well as humans—an ambitious species believed to have originated on the Core world of Coruscant.

Coruscant's humans may have come into dominance on their homeworld by defeating a near-human, gray-skinned species known as the Taungs in several series of legendary battles. The humans, who comprised the thirteen nations of the Battalions of Zhell, suffered an almost extinction-level defeat when a sudden volcanic eruption smothered their encampment. The towering plume of black ash loomed over the Taung army for two years, and the awed Taungs took the name Warriors of the Shadow—or, in the ancient tongue, *Dha Werda Verda*. The Battalions of Zhell recovered and claimed Coruscant for their own, while the Taungs may have become the Mandalorians, judging from what we have learned concerning similarities between the Mandalorian language and surviving Taung texts.

In the galactic Core, the big-brained Columi species achieved interstellar spaceflight approximately one hundred thousand years ago, and surveyed the "primitive" people of Coruscant and Duro before returning to a sheltered life on their homeworld of Columus. In the Outer Rim, the Gree civilization flourished, creating strange marvels of alien technology that have never been duplicated. The Gree reached their apex during the same era as the Columi, but modern Gree have been reduced to mere caretakers of decaying wonders. In opposition to the Gree empire, the reptilian Kwa constructed Infinity Gates, which allowed them to teleport between worlds. Unknown factors led to the decline of the Kwa, and their descendants eventually became the simpleminded Kwi lizards of Dathomir.

Approximately thirty thousand years B.B.Y., a species known as the Rakata achieved the highest extent of their own expansion. The Rakatan "Infinite Empire" stretched between worlds as far removed as Dantooine and Honoghr, but numbered few planets in total. The Rakatans used the

The Rakata urge their slaves to complete work on the Star Forge.
[ART BY TOMMY LEE EDWARDS]

Force to power much of their technology, and employed starship engines that allowed them to tunnel through hyperspace and reach other planets with Force-strong signatures. Some of the artifacts that the Rakata left on the worlds they visited triggered strange aftereffects, such as the stimulation of rampant plant and animal growth on Kashyyyk.

The Rakatans eventually became arrogant in their power. They forced entire populations of conquered worlds into slavery, including the Duros, the humans of Coruscant, and the trispecies mix of the Corellian system. Soon they had built a monument to their glory—the Star Forge, a living satellite that could build anything its creators desired using raw stellar material. The Star Forge fed off the aggression of its Rakata builders, amplifying the dark side in the vicinity of Rakata Prime and setting the species up for tragedy.

Three primary factors led to the implosion of the Infinite Empire, which occurred approximately 25,200 B.B.Y. A plague that affected only the Rakata spread to every corner of the kingdom, killing billions. The slaves, suddenly presented with an ideal opportunity, rose up and broke the Rakatan hold on the colonies. Finally, an apparent mutation of the plague virus stripped the surviving Rakatans of the ability to use the Force. Rakata Prime fell into civil war, then devolved into barbarism as its inhabitants forgot how to operate their technology. In orbit overhead, the mighty Star Forge sat empty.

No longer held under the yoke of the Rakatans, progress on Coruscant continued apace. The planet had birthed billions of humans, but so far its citizens had been unsuccessful in their bid to reach the stars. Limited to a single world, they dried up their planet's resources through generations of overuse. By the time the first "sleeper ships" (suspended animation vessels that took centuries to reach distant stars) came into use, impenetrable industry had choked every landmass and wreathed the planet in smoke and steam.

Aboard sleeper ships, Coruscant colonists spread to neighboring worlds such as Alsakan, Metellos, and Axum. On Alderaan (circa 27,500 B.B.Y.), another group of settlers discovered the empty spires of a vanished insectoid species, the Killiks, but nevertheless claimed the world for their own.

Improvements in hyperspatial theory led to the development of hyperspace cannons. Starships launched into hyperspace by a cannon could then induce a drag element and drop back into realspace, but needed a second hyperspace cannon to return to their origin point. A cannon network was developed to link the Core Worlds with the spacefaring Duros civilization.

Their experience with the Rakata had one positive effect on the people of the Core. Scientists on Corellia and Duro launched independent investigations into the Rakatan hyperdrive. If they could duplicate the technology, the Core would no longer consist of stagnant outposts separated by distance and expense.

First, however, the galaxy had to contend with Xim. Out in the Rim area now known as the Tion Cluster, a new power had arisen over the centuries, composed of alien castoffs and the human descendants of an ancient Core Worlds colony ship. Their hyperdrives fused bits of Rakatan technology with fixed-position hyperspace beacons, allowing for travel within a defined area but presenting potentially fatal dangers if they ventured outside the "lighthouse network." The Tionese, who had not yet discovered the length of the Perlemian superhighway hyperlane, remained isolated from the Core Worlds, but occasionally ran up against the sprawling borders of the young Hutt empire.

Xim, the "pirate prince," greatly expanded Tion space by raiding planets and enlisting governors to manage the new territory. Xim's father, himself a bloodthirsty raider, had carved out a corner of the Tion into the Kingdom of Cron during the Cronese sweeps a generation before. Xim soon came to be known as "the Despot." He plundered uncountable treasures from his father's holdings and housed them in a voluminous facility on Dellalt.

In the twenty-fifth year of Xim's rule, the Hutt empire demolished one of his fleets at Vontor in the Si'klaata Cluster. Two more battles followed, but by that point the Hutts had forged the Treaty of Vontor, which bound the Klatooinians, Vodrans, and Nikto to them as permanent slaves. In the Third Battle of Vontor (circa 25,100 B.B.Y.), the Hutt-allied conscripts vanquished Xim's war droids. Kossak the Hutt declared victory, and Xim died in shame as a prisoner in Kossak's dungeon. The Tion Cluster split into competing states.

THE REPUBLIC BEGINS
25,000 B.B.Y.

At approximately twenty-five millennia before the current era, Corellian scientists succeeded in "perfecting" the Rakatan hyperdrive by implementing technology-based workarounds for the Force-attuned components. Starships could now travel among Corellia, Coruscant, Alderaan, and Duro in only a few days. The worlds of the Core linked themselves in a democratic union called the Galactic Republic, then tested their newfound freedom by exploring the uncharted expanses of hyperspace. The discovery of the Perlemian Trade Route linked Coruscant with distant Ossus, and the Jedi became the Republic's guardians.

Little is known of the genesis of the Jedi. The study of the Force—and the science behind the microscopic midi-chlorians that act as symbiotic Force carriers in most living things—had previously been practiced by the paladins of the Chatos Academy, the Followers of Palawa, and the mystic order of Dai Bendu, on planets as diverse as Had Abbadon and Ondos. The specific tenets of the Jedi Order, however, are believed to have been set down on the dawn world of Tython where many Force-users harnessed a positive energy called the Ashla. Those who hungered to wield the Force for personal power dragged the planet into an exhausting conflict known as the Force Wars. From the ashes of this conflict, the Force users of Tython established the Jedi as a society of monastic warriors who obeyed the precepts of harmony, knowledge, serenity, and peace. Traditions of the Tython Jedi included a "Jedi Forge" initiation ceremony, in which hopeful members of the order channeled Force energy into metal-bladed swords, honing the weapons to a supernatural degree of sharpness and strength. In time, the Jedi of Tython would face threats from beyond their world. Using advanced offworld technology, the Jedi forges were able to "freeze" a laser beam, resulting in a weapon that would eventually become the lightsaber. Taking it upon themselves to liberate other worlds from oppression, a proactive faction of Tython Jedi decided to go out into the galaxy. These warriors became known as the Jedi Knights.

In time, a school of Jedi philosophy took root on the planet Ossus. The Force came to be understood according to the "dark side" and "light side" alignments, both reflecting aspects of the living Force (the in-the-moment manifestation of life energy) and the unifying Force (the cosmic expression of prophecies and destinies). The Jedi faced their first true test since the Force Wars when followers of the Force's dark side (known in Tython lore as the Bogan) formed the Legions of Lettow and made war against the young Order.

The Jedi emerged victorious. Xendor, a general of the Lettow legions, lost his life to the Jedi, but his lover, Arden Lyn, fell into a mystic sleep, not to be broken until the time of the Empire. The war between the Jedi and the Legions of Lettow marked the first of many Great Schisms between the light and dark sides of the Force.

Soon, scouts had blazed a portion of the Corellian Run hyperlane, and the wedge defined by the Corellian Run and the Perlemian Trade Route became known as "the Slice." Since hyperspace, particularly the stretch to the galactic west of Coruscant, was anomaly-riddled and impassable to Republic technology, galactic expansion radiated eastward to fill in the Slice's pie wedge. The Core Worlds' tip of the Slice was dubbed the Arrowhead, and soon colony ships had uncovered habitable worlds farther out, establishing the Colonies region. Ossus and other outposts were considered Wild Space, and the vast majority of the galaxy bore the label Unknown Regions. Duro established settlements on Neimoidia and elsewhere, while the Jedi conferred with the gentle people of Caamas over the proper use of power.

While the Republic percolated in the Core and Colonies, Ossus became a fortress world—standing as a bulwark against the crumbling Tion and Hutt space and preventing the Perlemian from becoming an invasion corridor. With its enemies at bay, the Republic grew for a millennium, faster than Coruscant would have desired, mostly due to independent states that petitioned for membership in an effort to protect themselves from the Hutts.

Growing Pains
24,000–7000 B.B.Y.

Approximately twenty-four thousand years B.B.Y., war broke out between the Republic and the Tion. Armadas streamed up and down the Perlemian, exchanging volleys of pressure bombs on the respective capitals of Coruscant and Desevro. The Republic claimed victory when its agents stirred up trouble in Hutt space and steered the angry Hutts in the direction of their old foes in the Tion. Within a century, most of the Tion Cluster swore allegiance to Coruscant.

The borders of the Republic steadily expanded over the millennia but sometimes seemed to defy logic, incorporating odd juts, asymmetrical lumps, and lonely outposts surrounded by light-years of unexplored space. This was a function of hyperspace. Clear and stable paths through hyperspace, known as hyperroutes or hyperlanes, became the bedrock of travel, communication, and commerce, but trailblazing such paths was difficult. The Slice remained the heart of navigable territory as the Republic expanded radially toward galactic east. Gradually the Republic began to bleed past the northern and southern borders of the Slice, but most of the galaxy remained unknown, save for isolated outposts in the wilds such as Ord Mantell (established 12,000 B.B.Y.) and Malastare (established 8000 B.B.Y.).

The space due west of Coruscant resisted exploration. No analogues to the Perlemian or Corellian Run were discovered in that direction, and progress was limited to treacherous one- or two-light-year hops into a briar-patch stretch of hyperspace anomalies.

Coruscant, as the heart of the Republic, bore the coordinates 0-0-0 on hyperspace maps, where the first digit represented west–east, the second north–south, and the third up–down. Due to the unbalanced geography of early colonization, almost all colonized planets had a positive first digit, which they considered a mark of pride. Apart from the Republic, galactic colonization occurred among the Taung exiles, who settled a world that they named Mandalore, in honor of their leader Mandalore the First. Mandalore's warriors slaughtered the planet's mammoth Mythosaurs, modifying the creatures' skeletons into haunting cities of bone.

The Republic's Great Manifest period (20,000–17,000 B.B.Y.) marked an increased movement into the Rimward territories of the Slice, which became known as the Expansion Region. The Republic's boom collapsed due to internal scuffling, as the planet Alsakan attempted to usurp Coruscant as the rightful galactic capital. Dueling economic and political volleys eventually led to both sides firing shots. Though falling short of civil war—most fighting occurred between Coruscant's and Alsakan's holdings in the Expansion Region—Alsakan could not be brought fully to heel. Seventeen uprisings, collectively called the Alsakan Conflicts, would occur between 17,000 and 3000 B.B.Y.

While the Republic busied itself with the first Alsakan Conflict, the geneticists of Arkania began what would be the first of many experiments on sentient populations. They took a sampling of six-armed Xexto from their homeworld of Troiken and changed them into a new species, the Quermians, on another world.

At 15,500 B.B.Y., Rim scouts made contact with the Duinuogwuin, a species commonly known as Star Dragons. Not surprisingly, the scouts reacted with fear at the sight of fifty-meter creatures that soared through space breathing atomic fire. After a disastrous first encounter, hundreds of Duinuogwuin followed the scout ships back to Coruscant and waged war against the capital. Supreme Chancellor Fillorean brought an end to the Duinuogwuin Contention by forging a peace with Star Dragon philosopher Borz'Mat'oh. In the aftermath, the two helped found the University of Coruscant.

By this time, the Jedi had developed their signature lightsabers, but the weapons were unstable and power-hungry. Able to be operated for only short periods before overheating, lightsabers of this era often were simply ceremonial.

During the Pius Dea period (12,000–11,000 B.B.Y.), the Republic came under the influence of a theocratic sect. Over the next several centuries, Supreme Chancellor Contispex and his descendants sanctioned a number of crusades against rival alien sects. The fallout from this deepened tensions between the Core and the Rim that would ultimately be exploited during the Rise of the Empire era.

The Rianitus period (9000–8000 B.B.Y.) is notable for the 275-year reign of Blotus the Hutt, who defied traditional Hutt stereotypes by becoming one of the most distinguished personages to ever hold the chancellor's office.

EMERGENCE OF THE SITH

THE HUNDRED-YEAR DARKNESS
7000 B.B.Y.

The next Great Schism between the light and dark sides of the Force occurred approximately 7000 B.B.Y. By this time lightsabers had become more robust, although each required the use of a plug-in power pack attached to the user's belt. Among the Jedi Order, a cadre of dark-siders made a significant discovery—Force of sufficient intensity could bend life itself. They pioneered the twisted science of dark side mutations, and the century-long war that followed is known as the Hundred-Year Darkness.

The exiled Jedi raised an animalistic army—some of their soldiers monstrous, others merely pitiful. During the war's later years, their science birthed Leviathans, living superweapons that shambled across battlefields and drew life-essences into the blister-traps that speckled their broad backs. The dark lords made a last stand on Corbos, where Jedi hunters and evil rivals obliterated most of them, along with nearly all other life on the planet. The surviving dark lords fled beyond the Republic's borders, emerging in uncharted space, where they discovered the Sith species.

The Dark Jedi were treated as gods by these powerful yet malleable people. With unlimited resources and willing slaves, the Jedi exiles forged the Sith civilization into a new empire, bringing about a golden age of evil while separated from the Republic by the vastness of the galaxy. Over millennia, the dark rulers of the Sith Empire lost their charts and hyperspace maps, so that they no longer even knew how to locate the Republic.

The Manderon period lasted from 7000 to 5000 B.B.Y. At approximately 5500 B.B.Y., merchants in the Tapani sector established what would later become the Rimma Trade Route. This hyperlane, coupled with the recently blazed Corellian Trade Route, opened up new paths into the galactic southern quadrant. Dedicated explorers had tamed a significant portion of the galaxy, though many distant sectors remained uncharted.

THE GOLDEN AGE OF THE SITH
5000 B.B.Y.

It was a time of rugged frontiers. Pioneers established homes on harsh new colony worlds, and alien races encountered humans for the first time. Convoluted paths through the wilderness of hyperspace were still being mapped, which made long-distance travel treacherous and uncertain.

Gav and Jori Daragon, brother-and-sister hyperspace mappers, sought new trade routes in their ship *Starbreaker 12*. They used their "luck" and their blind faith to avoid collisions with stars or black holes, and hoped to blaze a new trail that would earn them a substantial fee from the Brotherhood of Navigators.

With nothing but creditors waiting for them, the two embarked on a random hyperspace hop, intending to map out a run farther than any that had been done before. They succeeded in skipping from the Koros system in the Deep Core all the way to Sith Space in the Outer Rim, an unlikely route known today as the Daragon Trail.

The Sith Empire—cut off from the Republic by vast distances and unexplored pathways—had grown powerful over the past two millennia, dabbling in its own brand of sorcery

At the gravesite, the two strongest Sith opponents confronted each other: Naga Sadow, eager to expand Sith powers; and his rival Ludo Kressh, content with the existing borders and loath to risk a folly that could potentially cost them everything.

Sadow and Kressh engaged in a bloody duel that was interrupted by the unexpected arrival of *Starbreaker 12.* The Sith Lords seized Gav and Jori as alien spies and took them to the bleak planet Ziost for interrogation. The conservative Ludo Kressh saw the Daragons as precursors to an invasion, while his rival Naga Sadow viewed the unsuspecting Republic as a vast new field to conquer.

After a tribunal sentenced Gav and Jori to death, Naga Sadow sprang them from prison with help from his Massassi warriors, members of a specially bred soldier race. He took Gav and Jori to his own isolated fortress, but not before planting evidence indicating that agents of the Republic had freed the prisoners.

Playing innocent in the next Sith council meeting, Naga Sadow exploited doubts and fears regarding the Republic. He used the Daragons as scapegoats to galvanize the Sith Empire, convincing the other lords of an impending invasion. He insisted that they must strike first.

Back at his fortress, Sadow began to initiate Gav into the ways of Sith sorcery. Jori petitioned for the return of *Starbreaker 12*—because of the random route by which she and her brother had discovered the Sith Empire, the only safe path back to the Republic was stored in the ship's navicomputer.

Ludo Kressh discovered evidence that Sadow may have been behind the prisoners' escape, and gathered loyal Sith forces to assault Sadow's fortress and expose him as a traitor. Naga Sadow had planned for this and crushed his rival's "surprise" raid, declaring himself the Dark Lord of the Sith. Jori escaped during the attack in *Starbreaker 12,* leaving her brother behind in the Sith Empire under the promised pro-

Hyperspace explorers Gav and Jori Daragon
[ART BY MARK CHIARELLO]

and dark Force magic. But it had reached a time of crisis.

After a century of iron-handed rule, Dark Lord Marka Ragnos had died. The ensuing power vacuum sparked a great struggle, a brewing civil war that threatened to tear apart the Sith Empire. Hungry factions convened on the mausoleum planet of Korriban as Ragnos was laid to rest among the towering tombs. Even under the shadow-filled skies, the funeral was held with tremendous pomp and splendor, including sacrifices of Sith slaves, bonfires, and the completion of a spectacular new tomb.

tection of Naga Sadow. She vowed to come to his rescue as soon as she could, but she also knew that the Sith were gearing up for an attack on the Republic. Her top priority was to sound the alarm back home.

THE GREAT HYPERSPACE WAR
5000 B.B.Y.

Jori Daragon was unaware that her ship carried a homing beacon that would lead Naga Sadow and his forces directly to the heart of the unsuspecting Republic. She arrived back in the Koros system, where the Empress Teta commanded a navy that was busy with pacifying the system's seven worlds, in the final stages of what is now known as the Unification Wars.

No one believed Jori's claims of an impending Sith invasion. Port officials arrested her on charges of fraud, felony, and starship theft. Eventually, she won an audience with Empress Teta herself, whose Jedi advisers—including Memit Nadill, Odan-Urr, and Odan-Urr's Master, Ooroo—recalled the stories of the outcast Dark Jedi who had long ago vanished into obscurity. The advisers convinced the empress to prepare for invasion. Empress Teta rallied support among other political leaders on Coruscant, while the Jedi Knights spread the word throughout the Republic.

Back in the Sith Empire, Naga Sadow continued training his pliable captive, Gav Daragon. Sadow had consolidated the remaining Sith forces, and set off on a surprise raid against the vulnerable Republic. His entire fleet arrived in Empress Teta's system, weapons blazing.

The conflict spread across the Republic like a storm: a succession of battles that pitted war fleets and loyal Jedi Knights against Sith sorcery and firepower. One of the young heroes of these battles was the alien Jedi Odan-Urr, who would become a pivotal figure in the Sith War a thousand years later.

Empress Teta proved to be a talented commander, but the Sith were relentless—and unpredictable, partly because Naga Sadow had only limited knowledge of this sector of the galaxy. The battles went poorly for the Republic.

Finally, the combined Republic fleet made a stand

around the flare-active red giant star Primus Goluud, where Sadow duped Gav Daragon into facing the Republic forces alone. Gav ultimately redeemed himself, switching sides against the manipulative Naga Sadow just before the star went supernova. Sadow fled in his flagship as Empress Teta's forces hurled themselves after him.

With the changing tides of battle, the Republic rallied against the invaders, trouncing the Sith fleet. Memit Nadill and his team of Jedi Knights defeated enemy forces on Coruscant itself, while Odan-Urr won an important skirmish on the outlying planet of Kirrek, a victory that cost the life of the great Jedi Master Ooroo.

Naga Sadow called a retreat, taking his surviving warriors back to the Sith Empire. Limping home with tattered forces, Sadow returned only to discover that his old enemy Ludo Kressh was alive and well. Giving no quarter, Kressh mercilessly attacked Sadow's "traitors." At this point he had nothing to lose, and Naga Sadow fought back with wild abandon.

The pursuing Republic forces arrived in the middle of the fray to vanquish the Sith threat. They decimated the fleets of Sadow and Kressh in a hail of crossfire.

Naga Sadow took his most faithful followers and made a second getaway in his damaged flagship, sacrificing the rest of his forces. Republic ships again pursued him, but Sadow made one last sorcerous gambit. He flew his warship between a tight binary star, the Dena rii Nova, and used Sith powers to manipulate solar flares that destroyed the Republic ships in his wake.

Of all his former glory, Naga Sadow was left with merely a single ship and his Massassi crew. The Dark Lord went to ground on a little-known jungle moon around the gas giant Yavin. There on Yavin 4 he made his camp, entombed his warship, and left the Massassi behind as guardians. Using Sith technology and sorcery, he cocooned himself in a suspended animation chamber, hoping someone would pick up the dark teachings where he left off, and bring about the Sith

War beasts charge the Republic line during the Sith invasion of Coruscant. [Art by Tommy Lee Edwards]

Golden Age that the Dark Lord Marka Ragnos had foretold.

As he died on the battlefield of Kirrek, Master Ooroo had prophesied that his studious trainee Odan-Urr would found a great library, eventually dying among his beloved scrolls and books. Beginning with Master Ooroo's collection of arcane artifacts, as well as numerous items found among the wreckage of the Sith invasion fleet, Odan-Urr did indeed establish the greatest library of the Old Republic, the grand museum city on Ossus.

Following the Great Hyperspace War, the Jedi developed the modern lightsaber, which operated nearly indefinitely on a charge without the need of an external power pack.

These weapons came into use around the time of the Gank Massacres (4800 B.B.Y.), which coincided with the discovery of ryll spice on the half-burned, half-frozen Twi'lek homeworld of Ryloth. The Duros of Neimoidia, who had by this time evolved into a race distinctly different from their forebears, locked up distribution rights to ryll, but the drug whipped the Porporites, a newly discovered species, into a homicidal frenzy. Various factions hired the Gank mercenaries to protect them. After exterminating the Porporites, the Ganks embarked on a full-scale war until put down by the Jedi.

LEGACY OF THE SITH

The Sith Empire had crumbled, and victorious Republic observers could be forgiven their rosy optimism. New star systems were explored, and new races were taken into the fold as the galactic government slowly learned how to rule over many cultures and across vast distances.

Centuries passed with no further contact with the dark leaders or remnants of the Sith, but the evil influence would ultimately return in a different and more insidious form than before—a cancer from within.

THE SHADOW OF FREEDON NADD
4400 B.B.Y.

Six centuries after Naga Sadow had exiled himself on the jungle moon, an ambitious Jedi Knight, Freedon Nadd, followed rumors and his own intuition to the isolated Yavin system.

In the centuries since the defeated Dark Lord had sealed his essence beneath the focusing chamber of a primary temple, the Massassi refugees had degenerated into primitive but powerful savages. Nadd arrived and fought with them, and his use of the Force awed the Massassi into recalling their past. They showed him where the Dark Lord rested, waiting for someone like Freedon Nadd.

Nadd awakened the ancient Sith Lord, and Sadow in-structed the Jedi in the dark twistings of the Force. Freedon Nadd then killed his mentor and set about making himself a king on the primitive world of Onderon, outside the boundaries of the Republic.

Centuries before, the peaceful people of Onderon had been beset by horrible creatures that crossed over from the erratic moon Dxun. The predators took a terrible toll on the population until the people constructed a walled city, Iziz, for their protection.

Freedon Nadd, with his knowledge of Sith magic, easily made himself the leader of these people. Over the decades the city grew, implacably driving back the jungle. One of the policies Nadd instituted was to banish criminals outside the walls of Iziz, where they would be devoured by the voracious predators. However, some of these exiles managed to band together and survive, even learning how to capture the beasts and domesticate them. Riding on the backs of flying beasts and carrying handmade weapons, the survivors struck back against the city that had exiled them, thus beginning centuries of unrest and rebellion—a scattered guerrilla war that even Freedon Nadd's powers could not crush.

After Nadd's death, the sarcophagus containing his body became a focus of dark side energy that was used by his descendants. Nadd's legacy passed from generation to generation, but the civil war continued, with a cost in blood nearly as high as the earliest attacks from the beasts of Dxun.

During the Vultar Cataclysm (4250 B.B.Y.), the Jedi Order experienced its Third Great Schism. Following a Jedi civil war on Coruscant, the dark side followers fell back to the Vultar system in the Core Worlds. There they discovered ancient technology indicating that the system's planets were artificial constructs, the likely creations of the alien Architects who had built the Corellian system. The dark-siders harnessed the machines (including the extraordinary Cosmic Turbine) but could not control them, and soon annihilated themselves along with the entire planetary system. Corellia's role as a similarly engineered system would remain unconfirmed until the Corellian insurrection, many millennia in the future.

TRIALS OF THE JEDI
4000 B.B.Y.

The survival of the Republic was predicated on two factors: wise governing from administrators and lawmakers, and a preservation of harmony by the Jedi Knights. This harmony was threatened during the Great Droid Revolution (4015 B.B.Y.), when thousands of droids—everything from sanitation to protocol to military models—rose up en masse against their owners. The Jedi destroyed the ringleader, the assassin droid HK-01, and put down the mutiny with a minimum of casualties. The Great Droid Revolution dealt a crippling blow to the budding "droids' rights" movement.

At the time, Jedi often became "watchmen" of new systems, overseeing their transition into the Republic and assisting with local difficulties. Jedi Master Arca Jeth of Arkania received the stewardship and responsibility for the Onderon system. Rather than becoming the watchman himself, he sent his three students—the brothers Ulic and Cay Qel-

Jedi Knight Ulic Qel-Droma
[ART BY MARK CHIARELLO]

Droma and the Twi'lek Tott Doneeta. Arriving on the war-torn world, the three Jedi Knights were greeted by Queen Amanoa. She explained about the depredations of the beast riders and requested help from the Jedi. In a bold move, the riders soon attacked the palace itself, kidnapping Queen Amanoa's daughter Galia.

The Qel-Droma brothers and Doneeta set out to rescue the queen's daughter, but discovered that all was not as they had been led to believe. Galia and the warlord leader Oron Kira had planned the abduction. They intended to marry and unify the two societies, ending centuries of bloodshed.

Queen Amanoa, however, had no interest in peace. For years she had been tapping into Freedon Nadd's power, and in her outrage she called upon the dark side to destroy Oron Kira's people. The Jedi fought back, but they were out-classed—in the struggle Cay Qel-Droma lost his arm, which he later replaced with a droid prosthesis.

Only Master Arca's arrival was enough to prevent a catastrophe. Arca used Jedi battle meditation to influence the forces on the battlefield and turn the tide of the conflict. Galia and Oron Kira then worked to restore their world to peace and to bestow the benefits of civilization.

Elsewhere, the Jedi Knight Nomi Sunrider would become one of the greatest leaders of her age. Nomi had taken up the lightsaber after her Jedi husband, Andur, had died dur-ing an ambush in the Stenness system. On the bleak world of Ambria, she began her formal training with Master Thon, an armor-plated Tchuukthai of savage countenance and significant wisdom. Nomi Sunrider became a master in the technique of battle meditation.

After training Nomi for some months, Master Thon brought her to the Jedi learning center on Ossus, where he turned her over to Master Vodo Siosk-Baas. There, with other Jedi trainees, Nomi Sunrider learned even more of the Force and finally built her own personal lightsaber.

THE NADDIST REVOLT
3998 B.B.Y.

Following two years of relative peace on Onderon, unrest continued, sparked primarily by a grim sect that revered the memory of Freedon Nadd. In an attempt to remove the cancerous evil, Master Arca and his students prepared to move the sarcophagi containing Queen Amanoa's and Freedon Nadd's remains on the monster-filled moon of Dxun. During the funeral procession, followers of Freedon Nadd launched an unexpected attack from beneath the city

Queen Amanoa's funeral procession on Onderon
[ART BY TOMMY LEE EDWARDS]

of Iziz. The Naddist rebels captured the royal sarcophagi.

Arca then learned that Queen Galia's decrepit father, King Ommin, had been kept alive in a secret life-support facility. Suspicious, Arca, Galia, and Ulic Qel-Droma visited the dying old man, where they discovered that Ommin himself had been a follower of Freedon Nadd. The spirit-avatar of Nadd joined forces with Ommin, crippling Master Arca with blistering bolts of energy. Ommin fled with the paralyzed Arca to another dark side stronghold, where the stolen sarcophagi had been taken.

Hurt by his failure, Ulic Qel-Droma called for assistance from the Republic and the Jedi Knights. Republic military ships converged on the Onderon system, while another team of handpicked Jedi arrived from Ossus. Under fire, the Jedi reinforcements battled through the siege of Iziz to join Ulic and his companions.

In the midst of the chaos on Onderon, two other figures arrived: Satal Keto and his cousin Aleema, heirs to the now corrupt Empress Teta system (renamed from the Koros system following the Unification Wars). Spoiled, bored, and rich, Satal, Aleema, and their friends had dabbled in Sith magic, amusing themselves with artifacts recovered by the Jedi Odan-Urr during the Great Hyperspace War a thousand years earlier. These aristocrats dubbed themselves the Krath, after a fearsome childhood legend.

Satal Keto had stolen an ancient book of Sith secrets from a museum on Coruscant; egged on by the beautiful and ambitious Aleema, they departed for Onderon. Using freshly learned dark side skills as well as plain luck, the two made their way through the battle-ravaged city to the stronghold where King Ommin held Master Arca prisoner.

While a scribe diligently worked to reproduce the stolen Sith tome, the specter of Freedon Nadd appeared. With Republic troops pounding the city and the unified Jedi Knights on their way, Nadd knew that King Ommin would be defeated. Instead, Nadd threw in his lot with the two aristocrats, telling Satal Keto and Aleema that they alone held the key to the rebirth of the Sith Golden Age—and that he would guide them.

The Jedi Knights fought their way into Ommin's stronghold just as Master Arca was about to die in the grip of the dark side. Nadd withdrew his power and support from Ommin, and Ulic charged forward to kill the old man and rescue Arca.

Satal Keto and Aleema fled back to the Empress Teta system, bearing a wealth of Sith artifacts. Republic forces imposed order and martial law on devastated Iziz. The sarcophagus of Freedon Nadd was taken to an armored tomb on the moon of Dxun, sealed behind slabs of Mandalorian iron—which they hoped would last for millennia.

THE COMING RUIN
3997 B.B.Y.

With their Sith knowledge and artifacts, brash young Satal Keto and Aleema marshaled their Krath forces for a coup of the Empress Teta system. Killing old-guard aristocratic leaders proved far easier than actually subjugating the people, and the seven worlds revolted against the barbaric despots. However, Satal Keto and Aleema delighted in the chance to make use of their new Sith powers to crush the resistance.

Word of the revolt and the alarming use of Sith sorcery made its way to Onderon. Nomi Sunrider and Ulic Qel-Droma had grown close during the reconstruction of Iziz, and Master Arca decided to send them both to deal with the situation in the Empress Teta system.

Joining Republic military forces en route to the ferocious battles around the seven worlds, Ulic and Nomi assisted by using their Jedi abilities—but Aleema countered with her own powerful Sith illusions. In a suicide attack, one of the Krath ships nearly destroyed the bridge of the Republic flagship. Rebuffed, the Republic fleet retreated.

Around the same time, on distant Dantooine in Wild Space, Jedi Master Vodo Siosk-Baas trained three students: the Cathar mates Crado and Sylvar, and his most talented apprentice, Exar Kun. Kun easily defeated Crado in a lightsaber duel, then fought against Sylvar; as tensions escalated, she slashed him across the face with her claws. Master Vodo stepped in, and Kun met the challenge, defeating his own teacher.

Ambitious and curious, Kun had surreptitiously studied

the legends of the Golden Age of the Sith. He followed dark side clues to the tomb of Freedon Nadd on Dxun, and used his lightsaber to cut through the Mandalorian iron. When Kun cracked open the sarcophagus, he found a skeletal corpse clothed in black armor, but the ethereal form of Nadd's spirit shimmered to life.

The dark Jedi ghost revealed precious metal scrolls hidden in a compartment beneath his remains. He also told Kun that a great future awaited the young Jedi in the dark side. Continuing his explorations on the Sith tomb world of Korriban, Kun investigated a spectacular crypt, but the ceiling collapsed, crushing him.

As he cried out for help, the spirit of Freedon Nadd appeared, promising rescue only if Kun surrendered to the dark side. Kun made an empty promise to save his own life, but the vow sent him further down the slippery slope that he had already begun to walk. The flood of dark side power blasted away the rubble, knitted his broken bones, and left him lying naked on the dry clay of Korriban. Exar Kun let out a tremendous shriek that echoed across the galaxy, calling in despair upon Master Vodo, whom he had abandoned.

Master Vodo and all other Jedi had gathered on Deneba for a great convocation called to discuss the strife in the Empress Teta system. The historic meeting was called to order by Odan-Urr, who had spent the centuries after the Great Hyperspace War building Ossus into the foremost center of Jedi learning. In the audience were the premier Jedi of the period, including Master Arca, Master Thon, Nomi Sunrider, and Ulic Qel-Droma. Jedi witnesses spoke of the dangerous Sith sorcery unleashed by the Krath, and of the growing foothold of the dark side.

In the middle of the assembly, automated pods rained down through the atmosphere, unleashing hordes of Krath war droids that attacked the Jedi Knights. The Jedi defended themselves in a furious fight, but the battle left one tragic legacy—Master Arca died even as he saved the life of his student Ulic Qel-Droma. This became the pivotal event in Ulic's life, breaking his spirit and

Sith follower Aleema conjures an illusory herd of space grazers, menacing the Republic fleet. [ART BY TOMMY LEE EDWARDS]

leaving him open to the influences of the dark side.

As the Jedi Knights recovered from the onslaught, an anguished Ulic Qel-Droma vowed to go to the Empress Teta system, infiltrate the Krath despots, and destroy them from within. Master Thon warned him about the temptations of the dark side, but Ulic would not be swayed. His own pride did not allow Ulic to see the folly in his attempt to conquer the dark side by himself.

Disguised as a grim "fallen Jedi," Ulic infiltrated the iron-walled city of Cinnagar, where the Krath usurpers had crushed all dissent. He won acceptance into the Krath inner circle by killing an assassin who was gunning for Aleema. With innocent blood on his own hands, Ulic had taken another step on the road to his own damnation. Aleema intended to keep Ulic as her lover, though Satal Keto was jealous and highly suspicious. Keto interrogated and tortured Ulic, insisting that he was a Jedi spy. Finally, Keto injected Ulic with a Sith poison that affected the mind. Ulic became the Krath general in charge of military forces, and the personal pet of the evil Aleema.

As months passed with no word from Ulic, Nomi Sunrider joined Cay Qel-Droma and Tott Doneeta in an attempt to rescue the Jedi from the Krath. Nomi ended up as a prisoner inside the Cinnagar citadel, where Ulic—trying to maintain his cover—ordered her execution. When Nomi escaped, Satal Keto sent his men to kill Ulic, believing the Krath's new general to be a Jedi spy. Instead, Ulic killed Keto in a great duel, then took his place beside Aleema as the new ruler of the Krath.

On Korriban, Exar Kun had been healed and reborn in the dark side. The spirit of Freedon Nadd urged Kun to make his way to Yavin 4, the last resting place of Naga Sadow, who had instructed Nadd himself centuries before. On the jungle moon, Exar Kun discovered the degenerate descendants of the Massassi, who tried to sacrifice him to a gigantic monster beneath the main temple. Kun once again called upon the dark side in order to save himself.

Freedon Nadd reappeared, delighted with Kun's victory and claiming him as an ally and protégé—but Kun would hear none of it. Still simmering with the Sith powers he had mastered, Kun lashed out and obliterated Nadd for all time. Calling himself the Dark Lord of the Sith, Kun then subjugated the Massassi and had them construct huge structures based on Sith architecture, designed to focus dark forces. Beneath the sites of the ancient ruins, Kun uncovered Naga Sadow's Sith battleship and took it as his own.

An extremely powerful figure now, Kun dabbled in dark side alchemy, creating freakish two-headed avians and hulking terentateks that thirsted after Force-rich blood. He invented a glowing golden sphere that trapped the children of the Massassi and allowed him to feed off their energies. With his mind he reached across the galaxy and detected other users of Sith magic in the Empress Teta system. Knowing that his destiny was to bring about a new Sith Golden Age, Kun traveled to Cinnagar to destroy an unwanted rival, Ulic Qel-Droma.

The Jedi Knights Cay Qel-Droma, Nomi Sunrider, and Tott Doneeta executed a second rescue mission to drag Ulic away from the treachery of the Krath. Ulic responded to the Jedi attack with all of the military might at his disposal. Blind to his own delusions, he refused to join them, and the Jedi Knights withdrew in despair.

At that moment Exar Kun burst into the palace. He and Ulic fought with a blazing clash of Jedi blades—and during the conflict the Sith amulets both men wore began to shimmer. Before them appeared the image of the long-dead Dark Lord of the Sith Marka Ragnos—the Sith ruler whose death had triggered the civil war between Naga Sadow and Ludo Kressh a thousand years earlier. Ragnos commanded the two men to join forces, so that the alliance of Ulic Qel-Droma and Exar Kun could bring about the long-predicted return of Sith glory. Allies, not enemies, Kun and Qel-Droma clasped hands and vowed to do what was necessary to create such a future.

The Sith War
3996 B.B.Y.

Exar Kun and Ulic Qel-Droma consolidated their forces. Kun worked to create Sith converts among the weaker-willed Jedi, spreading his insidious teachings on Ossus as if he were some sort of prophet. Among the believers was Kun's former training companion, the Cathar male Crado. Crado's mate, Sylvar, remained loyal to the Jedi.

From the Jedi library, Kun stole the original Sith Holocron used by Naga Sadow. Caretaker Odan-Urr was killed during the theft, fulfilling the prophesy by Master Ooroo that Odan-Urr would die among his books. Kun then took his converts back to the Massassi temples on Yavin 4, where he unleashed a powerful Sith spell that bound the Jedi to him. Kun appointed Crado his second in command.

Ulic Qel-Droma took control of the war's strategic side. He forged an alliance with the Mandalorian warrior clans, who had left their homeworld of Mandalore behind and now searched the galaxy hungering for conquest. Ulic defeated their leader, Mandalore, in open combat, and the Mandalorian Crusaders agreed to become an arm of the Krath military. The Mandalorians and their Basilisk war-mounts, augmented by Aleema's Sith illusions, executed lightning strikes to gather supplies and weaponry from outposts and shipyards. Exar Kun had also constructed a Sith superweapon, the Dark Reaper, that was capable of drawing in the life-energies of thousands of combatants. Ulic unleashed the Dark Reaper against hundreds of Republic troops on the outpost world of Raxus Prime.

Believing that the time was right, Ulic, Aleema, and Mandalore launched a brash, all-out assault on Coruscant itself. The capital's loyal Jedi force joined together against the invaders. Surrounded by light and the Force, Ulic was captured and the invaders were driven back, while Aleema escaped. A prisoner stripped of his power, Ulic was taken to face trial for his crimes against the Republic.

The trial took place in the great Senate Hall on Coruscant. For a Jedi Knight, betrayal of the Republic was an unforgivable crime. Ulic, however, displayed no repentance. Master Vodo attended the trial, suspecting that Ulic wasn't acting alone; Vodo sensed the dark hand of his lost student Exar Kun.

During Ulic's sentencing, the doors crashed open and Exar Kun strode in, flanked by bestial Massassi bodyguards. Before the whole assembly, the new Dark Lord of the Sith

Fallen Jedi Knight Exar Kun
[Art by Mark Chiarello]

mission to assassinate their own Masters. The bloodbath of slaughtered Jedi Masters shook the Republic. Kun's lieutenant, Crado, attempted to kill his former Master, but Thon defeated him and Crado fled.

Crado then teamed with Aleema to execute a military strike using Naga Sadow's Sith flagship. Armed with the vessel's star-destroying weapon, they intended to destroy the suns of the Cron Cluster, not realizing that their Masters had set them up for a fall. The chain reaction triggered by the weapon consumed them as well, thus punishing Crado for his incompetence and Aleema for her lack of loyalty; she had tried to take over Ulic's forces while he was imprisoned. The blazing shock wave from the exploding stars streaked toward Ossus—exactly as Kun had hoped.

THE DEVASTATION OF OSSUS
3996 B.B.Y.

During the frantic evacuation of Ossus, the Jedi scrambled to retrieve as many vital artifacts as possible. Amid this chaos, Exar Kun and Ulic brought their forces to the library world to raid anything that remained. A tree-like Neti Jedi, Master Ood Bnar, had taken on the mantle of librarian after Odan-Urr's death. Knowing that he could not protect every item from the oncoming shock wave, Ood buried a priceless collection of ancient lightsabers just before the arrival of Exar Kun and his Massassi warriors. To protect his treasure, Ood called upon the Force inside the soil of Ossus and transformed himself into a gigantic tree. Gathering up the remaining plunder, Exar Kun departed Ossus.

As the waves of supernova fire drew closer, Ulic Qel-Droma fought against the rallying Republic and Jedi forces.

used his powers to hypnotize the observers and manipulate the president of the Senate. Master Vodo Siosk-Baas stepped in to battle his former pupil. Exar Kun, now armed with a double-bladed lightsaber and the tricks of Sith magic, struck down and killed Master Vodo. Ulic and Kun left the Jedi and Senators behind, returning to their stronghold on Yavin 4.

Vodo wasn't the only Jedi to die that day. Exar Kun had dispatched his Sith-possessed disciples on an insidious

Cay Qel-Droma attempted to stop his brother, but Ulic unleashed his anger and, in a devastating fury, struck down Cay, killing him. Staring at the body of his brother and realizing what he had done, Ulic collapsed in horror.

Nomi Sunrider and Tott Doneeta arrived too late to help Cay, but a distraught Nomi unleashed a wild Force ability that blinded Ulic to the Force, effectively stripping him of his powers. Utterly crushed, no longer even a Jedi Knight, Ulic Qel-Droma finally saw how much pain he had caused. He had traveled the dark path with the intention of avenging Master Arca, but instead had grown worse than his very enemies.

Knowing how the Sith War must end, Ulic offered to take the remaining Jedi to the headquarters of Exar Kun on Yavin 4. Kun realized that the Jedi were coming. He gathered the remaining Massassi into the Great Temple, then chained himself to the focal point of the pyramids. As the Jedi forces in orbit generated a wall of light that bombarded the thick jungles, Exar Kun drained the power from his Massassi slaves, triggering a final wave of Sith sorcery that liberated his spirit but preserved it inside the giant structures. Kun found himself trapped, unable to escape the prison he had created for himself.

The Jedi attack resulted in an immense conflagration in the jungles, obliterating the trees and scorching the temple complex so completely that nothing could survive. The victorious Jedi Knights departed and worked to pick up the pieces of their damaged Republic. The Mandalorian Crusaders, defeated during a battle on Onderon, fled under the leadership of a new Mandalore. The Republic seized control of the Empress Teta system, scattering the Krath. Surviving Sith forces retreated to territory that had historically been considered Sith space in the Outer Rim near Korriban, Thule, and Yavin. The Dark Reaper superweapon lay smashed on Raxus Prime, though its power source, the Force Harvester, remained intact and overlooked beneath garbage strata.

With Ossus ruined, the Jedi relocated their headquarters to their existing Temple on Coruscant, expanding the struc-

Jedi Master Ood gathers up Ossus's treasures before the arrival of a supernova shockwave. [ART BY TOMMY LEE EDWARDS]

ture that already sat on the site of a Force wellspring. They also increased their ties to the office of Supreme Chancellor.

THE GREAT HUNT
3993 B.B.Y.

With the Sith seemingly extinguished, attention turned to cleanup. For three years following the Sith War, the Jedi Knights were sent on a "dragon quest." Terentateks, Exar Kun's alchemically birthed monstrosities that fed on Force-strong blood, still prowled the Rim worlds. Each stood about half the size of a rancor and was a match for an entire squad of Jedi, making the extermination of terentateks the Order's highest priority at the time.

Three renowned Jedi Knights shored up their remarkable legends during this Great Hunt. Duron Qel-Droma, cousin of Ulic and Cay, joined with his lover, Shaela Nuur, and the hard-bitten brawler Guun Han Saresh to slay the mightiest terentateks. In the final days of the Great Hunt, Guun Han perished in the teeth of a terentatek in the shadow-lands of Kashyyyk. Duron Qel-Droma and Shaela Nuur were slain while fighting an-other of the killer beasts in the tombs of Kor-riban. Qel-Droma's Force-imbued robe, once worn by Cay Qel-Droma, would be found by Darth Revan decades later.

Jedi Knight Nomi Sunrider
[ART BY MARK CHIARELLO]

THE REDEMPTION OF ULIC QEL-DROMA
3986 B.B.Y

Ulic Qel-Droma, a disgraced war criminal, never regained his Jedi powers. A ruined man, he wandered from world to world and hid from history, haunted by the ghosts of his own guilt. Ten years after the Sith War, he went to the frozen world of Rhen Var to make his final

home in the ruins of an abandoned fortress.

Nomi Sunrider, too, was scarred by the loss of Ulic, the second man she had ever loved. She devoted much of her life to politics and to rebuilding the Order of the Jedi Knights. Intensely focused on her duties, Nomi failed to pay sufficient attention to her impressionable daughter. Young Vima Sun-rider did not receive adequate training as a Jedi—until she ran away from a Jedi Convocation at Exis Station and set out to find Ulic Qel-Droma, convinced that the legendary man would take her as an apprentice.

On Rhen Var, Vima persuaded the bitter Ulic to teach her what he knew of the Force. Even without the use of his powers, Ulic taught Vima about honor and duty, and his heart softened toward the girl; Vima came to love him like the father she'd never known.

Sylvar, the Cathar Jedi, had never overcome her anger at the death of her mate, Crado, during the Sith War. Placing much of the blame on Ulic, Sylvar vowed to find Vima—and to make Ulic pay for his crimes. Enlisting the aid of a scavenger pilot named Hoggon, Sylvar tracked her quarry to Rhen Var.

Sylvar and Nomi Sunrider confronted Ulic, but with assistance from Vima, overcame their anger and pain, and managed to forgive the man who had already paid so much for his crimes. But Hoggon—eager to make his own mark on history—shot Ulic in the back and killed him. To everyone's astonishment, though he had been blinded to the Force, Ulic Qel-Droma vanished into the light, a technique known only to a true Jedi Master.

With such a beginning to her career as a Jedi Knight, Vima Sunrider learned much and eventually became one of the greatest Jedi of her age.

THE MANDALORIAN WARS
3995–3961 B.B.Y.

Tue Mandalorian Crusaders had gained strength during the Sith War, but their leader Mandalore had died on the jungle moon of Dxun. Following tradition, a new soldier took up the name and identity of Mandalore, and this warrior led his "Neo-Crusaders" to triumphs that would be forever celebrated in the refrains of Mandalore skirmish-songs. Slowly at first, Mandalore conquered fringe worlds left defenseless in the Sith War's aftermath. Joining their war matériel to his own, within a decade Mandalore had accumulated a swath of "clan territory" that dwarfed Hutt space. Republic efforts to halt Mandalore's advance were halfhearted, until the warlord took advantage of his enemy's apathy and poured into Republic space.

Mandalore's top strategist, Cassus Fett, decided to punish the planet Cathar for opposing the Mandalorian clans in clashes long since silenced. Fett's Basilisk war-mounts decimated Cathar's primitive settlements, nearly driving the proud feline species into extinction. After the Cathar incident, the Jedi joined with the Republic fleet in head-to-head confrontations against Mandalore's armies, but the ineffectual Jedi Council called for caution, hobbling the war effort.

A pair of charismatic Jedi, Revan and Malak, turned the tide of the war through sheer force of will. Revan openly defied the Jedi Council and drove back Mandalore by co-opting his enemy's own tactics. Revan was willing to sacrifice the populations of some planets in order to win key victories elsewhere. This earned Revan the grudging respect of the Mandalorians and the contempt of the Jedi Council—but even they reluctantly admitted that the coldhearted strategy was successful. Revan and Malak liberated Taris, sparred with Cassus Fett at Jaga's Cluster, and annihilated a large portion of the Mandalorian army at Althir. At Malachor V, Revan drew Mandalore into a direct fight and killed him in hand-to-hand combat.

At last defeated by a worthy opponent, the Mandalorians destroyed their armor and war-mounts under the eyes of Revan and Malak. Some survivors returned to the planet Mandalore; others became guns-for-hire and were to be known informally as the "Mandalorian Mercs."

THE SECOND SITH WAR
3958–3956 B.B.Y.

During their string of victories in the Mandalorian Wars, Revan and Malak had acquired a taste for rebellion. In the spirit of seeking out what the Jedi Council would deny them, the two discovered artifacts created by the pre-Republic Rakata civilization on Dantooine, Kashyyyk, Tatooine, Manaan, and Korriban. Knowledge gained on Korriban, the Sith tomb world, may have proved too tempting for war commanders steeped in blood. They abruptly

Darth Malak, with his dark side apprentice, Bastila Shan
[ART BY TOMMY LEE EDWARDS]

announced themselves to the galaxy as the *new* Dark Lords of the Sith—Darth Revan and Darth Malak.

Many of the Republic crewers and Jedi Knights who had fought with Revan and Malak in the Mandalorian Wars joined their cause, eager for the chance to again serve the two great champions. At the shipyards of Foerost, Revan and his accomplices seized control of the bulk of the Republic fleet. This brash action initiated the Second Sith War.

Revan's fleet commander, Admiral Saul Karath, intimidated hundreds of key military worlds by threatening to slag their cities through orbital bombardment. Revan and Malak took up Sith holdings left dormant after the First Sith War, establishing a link between their ideology and that of Exar Kun, despite their lack of a connection to the Sith species itself. Many citizens admired this take-charge mentality, and much of the Sith territorial expansion was the result of Republic defections. Revan revitalized an existing Sith training academy on Korriban, ensuring that a corps of Dark Jedi would be ready to defend the new Sith Empire.

Revan and Malak, on the trail of the Rakatan clues they had uncovered, located a colony of surviving Rakatans on the species' original birthworld of Rakata Prime. Though the Rakata had fallen into relative primitivism since their golden age many millennia in the past, their Star Forge remained in orbit and possessed the power to create fully formed machines at the flip of a lever. Bolstered with ships of Rakatan design, the Sith forces drove the Republic to its knees. Absolute victory seemed within Revan's grasp.

The Jedi Knight Bastila Shan, a master of Battle Meditation, helped prevent the Republic's defeat, and soon the Jedi arranged a trap for Darth Revan. In the midst of a pitched fleet battle, Bastila and a strike team boarded Revan's flagship and subdued the Sith Lord. Darth Malak treacherously opened fire on his own Master's ship, but Bastila escaped

hoped that an amnesiac Revan might lead them to th Forge without presenting a threat to the Republic.

Malak, now the reigning Sith Lord, took Darth Ba as his apprentice and pushed ahead in the war. A ma gagement over Taris nearly netted him Bastila as wel combatant who had once been Revan. In Malak's eff capture them, he leveled Taris and destroyed the Jedi emy on Dantooine.

Bastila, working with Revan and a number of han including Mandalorian clansman Canderous Ordo and van's former assassin droid HK-47, found the location Star Forge and launched an assault to shut it down. A by the full Republic fleet, Revan—now in possession o memories the Council had erased—killed Darth Malak destroyed the Star Forge above Rakata Prime.

THE SITH CIVIL WAR
3951 B.B.Y.

Revan's fate following the Battle of Rakata Prime unclear, but the Sith Empire that had sworn fealt Revan (and later Malak) now found itself rudderless. Bandon had also perished during the recent fighting, so a host of potential Sith Lords rose up to fill the voi Darth Sion, Darth Kreia, Darth Traya, and Darth Nihilu among the many to take advantage of the Republic' ity to safeguard its holdings after the Second Sith Wa

As the Outer Rim descended into chaos and the Si again took hold, the surviving Jedi publicly disbanded going underground, they hoped to escape assassins th been dispatched by Darth Sion. Working to uncover th in secret, salvation came instead from a former Jedi w been excommunicated for assisting Revan during the dalorian Wars. This hero—aided in part by Canderous the new Mandalore heading the reemerging Mandalo

Darth Sion
[Art by Mark Chiarello]

Repercussions Through the Republic
3900–3000 B.B.Y.

Years of consolidation and recovery followed the two Sith Wars. At approximately 3900 B.B.Y., Queen Tasia of Grizmallt sponsored one of the last of her world's colonization missions. The three ships—*Beneficent Tasia, Constant,* and *Mother Vima*—departed Grizmallt and vanished from sight. Much later it was learned that they had reached the planet Naboo in the Wild Space of the southern galactic quadrant, where the colonists became embroiled in a war with the planet's native Gungans.

In the Kanz sector on the Republic's frontier, Provisional Governor Myrial of Argazda used the recent chaos to cover her attempts at establishing a military dictatorship. Myrial's armies bombed recalcitrant planets, including Lorrd, and sold their inhabitants into slavery. The Lorrdians, forbidden from speaking aloud by their slave masters, developed into geniuses at nonverbal communication, a trait still seen today. The Kanz sector eventually seceded from the Republic and existed as a totalitarian state for three centuries, until Jedi efforts toppled the regime at 3670 B.B.Y. More than five billion lives were lost during the Kanz Disorders.

Concurrent with the Sith War was the rise of the matriarchy in the Hapes Consortium. A few decades before Ulic Qel-Droma and Exar Kun nearly toppled the Republic, a band of Jedi Knights—including Master Arca Jeth—traveled into the densely-packed Hapan worlds and eliminated the barbaric Lorell Raiders who had preyed on Republic shipping for generations. The women of the Hapes Consortium, freed from their servitude to the Raiders, established a female-dominated society and placed all power in a single monarch, the Queen Mother. The Hapan Queen Mother sealed the borders to the star cluster centuries later (circa 3100 B.B.Y.), and the Consortium developed in near-total isolation for millennia until Princess Leia Organa broke down the barriers in a historic diplomatic achievement for the New Republic.

At 3000 B.B.Y., the legendary pioneer woman Freia Kallea blazed a remarkable new hyperspace route—the Hydian Way, which spanned nearly the entire north–south width of the galaxy. The Hydian finally opened up the galaxy to widespread colonization beyond the narrow wedge of the Slice and fundamentally altered the scale of galactic civilization.

The Hydian Way and the discovery of other super-hyperroutes including the Corellian Trade Spine helped spur the second great colonization of the galaxy. The Republic exploded into the galactic northern and southern quadrants, and simultaneously expanded out into new settlers' regions dubbed the Mid Rim and the Outer Rim Territories.

The New Sith
2000–1000 B.B.Y.

Two thousand years before the rise of the Empire, a rogue Jedi Knight broke away from the teachings of the Council and founded a new order of the Sith, marking another Great Schism. Over time, more Jedi Knights joined the renegade, and soon the Republic once again found itself threatened. The followers of the Sith grew in power and eventually made war against the Republic.

These centuries of strife, known as the Draggulch period (2000–1000 B.B.Y.), saw a consistent decline in Republic power as mineral mines ran dry and thousands of megacorporations went bankrupt. The Republic borders began to shrink for the first time in millennia, as colony worlds dried up and were abandoned. Hardship bred lawlessness, and the overextended Jedi took a more active role in government. In a move of desperation, several Jedi even served as Republic Supreme Chancellor. Scandal continued to plague the Jedi, most notably following the military strike against the Ubese that left the Ubese homeworld inhospitable and forced its survivors to live the rest of their lives beneath filtration helmets.

The Battle of Mizra (1466 B.B.Y.) saw the victory of a massive Sith army over the Jedi. It was immortalized by the poet Felloux, who described scores of Sith speeders bearing scores of Sith Lords, each vehicle bearing the name of a predatory creature—*Ng'ok, Hssiss, Sleeth*—that embodied the character of its rider. The Sith Lords' drawn lightsabers illuminated the ash-blackened sky, and their whining repulsorlift chariots drowned out the screams of the dying.

The final hundred years of the Draggulch period are sometimes called the Republic's "dark age." The Republic could no longer afford to maintain its communications network, dropping all settlements outside the Core off the grid and forcing them to rely on hyperspace courier ships. At the same time, an outbreak of the Candorian plague killed off as much as two-thirds of the citizens of some major population centers.

The Sith grew exponentially during the dark age, ravaging entire star systems while under the squabbling leadership of a host of Sith Lords, including Kaan, Bane, Qordis, Seviss Vaa, and Kaox Krul.

The Jedi, shaken out of their complacency by the galactic crisis, raised their own champions, such as the stalwart Lord Hoth and his Army of Light, the charismatic Kiel Charny, and Lord Farfalla, a foppish alien whose retinue and wooden-hulled battleship looked like elements of a forgotten fairy tale. Jedi casualties grew so common that the Order sanctioned recruiters to seek out able-bodied Republic citizens with any hint of Force sensitivity. Many of those recruited into the war were children.

Lord Hoth's Army of Light clashed with the Sith on countless worlds, and the Sith leaders clashed with one another. Lord Kaan eventually raised his own army, the Brotherhood of Darkness, numbering twenty thousand warriors and dedicated to the principle of "rule by the strong." Fearful that Bane would usurp his position as head of the Brotherhood of Darkness, Kaan poisoned his rival and left him for dead.

The Battle of Ruusan
1000 B.B.Y.

Jedi and Sith ultimately squared off on the planet Ruusan where they fought seven blood-soaked ground battles that left both sides demoralized. The Brotherhood of Darkness lost all but two of the battles, reducing their once fearsome army to a tenth of its original size.

Into this morass came Bane. He chose not to take revenge on Kaan for the failed attempt at poisoning, instead focusing his attention on the annihilation of Lord Hoth's forces. Gathering all the Sith Lords on a mountaintop, Bane sharpened their dark energies into a Force storm that aged the lush Ruusan landscape into dust and ash. Kaan used the opportunity to attack the reeling Jedi. Then the most devastating blow came from one of the Jedi army's own recruits, an untrained boy named Tomcat. He killed Kiel Charny with Charny's own lightsaber, then defected to the Sith side.

Unfortunately for the Sith, it was apparent that the power of the dark side had driven Lord Kaan mad. Kaan and his disciples hunkered in their underground chambers and used their powers to create a "thought bomb"—a volatile cauldron of seething Force energy.

The following morning, Lord Hoth and the Army of Light marched into the enemy encampment, past the severed heads and dangling corpses of Jedi. The Lord of Darkness and the Defender of Light confronted one another, and Kaan triggered the thought bomb. A furious explosion of energy annihilated nearly every member of both armies, sucking their disembodied spirits into an unbreakable state of equilibrium.

Bane was one of the few to survive the blast. Afterward, he sensed the latent power of a young girl named Rain, Tomcat's sister who had slipped into darkness while she was lost in the Ruusan wilderness. Bane approached her as a potential apprentice, telling her to find her way to Onderon if she wished to continue in her journey as a Sith.

Bane departed for Onderon's dark side–saturated moon, Dxun. In the tomb of Freedon Nadd, he meditated on Sith power as barnacle-like orbalisks covered him in a permanent suit of living armor. Bane believed that he had discovered the secret to the Sith's continued survival. Too many Sith Lords spread the energy of the dark side too thin, while also inviting power struggles. By establishing a strict dictate of only one Master and one apprentice at any time, the Sith could dwell in the shadows until they had consolidated more power than ever before. Darth Bane retrieved Rain from Onderon, and she became his apprentice—Darth Zannah.

Meanwhile, the Jedi could not free the spirits from the valley that encircled the Ruusan battle site. Lord Hoth's former apprentice petitioned the Senate to erect a memorial on the grounds, and the Valley of the Jedi soon boasted towering statuary and memorial inscriptions. But the Jedi Order wished to forget its failure, and deleted most mentions of the battle from their archives. The passage of time did the rest. Ruusan would be all but forgotten within a few centuries, save for an enigmatic prophecy made by Ruusan's natives: "A Knight shall come, a battle will be fought, and the prisoners go free." That prophecy would remain unfulfilled until a year after the Battle of Endor.

THE RUUSAN REFORMATIONS
1000 B.B.Y.

Ruusan went down as a Republic victory—Kaan's Brotherhood of Darkness was no more, and all the Sith Lords had either died or disappeared. But the ranks of the Jedi had suffered terribly during the war, and without their unifying police-like presence, more than two dozen self-contained kingdoms announced their intentions to follow the lead of the Hapes Consortium two thousand years earlier and withdraw from the Republic.

The chancellor at the time, Tarsus Valorum, knew that radical steps had to be taken to prevent the splintering of the once proud Republic. Proclaiming that the Republic as its citizens knew it no longer existed, Valorum ushered in a new era with the passage of the Ruusan Reformations. The act diminished the governmental authority of the chancellor and gave greater control to planetary systems and sectors, thereby giving the Senate unprecedented levels of power. The Republic vowed to dismantle its standing army (already decimated by the last Sith conflict) and assist territories in raising their own defense forces. Finally, the Reformations codified the Jedi Order as a branch of the Judicial Department, answerable to the Senate. Valorum even

The armies of the Jedi clash with the Sith Brotherhood of Darkness in the climactic Battle of Ruusan. [ART BY TOMMY LEE EDWARDS]

began a new calendar, with years starting over at 1.

The Ruusan Reformations may have saved the Republic, but by giving every Senator a powerful voice, Tarsus Valorum had invited gridlock and greed. Frustration with the system would continue to grow among the populace throughout the following centuries.

JEDI VALIANCY
1000 B.B.Y.

Over the next thousand years, the Sith Brotherhood remained in hiding. They meditated on the dark side and systemitized their teachings. Choosing not to recruit widely, they continued by the system of each Master training only one apprentice. Like monks in a hermitage, the Sith waited in isolation for a chance to strike at the Jedi. Yoda, born in 896 B.B.Y., would shape the Jedi Order during this era.

Even without the influence of the Sith, some Jedi were occasionally seduced by evil. The Council rarely executed these fallen Jedi Knights, preferring instead to banish the offenders, in the hope that in primitive isolation the outcasts might focus on their Masters' teachings and return to the light. Approximately 600 B.B.Y., a fallen Jedi named Allya was exiled to the savage forests of Dathomir, a rugged planet that had long served as a prison colony for some of the Republic's worst criminals. Allya used the Force to subjugate the other prisoners and to tame Dathomir's feral rancors. Over time Allya had many daughters, all of whom she taught to use the Force. A female-dominant society eventually took shape, led by "Witches" who viewed the Force as a form of atavistic magic.

Economic forces continued to shape the Republic. In 490 B.B.Y., the Corporate Sector was established in the fringes of the galaxy's Tingel Arm, where companies could buy and manage star systems in an early attempt at founding a free trade zone. In 470 B.B.Y., the Corellian sector invoked the ancient constitutional clause of *Contemplanys Hermi,* which

allowed them to temporarily withdraw from the Republic in a short-lived bid at territorial independence. In 350 B.B.Y., the Trade Federation came into existence to represent the needs of major shipping corporations. The Trade Federation, dominated by Neimoidians, became known for its greed.

Other Jedi, continuing their work across the Republic, laid the foundations for events that would have an impact centuries later. Approximately 400 B.B.Y., a Hutt Jedi hopeful, Beldorion the Splendid, traveled to Nam Chorios and discovered that the planet's crystal energy magnified his Force powers. Beldorion set himself up as a petty local dictator. Elsewhere, a tiny Kushiban named Ikrit journeyed to Yavin 4 and discovered the golden sphere that Exar Kun had created thousands of years earlier. Realizing that he was incapable of freeing the Massassi spirits trapped within the orb, Ikrit placed himself in stasis to await the arrival of one who could break the curse, even if it would take centuries. In 380 B.B.Y., the Corellian Jedi Keiran Halcyon defeated the *Afarathu* terrorists, a radical group of Selonians who wanted to eliminate humans from within the Corellian system's borders.

Dathomir's Witches came to the Republic's attention in 340 B.B.Y. when the massive Jedi training vessel *Chu'unthor* crashed on the planet's surface. A triumvirate of famous Jedi Masters—Gra'aton, Vulatan, and Yoda—along with many Jedi Knights and acolytes attempted to rescue the *Chu'unthor's* passengers by battling the native spellcasters. On a return visit, Master Yoda used his insight to negotiate a peaceful settlement with the leader of the Witches.

The Mandalorian warrior clans committed the greatest crime of this era. Having defeated the Ithullans in a war over a narcolethe distillery in 200 B.B.Y., the Mandalorians then went on to exterminate the entire Ithullan species. Unfortunately, the Jedi Council did nothing in response to the genocide, and several rogue Jedi allied with the Bounty Hunters' Guild to take down the ruling Mandalore.

PART TWO

The Fall of the Republic

Approximately two hundred years before the Battle of Yavin, the shape of the Force abruptly seemed to flux. The greatest Jedi Masters, those most in touch with the unifying Force, studied this puzzle in quiet meditation. All of them reported the same thing—the murkiness, the uncertainty, the looming sense of dread all pointed to the growing power of the dark side. At first, some proposed that the Sith had returned, but when no Dark Lords made an appearance, an alternate explanation gained credence. Under this theory, one championed by Master Yoda, the gathering darkness indicated the coming fulfillment of an obscure, millennia-old prophecy that a Chosen One would one day destroy the Sith and bring balance to the Force. Yoda believed that the dark side could not be fully defeated by anyone save the Chosen One, and Yoda knew that he was not that person. The Chosen One would be a vessel of pure Force, more powerful than any Jedi in the history of the Order.

Not every Jedi agreed with Yoda's interpretation of the Chosen One prophecy. Some even disputed that the dark side was mustering strength. Seventy years after the first discovery of the flux (approximately 130 B.B.Y.), a group of Jedi formed a breakaway sect called the Potentium. Their creed stated that the dark side didn't truly exist and that the Jedi should embrace the Force's benevolence without regard for the strictures laid down by the Jedi Council. Yoda led the campaign to expel the Potentium from the Jedi Order.

Under the gathering darkness, Jedi victories seemed to be offset by setbacks of injustice or self-indulgence. In 124 B.B.Y., the Wol Cabasshite Jedi Master Omo Bouri orchestrated the famed Treaty of Trammis, but later that same year the Republic Senate declared the Outer Rim a free trade zone. This permitted the Trade Federation to represent planets that chose to align with it, giving corporations voting power in the Senate.

THE MAKING OF DOOKU
89–53 B.B.Y.

Count Dooku, heir to the aristocracy of Serenno, became a ward of the Jedi at a very early age and spent years training with Yoda in the Jedi Temple on Coruscant. In 89 B.B.Y., at the age of thirteen, Dooku was chosen as the Padawan of Master Thame Cerulian. Scandal marred his ascension, however, when Dooku was caught up in a fellow student's plot to steal a Sith Holocron from the Jedi archives. Though the Council cleared Dooku of any wrongdoing, they expelled student Lorian Nod from the Order. The experience left Dooku wary of friendship, and inordinately curious about the teachings of the Sith.

In his early twenties, Dooku took on his own Padawan learner, Qui-Gon Jinn—an at-times rebellious pupil with a deep connection to the living Force. On one early mission, Dooku and Qui-Gon fought Dooku's former friend Lorian Nod, who had become a pirate following his banishment from the Jedi Order.

Qui-Gon eventually became a Jedi Knight, but his kindness stood in stark contrast to the severity of his Master. Qui-Gon would endure his own troubles, however. He took on an apprentice of his own named Xanatos, but the boy never fully appreciated the teachings of the Jedi. In 53 B.B.Y., Master Yoda asked Qui-Gon and Xanatos to mediate a dispute on Telos.

This was intended to be Xanatos's final test before Jedi Knighthood. Telos, however, had been Xanatos's home before his induction into the Jedi Order, and his father Crion now ruled the planet with an iron grip. Rather than aiding the rebels, Xanatos took command of his father's army. Qui-Gon brought an end to the civil war by killing Crion. Xanatos, vowing revenge against his Master for his father's murder, vanished.

Dooku considered the incident a natural outgrowth of Qui-Gon's reliance on the living Force—Qui-Gon's "feelings" had failed him, and Dooku knew that, in the end, everyone was capable of betrayal.

Failing Republic, Thriving Sith
52–46 B.B.Y.

The Republic had grown stagnant. As a sprawling representative government hobbled by numerous sets of checks and balances, even simple decision making had turned impossible. Many Senators and planetary governors began to take the view that the existing system of government would continue through sheer force of inertia. Laziness and complacency became the rule, and with this apathy came corruption.

The crafty Senator Palpatine studied the government's decay with a practiced eye and a knowing smile. Elected in 52 B.B.Y. to represent the citizens of Naboo, he knew the time was drawing near when the citizenry would cry out for strong leadership. Palpatine set wheels in motion behind the scenes.

It is unclear how Palpatine fell under the mentorship of the Sith Lord Darth Plagueis, and little is known of Plagueis's own career. A mystic obsessed with eternal life, Plagueis is believed to have possessed knowledge that could sustain those who were dying, and perhaps had even gained the ability to use midi-chlorians to draw new life directly from the wellspring of the Force. Palpatine—under the Sith name Darth Sidious—learned dark side traditions from Plagueis, but grew concerned over his Master's stated intentions to create life from nothing. The child that resulted from this Force miracle, Plagueis insisted, would be the living embodiment of the Force itself—and at that moment, Sidious knew that

his Master was discussing Sidious's *replacement.* Soon after, Sidious killed Darth Plagueis in his sleep. The work necessary to create a Force-conceived child continued, however. It is unclear whether Plagueis had initiated the process before his death, or whether Sidious instead implemented his former Master's scheme for his own dark purposes.

In keeping with the Sith rule, Sidious accelerated the training of his own pet project, the Zabrak child called Maul. Unknown to Plagueis, Sidious had taken the Zabrak from his homeworld of Iridonia and, in a dark reflection of the Jedi Order's own training methods, began tutoring Maul in the art of cruelty and manipulation. Droids did most of the day-to-day work, for Sidious needed to maintain his role as Senator of Naboo. But whenever Sidious returned to his secret Coruscant lair, he gave Maul lessons in how to take a blow without flinching and how to kill lesser creatures without mercy.

On Tatooine, the slave Shmi Skywalker had given birth to a child more powerful in the Force than any other in history—the apparent product of forbidden research initiated by Darth Plagueis and taken up by Darth Sidious. This boy, Anakin Skywalker, had seemingly not been conceived by a human father, but by the midi-chlorians themselves. Palpatine kept a close watch on Anakin as the boy grew. If trained as a Sith apprentice, such a child could be vastly more powerful than Maul.

Local uprisings began to afflict the Republic during these years, the first being the Arkanian Revolution in 50 B.B.Y. Centered on Arkanian space in the Colonies region, the incident pitted a noninterventionist faction of Arkanians against the hard-line geneticists of the Arkanian Dominion. The geneticists, who had forcibly reengineered a number of species over the millennia including the Quermians and the Yakas, now stood helpless in the face of a spliced-together army.

The revolutionaries had created fierce mercenary cyborgs, who slaughtered thousands until the Dominion appealed for help from the Jedi. The revolutionaries perished, but a few of their creations survived. One of them, the patchwork bounty hunter Gorm the Dissolver, would later battle a rising star in the Jedi ranks named Mace Windu.

In 47 B.B.Y., the Jedi lost one of their greatest warriors—Sharad Hett, "the Howlrunner." Hett vanished after discovering the murder of his birth parents, and was presumed dead. In truth he had fallen in with the Tusken Raiders on Tatooine, where he became the leader of a Tusken tribe.

In the Republic Senate, officials continued to throw money away on grandiose projects. One example was the *Katana* fleet, an armada of two hundred slave-rigged Dreadnaughts completed in 46 B.B.Y. Tragically, a hive virus caused the crew of the flagship *Katana* to go mad. They jumped their ship into hyperspace using random coordinates, and the slave rig brought the other 199 vessels along for the ride. The *Katana* fleet would remain undiscovered for more than half a century, and the fiasco further eroded public confidence in the Republic's leadership.

FATEFUL APPRENTICESHIP
44 B.B.Y.

Qui-Gon Jinn took his second Padawan this year, following his failure with his apprentice Xanatos. Thirteen-year old Obi-Wan Kenobi had originally been slated for a career in the Jedi Agricultural Corps, but earned his place alongside Qui-Gon following a crisis on Bandomeer.

Clues behind the Bandomeer mission indicated that Xanatos had reemerged, now reigning as the corrupt kingpin of the Offworld Mining Corporation and the new ruler of Telos. The ex-Padawan attempted to assassinate Yoda and destroy the Jedi Temple, but Qui-Gon and Obi-Wan caught up with him on Telos. In a final confrontation with his former Master, Xanatos killed himself in a pool of acid rather than surrender. His son, under the name Granta Omega, would make trouble for Obi-Wan nearly twenty years in the future.

THE STARK HYPERSPACE CONFLICT
44 B.B.Y.

Though its battles took place only on a single planet, the so-called Stark Hyperspace Conflict intensified calls for a Grand Army of the Republic and raised the fortunes of two key historical players—Senator Finis Valorum of Coruscant and Minister Nute Gunray of the Trade Federation.

The incident began with a bacta supply crisis. Iaco Stark, a charismatic Outer Rim pirate and head of the Stark Commercial Combine, raided cargo ships carrying bacta and sold the stolen goods at a huge markup. Senator Valorum proposed that the Trade Federation, the Republic, and the Stark Commercial Combine air their issues at a diplomatic summit on the Xexto homeworld of Troiken.

Jedi negotiators assigned to the Troiken summit included Tyvokka—a Wookiee Master serving on the Jedi Council—as well as Plo Koon, Qui-Gon Jinn, and Qui-Gon's new Padawan Obi-Wan Kenobi. Plans for a peaceful meeting, however, were doomed from the start. Senator Ranulph Tarkin of Eriadu, a devout militarist, had assembled his own armada. He was already en route to Troiken to crush Stark's pirate fleet and win himself glory.

Stark, knowing an attack was imminent, unleashed a computer virus that affected all Republic navicomputers. No longer able to plot courses through hyperspace, most of Tarkin's vessels collided with mass shadows or disappeared into black holes. Stark attempted to hold the delegates hostage, but they escaped and regrouped in the caverns of Troiken's Mount Avos.

Tyvokka succumbed to injuries, and Plo Koon—who had once been Tyvokka's Padawan—used the crisis to make himself a legend. In a series of punishing ground battles against Stark's troops, Koon rallied the Republic soldiers under his command and drove back the enemy despite overwhelming odds.

The Republic finally assembled reinforcements, but at this point Stark had decided that he couldn't win. In exchange for immunity, he supplied the patch to eliminate the navicomputer virus. But no one informed Ranulph Tarkin, who was determined to go out as a hero. Tarkin detonated an explosive charge at Mount Avos, killing himself and freeing millions of flesh-eating insects from the inner caverns that devoured the remainder of Stark's army.

The resolution of the crisis made Valorum a political star. Nute Gunray earned a promotion to viceroy. And Plo Koon honored his former Master's dying wish by taking Tyvokka's seat on the Jedi Council.

Months after the Stark incident, the Republic experienced the Kol Huro Unrest, in which a local despot used the Kol Huro factories to turn out an army of battle droids. The Jedi squashed the minor rebellion, but the use of droids in combat would become an increasingly hot topic as the Trade Federation moved to grow the size of its own automated "security force."

The Battle of Galidraan
40 B.B.Y.

The Battle of Galidraan marked the end of the Mandalorian Civil War, a conflict between the True Mandalorians and the Mandalorian Death Watch that had been sizzling for over a quarter century. Following the Mandalorians' extinction of the Ithullans a century and a half earlier, some clan members had expressed a desire to shed the amoral ways of the "Mandalorian Mercs." Eventually, the charismatic Jaster Mereel came to lead the clans as Mandalore, and set down an idealistic code of conduct in the Supercommando Codex. A Mandalorian named Vizsla attracted followers fond of the old ways, who formed the Death Watch faction. Armed conflict broke out approximately 60 B.B.Y.

Vizsla succeeded in killing Jaster Mereel, but Mereel's role as head of the True Mandalorians was filled by Jango Fett. After decades of infighting, Galidraan was to be the end of the Death Watch—but instead it proved to be the end of four thousand years of Mandalorian dominance.

The governor of Galidraan informed Jango Fett that he would give up Vizsla's location if Jango's troops terminated a group of local rebels. They did so, only to learn that the governor and the Death Watch had set Jango up. Protesting to the Republic that the True Mandalorians had slaughtered innocents, the governor called in a Jedi peacekeeping force led by Master Dooku and his Padawan, Komari Vosa. The Mandalorian army fought to the last man; only their commander Jango survived, to become the prisoner of slavers.

The once great Mandalorian power had been forever gutted. Besides Jango, only Vizsla and a few surviving Death Watch members remained active in the galaxy, while a small regiment of troopers remained on the planet Mandalore as a home guard.

MOVING INTO ALIGNMENT
40–36 B.B.Y.

In 40 B.B.Y., Finis Valorum began the first of two terms as Supreme Chancellor of the Republic. The influential Tarkin family helped push the election through, on the condition that Valorum posthumously decorate Senator Ranulph Tarkin for his role in ending the Stark Hyperspace Conflict.

Obi-Wan Kenobi continued to grow in his apprenticeship to Qui-Gon Jinn. The two found themselves running missions on behalf of Supreme Chancellor Valorum, who was a fan of the Jedi Order. Their assignments frequently paired them with Adi Gallia and her Padawan Siri Tachi. Obi-Wan grew fond of Siri, as both a colleague and . . . something more. In this, he was following the lead of his impulsive Master Qui-Gon, who held his own feelings for a fellow Jedi Master named Tahl. In 39 B.B.Y., Tahl died on a mission to New Apsolon, spurring Qui-Gon to vengeance—but he managed to pull himself back from the brink of rage.

Qui-Gon and Obi-Wan also helped Attichitcuk, leader of a Wookiee colony, establish a new settlement on Alaris Prime despite opposition from the Trade Federation. Attichitcuk's son Chewbacca would later become one of the greatest heroes of the Rebel Alliance.

In 36 B.B.Y., Finis Valorum won a second four-year term as Supreme Chancellor, though by this time many Senators were beginning to have doubts about his leadership. Opposition parties began considering possible replacements, a list that always seemed to include Naboo's Senator Palpatine.

THE YINCHORRI UPRISING
33 B.B.Y.

The Jedi Order numbered more than ten thousand members and could have vanquished any foe if permitted to attack en masse, but Judicial Department bureaucracy tied the hands of the Jedi and often left them shockingly

Padawans Anakin Skywalker and Siri Tachi, with their Masters, Obi-Wan Kenobi and Adi Gallia [ART BY TOMMY LEE EDWARDS]

ineffectual. No incident better captured this paralysis than the Yinchorri Uprising.

The reptilian Yinchorri controlled several worlds in their star system, including their home planet Yinchorr and the colony moons of Yitheeth, Yibikkoror, and Uhanayih. Stirrings of aggression against neighboring planets prompted Chancellor Valorum to dispatch a Jedi team to assess the situation. The Yinchorri dumped the bodies of the Jedi investigators on Valorum's doorstep.

Mace Windu sent only three Republic cruisers to put down the uprising. Though the cruisers carried some of the best Jedi in the order—including Windu, Adi Gallia, Eeth Koth, Plo Koon, Micah Giiett, Qui-Gon Jinn, and Qui-Gon's Padawan Obi-Wan Kenobi—the Yinchorri possessed cortosis-weave armor that could resist lightsaber cuts. They also had the advice and silent backing of Darth Sidious.

Yoda stopped a Yinchorri assault against the Jedi Temple on Coruscant, but Mace Windu's team walked into a bloodbath on the worlds of the Yinchorr system. The Jedi casualties included Micah Giiett, who sacrificed himself to slow the advance of Yinchorri troops. Ultimately, Valorum won Senate approval of an emergency measure to blockade the system, forcing the Yinchorri to surrender in the face of overwhelming power.

The Jedi Council failed to apply any learnings from the debacle, passing over the iconoclastic Qui-Gon Jinn for Micah Giiett's Jedi Council seat in favor of the by-the-book Cerean Jedi Ki-Adi-Mundi. Chancellor Valorum looked more ineffectual than ever, and political observers declared Valorum's career to be on life support.

Before Ki-Adi-Mundi accepted the Jedi Council's offer to serve as one of their members, he returned to his homeworld of Cerea. Unlike other Jedi of the time, Ki-Adi-Mundi had children and several wives, a unique dispensation given

Supreme Chancellor Finis Valorum
[Art by Mark Chiarello]

to Cerean Jedi due to the species' low birthrate. Ki-Adi-Mundi became involved in a dispute between the Cerean preservationists, who wished to outlaw technology, and the young people of his world, who were enamored with the high-speed swoopbikes imported by offworlders.

The Eriadu Summit
32.5 B.B.Y.

Darth Sidious had shaped Maul into a razor-honed weapon. The Zabrak apprentice, now a Dark Lord of the Sith, wielded a double-bladed lightsaber (patterned after the one used by Exar Kun during the Sith War) and wore a jagged red-and-black tattoo over his entire body. Sidious

Mace Windu whirls to face a charging Yinchorri warrior.
[Art by Tommy Lee Edwards]

wasted no time sending his agent out on missions. At a Iommite-mining colony on Dorvalla, Maul used stealth to pit two rival mining operations against each other, leaving the planet ripe for takeover by the Trade Federation.

The event solidified the hold that Darth Sidious had over Nute Gunray of the Trade Federation. Sidious also had contacts among the Nebula Front, a band of pirates and terrorists who fought the Trade Federation in the outlying systems. The violence between the Trade Federation and the Nebula Front had become a political hot button in the Republic Senate. From his darkened sanctum, Darth Sidious saw this as the perfect wedge. By pushing it, he could crush Chancellor Valorum and eventually split the Republic.

Sidious set things in motion with a second incident at Dorvalla. Space pirate Arwen Cohl, working on behalf of a radical arm of the Nebula Front, raided the Trade Federation freighter *Revenue* and made off with a stash of aurodium ingots worth two billion credits.

In response to the theft, Sidious—in his role as Senator Palpatine—convinced Chancellor Valorum to propose a tax on the Outer Rim trade routes, effectively abolishing the free trade zone that had made the Trade Federation so wealthy. Senator Lott Dod of the Trade Federation objected to this obvious check to its power, and demanded that his conglomerate be allowed to expand its droid armies to defend against the Nebula Front. To allow both sides to voice their concerns, Palpatine suggested that a summit be held on Eriadu, the Outer Rim home of the powerful Tarkin family.

On Coruscant, a Nebula Front assassin shot and wounded Valorum. In response, a Jedi task force

Darth Maul makes short work of Black Sun's defenders on Ralltiir. [Art by Tommy Lee Edwards]

smashed a Nebula Front base on Asmeru in the Senex sector, uncovering enough clues for Qui-Gon Jinn and Obi-Wan Kenobi to learn of a second assassination plot against Valorum, this time on Eriadu. Qui-Gon received unexpected help from pirate Arwen Cohl, who had had a falling-out with his Nebula Front confederates.

Valorum survived the Eriadu summit without a scratch. The true targets of the assassination proved to be the ruling members of the Trade Federation directorate, who were gunned down by their own security droids. This left Sidious's puppet Nute Gunray as the Trade Federation's ruling viceroy.

On Naboo, the corrupt King Veruna chose this moment to abdicate the throne. Padmé Naberrie, a fourteen-year-old girl currently serving as Princess of Theed under the "name of state" of Amidala, became Naboo's new monarch. Veruna, who was known to have had close ties with Senator Palpatine, later died under mysterious circumstances.

Showing little sympathy for the Trade Federation after the Eriadu disaster, the Republic Senate passed Valorum's taxation proposal. Sidious suggested to Nute Gunray that he retaliate in symbolic fashion by blockading a planet, preferably Senator Palpatine's homeworld of Naboo.

Chancellor Valorum suffered yet another blow when evidence, planted by Sidious, suggested that he had arranged for the two billion in stolen aurodium to be transferred to a small family company, Valorum Shipping, on Eriadu. Though formally cleared of charges, Valorum privately admitted that his rule had been crippled. Rumors swirled that he might be forced from office before the completion of his term.

FINAL PREPARATIONS
32 B.B.Y.

With his plans now inevitable, Darth Sidious moved to tie up loose ends. Darth Maul traveled to the Core world of Ralltiir in his newly acquired Sith Infiltrator starship *Scimitar*, aiming to kill the assembled mob bosses of the Black Sun syndicate. Maul buzz-sawed his way through the stronghold, eviscerating Black Sun leader Alexi Garyn and scores of underlings. The loss of Black Sun's entire command structure left the organization in disarray for many years. Following an intense power struggle, the Falleen prince Xizor assumed authority over the consortium.

Nute Gunray and the other Neimoidians were vital to Darth Sidious's plans, but they carried with them a huge risk—as a rule, Neimoidians had difficulty keeping their mouths shut. Sidious had revealed his plans for the invasion of Naboo to only three top-level Neimoidians besides Gunray, but one of them, Hath Monchar, decided that selling the information could make him very rich.

By the time Sidious realized the risk, Monchar had already fled to Coruscant with a holocron that contained full details on the Sith plot. Darth Maul set off in search of Monchar and the intelligence he carried.

The Neimoidian soon lost his head to Maul's dual-bladed lightsaber, but other people had already been exposed to the information, including Jedi Padawan Darsha Assant and data broker Lorn Pavan. Maul chased them through the undercity past cannibalistic Cthons and a train-sized taozin worm, and eventually killed the Padawan. Lorn Pavan foolishly tried to get the drop on Maul aboard an orbital space station, but received critical injuries during the fight. Before he died, Pavan gave Monchar's information to Senator Palpatine, never knowing that he had only brought it full circle, back to the original mastermind.

One month before the event now known as the Battle of Naboo, the Trade Federation carried through on its threat and blockaded Naboo in defiance of the taxation of the Outer Rim trade routes. Valorum realized he had to do something radical to shore up his crumbling support base. Exploiting his friendship with Jedi Master Adi Gallia, Valorum went directly to the Jedi Council to request mediators, breaking protocol by neglecting to inform the Senate of his decision. Mace Windu sent Qui-Gon Jinn and Obi-Wan Kenobi to Naboo to apply direct pressure on the Trade Federation viceroy and to force Gunray's vessels to stand down.

THE BATTLE OF NABOO
32 B.B.Y.

Qui-Gon and Obi-Wan received a poor welcome aboard the Trade Federation flagship. Viceroy Nute Gunray destroyed their landing ship and attempted to eliminate them with poison gas and droidekas. The two Jedi escaped to the planet's surface with the knowledge that the Trade Federation was planning a full-scale invasion of Naboo using a vast battle droid army.

In Naboo's capital city of Theed, Queen Padmé Amidala waited with a heavy heart for the Trade Federation's army. She had been Naboo's monarch for only six months, and for the past several weeks she had worked in vain to end the blockade. Columns of battle tanks approached the Palace, and Queen Amidala became the prisoner of battle droids.

In the Naboo swamps, Qui-Gon and Obi-Wan met a native Gungan named Jar Jar Binks, who introduced them to Boss Nass, ruler of the underwater city of Otoh Gunga. The trio borrowed a submersible to take them to Theed, where the Jedi freed Queen Amidala and her military aides. The group escaped Naboo aboard the Royal Starship, bound for Coruscant.

Unfortunately, a hyperdrive malfunction forced the ship to drop into realspace before it could begin its jaunt down the Corellian Run. In need of discreet repairs, the group had no choice but to touch down on the desert planet Tatooine.

Qui-Gon took it upon himself to obtain a replacement hyperdrive generator. In Mos Espa he found a Toydarian dealer with the parts Qui-Gon needed. The Toydarian also owned a nine-year-old slave, Anakin Skywalker. Anakin's mother, Shmi, confirmed in her own words what Qui-Gon had already suspected—the boy was immeasurably strong in the Force. Neither knew of Darth Plagueis's suspected involvement in inducing midi-chlorians to create life, though Shmi informed Qui-Gon that Anakin had no natural father.

Queen Padmé Amidala of Naboo
[ART BY MARK CHIARELLO]

By wagering that Anakin would win Mos Espa's Boonta Eve Podrace, Qui-Gon obtained the hyperdrive parts, and he secured Anakin's freedom. Tearfully, the boy bid farewell to his mother, promising to return one day to free her. He also left behind C-3PO, a protocol droid he had built from spare parts.

Darth Sidious learned of his enemies' arrival on Tatooine. He dispatched his apprentice Darth Maul in order to prevent the Jedi from meddling with Anakin Skywalker's fate. Maul engaged Qui-Gon in a frenzied lightsaber attack, but failed to prevent the Jedi from bringing both Anakin and Queen Amidala to Coruscant.

Qui-Gon brought Anakin before the Jedi Council. Yoda and Mace Windu remained unconvinced that the boy could be the Chosen One of prophecy who would restore balance to the Force. In the Republic Senate, Queen Amidala begged for help on behalf of her conquered homeworld. When her pleas failed to move anyone to action, she gave in to Senator Palpatine's advice and called for a vote of no confidence in Chancellor Valorum.

Rather than wait for the Senate to determine Valorum's successor, Amidala decided to return to Naboo and stand beside the people she had sworn to represent. Qui-Gon, Obi-Wan, and Anakin accompanied her with the blessing of the Jedi Council. The Queen enlisted the help of Boss Nass's Gungan army to provide a diversion on the great grass plains so that Amidala's group could sneak into the Palace and capture Nute Gunray.

A strike team captured the Theed hangar and seized its N-1 starfighters, taking off to attack the Trade Federation's orbiting Droid Control Ship. Anakin Skywalker inadvertently joined this group along with the astromech droid R2-D2, and Anakin's natural skill with the Force led to the destruction of the Droid Control Ship with a pair of proton torpedoes. The explosion of the vessel triggered the collapse of the Trade Federation's droid army, saving Boss Nass's Gungans from annihilation in the ground battle below.

Queen Amidala scaled the Palace walls and forced the surrender of Viceroy Nute Gunray, while Qui-Gon and Obi-Wan battled Darth Maul above the bottomless abyss of the Theed power generator. During the fighting, impenetrable electron walls closed to separate Obi-Wan from his Master. Obi-Wan watched in helpless shock as Maul stabbed Qui-Gon through the chest with his double-edged light-saber.

As soon as the electron walls dropped, Obi-Wan attacked in a haze of grief and sliced Darth Maul in half. Later, in the Palace turret room, Yoda promoted Obi-Wan to the rank of Jedi Knight. He also passed along the Council's recommendation that Anakin be trained as Obi-Wan's new apprentice. The Jedi Order realized that Darth Maul had been a Sith, and Yoda began the search for the second Sith—the one who would have trained Maul and possibly even orchestrated the Naboo invasion. The reemergence of the Sith also seemed to confirm Yoda's interpretation of the prophecy of the Chosen One.

In a final celebration on the Palace steps, Queen Amidala and Boss Nass presided over the long-overdue unification of their two civilizations. Behind them, Palpatine, the newly elected Supreme Chancellor of the Republic following Valorum's forced ouster, looked on with satisfaction.

At this time, Nute Gunray, viceroy of the Trade Federation, began the first of what would be four trials in the Supreme Court for his actions in the invasion of Naboo. Exonerated time and again by his timid prosecutors, who didn't want to upset the Trade Federation economic engine, Gunray held on to his title and status. Eventually, the Republic announced the public disarmament of the Trade Federation's battle fleet and droid army, but no significant reductions followed.

THE LOST TWENTY
32 B.B.Y.

Master Dooku, hero of the Battle of Galidraan, had become a thorn in the side of the Jedi Order. Dooku's first Padawan, Qui-Gon Jinn, had died at Naboo, while his second, Komari Vosa, had disappeared after Galidraan. Dooku had since become a very public critic of the Republic's corruption and the Jedi Order's complicity in

propping up a broken system. His protestations disturbed the Jedi Council, but none of its members were aware that Dooku had already fallen under the sway of Darth Sidious.

One of Dooku's close friends within the Order, Master Sifo-Dyas, perceived the events surrounding the reappearance of the Sith and believed that the Republic could not survive without additional defenders. Without the knowledge of his Jedi colleagues, Sifo-Dyas placed an order for a massive clone army with the geneticists of Kamino. Darth Sidious learned of the plan and moved to secure the army for his own purposes. As a final test of loyalty for his would-be apprentice, he ordered Dooku to kill Sifo-Dyas.

After the clandestine murder, Dooku erased all traces of Kamino from the Jedi archives and announced his intention to leave the Order. Now a true Sith Lord, Dooku took the secret name of Darth Tyranus. He returned to his native Serenno, taking up the title and holdings due to him as the planet's hereditary Count, then disappeared from public view. Dooku became the newest Jedi Master to leave the Order, making the Lost Nineteen into the Lost Twenty.

Jango Fett
[Art by Mark Chiarello]

THE PRIME CLONE
32 B.B.Y.

Dooku knew that the Kaminoan clone army had to be flawless if it hoped to stand a chance against the forces of industry he would soon marshal on the opposite side. For the genetic template that would become the Prime Clone, Dooku had his eye on Jango Fett, the greatest (and one of the last) of the Mandalorians. Jango had escaped from two years spent as a slave, following his capture in the Battle of Galidraan—a battle that Dooku had orchestrated. After once again donning the armor of the Mandalorians, Jango reinvented himself, this time as a

The Gungan Grand Army prepares to engage Trade Federation forces on Naboo. [Art by Tommy Lee Edwards]

bounty hunter. Having heard that Jango had also tracked down and killed Vizsla of the Mandalorian Death Watch, it was clear to Dooku that slavery had done nothing to dull Jango's edge.

Dooku chose to test Jango and the galaxy's other top bounty hunters by posting a five-million-credit bounty on the head of his former Padawan Komari Vosa, who had become the leader of the Bando Gora cult. Jango's quest took him to the penitentiary on Oovo IV, where he fought his way through a jailbreak alongside fellow hunter Zam Wesell, who revealed herself as a shape-shifting Clawdite. Jango escaped by stealing a prototype *Firespray*-class police interceptor, which replaced his former vessel, *Jaster's*

Legacy. Jango christened his new ship *Slave I.*

Jango tracked Komari Vosa to Kohlma, one of the Bogden moons. There he defeated an old Mandalorian rival named Montross to claim the five-million-credit bounty. Although Jango got the drop on Komari Vosa, it was Dooku who delivered the killing blow.

Now confident of Jango's skills, Count Dooku summoned the bounty hunter to his retreat on one of the moons of Bogden, engaging him in a test of wits involving mutual poisonings. At last satisfied with each other's sincerity, Jango agreed to Dooku's offer and accepted a lucrative and low-effort contract as the Kaminoan Prime Clone. Jango made one special request—he wanted an unaltered clone to raise as his own. He would name this clone Boba Fett.

The Kaminoans set to work growing soldiers based on the Fett genetic template. Within ten years, the Republic would have the finest army in the galaxy. As leader of the Republic, Chancellor Palpatine would control the clones, while Dooku would raise an opposing army of corporate droids. The two sides, each under the control of a Sith Lord, would then fight a sham war that would decimate the Jedi and make the public hunger for a centralized government.

As a final step, Sidious ensured that every clone received special training for even the most extreme eventualities. When Sidious felt the time was right, he would activate this contingency plan by issuing "Order Sixty-Six."

DUTIES OF THE JEDI COUNCIL
32–30 B.B.Y.

To some, the Naboo crisis appeared to represent a new culture of lawlessness. The members of the Jedi Council had their hands full over the next year, putting down emergencies large and small.

Ki-Adi-Mundi returned to Tatooine to investigate reports that the legendary Jedi Knight Sharad "Howlrunner" Hett had reappeared after a fifteen-year absence. Sharad had apparently gone native and now controlled a tribe of Tusken Raiders. His young son, A'Sharad Hett, wore the mask and wrappings of a Tusken but wielded the lightsaber of a Jedi.

The mission was complicated by a local Hutt gang war between Gardulla and Jabba, as well as the appearance of Aurra Sing—a failed Padawan who had become a bounty hunter and assassin, collecting the lightsabers of the Jedi she murdered. Sing killed Sharad Hett, and Ki-Adi-Mundi took A'Sharad back to Coruscant as his new apprentice.

Months later, Mace Windu led a mission to Malastare to help mediate a dispute between the government of Lannik and a Lannik terrorist organization, the Red Iaro. The Jedi prevented the terrorists from feeding the Lannik prince to akk dogs, ravenous beasts hailing from Windu's homeworld of Haruun Kal. Mace Windu and Depa Billaba later smashed the illegal Nar Shaddaa operation that had been trafficking in akk dogs.

Aurra Sing made a reappearance in 30 B.B.Y., slaying Jedi Knights in the Coruscant undercity. Adi Gallia, along with Ki-Adi-Mundi and his new Padawan A'Sharad Hett, received the assignment to track Sing down. On a tropical planet buffeted by meteorites, A'Sharad tried and failed to take his revenge on the woman who had murdered his father. Even the arrival of the Dark Woman, Aurra Sing's former Master, was not enough to eliminate this dire threat to the Jedi.

QUINLAN VOS'S ROAD BACK
32–30 B.B.Y.

Jedi Knight Quinlan Vos had served the Order with honor. Former Padawan of Master Tholme, Quinlan possessed the Kiffu talent of psychometrics, allowing him to read memories and impressions directly off the surface of objects. He had recently taken the Twi'lek Aayla Secura as his Padawan.

Aurra Sing fights for her life against Jedi Padawan A'Sharad Hett.
[ART BY TOMMY LEE EDWARDS]

On a mission to investigate a new spice drug called glitteryll, Quinlan Vos and Aayla found themselves too close to a glitteryll-processing operation on Ryloth. Aayla's uncle, Pol Secura, wiped the memories of both Jedi and took Aayla as a house slave. Quinlan Vos awoke on Nar Shaddaa with no memory of who he was or how he had arrived there.

The Devaronian scoundrel Vilmarh "Villie" Grahrk helped Quinlan recover bits and pieces of his life history. Burning with rage, and no longer bound by the forgotten rules of his Jedi training, Quinlan would have murdered the Twi'lek Senator behind the glitteryll plot if not for Mace Windu's intervention. Quinlan agreed to return to the Jedi Temple for retraining.

In a field test of his reemerging abilities, Quinlan Vos executed a solo mission to Dathomir. Six hundred years after the arrival of Allya, the Witches of Dathomir had developed into primitive, Force-wielding clans. One of their more malevolent members, the Witch Zalem, had discovered a teleportational Infinity Gate buried in the heart of the planet by the pre-Republic Kwa species. Zalem triggered the Gate and unleashed a wave of energy directed at Coruscant, but Quinlan engineered the machine's destruction.

Aayla Secura, still tormented by her damaged memories, accidentally became stranded on the prison world of Kiffex. She freed the fallen Anzati Jedi Volfe Karkko from a stasis field, and Karkko rallied an army of his fellow Anzati vampires that overran Kiffex and terrorized the prisoners. Quinlan Vos, with help from his former Master Tholme, killed Karkko and freed Aayla Secura from his Anzati spell. Master Tholme agreed to train Aayla during her long path to recovery.

Nearly two years after the glitteryll incident, Aayla's homeworld of Ryloth became a trouble spot once more. Lon Secura, another of Aayla's uncles and ruler of Clan Secura, invited his niece and Master Tholme to mediate a clan dispute. Soon after their arrival, Kh'aris Fenn, an ambitious Twi'lek in league with Count Dooku, hired two Nikto of the Morgukai warrior tradition to kidnap Lon Secura's son Nat. In the lava fields of Kintan, Quinlan Vos and Aayla Secura defeated the two Morgukai and freed the young heir. For their roles in the rescue, the two Jedi received promotions—Quinlan Vos became a Jedi Master, while Aayla Secura graduated to Jedi Knight.

Mission to Zonama Sekot
29 B.B.Y.

The Tarkin family of Eriadu played a critical, but mostly offstage, role in shaping galactic politics. Wilhuff Tarkin had once been a commander in the Republic Outland Regions Security Force and had recently served as the lieutenant governor of Eriadu. Like his cousin Ranulph—who had kick-started the Stark Hyperspace Conflict fifteen years earlier—Wilhuff Tarkin was an instigator.

Tarkin had already been contacted by Darth Sidious and was seduced by the Sith Lord's vision of a Human High Culture in which aliens would be pushed from power and forced to grovel as slaves. Tarkin enlisted his friend Raith Sienar, the genius starship engineer behind Republic Sienar Systems. Raith Sienar had designed Darth Maul's ship *Scimitar* and had already begun conceptual work on a moon-sized battle station, but Tarkin believed he could locate an even greater weapon.

Tarkin learned that the Jedi Council had dispatched Obi-Wan Kenobi and his Padawan Anakin Skywalker to the far-flung Gardaji Rift, the rumored location of the mythical "living planet" Zonama Sekot. A Jedi Knight named Vergere had vanished on a mission to Zonama Sekot one year prior. Obi-Wan and Anakin hoped to find Vergere, while Tarkin wanted to exploit Zonama Sekot's strange ability to fuse organic and high tech into starfighters faster than anything else in the galaxy. Sienar and Tarkin followed the two Jedi to Zonama Sekot with a Trade Federation armada.

The number and variety of living things in the jungles of Zonama Sekot left Anakin and Obi-Wan speechless. The planet's colonists, many descended from the expelled Jedi sect known as the Potentium, sold organic "seed-partners" that bonded to their hosts, allowing the living planet to grow ships personalized for each customer. Anakin attracted twelve seed-partners, more than anyone in history, and named his living starship *Jabitha* after the daughter of Zonama Sekot's ruling Magister.

By the time Tarkin arrived with a force sufficient to subjugate the planet, Obi-Wan and Anakin had learned that Zonama Sekot possessed a sentient consciousness. The planet revealed to them that a year earlier, Vergere had given herself up to scouts from an extragalactic species called the "Far Outsiders" (known to modern historians as the Yuuzhan Vong) in order to prevent them from attacking Zonama Sekot. Anakin and Obi-Wan's original mission could no longer be carried out, but they suddenly had a more pressing problem—halting Tarkin's attack and making it off the planet alive.

Anakin killed Sienar's Blood Carver bodyguard in a fit of rage, telekinetically burning the alien from the inside out. Anakin also met Wilhuff Tarkin for the first time, as a prisoner aboard his flagship. Obi-Wan Kenobi destroyed Tarkin's vessel, and the fighting gave Zonama Sekot sufficient time to initiate its planetary hyperspace engines. The entire planet vanished in a blink, presumably bound for the safety of the Unknown Regions.

Anakin did not get to keep *Jabitha*. Away from her creator-planet, the organic starfighter sickened and died. Sienar and Tarkin both returned to Republic space, winning forgiveness for the debacle by presenting the plans for Sienar's moon-sized Expeditionary Battle Planetoid to Supreme Chancellor Palpatine. When the battle station project shifted from conceptual stage to architectural planning, work moved to the planet Geonosis. There, engineer Bevel Lemelisk teamed with the hive-minded Geonosians to hammer out structural and power supply issues.

EDUCATION OF THE CHOSEN ONE
29–27 B.B.Y.

At this point in his apprenticeship, Anakin had progressed enough in his training to construct his own lightsaber, which he did inside the sacred crystal caves on the snow-wrapped planet of Ilum. He also notched his second kill in anger, following his execution of the Blood Carver on Zonama Sekot. On a mission to take down Krayn, the infamous pirate and slaver, Anakin allowed the pain and humiliation he had experienced in his former life as a slave to overtake his propriety as a Jedi. Though Krayn could have been apprehended, Anakin used his new lightsaber to burn a hole through the slaver's chest.

As Anakin grew further into his training, he struggled with the issue of mentorship. He had never known a father, and Qui-Gon Jinn had died mere days after taking Anakin from his mother. Obi-Wan was now his master—though Anakin suspected that Obi-Wan had agreed to the training only out of obligation to Qui-Gon's dying wish—and Supreme Chancellor Palpatine had become another influence, dispensing advice and veiled flattery to the Chosen One. Among his peers, Anakin found a friend in Padawan Tru Veld and a rival in Ferus Olin, the apprentice of Obi-Wan's close companion Siri Tachi.

THE OUTBOUND FLIGHT PROJECT
27 B.B.Y.

Two years after the Zonama Sekot catastrophe, Jedi Master Jorus C'baoth brought a new exploratory proposal before Supreme Chancellor Palpatine. C'baoth's project, named Outbound Flight, would send almost 45,000 colonists on a swing through the Unknown Regions, with the ultimate goal of reaching a nearby galaxy.

Extra-galactic travel had long been thought impossible due to the intersecting ripples formed in hyperspace by galactic masses. C'baoth believed that the Jedi could use the Force to smooth this zone of turbulence. He tested his theory on the briarpatch border of the Unknown Regions, then recommended that he, with seventeen other Jedi Knights and Masters, accompany the Outbound colonists on their journey.

Palpatine remained cool on the concept, but intrigued with the possibility of sabotaging the project and causing the deaths of a number of prominent Jedi, he allowed C'baoth to move forward.

The Outbound Flight project—six dreadnaughts linked in a ring around a central fuel tank—launched from Yaga Minor.

Among the Jedi aboard were Obi-Wan Kenobi and Anakin Skywalker, but Palpatine—who knew that Anakin would play a critical role in events yet to come—arranged for them to disembark after the first leg of the trip. Outbound Flight continued on under the command of Jorus C'baoth until it reached the Unknown Regions, where it ran head-on into the Chiss Ascendancy, and the brilliant alien mastermind who would someday become Grand Admiral Thrawn.

As far as the rest of the galaxy was concerned, Outbound Flight mysteriously disappeared somewhere in the Unknown Regions. Not until decades later, when its remains were found by the Chiss and returned to the New Republic, would its true fate be discovered.

DEATHS ON THE JEDI COUNCIL
27–26 B.B.Y.

The Jedi Council lost one of its members when the Quermian Jedi Master Yarael Poof tracked down a rogue Annoo-dat general, who had hoped to use the ener-gies of an alien religious idol to destroy Coruscant. Deep in the heart of the capital planet near the core power relays, bounty hunters Jango Fett and Zam Wesell stopped the doomsday plot, but could not prevent the death of Master Poof. Master Coleman Trebor assumed a post on the Council to fill the vacancy.

As their Master–Padawan bond deepened, Obi-Wan and Anakin made a powerful enemy of Granta Omega, the son of Qui-Gon's fallen apprentice Xanatos. Omega lacked any connection to the Force, but his extreme wealth had allowed him to become an expert in Sith lore. By killing the Jedi heroes, Omega hoped to attract the attention of the Sith Lord Darth Sidious. Obi-Wan and Anakin clashed with Omega several times over the years, but the would-be Sith committed his greatest crime on the war-torn world of Mawan. There, Jedi Council member Yaddle sacrificed her life to prevent Omega from poisoning the population with dihexalon gas. Shaak Ti, a red-and-white striped Togruta, took Yaddle's place on the Council.

THE SEPARATIST MOVEMENT
24 B.B.Y.

After eight years out of the limelight, Count Dooku made his first public reappearance on the industrial powerhouse of Raxus Prime. Decrying the corruption that consumed the Republic like a Raxan garbage-worm, Dooku rallied star systems to join his new government, the Confederacy of Independent Systems, or CIS.

In public, he swayed planets and commercial concerns to his side. In private he trained a number of Force-sensitive individuals in the ways of the dark side, and recruited high-powered killers to silence his enemies. Among Dooku's dark side minions was Asajj Ventress, a pale-skinned native of Rattatak who had learned a heavily distorted version of the Jedi way from a shipwrecked Jedi Knight. Others included Sev'rance Tann, a Chiss who had been brought into civilized space with her lover Vandalor by Darth Sidious, and Saato, a Witch from Dathomir with a fearsome tattooed face.

The soldiers in Dooku's employ included Durge, an armored Gen'Dai who had recently awakened from a century-long hibernation following a battle with Mandalorians, and Cydon Prax, a reptilian Chistori who concealed his identity behind a battle suit. But the greatest among them was Grievous, an alien battlefield commander who had been critically injured in a shuttle crash arranged by San Hill of the Inter-Galactic Banking Clan. Hill then had Grievous rebuilt as a cyborg. Dooku, who taught the half-machine killer to wield four blades at once, would eventually name Grievous the supreme general of the Separatist droid armies.

Not coincidentally, Dooku's reemergence corresponded with the end of Chancellor Palpatine's eight years in office. To lead the Republic through the crisis of Separatism, Palpatine won an indefinite extension of his term—despite the measure's clear unconstitutionality. Most observers hoped that Palpatine would bring about a swift end to what looked like the foolhardy act of a political dreamer.

Obi-Wan and Anakin battle Granta Omega on Mawan.
[ART BY TOMMY LEE EDWARDS]

THE DEATH OF GRANTA OMEGA
24 B.B.Y.

Obi-Wan Kenobi and Anakin Skywalker eventually caught up with their enemy Granta Omega on the Sith world of Korriban. Following an incident in which the Senate chamber had nearly been poisoned by Separatist scientist Jenna Zan Arbor, both Zan Arbor and Granta Omega had arrived on Korriban to receive new assignments from their secret commander, Count Dooku.

A Jedi task force led by Obi-Wan Kenobi moved in to capture the plotters. Dooku and Zan Arbor escaped, but Obi-Wan killed Granta Omega in a final showdown. Jedi Padawan Tru Veld inadvertently caused the death of a fellow Jedi when his lightsaber malfunctioned in the heat of battle. Ferus Olin and Anakin Skywalker had both known about the lightsaber malfunction beforehand, but neither had told their Masters. Anakin remained silent, but Olin stepped forward to take the blame for the incident. He voluntarily resigned from the Jedi Order.

Elsewhere, on Maramere, the Trade Federation contended with a new threat as the Feeorin mercenary Nym joined forces with pirate Sol Sixxa to drive all traces of Nute Gunray's conglomerate out of the system. Since Maramere had become a repository for invisibility-generating stygium crystals from Aeten II, the Trade Federation tied up many of its assets in the recapturing of Maramere in order to ensure the future of cloaking technology.

THE CONFEDERACY TAKES SHAPE
23 B.B.Y.

In one year, Count Dooku's Separatist movement had grown significantly more powerful. Every day saw news of another planet joining the Confederacy of Independent Systems. Many Senators thought the chancellor should simply let them go, allowing the Confederacy to exist side by side with the Republic. Others pushed for the passage of a Military Creation Act that would create a Grand Army of the Republic to bolster the meager Judicial security forces.

Dooku had made great strides in soliciting the help of the galaxy's six major industrial powers. Though none of them had yet signed on as official members of the CIS, their financial assistance had proven invaluable to Dooku. The Baktoid Armor Workshop's foundries on Geonosis produced thousands upon thousands of battle droids. The InterGalactic Banking Clan of Muunilinst was both a financial hub and a manufacturer of hailfire and IG-style droids. The Commerce Guild controlled raw materials under the leadership of Gossam magistrate Shu Mai. Wat Tambor of the Techno Union provided dozens of "mechworlds" dominated by smoke, fire, and machinery. The Corporate Alliance, which regulated the distribution of retail products, remained a quiet backer. Nute Gunray of the Trade Federation insisted that Dooku deliver Padmé Amidala's "head on his desk" before he would sign on with the CIS.

Palpatine claimed that he would not allow the Republic to be split in two, but did not publicly advocate the creation of the Grand Army. The Senate chamber on Coruscant rang with the shouts of angry legislators debating the pros and cons of the movement and complaining about the endless delays in bringing the issue to a vote. Beginning with the Battle of Antar 4, events quickly snowballed and left the chancellor with no options besides armed conflict.

THE BATTLE OF ANTAR 4
22.5 B.B.Y.

Over a thousand worlds had already joined the CIS, but violence had thus far been limited to the wounded pride of spurned diplomats. The blood spilled on the moon Antar 4 changed that and cast the conflict in a new and deadly light.

Home to the furry, flat-faced Gotals, Antar 4 had given rise to the Roshu Sune, a militant splinter branch of the Gotal Assembly for Separation. During New Year Fete week, Roshu Sune terrorists activated the undercover agents that they had infiltrated into Antarian Ranger chapter houses across the moon, decimating the Jedi-allied Rangers and throwing Antar 4 into chaos. The Roshu Sune then issued a declaration of secession.

The Republic refused to honor terrorist proclamations. Antarian Rangers from across the galaxy descended on the moon, eager for revenge against those who had desecrated the chapter houses where their order had originated. Following close on their heels came battalions of Jedi Knights led by Masters Coleman Trebor and Saesee Tiin.

The first assault proved disastrous, resulting in heavy casualties to both Jedi and civilians. The second assault used an electromagnetic pulse to overwhelm the Gotals' sensitive head cones. This tactic eventually succeeded, but at the cost of the goodwill of the people of Antar 4, who were incapacitated by the pulse and blamed the Jedi for sloppy tactics.

Separatist-leaning planets across the galaxy looked at Antar 4 and realized that the Republic wasn't omnipotent. The Jedi Council, however, refused to trace any direct link between the Roshu Sune and Count Dooku. The Council's denials persisted even as random terrorist bombings began striking Coruscant, despite Dooku's failure to condemn the killings being done in his name.

SPLINTERING OF THE REPUBLIC
22.5–22 B.B.Y.

The final months leading up to the Clone Wars were a chaotic dance of shuffling alliances and desperate overtures. When war eventually broke out, it almost came as a relief.

The secession of the planets Ando and Sy Myrth three months prior to the Battle of Geonosis marked a sort of tipping point. The two worlds and their sector fiefdoms brought the total of Separatist planets to more than six thousand. The Refugee Relief Movement struggled to contain displaced citizens, leading to civil unrest. Angry showdowns occurred throughout the galaxy, such as the one on Naboo, where kassoti-spice miners on one of the planet's moons refused to give up their landing slip to accommodate refugee freighters.

Ando in particular became a microcosm of the greater galactic conflict when the Aqualish of the Andoan Free Colonies refused to acknowledge the secession ordered by their walrus-faced brethren on the homeworld. The always belligerent Aqualish now looked as if they might tear themselves apart regardless of what happened outside their borders.

Weeks later, Senator Garm Bel Iblis of the Corellian sector announced that his sector had closed its borders and would no longer participate in future discussion. With a cry of "Corellia for Corellians," the Republic lost the support of one of its founding Core Worlds.

Chancellor Palpatine responded to Corellia's withdrawal with an offer to Count Dooku to negotiate a peaceful solution to their differences. Dooku didn't show and the Republic shook from a rapid-fire string of prominent secessions.

The Elrood, Danjar, Tantra, and Sluis sectors all joined the CIS, making the entire Rimward leg of the Rimma Trade Route inaccessible to Republic shipping. The Lahara sector followed suit, bringing with it the planets of Agamar and Oorn Tchis and the Mirgoshir hyperspace crossroads. The Abrion sector gave the CIS more than two hundred farming planets when it seceded. The Expansion Region planet of Tynna joined the Separatists following an outbreak on their world of building-eating insects called stone mites, believed to be a biologically engineered terrorist weapon. The mathematical Givin of Yag'Dhul left when their ruling Body Calculus determined that the risks of staying with the Republic were "greater than or equal to" the risks of seceding.

Not everyone on the Republic side was content to sit and watch. On board the Republic Judicial Department corvette *Scarlet Thranta,* Captain Zozridor Slayke and his crew withdrew from Republic service to wage their own private war against Separatist forces in the Sluis sector. Slayke's army soon became known as Freedom's Sons.

Two weeks after Slayke's resignation, the Republic dispatched a Jedi-led task force to reign in the rogue captain. Master Nejaa Halcyon, a Corellian Jedi and descendant of early Jedi hero Keiran Halcyon, commanded the cruiser *Plooriod Bodkin* on its mission to the Sluis sector. It took weeks, but Halcyon eventually pinned down Slayke—who promptly turned the tables on the Jedi Master and stole the *Plooriod Bodkin.*

Mission to Ansion
22 B.B.Y.

Not every development was disadvantageous for the Republic. The simple world of Ansion in the Mid Rim responded favorably to a Jedi diplomatic mission and elected to remain a member of the Republic, rejecting a Separatist invitation extended by Commerce Guild magistrate Shu Mai. The Jedi team of Anakin Skywalker, Obi-Wan Kenobi, Luminara Unduli, and Bariss Offee received credit for the outcome. Though Ansion had little to offer in the way of natural resources, its involvement in a number of ancient treaties including the Malarian Alliance and the Keitumite Mutual Military Treaty meant that Ansion's defection would have pulled an entire web of planets into the Separatist fold.

But a closer look at the Ansion victory revealed an unpleasant truth—if the Republic's successes occurred only when it managed to *prevent* a defection, the Confederacy could not help but gain in power. Calls for the passage of the Military Creation Act increased in volume. Terrorist bombings on Coruscant continued.

Diplomacy could not stanch a bleeding artery. Unless the Republic wanted to concede victory already, war appeared inevitable.

THE CLONE WARS

The Battle of Geonosis
22 B.B.Y.

Formerly the planet's Queen, Padmé Amidala had become Naboo's representative to the Republic Senate after the ascension of Queen Jamillia. Padmé had also become one of the most vocal opponents of the Military Creation Act. Upon arriving on Coruscant to vote on the measure, her starship exploded on the landing pad. Padmé survived the assassination attempt, which had been ordered by Count Dooku on behalf of Nute Gunray and contracted out to Jango Fett—who had enlisted his own subcontractor, Zam Wesell. The Jedi Council assigned Obi-Wan Kenobi and

Count Dooku
[Art by Mark Chiarello]

locate anything about the planet in the Jedi archives—thanks to Dooku's erasure of the information ten years prior—and so decided to travel to Kamino himself.

The Kaminoans were happy to host a representative from the Jedi, still believing that their growth-accelerated army, now nearly one million strong, belonged to Jedi Master Sifo-Dyas. During his tour of the Tipoca City facilities, Obi-Wan met Jango Fett, the army's Prime Clone, and his son Boba Fett. Convinced that Jango had been behind the attacks on Padmé, Obi-Wan tried to bring the bounty hunter to Coruscant for questioning. Jango bested Obi-Wan in combat and escaped with Boba in *Slave I*.

Anakin had recently been disturbed by vague and disturbing nightmares of his mother's torture. He left Naboo with Padmé and traveled to Tatooine, where he learned that Shmi Skywalker had been freed from slavery years ago, to become the wife of local moisture farmer Cliegg Lars. At the Lars homestead, Anakin met Cliegg's son Owen Lars and Owen's girlfriend Beru, and enjoyed a reunion with C-3PO, Anakin's home-built protocol droid. But Shmi was not there. She had been kidnapped by a tribe of Tusken Raiders weeks before.

Anakin tracked down his mother, who had been tortured and was near death, in a Tusken camp. When she died in his arms, Anakin welcomed the liberating fury of the dark side. He slaughtered the entire Tusken clan, including the children.

After burying Shmi, Anakin intercepted an urgent message from Obi-Wan, who had tracked Jango Fett to the droid foundries on Geonosis. Obi-Wan had learned of Count Dooku's involvement with the galaxy's major commerce factions. With the Trade Federation, Techno Union, Commerce Guild, Corporate Alliance, and InterGalactic Banking Clan officially joining the Separatist cause, the Republic faced grave danger. Obi-Wan would not escape to deliver his news,

Anakin Skywalker to protect the Senator.

A second attempt on Padmé's life, involving poisonous kouhuns, also failed, but this time the Jedi apprehended Zam Wesell. Before the Clawdite shapeshifter could reveal the identity of the other plotters, Jango Fett killed her with a toxic dart.

In light of the violence, the Council decided that Padmé would be safer on her homeworld. Anakin accompanied her to Naboo, where he found himself struggling with his increasingly powerful feelings of infatuation. Padmé tried to resist her own attraction to Anakin, but the two soon fell in love.

On Coruscant, Obi-Wan investigated Jango Fett's dart and connected it to the cloners of Kamino. He could not

Clone troopers and gunships take out Geonosian defenses during the Battle of Geonosis [Art by Tommy Lee Edwards]

however—a squad of droidekas had captured him and locked him in the Geonosian dungeons. Anakin and Padmé rushed to free their friend, but became prisoners themselves.

Back on Coruscant, Chancellor Palpatine, Mace Windu, and Master Yoda agreed that war was the only way to stop the Separatists. Representative Jar Jar Binks put forth a motion that gave emergency war powers to Palpatine, who then announced the creation of the Grand Army of the Republic.

Yoda departed for Kamino. While the Jedi still weren't sure who had orchestrated the clone army's creation, they could not afford to wait for volunteers and conscripts to build up a standard army. And if the Separatists were involved in creating the clone army (as Jango Fett's dual role seemed to indicate), the Jedi wanted to prevent Dooku's forces from claiming the clones for themselves. The Kaminoans gladly turned over the first two hundred thousand clones to Yoda, and he led them to Geonosis at top speed.

Obi-Wan, Anakin, and Padmé received death sentences from Dooku, to be carried out by the teeth and claws of wild beasts in the Geonosian execution arena. Meanwhile, two hundred Jedi Knights, led by Mace Windu, arrived outside the arena in their Jedi starfighters. They failed to force a surrender from Count Dooku, and the arena exploded in violence as Dooku unleashed his super battle droids. Mace Windu beheaded Jango Fett, yet Dooku's forces held the upper hand until Yoda's armies arrived aboard laser-spewing Republic gunships.

The battle quickly moved to the dust plains of Geonosis, where both sides' heavy equipment clashed with stunning might. Geonosian starfighters sparred with clone gunships. Commerce Guild spider droids blasted beetle-like AT-TEs. Huge SPHA-T cannons carved up Trade Federation core ships. Elsewhere on the battlefield, trained acklays and nexus devoured clone troopers, and Count Dooku's lowest-ranking dark acolytes lost their lives in a tank battle with Mace Windu.

Dooku himself escaped to a secret hangar, where he was confronted by Obi-Wan and Anakin. The count left Obi-Wan beaten and Anakin without his right arm, and may have killed them both if not for Yoda, who arrived and launched a whirlwind attack. Dooku barely escaped with his life.

By the battle's conclusion, only Republic soldiers remained. Though considered a victory, the cost to the Republic was high—thousands of clone trooper deaths and scores of fallen Jedi. Most of the Confederacy's battle droids and heavy equipment escaped into space aboard core ships.

Geonosian leader Poggle the Lesser was nowhere to be found, although his second in command, Sun Fac, had been assassinated by a squad of clone commandos during the fighting. The Geonosian workers retreated into the catacombs far beneath the spire-hives, where they resisted every effort to dislodge them.

War had been joined, and the Republic's new clones would give a name to the conflict that had begun. Before the next round of attacks, Anakin escorted Padmé back to Naboo, where they were secretly married. The only witnesses, besides the Naboo holy man who presided over the ceremony, were C-3PO and R2-D2.

THE SHAPE OF WAR
22 B.B.Y.

Had the Republic pressed the advantage, they most likely could have overrun Confederacy space before the CIS had time to fortify its positions. The Republic had one glaring problem, however—it wasn't ready for war. Until all the clones could be activated and new warships launched, the Republic didn't have enough assets to fight on a galactic scale.

Meanwhile, the Confederacy deployed along the major hyperspace lanes into Separatist space, solidifying its defenses. The Republic had no choice but to rely on harassment tactics for the time being, guaranteeing that the war would not have a swift end.

Victories did not always come only on the battlefield. On isolationist Corellia, the Twi'lek Jedi Aayla Secura and the Caamasi Jedi Ylenic It'kla helped take a defecting Techno Union researcher into Republic custody. Unexpected assistance came from the Corellian Jedi Master Nejaa Halcyon, recently returned from his failed mission to stop the Freedom's Sons vigilantism in the Sluis sector.

The dead had just been recovered from the red sands of Geonosis when the Clone Wars exploded to life on new worlds. Atraken, a tiny mining planet of great strategic value, became one of the brightest-burning flashpoints.

A Confederacy world, Atraken had both the blessing and curse of being rich in the rare metal doonium. Republic assault ships touched down on Atraken's crust, unloading clones who besieged the doonium mines. Digging out the enemy on Atraken would consume most of the year, with the seeming futility of the efforts proving to many Jedi that they should not fight in a war this nihilistic.

The green-scaled Trandoshans, inhabitants of a planet orbiting the same sun as the Wookiee homeworld of Kashyyyk, had long exploited the Wookiees as slave labor. Now the Trandoshans had allied themselves with the Confederacy of Independent Systems. Armed with the latest in Separatist weaponry, rowdy bands of Trandoshan brawlers roamed the spaceways and stirred up trouble for Republic ships.

The Republic sent units of clone commandos to Kashyyyk to prepare for a possible invasion. Upon their arrival, the clones discovered that Trandoshan slavers had already set up containment camps for Wookiee captives, and the full force of the Separatist army soon followed. Though the clone troopers beat back the first incursion, Kashyyyk would be a contested world for the remainder of the war.

The Jedi as Generals
22 B.B.Y.

At Geonosis, Atraken, and Mirgoshir, the Jedi and the clone troopers fell into a natural battlefield hierarchy—Jedi Masters, Jedi Knights, and Jedi Padawans commanding the clone ranks of commanders, captains, lieutenants, sergeants, and troopers. Jedi, regardless of their experience, always outranked clones.

One month into the war, Supreme Chancellor Palpatine made the role of the Jedi official. Most Jedi Knights and Masters would henceforth be given the rank of general in the Grand Army of the Republic; most Padawans, the rank of commander.

This clarified the military command process, but it also had the effect of *requiring* that all Jedi take an active role in the war. For many reasons—frustration with Republic corruption, devotion to the ideal of peaceful contemplation—some Jedi refused to obey the Council's order to return to Coruscant and receive their promotions. Although most Jedi accepted their assignments and left to defend Ossus and retake Excarga, the dissident Jedi remained a mounting problem.

The Hunt for the Decimator
21.95 B.B.Y. (1 month after the Battle of Geonosis)

Only one Confederacy general held more sway than Grievous during the war's first month—the Chiss Force user Sev'rance Tann. General Tann saw her first true battlefield test on sunbaked Tatooine, where Separatist spies had learned of a new Republic weapon known only as "the Decimator."

On Eredenn Prime, Tann captured several Decimators for herself. The weapons—tanks with giant turbolaser cannons mounted atop—proved stunningly destructive. She raided the Wookiee colony of Alaris Prime (which had just recovered from the attack during the Dark Reaper crisis), and made a bold strike against the Core world of Sarapin.

A crucible of flame and magma, Sarapin generated enough geothermal energy to supply a significant fraction of the power for the Core Worlds. Scaling the slopes of Mount Corvast, Tann's captured Devastators vaporized the Republic's geothermal generators. Dozens of Core Worlds plunged into darkness.

General Echuu Shen-Jon, Sev'rance Tann's counterpart on the Republic side, held a personal grudge against the enemy commander, for Tann had murdered Echuu's Padawan during the Battle of Geonosis. Echuu led a massive Republic counterattack to recapture Sarapin, then ultimately caught up with his quarry on the snow-dusted tundra of Krant. Calling on the power of the dark side, Echuu Shen-Jon cut Sev'rance Tann in half with a mighty sweep of his energy blade.

Although the Separatists had lost their stolen Decimators, Echuu Shen-Jon had also crossed a line. Telling his surviving troops to return to the Republic, he vanished into the wilderness of Krant to wander and forever contemplate his moral failure.

THE DARK REAPER PROJECT
21.9 B.B.Y. (1 month after the Battle of Geonosis)

Buried for thousands of years on Raxus Prime lay the Force Harvester, an artifact of Sith technology capable of sucking the life from every living thing within a number of kilometers. During the First Sith War, the Force Harvester had been used as a power device for an even greater monstrosity—the Dark Reaper.

The Dark Reaper had not been seen in millennia, but Count Dooku knew that some Force spirits persisted even after death. Dooku sent a Trade Federation fleet to frozen Rhen Var to secure Ulic Qel-Droma's crypt. Guided by the ancient Jedi ghost, Dooku began excavating for the buried Force Harvester on Raxus Prime.

The Jedi Council mobilized an attack. Marching through a forest of rusted girders, the Republic's new AT-XT scout walkers blasted Separatist mortar tanks, while nimble Jedi hovertanks cleared out gun turrets. When Dooku made an appearance, Anakin chased him aboard a starship, which then blasted into orbit. Left behind, Obi-Wan defeated the Count's going-away present: a giant, crablike siege weapon called a protodeka.

On board Dooku's vessel Anakin sat in a holding cell, having fallen victim to a sneak attack by Dooku's mercenary Cydon Prax. Soon the ship reached the Wookiee colony of Alaris Prime, where Dooku tested his Force Harvester. Anakin escaped only centimeters ahead of the weapon's shock wave, and sent an SOS to the Republic. By the time a clone legion arrived, Anakin had Alaris Prime well on its way to freedom.

Meanwhile, Count Dooku unleashed the Force Harvester on Mon Calamari, Bakura, and Agamar. The Republic counterattacked on Thule, a crumbling planet that had once been part of the glorious Sith Empire. The Republic army advanced on the old Sith city of Kesiak, but the deadliest weapon in their arsenal proved to be Anakin Skywalker. When Cydon Prax destroyed Mace Windu's vehicle in a tank-versus-tank showdown, Anakin killed Prax in a fusillade of energy darts. Anakin

The ancient Dark Reaper superweapon
[ART BY TOMMY LEE EDWARDS]

then penetrated the Dark Reaper and destroyed the alchemical monstrosity with old-fashioned Republic ordnance.

Though counted as a victory, the Republic's preoccupation with the Dark Reaper allowed the Separatists to seize Bespin's Tibanna gas refineries as well as the historic Jedi stronghold of Ossus.

THE BATTLE OF KAMINO
21.83 B.B.Y. (2 months after the Battle of Geonosis)

Jedi Master Quinlan Vos had gone deep undercover on the seedy gambling station known as the Wheel. Among the Jedi, Quinlan Vos had acquired a reputation for undisciplined behavior, but this time his intelligence coup was of epic proportions. A decrypted data disk revealed a Separatist plan to assault the Republic cloning laboratories on Kamino.

Count Dooku appointed Corporate Alliance Magister Passel Argente as the ranking Confederacy officer for the attack, though Argente's military experience was nonexistent. Mon Calamari Commander Merai joined the CIS navy following the attack on his homeworld by the Force Harvester, and received the honor of leading the assault. Outfitted with submersible starfighters, Commander Merai believed his expertise in amphibious warfare would carry the day.

Republic forces on Kamino were keenly aware of the threat—only a few weeks earlier, a traitor among the Kaminoans had attempted to murder the clones by releasing a nanovirus. The Jedi hoped to defend Kamino with a three-pronged battle plan. Obi-Wan Kenobi and Anakin Skywalker would shoot down landing ships with a squadron of Jedi starfighters, Master Shaak Ti would defend Tipoca City itself, and Oppo Rancisis and a Republic armada would wait for their cue to leap into the system and squeeze the Separatists in a vise.

The day of battle dawned, rainy as always on storm-rocked Kamino. Commander Merai sent down his landing ships accompanied by a thick droid starfighter escort. Obi-Wan and Anakin could not stop them all, and dozens of fully stocked transports landed on Tipoca City.

Shaak Ti activated Kamino's "secret weapon"—a special batch of clone troopers who had been bred for greater au-

tonomy. These ARC (Advanced Reconnaissance Commando) troopers had been trained by Jango Fett himself. The ARC troopers and Shaak Ti mowed through the advancing super battle droids, scattering body fragments like metallic sawdust.

Commander Merai personally piloted his custom submersible *Shark* in an attempt to destroy the city's shield generator. When he discovered that no generator existed, Merai began to suspect that someone had tampered with Separatist intelligence. In a last act of defiance, Merai rammed his vessel into the Jedi starfighter hyperspace rings, a spectacular but ultimately futile gesture. Passel Argente executed a full Separatist retreat.

What neither side had realized was that the Battle of Kamino had been an intentional stalemate in the larger game being orchestrated by Darth Sidious. Count Dooku had ensured that the Separatists would attack Kamino, and had also guaranteed that the assault would prove a failure. The war would now drag out for years, consuming billions of lives and trillions of credits as the people cried out for firm, decisive leadership.

Within a few weeks, Kamino's million battle-ready clones went out to join the two hundred thousand already in service. The Republic began investigating alternate cloning methods (with Spaarti Creations coming into prominence within the next year). Conscription, however, was a necessary reality. Countless beings of every species became draftees into the Grand Army of the Republic.

Meanwhile, ARC troopers bolstered the Republic's ground forces. Clad in modified clone trooper armor, they boasted a touch of Jango Fett's dry wit, and often questioned their superiors' orders if they conflicted with their own tactical training. One ARC trooper, assigned to General Obi-Wan Kenobi, received the nickname "Alpha" from Anakin Skywalker.

THE DEFENSE OF NABOO
21.8 B.B.Y. (2.5 months after the Battle of Geonosis)

The destruction of the Dark Reaper only made the Separatists strive to develop even deadlier weapons. On the Techno Union mechworld of Queyta, Separatist researcher Dr. Jenna Zan Arbor succeeded in bottling a virulent aerosol poison. Nicknamed "swamp gas," the green mist raised blisters on the skin and caused shuddering death in most humanoid species. Commander Asajj Ventress decided to test this toxin on the Gungan settlers of Ohma-D'un, one of the inhabited moons orbiting Naboo.

All of the Gungans died instantly. A Jedi investigative team soon followed. Amid the corpses they found super battle droids outfitted with swamp gas sprayers, accompanied by Dooku's welcoming committee—Asajj Ventress and the bounty hunter Durge.

The two Separatist warriors laid into their enemies with glee. Several Jedi perished, but Anakin Skywalker and Obi-Wan Kenobi managed to keep Durge at bay. Asajj Ventress retreated, satisfied with the deaths she had caused. Meanwhile, the ARC trooper Alpha destroyed the Separatist landing ships that would have carried the swamp gas to the planet Naboo.

THE BATTLES OF LIANNA AND TEYR
21.77 B.B.Y. (3 months after the Battle of Geonosis)

Lianna, in the Tion Cluster, was a vital Republic manufacturing world home to a Sienar starfighter facility. Raith Sienar and his engineers had been enlisted by the Republic to develop new starfighters for the clone troopers, and the Lianna facility held all the secrets to Sienar's Twin Ion Engine project. Jedi Master Cei Vookto led the campaign to preserve Lianna, using his powers of elemental summoning to cleanse the planet with twin pillars of fire and water. The strain cost Vookto his life.

On Teyr, the Whiphid Jedi Master K'Kruhk led an army of clone troopers against a Trade Federation battleship that had made a hard landing on the planet's surface and was now serving as a Separatist bunker. Trudging on foot through Teyr's Great Canyon, K'Kruhk watched as spider tanks shredded his clone troopers with laser barrages. Master K'Kruhk managed to lead his army to the lip of the canyon, where they destroyed the great battleship, but only K'Kruhk survived the final assault. Shell-shocked, he fled Teyr without telling the Council that he still lived, and joined other dissident Jedi opposed to the war.

JEDI SCHISM
21.75 B.B.Y. (3 months after the Battle of Geonosis)

Hundreds of Jedi had refused to honor Chancellor Palpatine's decree that made them generals, and had formed a growing movement of dissidents. Few of them had actively joined the Separatists, but their refusal to fight for their Commander in Chief threatened to divide the Jedi Order.

Mace Windu decided to meet with the defectors on the Weequay moon of Ruul. Sora Bulq, leader of the dissidents, had earned respect in Mace's eyes for his devotion to Form VII ("Vaapad") lightsaber combat—an aggressive style that took its user to the edge of the dark side. Bulq, however, had secretly joined Count Dooku, and Ruul was a trap.

Asajj Ventress raided the Ruul gathering, hoping to kill some of the dissidents and blame their deaths on the Jedi Council. But Mace had deduced Sora Bulq's true nature, and forced Bulq and Ventress to flee offworld. Despite the incident, the dissident Jedi remained split. While shocked at Master Bulq's betrayal, many still had hostile feelings toward a Republic that they considered irredeemably corrupt. K'Kruhk, however, returned to Coruscant to resume his role as a Jedi general.

RAID ON PENGALAN IV
21.75 B.B.Y. (3 months after the Battle of Geonosis)

From Pengalan IV, a dry, sparsely populated world in the Inner Rim, came word of a Separatist military breakthrough—diamond boron missiles designed to punch through the shielding of most Republic starfighters. But the Republic's attack against the "secret factory" proved to be a trap. Gun emplacements and droid starfighters opened up on the invaders, destroying a wave of gunships and sending the survivors limping away in defeat.

One gunship, carrying republic observer Joram Kithe and a crew of clone troopers, crashed in a canyon near the tiny village of Tur Lonkin. On foot, this small band infiltrated Tur Lonkin and discovered that the Confederacy's *real* missile factory lay deep underground in a shielded bunker. The clone troopers destroyed the facility at a great cost of lives within their own ranks. Upon returning to Coruscant, Kithe

reported that the Republic had purchased an army that was nothing short of remarkable.

In the hostile wilderness of Qiilura, a group of clone commandos provided further support for Kithe's glowing assessment. In a mission to capture a Separatist scientist and destroy a bioweapons facility, the commandos, with help from an untested Jedi Padawan, dealt with the proliferation of an anti-clone nanovirus.

MISSION TO QUEYTA
21.7 B.B.Y. (4 months after the Battle of Geonosis)

Following the "swamp gas" outbreak on the Gungan moon, four Jedi Masters united in a strike against the guilty laboratory on Queyta before the Separatists could target a second world. Obi-Wan Kenobi earned a fifth spot alongside this dream team due to his familiarity with the toxin. The Queyta chemical plant floated atop a lava river, and its Skakoan workers exploded like proton bombs when their pressurized armor shells were ruptured. Asajj Ventress and Durge lay in wait for the team, and killed all four Jedi Masters. Only Obi-Wan Kenobi survived, and he returned with the plague's antidote.

Unknown to the Republic, a second laboratory on the far side of Queyta had installed its equipment aboard the science vessel *Gahenna,* and then abandoned the compromised world. For the next two years *Gahenna* would cruise the Outer Rim, perfecting a new strain of toxin.

THE STORM FLEET DESTROYERS
21.67 B.B.Y. (4 months after the Battle of Geonosis)

The heavily armed bulk freighters of Count Dooku's Storm Fleet had been produced by the shipbuilding conglomerate Kuat Drive Yards. Once a member of the Techno Union, KDY had broken ranks with the Separatist organization at the start of the war so that it could continue producing assault ships for the Republic Navy. Yet KDY's new Storm

Sith hopeful Asajj Ventress and bounty hunter Durge
[ART BY TOMMY LEE EDWARDS]

Fleet went straight to the Confederacy—grounds for treason, but Palpatine's investigators chalked it up to mistaken corporate connections, and KDY escaped repercussions.

Of course, that didn't help the Republic vessels no w terrorized by the Storm Fleet. Up and down the Perlemian Trade Route, the Storm Fleet intercepted convoys of medicine and munitions, opening their victims' hulls to the cold vacuum of space.

Anakin Skywalker and Obi-Wan Kenobi, at the Llon Nebula's Kronex spaceport during a mission layover, encountered the Storm Fleet as it came in for refueling. Against the wishes of his master, Anakin followed the Storm Fleet as it left Kronex and flew his Jedi starfighter between the larger ships like a flitnat among banthas. When the bridges of the two vessels crumpled under asteroid impacts, the Storm Fleet limped back to Kronex for repairs.

The encounter delayed the Storm Fleet's mission just long enough for a Republic fleet to arrive at their target of Cyphar. In the Battle of Cyphar, the Storm Fleet lost nearly half of its vessels, and Cyphar remained an open port.

THE FORTRESS OF AXION
21.67 B.B.Y. (4 months after the Battle of Geonosis)

At the Battle of Geonosis, Master Yoda had proven himself a superior battlefield commander. Since then, Chancellor Palpatine had requested that the centuries-old sage be kept far from the front lines.

Master Yoda still found ways to insert himself into strategic combat. One such situation presented itself on Axion. Once inhabited by humans, the planet had been bought out by the cannibalistic Colicoid insects and now served as a Separatist research and development center. One Colicoid engineer, responsible for the design of the protodekas used during the Dark Reaper crisis, had been sealed away in Axion's corporate fortress by his brethren. He made a tempting target for a Republic extradition mission.

Several companies of clone troopers, along with their

Jedi Master Kit Fisto, who led clone scuba troopers in the Battle of Mon Calamari [ART BY TOMMY LEE EDWARDS]

heavy equipment, made planetfall on Axion, led by Commander Brolis—one of the outside military advisers hired by the Kaminoans to fine-tune the clones into fighting shape. Within two days, the small force had penetrated the fortress through a hole in its foundation. Two days, however, was all the time that the Colicoids needed to call in the Separatist army.

Super battle droids flushed the clones from the fortress and killed every last clone in vicious house-to-house fighting. Soon only Commander Brolis remained, holed up in the bombed-out shell of a residential apartment, his call for reinforcements apparently ignored by Republic High Command.

He awoke to the sight of Master Yoda—his single reinforcement. Armed with only a lightsaber, Yoda reduced the advancing battle droid line to scrap, and engaged a hoop-wheeled hailfire droid tank in a strangely elegant duel. Finally, Yoda tricked the robot into burying itself beneath twelve tons of collapsing rock. Yoda escaped with Brolis, but the overall mission to Axion had failed.

THE BATTLE OF MUUNILINST
21.66 B.B.Y. (4 months after the Battle of Geonosis)

San Hill, the arrogant chairman of the InterGalactic Banking Clan, had worked to make his homeworld of Muunilinst an unassailable castle keep. The Republic countered with sheer numbers, sending hundreds of assault ships, each one groaning from the weight of troopers and war machines. Many vessels reached the surface only as smoldering hulks; others found themselves cut off from their drop zones, forced to make landings behind enemy lines. General Obi-Wan Kenobi took command of the ground assault, while Anakin Skywalker fought for control of space in his Jedi starfighter.

Panicked, San Hill turned to Count Dooku's "special reinforcements"—the mercenary Durge and his droid team of IG-series lancers. Armed with laser lances and mounted on speeder bikes, the killers roared forth to decimate the Republic's field headquarters.

Like dark knights from the tales of the pre-Republic, Durge's crew rode into the camp. Obi-Wan Kenobi mounted his own speeder bike and led a squad of Republic lancers in a classic joust that ended with Durge's defeat. Obi-Wan capitalized on his success by hooking up with some lost ARC troopers and staging a final offensive against the IBC command center.

In space, Asajj Ventress toyed with Anakin Skywalker, leading her prey into hyperspace. They emerged at the jungle world of Yavin 4, and were soon joined by a company of clone troopers whom Obi-Wan had dispatched as backup. Anakin led the troopers through the sticky Massassi rain forest, watching helplessly as Ventress eliminated his men one by one.

Finally, the two crossed blades atop a vine-blanketed ziggurat. Neither fighter could gain an advantage in a contest where they seemed to be evenly matched, but Anakin found his edge by tapping into his own rage. Knocked from the pyramid, Ventress vanished into the jungle below.

On Dantooine, Master Mace Windu used his martial arts talents and the invisible punch of the Force to defeat a Separatist droid battalion, then carved up a hovering seismic charge minelayer. Master Yoda, Luminara Unduli, and Bariss Offee prevented cloaked "chameleon droids" from destroying the crystal caverns of the sacred Jedi planet Ilum. On Mon Calamari, Kit Fisto led a regiment of clone scuba troopers against the Quarren Isolationist League, defeating the Separatist-allied faction with help from the ancient order of Mon Calamari Knights.

On Hypori, a factory world, General Grievous chose a key moment to attack Republic forces and nearly killed the Jedi Masters Ki-Adi-Mundi, K'Kruhk, Shaak Ti, and Aayla Secura. A squad of ARC troopers burst in before the Jedi could be slaughtered.

Grievous's sudden appearance on Hypori stunned the Jedi Council. While they had been aware of the existence of the Separatist general—Republic commandos had fought him in the catacombs during the Battle of Geonosis—none of them was prepared for the ease with which he took apart a knot of fully trained Jedi.

THE BATTLE OF BRENTAAL
21.6 B.B.Y. (5 months after the Battle of Geonosis)

It would be difficult to overstate the importance Brentaal IV had to the Republic. An ancient Core world home to noble families and trade guilds, it sat at the crossroads of the Perlemian Trade Route and the Hydian Way—two of the galaxy's most vital hyperroutes. At the time, no one realized that the population ached for a new life under the leadership of the Confederacy of Independent Systems.

Brentaal clan leader Shogar Tok incited his people to riot. The Republic moved to secure their hyperspace junction, but by then Shogar Tok already held the triggers of Brentaal IV's formidable magna-guns. Republic strategists assembled an invasion force led by Jedi generals Shaak Ti, Plo Koon, the Zabrak Agen Kolar, and Shon Kon Ray.

General Plo Koon commanded the fleet, while the other three led the invasion armies. Things began to go wrong almost immediately. General Shon Kon Ray perished aboard an exploding gunship. General Kolar became a captive of the enemy. General Shaak Ti survived long enough to make it to a prison facility, where she recruited a few allies, including Lyshaa, the murderer of Shaak Ti's former Padawan. Lyshaa betrayed her rescuer to Shogar Tok at the earliest opportunity. Fortunately for the Republic, the rest of Shaak Ti's prison recruits sabotaged Brentaal's shield generator and wrecked its magna-guns. Plo Koon's fleet landed inside the hour, pacifying the planet and disposing of Shogar Tok's body.

Meanwhile, a similar situation had occurred on the neighboring Core world of Esseles. When a Separatist-funded government faction declared that Esseles had joined the Confederacy, a resistance movement of Republic loyalists forced the faction out in a bloody five-day battle.

DEFECTION ON NAR SHADDAA
21.52 B.B.Y. (6 months after the Battle of Geonosis)

Jedi Master Quinlan Vos had always played in the moral "gray zone" of the Jedi Code. But after faulty intelligence surrounding the Battle of Brentaal IV became associated with him, some Jedi thought that Quinlan might be a traitor.

The Jedi Council still trusted their agent, but saw the suspicion opening up an opportunity for enemy infiltration. Delib-

Korunnai warrior Kar Vastor holds an akk dog as Republic war machines attempt to pacify Haruun Kal. [ART BY TOMMY LEE EDWARDS]

erately giving Quinlan the latest military codes, they allowed him to return to his undercover life as an information broker. Days later, the Council sent Master Agen Kolar to capture Quinlan, telling the Zabrak that Vos had stolen the codes.

The two Jedi had their showdown on the Smugglers' Moon, Nar Shaddaa, in neutral Hutt space. Fully convinced of the rightness of his mission, in his zeal Agen Kolar nearly killed his target. But, as planned, Quinlan eluded capture, and now possessed the perfect reputation of "Jedi fugitive" to ease his penetration of Count Dooku's inner circle.

THE HARUUN KAL CRISIS
21.51 B.B.Y. (6 months after the Battle of Geonosis)

With their Force-given powers, Jedi Knights could be supernatural in battle. But even with the clone troopers at their disposal, the Jedi could not win the war on their own.

Local militias became the unsung heroes of many conflicts. Clone troopers had been trained to recruit native forces and set up independent chains of command, making it possible for a handful of clones to trigger a planetwide uprising. After seeing the success of the "militia model" on Malastare and Giju, the Jedi Council decided to try an extreme version of the model on the Separatist-controlled jungle world of Haruun Kal. This time, they sent Jedi Council member Depa Billaba to rally the locals.

Other than the fact that Haruun Kal sat at a hyperspace crossroads called the Gevarno Loop, the planet had little to recommend itself. Its "cloudsea" of toxic volcanic gases made colonization possible only on the highest mountain peaks. Nevertheless, two distinct societies had arisen on Haruun Kal—the Korunnai (Mace Windu's people), Force-sensitive jungle dwellers descended from shipwrecked Jedi, and the Balawai, more recent settlers concentrated in the capital city of Pelek Baw. The two sides had fought one another for generations in a bitter conflict known as the Summertime War.

Haruun Kal supported a heavy Separatist presence, but Depa Billaba formed a guerrilla force called the Upland Liberation Front. Shortly after her arrival, the Separatist force

withdrew. But just when Depa should have returned to Coruscant, the Jedi Council received the disturbing news that she had gone native, massacring Balawai settlers and refusing to answer the Council's inquiries. Mace Windu went to Haruun Kal to bring back his former Padawan.

The reality of the Summertime War proved to be more brutal than Mace had believed possible. The Balawai and Korunnai loathed one another with such ferocity that atrocities of war were commonplace. Mace eventually located Depa deep in the jungle, protected by the Korunnai shaman Kar Vastor. A primal warrior, Vastor defeated Mace in a one-on-one brawl by turning the living jungle against his opponent. Depa had completely lost focus, insisting that the Jedi would have to become creatures like Kar Vastor if they hoped to survive the Clone Wars.

Meanwhile, the Balawai military commander, Colonel Geptun, launched an all-out attack against the Korunnai hideout with help from Separatist droid starfighters. Mace responded by taking the battle to Pelek Baw, where he smashed Geptun's defenses and forced a surrender from the colonel. The Republic took control of Haruun Kal and forced both the Balawai and Korunnai to disarm.

Depa Billaba was sent back to the Temple on Coruscant, where she remained in a near-catatonic state. Jedi healers saw no hope for improvement.

ASSASSINATION ON NULL
21.5 B.B.Y. (6 months after the Battle of Geonosis)

Count Dooku liked to use the term *old friend* in conversations with his business associates, but most suspected that the aloof aristocrat had no real understanding of the concept. During his years as a student in the Jedi Temple, Dooku had formed a friendship with fellow trainee Lorian Nod, a relationship that had ended with finger-pointing and betrayal over the theft of a Sith Holocron. Dooku's past connection to Lorian Nod would come back to haunt the Count in an encounter on the planet Null.

Set amid the stars of the Mid Rim, the planet Junction V and its sister systems of Bezim and Vicondor sat at the nexus of several hyperspace lanes. Bound together by ages-old treaties, the rulers of the three worlds and the Delaluna moon vowed to move as one when choosing sides between the Republic and the Separatists (similar to the prewar diplomatic dance that had centered on the planet Ansion). The four entities also controlled the Station 88 spaceport, the "gateway to the Mid Rim." The loss of one system would mean the loss of all, with Station 88 thrown in to boot—potentially an eviscerating blow to the Republic.

Dooku arranged a conference with the leaders of the worlds on the neutral planet of Null. Lorian Nod was now the ruler of Junction V. The ensuing decades had further poisoned the bad blood between them. Nod decided to pay lip service to Dooku's overtures, while secretly working with the Jedi Council to bring his fellow delegates in on the side of the Republic.

In Dooku's private cliffside villa on Null, the Count prepared to host the Mid Rim delegates. Dooku tried to assassinate one of the delegates in order to swing the vote in his favor, but the hit failed, and Lorian Nod reaffirmed his Republic loyalties. Station 88 and its systems would now support the Republic.

Count Dooku did not take his defeat well. Locking the doors to the meeting room, he ordered a squad of super battle droids to murder everyone inside. Obi-Wan Kenobi and Anakin Skywalker helped mangle the machines, while Lorian Nod followed Dooku to his escape ship. Nod hoped to force Dooku into a final reckoning for his crimes, but Dooku stabbed his "old friend" through the heart with his crimson lightsaber.

Anakin remained haunted by the thought that *he* could have stopped Dooku had he not been constrained by Obi-Wan's orders. First on Raxus Prime and now on Null, Anakin had squandered two chances to end the war by killing the Separatist leader. Soon, Anakin vowed, Dooku would feel the bite of his lightsaber blade.

THE DEVARON RUSE
21.41 B.B.Y. (6 months, 1 week after the Battle of Geonosis)

Aurra Sing, Jedi killer and professional assassin, accepted a contract from Senator Vien'sai'Malloc of Devaron. Behind the backs of her constituents, the Senator had started a smuggling operation that waylaid Republic freighters traveling near Devaron and stole their cargo. Aurra Sing's role was to eliminate anyone who came too close to discovering the truth.

The attacks had already hobbled the Republic's resupply efforts at Bestine as well as points beyond. A Jedi task force consisting of Kit Fisto, Aayla Secura, the Dark Woman, Master Tholme, and the Neti Jedi T'ra Saa arrived at Devaron with orders to find the smuggler base and crush it. They soon uncovered Senator Vien'sai'Malloc's treachery and moved against her hired raiders at their hideout in Devaron's mountains. But Aurra Sing lay in wait. Incapacitating Tholme and her own former Master, the Dark Woman, Aurra Sing then used her captives as bait to lure Aayla Secura into a trap.

Aayla, however, proved more resourceful than Aurra Sing had anticipated. In a lightsaber duel that became a test of wills, Aayla defeated the notorious mercenary and rescued the wounded Jedi. Kit Fisto's subsequent destruction of the pirate hideout ensured that Devaron space would remain safe for the time being.

Aurra Sing arrived at the Oovo IV asteroid prison under heavy guard. Within a few months she would be free again, beneficiary of an early release—in exchange for vital intelligence regarding a bounty that had recently been posted by an anonymous party on the heads of Jedi Knights.

The Descent of Quinlan Vos
21.38 B.B.Y. (7.5 months after the Battle of Geonosis)

The Gotal moon of Antar 4, site of one of the pre–Clone Wars uprisings, had become a battlefield once more, as Separatist loyalists struck back against the militant Antarian Rangers who now kept order. Count Dooku's orbital bombardment decimated the Rangers, and the Count set up a new command HQ on Antar's surface, notching himself another triumph.

It was here that Quinlan Vos grew into his role as one of Dooku's Dark Jedi. Dooku, who knew the truth behind Quinlan's undercover mission, allowed the spy to sink into the part. The Count could see that Quinlan already walked close

to the dark side. It would not take much to make the deception a reality.

Quinlan worked with three of Dooku's other Dark Jedi—Kadrian Sey, Tol Skorr, and Master Sora Bulq—on missions including the Separatist conquest of the planet Tibrin. To the cheers of thousands of liberated Ishi Tib, Dooku executed the cruel dictator Suribran Tu, and hung Tu's corpse out for public display.

Quinlan's undercover assignment came to a head on his homeworld of Kiffu. There Dooku hoped to construct a secret Separatist base with the cooperation of Sheyf Tinté, the ruler of Kiffu and Quinlan's great-aunt. When the arrogant Tinté spurned Dooku's offer, the Count ordered her death. Quinlan, caught in a crisis of conscience, cut down Kadrian Sey in order to save his aunt's life.

Dooku, however, had his pawn right where he wanted him. After the Count hinted to Quinlan that Sheyf Tinté held a secret, Quinlan used his own psychometric power to read past events hidden in his aunt's mind. What he saw sent him into a blood rage. Years earlier, Sheyf Tinté had sacrificed Quinlan's parents to Anzati vampires as part of an unholy business deal. With a surge of dark side power, Quinlan butchered his terrified aunt.

Satisfied, Count Dooku welcomed Quinlan Vos to the Separatist side, knowing that this time, the conversion was no act.

The Bassadro Massacre
21.25 B.B.Y. (9 months after the Battle of Geonosis)

For a Republic that had enjoyed total control over the media through government seizure of the HoloNet, the emergence of a Confederacy pirate "shadowfeed" broadcast became a vexing problem. Now the public had dueling propaganda to choose from. A case in point was the so-called Bassadro Massacre.

A volcanic mining planet, Bassadro became the nucleus of a twelve-day battle when Jedi Knight Empatojayos Brand led a clone force to dislodge entrenched Separatists in the Agao Ranges. Brand's decision to fire concussion missiles at the overhanging ridge filled the air with millions of glassy shards, shredding the Separatist troops—along with a village of four hundred unaffiliated miners. Both sides put their own spin on the story, and the Republic could not manage to shut down the shadowfeed.

The propaganda streams further polarized segments of the population, turning some Republic citizens rabidly loyal. One outgrowth of this was the Commission for the Protection of the Republic (COMPOR), a primarily human group of civilians given to marches and rallies.

In other war theaters, Jedi died in the ongoing Aqualish conflicts between the Republic's Andoan Free Colonies and the Separatist planet of Ando. The Republic also lost the world of Ord Canfre to the Separatists. Good news, however, came in for the Republic from Balamak in the Mid Rim, where Anakin Skywalker again proved his stratospheric talent by firing missiles that destroyed a Droid Control Ship—a ship that happened to be carrying a prototype communications jammer that could have taken out an entire HoloNet node.

RISE OF THE CORTOSIS BATTLE DROIDS
21.17 B.B.Y. (10 months after the Battle of Geonosis)

On the Techno Union mechworld of Metalorn, Wat Tambor's engineers invented battle droids that incorporated cortosis into their chassis, making them resistant to lightsaber blades.

Tambor had obtained his cortosis through Jabba the Hutt. Anakin Skywalker, dispatched to investigate Jabba's operations, killed Dooku's Sith witch Saato. Bounty Hunter Aurra Sing also tried to kill Anakin, although she escaped with her head still attached to her shoulders.

The first of the cortosis droids then attacked Coruscant and overran the Jedi Temple. Anakin chased off the rest of Dooku's droid raiding party, but the damage had been done. With the Sarapin blackout and now this latest attack, Coruscant's citizens no longer felt safe from the war's ravages.

The Jedi Council ordered Anakin to destroy the cortosis droid factory on Metalorn. While planting detonators, Anakin encountered and killed three more of Dooku's second-tier lieutenants: the dark side brothers Vinoc and Karoc, and the Chiss bounty hunter Vandalor. Enraged by the indiscriminate slaughter of his staff, Count Dooku confronted Skywalker himself. Their lightsaber battle was brutal and short. Prodded to berserker fury through the Count's taunts, Anakin struck his opponent down, though he later learned that this Dooku may have only been a clone doppelgänger.

Anakin returned to Coruscant with Techno Union leader Wat Tambor as his prisoner, leaving behind a radioactive crater where Metalorn's cortosis droid plant had stood.

THE DEATH OF ATRAKEN
21.1 B.B.Y. (11 months after the Battle of Geonosis)

On Atraken, fighting had persisted for a year in a murderous string of stalemates. At last the Republic gained the upper hand with Operation Katabatic, but the Separatists viewed their own impending defeat as an excuse to spit in their enemy's victory cup. A virulent biochemical toxin was released into Atraken's water table. By the time a triumphant clone trooper raised the Republic banner over the capital city, Atraken was already a dead planet.

If the first months of the Atraken campaign had convinced the dissident Jedi that the Clone Wars were futile, the final days assured them that the war was morally repugnant. Atraken proved that it was impossible for the Republic to wage a "clean" war. Republic High Command admitted that victory might have to come by any means necessary.

Anakin Skywalker's capture of Wat Tambor during the Metalorn mission had caught Darth Sidious by surprise. The move could have potentially destabilized the war, and so Sidious, as Chancellor Palpatine, ordered that Wat Tambor be relocated to a prison on distant Delrian.

Tambor received a visit from two legal deputies, both pressure-suited Skakoans like himself. The two Skakoans proceeded to breach their pressure suits, and the release of their compressed methane atmospheres detonated like twin bombs. In the chaos, a third member of their party—a Clawdite shapeshifter known as Nuri—slipped in to free the Techno Union foreman. With the Techno Union again active, the balance of power between the Separatists and the Republic tipped back into a dead heat.

The Spaarti Incident
21 B.B.Y. (12 months after the Battle of Geonosis)

Cartao, trading hub of the Prackla sector, had remained unaligned in the war thus far. But Cartao sheltered Spaarti Creations, one of the most remarkable (and least known) factories in the galaxy. By using a "fluid retooling" process unique to their species, the native Cransoc could adjust the Spaarti factory overnight to produce virtually any product, and the results were almost always superior to similar items on the market. Darth Sidious saw in Cartao an opportunity to turn Spaarti Creations to his own ends, while discrediting his enemies in the process.

Kinman Doriana, Chancellor Palpatine's aide, became the agent of Cartao's ruin. Doriana had been double-dealing since the outset of the war, believing that he had successfully created *two* lives—one to serve Chancellor Palpatine and the other to serve Darth Sidious. On Sidious's orders, Doriana used his credentials to seize Spaarti Creations in the name of the Republic. Immediately, the factory began churning out cloning cylinders that could grow battle-ready soldiers in less than a tenth of the time it took the Kaminoans to do the same.

But the Separatists had a similar idea, intending to use Spaarti to produce a new variety of battle droid. Their invasion force seized the facility. Since no one wanted to wreck the factory in a careless crossfire, the two sides fought a very precise battle; the factory changed hands several times over the next few weeks. Finally, one of Darth Sidious's agents remote-steered a Republic gunship into the roof of the Spaarti complex, sparking a fire that melted the priceless Cransoc technology.

Darth Sidious had achieved what he wanted. The Jedi, implicated in the gunship crash through false evidence, suffered another blow to their credibility. Spaarti Creations could no longer be used by potential rivals. And the Republic took a delivery of thousands of Spaarti cloning cylinders. These cylinders saw heavy use following their installation on Wayland and other planets. Spaarti clones became increasingly common during the war's final year.

The Bio-Droid Threat
21 B.B.Y. (1 year after the Battle of Geonosis)

Ord Cestus, a relatively forgotten planet in the far reaches of the Outer Rim, had established a booming economy based on the manufacture of bio-droids—robots with a unique living circuit composed of a sleeping Dashta eel. These eels, found only in a single underground lake beneath Ord Cestus's mountains, had a powerful connection to the Force. When wedded to a security droid's circuitry through a secret Cestian procedure, the resulting biological–mechanical gestalt could seemingly react to threats before they happened. This slight precognitive ability made bio-droids the only battle droids that could efficiently stand up to a Jedi in one-on-one combat, giving them the nickname "Jedi Killers."

Dooku's lieutenant Asajj Ventress soon approached Ord Cestus's leaders with an offer they couldn't refuse—an order for hundreds of thousands of bio-droids, and the machinery and tissue-cloning tanks needed to fulfill that order. The huge influx of credits would be enough to ensure Ord Cestus's survival in the uncertain postwar future.

Word of the deal soon reached the Jedi Council. They could not let the bio-droid army reach completion, but neither did the Council wish to antagonize neutral planets by bullying Ord Cestus into submission. Obi-Wan Kenobi, Kit Fisto, and a squad of clone troopers received the Ord Cestus assignment. The clones would follow the textbook "militia model" by organizing the planet's low-caste workers into a fighting force. If negotiations failed, sabotage would follow. If *both* options failed, a Republic assault ship stood ready to bombard the bio-droid factories into oblivion.

Out in the planet's countryside, the clone troopers created their ragtag militia. Obi-Wan and Kit Fisto soon joined them, and the small army began to strike the high-end bio-droid factories. The Cestian government scrambled the bio-droids to fight the insurgents. Hundreds died under the guns of the unstoppable automatons.

The two sides reached a stalemate. A Republic orbital bombardment—and the complete destruction of Ord Cestus society—seemed inevitable. But something remarkable and unprecedented had happened to the clone captain. During the recruitment of the local militia, he had fallen in love with a transport pilot, who had awakened a need in him that went beyond the imprinted loyalty he had to his corps. In the end, the clone captain sacrificed himself to destroy the control center for the bio-droid production line. With his death, the specter of a vast bio-droid army evaporated.

MASSING THUNDERHEADS
20.9–20.8 B.B.Y. (1 year, 1–2 months after the Battle of Geonosis)

Eriadu in the Seswenna sector held a strategic Republic position, straddling both the Rimma Trade Route and the Hydian Way. The Rimward end of the Rimma had turned unfriendly since before the Battle of Geonosis, with major worlds such as Sluis Van and Clak'dor VII defecting to the Separatist side. The nearby planet Sullust, a major manufacturing center, had remained in the Republic stable. For more than a year Eriadu and Sullust had served as bastions, stemming the tide of Separatist incursion. That is, until Sullust's secession.

The Republic was quick to respond lest they lose control of the Hydian. Eriadu had by now become the preeminent Republic staging point for all battles in that quadrant, boasting a full fleet under the command of Brigadier Gideon Tarkin—Wilhuff Tarkin's brother—and numerous wings of Jedi starfighters. Brigadier Tarkin merged various planetary navies into "priority theaters" and launched t hem from Eriadu.

Ultimately, a betrayal in the Republic ranks led to their defeat in the Battle of Sullust, yet the overall campaign eventually resulted in the Republic's partial recapture of the Sluis sector.

Violence across the galaxy continued to build as if heating to a boiling point. Kuat and Neimoidia—key members of the Republic and Confederacy, respectively—escalated their military standoff by saturating the space around their sectors with mines, effectively shutting down a crucial leg of the Hydian Way. In another part of the galaxy, Anakin and Obi-Wan helped bring peace to the embattled planet of Skye. Along the Rimma Trade Route, Mace Windu foiled a Separatist plot to mine the route, chasing a battle droid

army from the Squib homeworld of Skor II.

Elsewhere on the Rimma, in the Separatist-aligned Sluis sector and neighboring space, Freedom's Sons continued to score victories under the leadership of Captain Zozridor Slayke. Hoping to take control of the situation, the Republic sent diplomats to negotiate with the Sluis sector rulers, but both sides' negotiators were killed when the space station hosting the meeting exploded.

THE BATTLE OF JABIIM
20.79–20.67 B.B.Y. (1 year, 2–4 months after the Battle of Geonosis)

Republic negotiations again fell apart over the fate of Jabiim, a soggy ball in the Outer Rim rich in minerals. The charismatic Alto Stratus, who had recently seized control of Jabiim in a coup, had allied his majority government with the Separatists, despite the presence of Republic loyalists on his world. Chancellor Palpatine authorized the use of force to protect the loyalists from Stratus's aggression, though unofficially the Republic was more concerned about going after Jabiim's ore.

Rain fell around the clock on Jabiim. The world was a mess, too stormy for atmospheric flight and too muddy for most heavy equipment. Nevertheless, the Republic chose Jabiim to be a field test for its newest walker, the All Terrain Armored Transport, or AT-AT. These four-legged behemoths packed enough firepower to decimate any Separatist AAT or spider droid. Combined with six-legged AT-TEs and two-legged AT-XTs, the Republic battle line appeared unstoppable.

Unfortunately, the Republic ran into trouble almost immediately, and it wasn't the mud. Alto Stratus and his elite Nimbus commandos employed native technology like repulsor boots to skate above the quagmire that passed for a surface. It took weeks for the Republic to score a major victory at Camp Aurek. After that, their successes seemed to come quickly—Point Down and Outpost Shear fell within days. But the Republic's forward march was taking them farther and farther from their main HQ, Shelter Base, precisely as Alto Stratus had intended.

In a brutal raid, Stratus's hailfire droids pummeled Shelter

Base and killed hundreds. General Obi-Wan Kenobi and the ARC trooper Alpha were believed to be among the dead. Unknown to their fellow soldiers, the two survived, only to become prisoners of Commander Asajj Ventress.

Now Masterless, Anakin received a transfer to the "Padawan Pack," a group of orphaned apprentices bunched together in the hope that several Padawans would be equal to one Jedi Knight. With Obi-Wan's disappearance, the Jabiim campaign fell to General Leska, who moved her surviving troops to the Razor Coast in an effort to kill Alto Stratus.

The Battle of Jabiim dragged into its second month. Alto Stratus had a new target in mind—reinforced with fresh battle droids, he marched against the Republic's Cobalt Station with an army ten thousand strong.

General Leska perished in the offensive, and Republic High Command had no choice but to order a full evacuation of Jabiim. The Padawan Pack agreed to delay Stratus's troops long enough for a full evacuation. Staging from Cobalt Station, they fell one by one in a last stand against overwhelming odds. Anakin, however, wasn't with them. Ordered by Chancellor Palpatine to assist with the evacuation, the Chosen One was kept safely away from the grinder that soon claimed the lives of every member of the pack.

The evac transports didn't have room to carry the native Jabiimi loyalist fighters. They were left behind to face certain execution at the hands of Stratus's conquerors. Any Jedi wounded in the Battle of Jabiim went to the medical planet New Holstice for treatment, while Anakin received temporary orders to pair with Jedi Knight A'Sharad Hett on a mission to Aargonar.

THE DRAGON OF AARGONAR
20.67 B.B.Y. (16 months after the Battle of Geonosis)

The desert planet Aargonar had little value save its location, which at this point in the war happened to be directly on the border between Republic and Confederacy space. To beat back Separatist encroachment, the Council sent Jedi Master Ki-Adi-Mundi and Jedi Knight Bultar Swan to lead an Aargonar attack. Also contributing were A'Sharad Hett and Anakin Skywalker.

Early in the battle, the gunship carrying A'Sharad and Anakin crashed behind enemy lines. Though the two Jedi had much in common, having both come late to the Temple following Tatooine childhoods, A'Sharad remained steeped in the Tusken Raider culture of his upbringing. Anakin hated him. Unable to forget his mother's murder at the hands of Tuskens, Anakin slipped into a nightmare in the Aargonar heat and screamed out the secret that he had kept from everyone—that in his fury following his mother's death, he had slaughtered an entire Tusken village.

A'Sharad chose not to reveal Anakin's secret, calling it a burden that the Padawan must bear alone. The two Jedi made it back to the Republic line, where Ki-Adi-Mundi and Bultar Swan held a rapidly crumbling position in the Vondar Canyon. By luring a hovertrain-sized gouka dragon onto the battlefield, Anakin managed to break up the Separatist offensive and allow for a Republic evacuation of Aargonar.

Anakin refused to give up hope regarding Obi-Wan's survival on Jabiim, but the Council did not share his optimism. Recognizing the need to keep Padawans paired with more experienced Jedi following the deaths in the Padawan Pack, the Council reassigned Anakin to Jedi Master Ki-Adi-Mundi. Though Master Mundi was hardly a typical Jedi—he had once married and raised a family—Anakin found it difficult to open up to him. Ki-Adi-Mundi was a dour man with other things on his mind than training a Padawan.

The two spent much of their time away from the war's front lines. Pirates, the perennial scourges of the spaceways, had become emboldened by preoccupation of the Republic security forces. To send an unmistakable message to these criminals, the Republic dispatched special task forces to cut the strongest pirate fleets to ribbons.

ESCAPE FROM RATTATAK
20.66 B.B.Y. (1 year, 4 months after the Battle of Geonosis)

Obi-Wan Kenobi and the ARC trooper Alpha were now prisoners of war, imprisoned in Asajj Ventress's citadel on Rattatak. Ventress tormented Obi-Wan with muscle maggots and a Sith torture mask, hoping to prove to Dooku that the Jedi was unworthy of his attention as a potential apprentice.

Obi-Wan sprang himself and Alpha from their holding cell and tore through Ventress's guards. Ventress intercepted him on the landing pad, but couldn't prevent Obi-Wan from stealing her own ship and flying himself and Alpha back to civilization.

Separatist starfighters perforated the hyperdrive of Obi-Wan and Alpha's escape vessel, however, and it crashed on a forgotten planetoid. Their Separatist pursuers followed them

A Republic clone commando
[Art by Mark Chiarello]

Anakin Skywalker makes a run on the Separatist flagship during the Battle of Praesitlyn. [Art by Tommy Lee Edwards]

down, but fell in a shower of blasterfire, the victims of bounty hunters eager to claim the price on the heads of Jedi posted by Asajj Ventress. Yoda and Mace Windu had an open bounty posting of 1,250,000 credits each, and Anakin Skywalker, still a Padawan, fetched 225,000 credits, dead or alive.

Anakin Skywalker and Ki-Adi-Mundi rescued Obi-Wan from the hunters. Obi-Wan Kenobi returned to the Republic as a war hero. With his master's safe return, Anakin's brief apprenticeship to Ki-Adi-Mundi came to a close.

Alpha, meanwhile, returned to Kamino to train new clones. Obi-Wan joked that Alpha should give the clones *real* names, and Alpha took him at his word. The next batch of commanders to arrive from Kamino bore simple one-word names in addition to their numeric designations. The new commander assigned to Obi-Wan called himself Cody.

DEATH OF A CHANCELLOR
20.65 B.B.Y. (1 year, 4 months after the Battle of Geonosis)

On Coruscant, Chancellor Palpatine took advantage of every development in the war, both setbacks and victories, to acquire more power for himself. The passage of the so-called Reflex Amendment gave him authority over planetary and sector matters. Critics speculated that it was only a matter of time before Coruscant-appointed territorial governors stripped all control from local governments.

Bail Organa, Senator of Alderaan, was one of a growing number of politicians who mistrusted Palpatine's expanding power base. In the eleven years since he had replaced Chancellor Valorum, Palpatine had far outlasted his eight-year term limit, as well as taken on emergency powers.

The Republic's latest failures became more fod-

der for Bail Organa's Senate colleagues. Agora in the Sluis sector had fallen to the Separatists, despite last-minute resistance by Freedom's Sons. On Cerea, Commerce Guild spider droids befouled the paradise world in a monthlong battle that ended when Gossam commandos assassinated Cerea's President Bo-Ro-Tara. Pirates had even attacked Bail Organa's ship. In response to the news, Palpatine called for even more draconian security measures. When Senator Seti Ashgad argued against the installation of new surveillance cams in the Senate Building, he suddenly disappeared. Much later it emerged that he had been exiled to the prison planet Nam Chorios.

Organa had already formed an alliance with the like-minded senator Mon Mothma of Chandrila. Now he received a surprising visit from Finis Valorum. Over the past decade, the ex-chancellor had collected reams of stories concerning Palpatine, including the fact that, as with Seti Ashgad, his critics often mysteriously vanished. Initially, Organa couldn't be sure that Valorum's words weren't the bitter griping of a man forced from power, but two facts changed Organa's mind. The first was the suspicious explosion of Valorum's transport as it lifted off from a Coruscant starport, killing Finis Valorum and everyone else aboard. The second was Palpatine's exploitation of the incident to pass another security bill, which gave him unprecedented central power.

Clearly, aboveboard politicking was not enough. Over

the next several months, Bail Organa and Mon Mothma, with the occasional help of other Senators including Garm Bel Iblis of isolationist Corellia, began laying the groundwork for a political alliance opposed to Palpatine's rule.

Coruscant Assassination
20.63 B.B.Y. (1 year, 4 months after the Battle of Geonosis)

Dooku wasted no time sending his new agent, Quinlan Vos, on missions. On the Sith tomb world of Korriban, Quinlan retrieved a holocron once belonging to the Sith Lord Darth Andeddu from a booby-trapped catacomb. On Coruscant, Quinlan assassinated a double-dealing Senator who had displeased Dooku. While escaping from Coruscant, he ran afoul of the Whiphid Jedi Master K'Kruhk, hero of Teyr and former dissident Jedi. K'Kruhk nearly died in his pursuit of Quinlan through the vertical city. Even those in the Order who knew of Quinlan's undercover mission became convinced that his cover story could no longer explain his deeds. Quinlan continued to delude himself, believing any actions to be justified if they ingratiated him with Dooku and got him closer to uncovering the identity of Dooku's Master, the "second Sith."

The Hero with No Fear
20.3 B.B.Y. (1 year, 10 months after the Battle of Geonosis)

Though some segments of the population continued to distrust the Jedi, planets liberated from Separatist control often viewed the Jedi as heroes. Anakin Skywalker had already received more than his share of the glory. Following his exploits at Jabiim and Aargonar, the newsnet media had dubbed him "the hero with no fear." Entire worlds began expecting Anakin to free them singlehandedly. In a surprising number of cases, they weren't disappointed.

On Virujansi, Anakin defeated a Separatist occupation force by taking command of the planet's Rarefied Air Cavalry and luring the enemy's vulture fighters into a treacherous warren of mountain caverns. The grateful Virujansi named Anakin their "warrior of the infinite."

At Togoria, the Republic suffered a total defeat. The planet, homeworld of the fierce feline Togorians, became a flashpoint when General Grievous's troops arrived in force—apparently menacing Togoria's small shipyard. The Republic dispatched General Bridger to the rescue, only to realize that Togoria had voluntarily gone over to the enemy. Togorian warriors tore General Bridger's landing party to shreds with their claws. Grievous spared Bridger and challenged him to a duel. The fight lasted less than twenty seconds, and Grievous left the body on the dirt to feed the mosgoths.

The Battle of Dreighton
20.2 B.B.Y. (1 year, 10 months after the Battle of Geonosis)

Cloaking technology had been one of the greatest breakthroughs of the last five millennia, yet it was rarely used in the Clone Wars. Making a starship invisible could only be done with stygium crystals, and the stygium mines had gone dry years earlier on the planet Aeten II. The space pirate Nym's stygium cache on Maramere had likewise run empty.

Both the Republic and the Confederacy hoped to locate undiscovered caches of stygium on Aeten II. Dreaming of invisible fleets, they clashed in the monthlong Battle of Dreighton, named for the nebula that shrouded Aeten II from outside eyes. The Republic received support from an independent army known as the Pendarran Warriors, but it proved to be of little use. The conflict cost the lives of more than a hundred Jedi, many of them killed when Hutt and Black Sun forces moved in to rout the weakened combatants.

There was no victor at the Battle of Dreighton. Aeten II was declared barren of military resources and soon forgotten, again emerging into importance decades later in the middle of the Galactic Civil War.

Closer to home, General Grievous personally led the Confederacy's boldest push yet—an assault on the Core world of Duro, one of the founding members of the Republic and home to key corporate and shipbuilding concerns. Separatist naval forces hammered the Republic *Acclamator*-class warships tasked with Duro's defense, and captured a key orbital city after less than a week of fighting. Using the city's command codes to drop Duro's planetary shields, Grievous unleashed an orbital bombardment followed by a mass landing of his droid troops on the planet's polluted surface.

BREAKING THE FOEROST SIEGE
20.1 B.B.Y. (1 year, 11 months after the Battle of Geonosis)

The shipyards of Foerost lay practically in Coruscant's backyard. During the Great Sith War they had been used as a military staging area, and in more recent centuries they had been purchased by the Techno Union. At the start of the Clone Wars, the Republic had simply blockaded Foerost space. Without access to Separatist supply lines, the Republic hoped the shipyards would wither into decay.

For nearly two years the standoff continued, until the besieged Techno Union engineers exploded from Foerost with warships that no one had imagined. The engineers called the design the Bulwark Mark I—a kilometer-long behemoth with turbolasers, ion cannons, and enough armor to ram small ships with impunity. With the old Sullustan Dua Ningo in charge of the armada, the Bulwark Fleet broke through the Republic's blockade and proceeded to smash military outposts throughout Coruscant's Sector Zero. To stop Ningo, the Republic launched its newest warship—the *Victory*-class Star Destroyer—nearly six months early.

These arrowhead-shaped craft measured nine hundred meters from stem to stern, boasting ten tractor beam projectors and 80 concussion missile launchers. Born of the Victor Initiative Project between Kuat Drive Yards and Rendili StarDrive, they performed with distinction in a shakedown cruise that became a naval slugging match for the heart of Core space. Captains Terrinald Screed and Jan Dodonna led the two task forces that made up the Victory Fleet, surviving clashes with Ningo at Ixtlar, Alsakan, and Basilisk.

The final showdown came in the skies above Anaxes. Dodonna, under heavy fire with dead wrecks from his task force plunging planetward, held out long enough for Screed to pop in from hyperspace and disintegrate Ningo's flagship with a broadside fusillade. Screed required cybernetic reconstruction to survive the injuries he received in the Battle of Anaxes, but both men returned to Coruscant as heroes.

THE CASUALTIES OF DRONGAR
20 B.B.Y. (2 years after the Battle of Geonosis)

War is hell, goes the saying, and no one knows it better than field surgeons. Battlefield medics experience a near-continuous parade of severed limbs, exploded torsos, and gushing arteries. During the Clone Wars, giant MedStar frigates accompanied most Republic fleets into battle, deploying mobile field hospitals known as Republic Mobile Surgical Units or RMSUs—"Rimsoos." On contested Drongar, one Rimsoo had to choose sides over the fate of the planet.

Drongar was a young world of steam fissures and lightning strikes with no plant life more advanced than fungus. Bota, an ugly native mold, had the curious quality of being useful to nearly every species as an antibiotic, painkiller, or intoxicant. Since bota, once picked, deteriorated quickly, both the Republic and the Confederacy maintained harvesting operations on-planet and fielded armies to fight for control of the bota fields.

The planet's atmospheric spores contaminated airspeeder engines and made airborne warfare impossible, so battle on Drongar came down to face-to-face shootouts. Hundreds of bleeding clone troopers arrived every week at the Rimsoos, only to be patched up and sent back into the fray.

The war on Drongar had been burning for more than a year when Padawan Barriss Offee, who had participated in such earlier conflicts as the mission to Ansion and the Battle of Ilum, arrived to practice her skills as a Jedi healer. At Rimsoo Seven in the Jasserak Lowlands she encountered Dr. Jos Vondar, a young surgeon whose cynicism covered his idealistic hope that he could save the lives of every clone to come under his laser scalpel. The Rimsoo personnel aided in uncovering evidence that Admiral Bleyd, commander of the Drongar MedStar, had masterminded a bota-skimming ring to line his own pockets.

Bleyd's scheme ended with his death, but the Drongar operation continued to be plagued by Separatist spies and saboteurs who attacked the bota fields. Barriss Offee discovered that the bota acted as a Force magnifier for her Jedi perceptions, and briefly flirted with an addiction to the medicinal mold. The Republic used Drongar to test its own superlaser project, using an enhancement of the weaponry employed by SPHA-T heavy cannons. After much refinement, the superlaser ultimately would see use aboard the first Death Star following the rise of the Empire.

Eventually, the fighting resulted in the destruction of the Drongar operation, as most settlements were bombed out of existence. Dr. Vondar went on to other assignments, and Barriss Offee returned to Coruscant, secure in her new status as a Jedi Knight.

DISASTER ON HONOGHR
20 B.B.Y. (2 years after the Battle of Geonosis)

At this point in the war, the Republic believed that it had blunted the threat of Separatist biological warfare. By enlisting the experts of the Lurrian Genetic Enclave to study the "swamp gas" antidote recovered from Queyta, the Republic had cracked the enemy's bioweapon signature.

Across the galaxy, however, one Separatist commander struggled to create a toxin that could *never* be cured. The lab aboard his scientific vessel *Gahenna* had been rescued two years earlier from Queyta. The *Gahenna* developed a poisonous defoliant, TriHexalophine1138, and headed back toward Naboo to complete the planned mission that had seen the devastation of Ohma-D'un. But a Republic cruiser got wind of the plan and drove the *Gahenna* to ground above a forgotten world called Honoghr.

The Scientific Information Packet aboard the ship contained all the details on the TriHexalophine plot, and both the Republic and the Separatists scrambled to secure it. The planet's native Noghri, however, had already taken the SIP to the heart of a sacred temple built there thirty millennia

Jedi Knight Aayla Secura and Jedi Master Quinlan Vos
[ART BY MARK CHIARELLO]

before by the ancient Rakata.

Quinlan Vos headed into the temple to retrieve the SIP for Dooku. Opposing him were Aayla Secura and Commander Bly, one of the newest clone commanders to come from Kamino. The two sides teamed up to defeat the temple's booby traps, but Quinlan betrayed his former Padawan and tried to make off with the SIP for himself. By forcing Quinlan into a position where he might have to kill her, Aayla made him realize that his obsession with rooting out the "second Sith" might not be worth the choices he had made. Doubting himself for the first time in months, Quinlan escaped Honoghr empty-handed.

Honoghr suffered mortal damage as the *Gahenna*'s toxins leaked from the cracked laboratories and devastated the ecosystem, leaving almost no plant life, save for dry plains of kholm-grass. Forgotten by the Republic, the Noghri bore their misery in stoic silence.

TARGET: GRIEVOUS
20 B.B.Y. (2 years after the Battle of Geonosis)

General Grievous energized the Separatist armies during this phase of the war, chewing through Republic territory like a logger droid felling deadwood. On Vantos, Nadiem, and dozens of other worlds, Grievous slaughtered clone troopers and civilians alike, collecting lightsaber trophies from the Jedi Knights whom he beheaded.

Grievous's atrocities led to the rise of a splinter faction within the Jedi Order, whose members advocated the general's assassination. Master Yoda opposed this radicalism, fearing that the actions of Jedi assassins could drive them to the dark side, but a few risked excommunication to dish out what they perceived as frontier justice.

One Padawan, Flynn Kybo, joined up with the Coway Jedi Master B'dard Tone and several others to track down Grievous in the Ison Corridor. The general's droid armies had conquered the Ugnaught homeworld of Gentes, strip-mining the landscape and massacring thousands of Ugnaughts after the species showed little value as slaves. Grievous also imprisoned a group of young Padawans on Gentes, planning to lobotomize them and turn them into cyborgs like himself. Kybo and Master Tone freed the Padawans, but both died before they could take out Grievous.

STONE MITES OF ORLEON
19.9 B.B.Y. (2 years, 1 month after the Battle of Geonosis)

Stone mites, bioengineered insects that could devour building foundations, had ruined many worlds since their introduction in the months prior to the Battle of Geonosis. The Separatist scientist Jenna Zan Arbor had created the stone mites with help from Arkanian geneticists,

but the Republic had been looking for a chance to turn the creatures to its own ends.

An opportunity presented itself when the freighter *Spinner*, on approach to Coruscant's busy Westport, fell like a rock into Kishi. The *Spinner* had been crawling with stone mites, and the creatures quickly overtook the Kishi. The stone mite outbreak resulted in the total collapse of the Pillar Zone before Jedi healers skilled in the art of *Morichro* snuffed out the lives of every last mite.

Armand Isard, head of the Senate Bureau for Intelligence, labeled the incident an act of terrorism. Isard's agents traced the *Spinner* back to a previous stopover on Orleon, a small Mid Rim planet of little note. Believing that Orleon held Separatist bioweapons facilities, Isard authorized the release of Republic-altered, mutant stone mites onto the world. Carbonite canisters fired from high orbit thawed on impact and released thousands of hibernating mites.

But Isard was wrong—Orleon had no biolabs, and might have escaped the Clone Wars untouched had it not been for the unlucky *Spinner*. Nothing could stop Isard's mites. Structures that had stood for thirteen thousand years crumbled into powder within a week. Orleon's entire population of eight hundred million fled offworld, and hordes of breeding stone mites set to work devouring the planet's crust.

BPFASSH UPRISING
19.75 B.B.Y. (2 years, 3 months after the Battle of Geonosis)

The Sluis sector continued to boil. Assailed by relentless internal raids from Captain Slayke's Freedom's Sons and pressured from the outside by the Republic fortress at Eriadu, the sector had known nearly continual fighting since the outset of the war.

Bpfassh, one of the Sluis sector's lesser lights, boasted a satellite Jedi training facility similar to the one on Kamparas. Due to its remoteness, the Jedi Council had always had trouble with the Bpfassh enclave, putting down minor insurrections from time to time when inexperienced students unwisely decided to flex their power. At the start of the Clone Wars, the Bpfasshi academy joined the dissident Jedi movement.

The ongoing stress of the Sluis sector battles is believed to have triggered an outbreak of fanatical militarism among the Bpfasshi Jedi. Fully in the grip of the dark side, and quite mad, the Bpfasshi Dark Jedi set themselves against Freedom's Sons and slaughtered everyone who got in their way. Soon opposed in battle by loyal Coruscant Jedi, the Bpfasshi Jedi fell one by one, until their leader ultimately perished in an epic Force clash with Master Yoda.

ATTACK ON AZURE
19.59 B.B.Y. (2 years, 5 months after the Battle of Geonosis)

Obi-Wan Kenobi and Anakin Skywalker, accompanied by fellow Jedi Siri Tachi, acquired a foolproof codebreaker developed by technical genius Talesan Fry. When they delivered the codebreaker to the Republic-controlled spaceport of Azure, the Separatists launched a massive attack in an attempt to seize the gadget for themselves.

Though the Republic repelled the assault, Siri Tachi died from wounds sustained in battle. Obi-Wan, who had always allowed a part of him to love Siri despite the Jedi principles of nonattachment, now allowed himself to feel the pain of loss.

THE PRAESITLYN CONQUEST
19.5 B.B.Y. (2 years, 6 months after the Battle of Geonosis)

The first strike in the Battle of Praesitlyn came without warning. Recently recaptured from Separatists, the planet held a cutting-edge communications complex that linked datafeeds throughout the galactic quadrant. Praesitlyn itself had few defenses. Concerned that the planet could again become a Separatist target, the Republic hoped to dispatch a fleet from the nearby Sluis Van shipyards.

Dooku's lieutenant Asajj Ventress soon revealed the flaw in the Republic's strategy. She dispatched a fleet under the command of InterGalactic Banking Clan bigwig Pors Tonith,

while also blockading the Sluis Van system. With Sluis Van's warships stuck in stardock, the bulk of Tonith's fleet zipped to Praesitlyn and landed an invasion force tens of thousands strong. The Separatists soon held Praesitlyn, and—thanks to a system-blanketing jamming field thrown out by Tonith's fleet—no one in the Republic had any idea of the problem.

Fortunately for the Republic, they had a local ally—Captain Zozridor Slayke of Freedom's Sons. His fleet had been operating in the area when the Praesitlyn invasion occurred. Slayke dispatched a message to Chancellor Palpatine, who agreed to send a relief force of clone troopers and Jedi. But Slayke, who viewed himself as a charmed figure, landed his entire volunteer army without waiting for the Republic's reinforcements. This time, Slayke badly miscalculated. Though hundreds of droids fell, the ground oozed red with the blood of Slayke's soldiers.

But the Republic reinforcements were soon on their way, streaking through hyperspace under the command of Master Nejaa Halcyon and Padawan Anakin Skywalker. For Halcyon, this was another opportunity to prove himself against the pirate who had shamed him two and a half years earlier by stealing his starship *Plooriod Bodkin*. For Anakin, it was another chance to show the Council that no enemy could stand against the Chosen One.

With twenty thousand clone troopers under their command, Anakin and Master Halcyon made planetfall on Praesitlyn and linked up with Slayke's harried forces. Anakin seized the communications complex with a company of clone troopers, but his sense of triumph on rescuing the hostages turned to boiling fury when a second force of droids murdered most of the hostages in an indiscriminate crossfire.

Hate had fully enveloped him now, weighing on his shoulders like a heavy robe. Anakin didn't bother to wait for support from Halcyon's or Slayke's lines; he pushed deeper into the encampment, penetrating Tonith's fortified HQ. When Tonith presented himself for surrender, Anakin nearly cut him in half before forcing himself back from the raw edge of fury.

Nejaa Halcyon focused his attention on mopping up the enemy fleet in orbit. Once in space, Anakin made a suicidal run on the enemy flagship's bridge, and he vanished in the explosion that followed. Anakin soon reappeared, revealing that he had made a risky, last-instant hyperspace hop. On the ground and in space, with little regard for his own life, Anakin had won the Battle of Praesitlyn.

Shortly after, on Susevfi, Nejaa Halcyon lost his life in a duel against the Anzati Dark Jedi Nikkos Tyris. The Anzati also perished in the battle, turning his Force-using followers, the Jensaarai, against the Jedi Order. The Jensaarai would develop their teachings in secret until being discovered by Luke Skywalker decades later.

LURE AT VJUN
19.49 B.B.Y. (2 years, 6 months after the Battle of Geonosis)

As an ex-member of the Jedi Order, Count Dooku stood alone among the Separatist leaders as a former friend to those he now fought. The Count had a special connection to Yoda, having learned much at the Jedi Master's side in the years before Dooku's apprenticeship to Thame Cerulian. Dooku believed that he could exploit this bond, tempt Yoda into a private meeting, and kill him.

Dooku drew Yoda to his new base on Vjun with the hint that he, Dooku, was willing to discuss the terms of his defection. Yoda suspected treachery, but didn't want to throw away the possibility of bringing a lost Jedi back into the fold. In a bit of misdirection arranged by Republic Intelligence, an actor famous for playing Yoda on the stage made a public departure from Coruscant in a Jedi starfighter. The real Yoda, concealed within the shell of an R2 unit, boarded a passenger liner with a quartet of Jedi guardians, bound for Vjun.

The Jedi Masters Jai Maruk and the Gran female Maks Leem, with their respective Padawans, Scout and Whie, made up Yoda's escort. Scout, a rebellious girl with low Force sensitivity, was embarking on her first mission outside the Temple walls. Whie had been heir to the House Malreaux on Vjun before the Jedi had brought him to the Temple as a child. Vjun itself had fallen into utter madness in subsequent years, brought on by generations of interbreeding to produce Force-strong traits in the populace.

Commander Asajj Ventress, eager to please Dooku, tracked down the Yoda decoy and blasted his ship to shards, taking the actor prisoner. Once she realized her error, Ventress caught up with the real Yoda at the Phindar Spaceport. As her assassin droids tore up the concourse, Ventress killed both Jai Maruk and Master Leem in a test of lightsabers. The two Masterless Padawans located Yoda and continued to Vjun under his protection.

The final confrontation within Vjun's Château Malreaux ended in a draw. Whie and Scout, aided by Whie's family droid, Fidelis, survived an inconclusive battle with Asajj Ventress. Dooku failed in his attempt to sway Yoda to the dark side with words; nor could he deliver a killing blow with a lightsaber. Dooku fled Vjun to regroup and plan the war's final stage.

For his heroism in the war to date, the Jedi Council inducted Obi-Wan Kenobi into their ranks, and he received a promotion to Jedi Master as dictated by tradition. Obi-Wan also used the opportunity to construct a new lightsaber.

In a related move, the Council agreed to grant Anakin Skywalker the rank of Jedi Knight. Anakin had accomplished great things and was no longer dependent on the guiding influence of his Master. In a small, private ceremony inside the darkened Council chamber, Yoda and the other members ignited their light-sabers in a ritualistic display of honor for the Chosen One. Yoda gently admonished Anakin, telling him that proper Jedi trials could not be conducted with a war on, and that his greatest test was still to come.

DREADNAUGHTS OF RENDILI
19.48 B.B.Y. (2 years, 6 months after the Battle of Geonosis)

The planet Rendili, home to a critical shipbuilding operation, voluntarily joined the Separatists. Rendili's home defense fleet consisted of state-of-the-art Dreadnaughts that could bolster the CIS—but the commander of the fleet had not yet decided where his allegiances lay. The Republic Navy, led by Saesee Tiin and Plo Koon, arrived in full force in the Rendili system. If the Dreadnaughts did not agree to join the Republic, Master Tiin had orders to destroy them.

During negotiations, Plo Koon and Republic Captain Jan Dodonna (a rising naval star who had participated in both the Stark Hyperspace Conflict and the Foerost Siege) became prisoners of the younger, Separatist-leaning officers in the Rendili fleet. With hostages, these officers hoped to break the Republic blockade. Saesee Tiin refused to back down from his ultimatum.

During the standoff, Obi-Wan Kenobi and Jedi renegade Quinlan Vos arrived together, having rescued each other from Asajj Ventress's trap aboard a derelict spacecraft. Quinlan claimed that his role as a double agent was over, since Count Dooku wanted Quinlan dead for his failure to recover the SIP from Honoghr. Both Obi-Wan and Quinlan helped rescue the hostages from the Rendili fleet, then joined the fight against the Separatist starfighters. Anakin Skywalker disabled the Rendili Dreadnaughts to prevent their escape to hyperspace.

The captured vessels were refitted to serve as prisoner transports. Chancellor Palpatine issued an order that immediately nationalized all similar, planetary-level defense fleets.

Quinlan Vos appeared before the Jedi Council, admitting that he had fallen into the shadows during his undercover mission and presenting himself for sentencing. The Council agreed to accept him back into the Order after he went through a period of meditation and repentance. Quinlan, however, was still working for Dooku as part of an elaborate triple cross—by maintaining his "dark" role, he felt that he could earn Dooku's complete trust and uncover the identity of the second Sith.

Burning with hatred toward Obi-Wan Kenobi for escaping her on Rattatak, Asajj Ventress slipped undetected onto Coruscant. She resolved to kill Obi-Wan's Padawan. In a battle on an industrial catwalk high above the city canyons, Ventress scarred Anakin Skywalker's face with her lightsaber. Anakin soon turned the tables, holding Ventress in a Force grip above an abyss and then letting her drop. Believed killed, Ventress barely survived by riding a thermal updraft. She escaped Coruscant soon after.

THE OUTER RIM SIEGES
19.48 B.B.Y. (2 years, 6 months after the Battle of Geonosis)

For the first time since the war began, it appeared that the Republic had momentum on its side. Battles on Duro, Commenor, and Balmorra cleared the CIS from key holdings in the Core and Colonies, forcing much of the Separatist navy to retreat to the Mid and Outer Rims.

Sora Bulq, the fallen Weequay Jedi, established a base on Saleucami, where he continued to serve the interests of Count Dooku. Bulq hired teachers from the elite Anzati assassin school to train his own clone soldiers, grown from the genetic material of Nikto Morgukai warriors. Jedi Master Tholme helped put an end to Bulq's plans. Months later, during the Siege of Saleucami, General Quinlan Vos led a brutal ground assault intended to drive home the horrors of war to the Separatist combatants.

The Confederacy reinforced its positions within the Rim territories, particularly its vast holdings on either side of the Slice. Confident that steady pressure would crumble the Separatist bulwarks and trigger a Confederacy surrender, nearly every fleet element and troop carrier pushed to the Rim borders to assail CIS bases on Ord Radama, Ossus, Ryloth, and elsewhere. Thus began the Outer Rim Sieges.

BETRAYAL AT BOZ PITY
19.43 B.B.Y. (2 years, 7 months after the Battle of Geonosis)

The Outer Rim Sieges marked the final stage of the Clone Wars. Fittingly, the battles saw the end of several of the Confederacy's top commanders. Obi-Wan Kenobi, still burning with shame over the torture that he had endured while a prisoner in Asajj Ventress's citadel, had requested of the Jedi Council that he be allowed to find and neutralize Ventress. Obi-Wan's single-minded fixation on his target violated the Jedi Code's rules against passion and emotion, but Yoda and Mace Windu hoped that Kenobi's solo quest would free up troops needed on the front lines.

Obi-Wan recruited the assistance of Anakin Skywalker,

though the two no longer held the connection of Master and Padawan. A tip from a crimelord led them to believe that Ventress would attack a space yacht, but when the Jedi investigated the ship, they discovered a trap set by Durge.

Anakin battled Durge as explosive charges burst and the vessel disintegrated around them. The hulking Gen'Dai put up a brutal fight, but Anakin succeeded where other Jedi had failed by mainlining the power of the dark side. Forcing the beaten Durge into an escape pod, Anakin sent the pod into the burning arms of a nearby sun.

That left Commander Ventress. The ship's logs indicated that she could be found at a major Confederacy base on Boz Pity. Obi-Wan put aside his pride and called in a full Republic assault force. Bail Organa, one of the mission commanders, hoped that the combined effort could eliminate Ventress, Grievous, and Dooku in one motion.

The attack went better than planned. In short order, Republic troops had secured most of Boz Pity's surface installations, allowing the Jedi to raid the HQ. Obi-Wan caught up with Ventress, but refrained from striking a killing blow. He believed that what he had learned of Ventress's history during his imprisonment on Rattatak painted the picture of a woman who could yet be saved from the lure of the Sith. He tried to reach her with words, but the battlefield actions of her "allies" proved more persuasive. Dooku fled Boz Pity with General Grievous, leaving Ventress behind to face capture or death. Stung by Dooku's betrayal, Ventress apparently perished in her final duel with Kenobi. Her dying words, "Defend Coruscant," provided a hint to the Separatists' future plans and indicated a deathbed change of heart. Obi-Wan ordered that Ventress's corpse be shuttled back to Coruscant for a Jedi cremation.

A curious footnote to the proceedings came with the word that the ship bearing Asajj Ventress's body had never arrived at its destination. Investigators later learned that she had merely muffled her life functions on Boz Pity to achieve a state of near-death stasis.

Commandeering the shuttle, she had leapt into hyperspace, bound for parts unknown.

The Xagobah Citadel
19.42 B.B.Y. (2 years, 7 months after the Battle of Geonosis)

Almost forgotten in the larger sweep of events, Boba Fett had survived the death of his father, Jango, in the Battle of Geonosis, and now moved to secure his status as the best bounty hunter in the galaxy. After signing on with Jabba the Hutt as a freelance agent—and acquitting himself against Dooku's Gen'Dai mercenary Durge—Boba accepted a Republic bounty on Techno Union foreman Wat Tambor.

Supreme Chancellor Palpatine
[Art by Mark Chiarello]

Knowing his enemies would besiege him, Tambor had taken refuge in a fortress on the Outer Rim planet of Xagobah. Although Boba Fett succeeded in penetrating Tambor's citadel, General Grievous humiliated Boba in combat and ensured the escape of the Separatist leader.

During the Xagobah incident, Boba Fett ran into Anakin Skywalker, who helped Boba repair his damaged starship *Slave I*. Anakin assisted in arranging a meeting between Boba and Chancellor Palpatine, who was singularly unimpressed by Boba's revelation that Count Dooku and the "Tyranus" who had recruited Jango as a clone template were one and the same. Boba departed Coruscant, though it would not be the last time that he would attract the attentions of either Palpatine or Anakin Skywalker.

Elsewhere, the Mandalorians staged an unlikely resurrection following their decimation in the Battle of Galidraan. Alpha-02, an aberrant Kaminoan clone of Jango Fett, became obsessed with rebuilding the clans, and recruited two hundred soldiers from police units on the planet Mandalore, along with former members of the Death Watch. These new Supercommandos comprised the Mandalorian Protectors, and they struck against the Republic at Null, Kamino, and New Bornalex. Following many bloody battles, only two recruits remained—Tobbi Dala and Fenn Shysa, both of whom returned to Mandalore.

THE HUNT FOR DARTH SIDIOUS
19.1–19 B.B.Y. (2 years, 11 months–3 years after the Battle of Geonosis)

A series of strikes led by Obi-Wan Kenobi and Anakin Skywalker eliminated the remaining Separatist bases on the Neimoidian colonial purse worlds of Cato Neimoidia, Deko Neimoidia, and Koru Neimoidia. The final assault on the Neimoidian homeworld pitted AT-ATs and juggernaut tanks against the delicate Trade Federation citadels. The planet suffered greatly in the onslaught that followed, and the destruction of the grub-hatcheries spelled bad news for the future viability of the Neimoidian species.

But Viceroy Nute Gunray's greed burned so brightly that he risked capture and death by returning to Cato Neimoidia, hoping to salvage his treasures. Republic Captain Jan Dodonna led an assault that failed to capture the viceroy, but in his haste to escape, Gunray left behind his walking throne. This custom-crafted piece of furniture contained a holoprojector that broadcast on an encrypted channel, allowing Gunray to communicate directly with Darth Sidious. If the Republic could crack the code, it would take a giant step forward on learning the whereabouts of the elusive second Sith.

Like Gunray, Corporate Alliance Magistrate Shu Mai couldn't resist returning to her headquarters on Felucia to make arrangements regarding the disposition of her holdings. Jedi Knight Bariss Offee tried to move against Shu Mai, but Offee wound up a prisoner, requiring a rescue by Aayla Secura and her top clone, Commander Bly. Shu Mai then escaped, but not before unleashing a poisonous biological agent that spread through Felucia's water distribution infrastructure.

General Grievous, on orders from Darth Sidious, collected Gunray, Shu Mai, and the other bickering members of the Separatist Council and looked for a secure place to stash them. His first choice, the Outer Rim planet Belderone, became known to the Republic after a transmission was intercepted via Gunray's mechno-chair. Republic battleships lay in wait at Belderone, led by Anakin Skywalker and Obi-Wan Kenobi. Skywalker again added to his legend by flying through a screen of turbolaser fire and taking repeated potshots at the bridge of Grievous's flagship, *Invisible Hand*. Grievous escaped the trap by opening his ship's cannons on a refugee convoy, killing ten thousand innocents.

By ambushing Grievous at Belderone, the Republic had revealed its advantage regarding its receipt of the mechno-chair messages. But Gunray's throne would still be useful in other ways. Reverse-engineering the device revealed hints regarding its manufacture, and soon Republic Intelligence had discovered Darth Sidious's secret lair—an abandoned industrial building in the heart of The Works, Coruscant's decaying factory sector.

Darth Sidious may have sensed that his disguise could

not hold for much longer. As Supreme Chancellor Palpatine, he delivered a State of the Republic address that identified three targets in the Outer Rim Sieges—Saleucami, Mygeeto, and Felucia, which he called a "triad of evil"—and committed more than half of Coruscant's defense fleet to the continued pacification of those worlds. At the same time, he ordered General Grievous to initiate an assault on Coruscant, using secret hyperlanes that cut through the Deep Core. It was to be the opening act of Sidious's endgame.

Anakin Skywalker was preoccupied with events on the Outer Rim planet of Nelvaan. After slaying a gargantuan monster in the thicket of the alien jungle, Anakin earned the admiration of the Nelvaan natives. They took his arrival as a sign that the gods had delivered a champion to eradicate the evil presence that stained their land.

His face smeared with ceremonial warpaint, Anakin set off to restore the spiritual balance on Nelvaan. After experiencing a vision quest in the darkness of an ill-omened cavern, Anakin uncovered a Separatist research facility where CIS scientists had been experimenting on captured Nelvaan warriors. Anakin shut down the facility, but, more importantly, he touched the minds of the mutated natives and convinced them to return to their village, demonstrating his fitness as a Jedi.

General Grievous
[ART BY MARK CHIARELLO]

ANAKIN TURNS TO THE DARK SIDE
19 B.B.Y. (3 years after the Battle of Geonosis)

General Grievous executed an attack against the capital world that stretched on for a week and struck terror into the hearts of all Coruscantis. The planet had suffered wounds in the past, such as the invasion of the cortosis battle droids ten months into the war—but never before had an enemy battle fleet slugged it out with home defense forces in the skies above the Senate District, for all to see. And never before had a Coruscant strike been orchestrated directly by General Grievous, butcher of a thousand worlds.

As smoking wrecks fell from orbit and turned into bombs on impact, Grievous and a squad of his IG 100-series MagnaGuards slipped through the orbital scrum and flew to Chancellor Palpatine's apartment in 500 Republica. Palpatine's Jedi defenders, including Mace Windu, Kit Fisto, Stass Allie, and Shaak Ti, hustled the chancellor to a hovertrain, and then a hardened command bunker, but none of them could stop Grievous. The Separatist general captured Palpatine and then spirited him to the waiting *Invisible Hand.* No one knew, of course, that Palpatine had wanted to be abducted, and had in fact arranged it as a test for Anakin Skywalker.

Both Anakin and Obi-Wan had been occupied elsewhere per Sidious's design, pursuing Count Dooku on the ruined world of Tythe. They leapt to Coruscant's defense in their Jedi starfighters. Punching through a thicket of buzz droids and droid tri-fighters, they landed aboard *Invisible Hand* to stage an against-the-odds rescue of the Supreme Chancellor.

Palpatine was their object of rescue; Grievous, their anticipated opposition. Neither Jedi expected Count Dooku to confront them in the General's quarters, but he swiftly became a target of opportunity. Palpatine, bound in a chair, urged Anakin to bloodlust, and Dooku fought for his life. Dooku may have expected to be taken into custody by the Jedi after putting on a good show for his Master, to later assume a role in the new government when Palpatine made their intentions clear to the galaxy. Dooku never guessed that Palpatine would order his death. Anakin beheaded the Count and fled with the chancellor.

General Grievous failed to prevent their escape, and he abandoned *Invisible Hand* in an emergency pod as the ship disintegrated. Anakin amazingly crash-landed the remains of the unflyable wreck of the *Hand* on Coruscant, further bolstering his legend.

Palpatine then insisted that Anakin receive a position on the Jedi Council as his personal representative. Yoda and Mace Windu obeyed the chancellor's wishes, but refused to grant Anakin the rank or privileges of a Jedi Master. Anakin, whose ego had been growing throughout the Clone Wars, now had targets for his arrogant scorn.

Based on Republic Intelligence's investigation of the Sith hideout in The Works and the discovery of a tunnel leading to the apartment building 500 Republica, the Jedi Council concluded that Darth Sidious was an agent in Palpatine's inner circle of advisers. With this knowledge, they at last confirmed that the Clone Wars had been a Sith plot all along. Sidious had controlled one side, his apprentice Dooku the other, both with the intention of bleeding the Jedi dry. The Council decided to force Sidious's hand by capturing or killing General Grievous. If the war continued, even after such a decisive move, the Jedi would arrest Palpatine as a pawn of the Sith.

Obi-Wan Kenobi drew the Grievous assignment, and caught up with the general on the sunken planet Utapau. Grievous dueled Kenobi using four lightsabers, and then led the Jedi on a wild chase along the sinkhole walls. But it was not enough. Obi-Wan shot Grievous in the gut with a blaster, killing him.

With news of Grievous's death, Mace Windu prepared to confront Palpatine—but he soon learned the stunning truth from Anakin Skywalker. Anakin had recently learned that Padmé was pregnant, and had been haunted by visions of his wife dying during childbirth. Palpatine had carefully cultivated Anakin's hopes for preventing this dire premonition, and had revealed everything to Anakin: Palpatine's secret identity as Darth Sidious. His murder of his own Master, Darth Plagueis. The role that the Sith had played in creating Anakin by manipulating the midi-chlorians. And the hint that by studying the ways of the Sith, Anakin could learn to conquer death.

Upon Anakin's confirmation that Palpatine was a Sith Lord, Mace Windu assembled the Jedi Masters Saesee Tiin, Kit Fisto, and Agen Kolar to confront Palpatine in his chambers. Palpatine at last dropped the façade and unleashed his full fury, killing the three lesser Jedi. As Anakin arrived on the scene, Master Windu appeared to have gotten the drop on Palpatine, but Anakin—panicked that the knowledge to save Padmé would be lost with Palpatine's death—hacked off Mace's arm. Palpatine then charred Master Windu with Force lightning, sending Mace out the window to his death.

By giving in to his darkest nature, Anakin Skywalker had become Darth Vader. At Palpatine's command, he led a clone assault on the Jedi Temple, slaughtering hundreds, including even the youngest students. He then left for the volcano world of Mustafar, current hiding place of the Separatist Council, and executed Nute Gunray, Wat Tambor, San Hill, Shu Mai, and all the other corporate tycoons whom Palpatine no longer had any use for. Palpatine also prepared to shut down every battle droid in the galaxy using a master control signal, knowing that the Clone Wars had fulfilled their objective.

Anakin Skywalker and Obi-Wan Kenobi duel on Mustafar.
[Art by Tommy Lee Edwards]

But while the droids no longer served a purpose, Palpatine had a final task for his clone troopers. He commanded his soldiers to execute "Order Sixty-Six." The instructions were one of several contigency plans to deal with varying threats to the Republic, both internal and external. On Felucia, Commander Bly and other clone troopers abandoned the effort to reverse the poisoning of the water supply, and killed Aayla Secura and Barriss Offee. On Mygeeto, Ki-Adi-Mundi died when his clones turned on him during an assault on Confederacy forces. Plo Koon was shot down by clones in the skies of Cato Neimoidia. Saleucami became a death trap for Stass Allie when clone troopers destroyed her speederbike. Obi-Wan Kenobi barely survived an attack by Commander Cody on Utapau, while Yoda escaped from his clone troopers when they turned traitor on Kashyyyk.

Palpatine moved to secure his public standing on Coruscant. Claiming that he had been the victim of a Jedi assassination attempt, he instituted martial law, making a speech before the Senate where he proposed a new society, an "Empire that will stand for a thousand years." As the new dictator-for-life, Palpatine looked out over a cheering Senate, declaring that day as the first Empire Day.

Not all Senators joined in the jubilation. Days earlier, Bail Organa and Padmé Amidala had joined with others, including Mon Mothma, Fang Zar, and Giddean Danu, in opposition to Palpatine's Sector Governance Decree, which placed the chancellor's lackeys as governors to oversee every planet in the Republic. The opposers had presented Palpatine with the dissenting Petition of the Two Thousand, but now many of the two thousand senators who had signed the document had been arrested. Bail Organa decided that he could do more to undermine Palpatine's rule if he appeared to support him in public, while plotting to overthrow him in secret.

Obi-Wan Kenobi and Yoda were the only Jedi left in a position to do something about the disaster. Yoda went after Palpatine in the empty Senate chamber, but could not defeat the most powerful Sith Lord in history. Yoda barely escaped offworld. Obi-Wan Kenobi stowed away on Padmé's ship, confronting Anakin Skywalker on Mustafar. Anakin, assuming that Padmé had betrayed him, locked her in a Force choke that left her near death. Obi-Wan faced his former apprentice in battle.

The contest left both combatants bruised and exhausted, but in the end Obi-Wan maimed Anakin, cutting off his legs and his left arm. Anakin, beaten, lay at the edge of a lake of lava, his head and torso igniting.

Emperor Palpatine's surgical droids rebuilt Darth Vader, and his ebony skull mask reflected the darkness of the spirit within. Encased forever in a walking coffin, his every wheezing breath pure agony, Darth Vader was doomed to live with Palpatine's revelation that Padmé had died from her injuries. He, Vader, had killed the only thing he had loved.

Palpatine, however, didn't know the whole truth. At a secret location in the Polis Massa asteroid belt, Padmé had given birth to twins before her death. The girl, Leia, would be raised by Bail Organa and his wife on Alderaan. The boy, Luke, would be placed with Anakin's stepbrother Owen at the Lars moisture farm on Tatooine, where Obi-Wan would watch over the child's development as the hermit "Ben Kenobi." The overly talkative droid C-3PO received a memory wipe, and he and R2-D2 received new assignments in the service of Captain Raymus Antilles of Alderaan.

Yoda planned to go into hiding on the swamp planet of Dagobah. When Anakin's children reached the appropriate age, Yoda believed that the Force would bring one or both of them to him. At that time, he would craft them into weapons that would spear the heart of Palpatine's dark Empire.

Darth Vader on an early mission, flying an Eta-2 starfighter [Art by Tommy Lee Edwards]

PART THREE

The Empire and the New Order

THE DARK TIMES

JEDI SURVIVORS
19–0 B.B.Y.

A few Jedi, such as the blind archaeologist Jerec, embraced the dark side to save their own lives. Other Jedi survivors went underground. Among these were the Whipid master K'kruhk, who took a young Padawan under his wing and followed clues to the mysterious "Hidden Temple," a rumored place of refuge for harried Jedi to hide from the Emperor's hunters. A'Sharad Hett returned to live among the Tusken Raiders of Tatooine where he planned his own war of revenge. Jeisel, a female Devaronian, found herself forced into the life of a fugitive, pursued by bounty hunters and agents of Darth Vader. It seemed impossible, but the 25,000 year-old Jedi Order had vanished. The Sith had finally exacted their revenge.

Still adjusting to life inside his armored suit, Darth Vader constructed a new lightsaber containing a crimson Sith crystal provided by Palpatine. The Emperor, wishing to test the extent of his apprentice's diminished powers, sent Vader on a series

of missions to give him focus and prevent him from wallowing in self-pity. These took him in search of Jedi who had escaped Order 66, and led to the enslavement of the Wookiees on Kashyyyk. With the help of the Trandoshans, the Empire took control of the entire planet, and the wookiees were assigned to work gangs, forced to labor on Imperial construction projects.

Obi-Wan Kenobi soon learned the awful secret of the Emperor's new apprentice —that the black-armored cyborg suit concealed the burned, limbless body of Anakin Skywalker. Other than Obi-Wan's allies (Yoda, Bail Organa, Owen and Beru Lars, and Artoo-Detoo), the galaxy's citizens did not know of Vader's true origin.

As Emperor Palpatine instituted his New Order across the civilized galaxy, Vader recruited his own cadre of bodyguards by visiting the Noghri of Honoghr and promising to restore their poisoned world in exchange for their unquestioning loyalty. The Emperor's agents also enlisted the help of Mitth'raw'nuruodo, the Chiss commander who had crippled the Outbound Flight mission in the Unknown Regions. Thrawn had since become an exile from his people, and came to the Empire to study at their finest military academies.

In his hovel on Tatooine, Obi-Wan tried to settle into his new life as Ben Kenobi. Yoda had helped him connect with the Force spirit of his former Master Qui-Gon Jinn, and Obi-Wan entered a second apprenticeship under Qui-Gon's ethereal guidance. He found himself compelled to leave Tatooine for short missions to aid the few surviving Jedi, or to protect the identities of Anakin's twins..

During the first year of his exile, Obi-Wan crossed paths repeatedly with former Jedi Knight Ferus Olin. The Emperor, who had established a corps of Jedi hunters and "truth officers" called the Inquisitors, sent many of his agents after Olin, trying to thwart Olin's plans to create a Jedi shelter. Tragically, many Jedi fell to the Inquisitors, while others turned traitor and joined their ranks. Palpatine encouraged these defections—which swelled the ranks of his "Dark Side Adepts"—despite the public's continued ignorance of the Sith. From these, Palpatine secretly hoped to train an apprentice to replace Vader, whom he viewed as a disappointment due

to the crippling accident on Mustafar. Vader began looking for his own apprentice, knowing he lacked the power to overthrow Palpatine on his own.

The Emperor's Inquisitors also awoke Arden Lyn of the Legions of Lettow after a sleep of twenty-five millennia. Lyn killed one Inquisitor, but lost her arm to another. Palpatine recognized her power and, after outfitting her with a prosthetic limb from a war droid, invited her to become part of a new cadre of elite, Force-using agents called the Emperor's Hands. The Hands answered only to Palpatine, and included top assassins and experts in physical and psychological combat. Each of them labored under the delusion that he or she was the only Emperor's Hand.

A separate branch of Palpatine's agents, the Secret Order, consisted mostly of spies. Identified by their hooded cloaks and the Sith tattoos on their forearms, the members of the Secret Order skulked around the bridges of Star Destroyers, giving special assignments to those who had won the Emperor's favor. The Prophets of the Dark Side, mystics who could tell the future by reading the unifying Force, composed a distinct subgroup of the Secret Order.

One Imperial warship, a gargantuan, asteroid-shaped battlemoon called *Eye of Palpatine,* existed only to crush hidden Jedi enclaves on distant worlds. The *Eye* targeted a small enclave on Belsavis that sheltered youngling survivors from the Jedi Temple massacre, but two Jedi Knights—Callista and Geith—sabotaged the death-engine before it could attack. The Belsavis refugees fled to parts unknown.

BIRTH OF THE EMPIRE
19–0 B.B.Y.

Emperor Palpatine's hold on the galaxy tightened. The power of the Senate waned as Palpatine erected his own system. Planetary governors soon were overseen by Moffs, who possessed power over entire sectors. Moffs who reached for too much power, like Flirry Vorru of the Corellian sector, found themselves imprisoned in the Kessel spice mines. Entities such as the Trade Federation and the Commerce Guild were absorbed, their interests reflected through Imperial-friendly entities such as the Mining Guild.

Grand Moff Wilhuff Tarkin
[Art by Mark Chiarello]

Emperor Palpatine's New Order took root and thrived, particularly in the Core Worlds. Coruscant became Imperial Center. Civilians received only restricted access to the HoloNet communications system, stifling any news that wasn't Imperial propaganda. Under the guidance of Ishin-Il-Raz, COMPOR became COMPNOR, the Committee for the Preservation of the New Order, and rapidly became a humans-only organ of Imperial propaganda. Disdain for alien species became the norm under the New Order principle of Human High Culture. It wasn't long before entire species—including the proud Wookiees and the dauntless Mon Calamari—became officially sanctioned slave labor.

Nonhuman population centers in the Core found them-selves marginalized—or worse. Caamas, a member of the Republic since its earliest days, protested the destruction of Republic principles and advocated "peace through moral strength" as an alternative. The beloved Caamasi soon found themselves under attack and their world ruined by an outbreak of firestorms, triggered when Bothan saboteurs brought down the shield generators and left the planet defenseless against assault. Other alien species quickly learned to keep their mouths shut.

The most visible expression of Emperor Palpatine's New Order became the military. New clone hosts and new cloning facilities swelled the ranks of the stormtrooper corps, as did the forced conscription of young humans from occupied planets. With a few exceptions (such as the Khommites and the Lurrians), the Emperor banned the science of cloning for non-Imperial projects. Palpatine greatly expanded the army and navy, instituting new tools of war including the *Imperial*-class Star Destroyer and the TIE fighter, a nimble attack craft born from Raith Sienar's advances in Twin Ion Engine technology.

Under the guiding hand of Wilhuff Tarkin, the moon-sized battle station first proposed by Sienar began to take shape in the Outer Rim. The project bore the code name *Death Star.* When completed, the weapon would be able to destroy entire planets with its hypermatter-fueled superlaser.

Dawn of Dissent
19–0 B.B.Y.

Eventually, both Palpatine and Vader ceased to view the scattered Jedi holdouts as a threat, and made no concerted effort to root them out. The Jedi, in turn, lived their fugitive lives as quietly as possible. The flame of rebellion endured in the hearts of some politicians, such as Bail Organa, Mon Mothma, and Garm Bel Iblis. Small resistance cells sabotaged Imperial efforts, including numerous strikes against the Death Star construction project. Isolated groups of Separatist fighters, who had fought against Palpatine dur-

ing the Clone Wars for ideological reasons, became unexpected allies.

The Ghorman Massacre finally proved that the Emperor's excesses could not be reined in by a bureaucratic system of checks and balances. In the Sern sector near the Core Worlds, the citizens of Ghorman massed in the capital square to protest a new Imperial tax. When a warship arrived under the command of Wilhuff Tarkin, it landed on *top* of the protestors and killed hundreds. The Ghorman Massacre horrified many, but the Emperor wasn't among them. In response to the incident, he gave Tarkin a promotion.

After the rise of the Empire, Captain Jan Dodonna had resigned from the navy rather than serve what he considered a corrupt regime. When the Empire decided it could not retrain or convert Dodonna, a secret order was issued for his execution. Mon Mothma warned him, trying to sway him to her cause, but Dodonna initially refused—according to his rigid outlook, the Rebellion represented treason against the lawful government, though he himself had come to hate what the Emperor stood for. When Imperial assassins charged in and tried to kill him in cold blood, Dodonna fled in his nightshirt, fighting his way out. Dodonna became a staunch ally of the budding revolution. Elsewhere, an insurgent leader named Cody Sun-Childe briefly became the charismatic face of the opposition, but he soon vanished, and resistance carried on in secret.

Bail Organa and Mon Mothma, sometimes accompanied by Corellian Senator Garm Bel Iblis, began holding regular meetings in Organa's Cantham House residence on Coruscant to discuss organized rebellion. Mon Mothma was far more outspoken in her opposition. After many years of secret plotting, the firebrand Senator was accused of treason. Mon Mothma went underground to escape a certain death sentence, visiting oppressed planets and speaking to fledgling guerrilla movements. Sedition spread from world to world, though it was still disorganized and unfocused.

The X-wing prototypes blast away from the Incom design facility.
[ART BY TOMMY LEE EDWARDS]

Senators Mon Mothma and Bail Organa
[Art by Mark Chiarello]

Organa, Mon Mothma, and Garm Bel Iblis.

The Alliance to Restore the Republic, more commonly known as the Rebel Alliance, had a clear command hierarchy with Mon Mothma at its head. It also possessed an enthusiastic and growing military. Mon Mothma negotiated a secret arrangement with the Mon Calamari shipyards that gave the Rebels access to top-of-the-line capital ships, while a team of defectors from the Incom Corporation provided the Alliance with prototypes and blueprints for a new precision attack craft—the T-65 X-wing starfighter.

Though the Alliance had countless cells on thousands of planets, a single command headquarters was necessary for the Rebel leadership to rest and plan strategy. The first of these top-secret bases was established on a tiny planetoid in the Chrellis system, though the HQ was designed for continual relocation. From Chrellis the base moved to Briggia, Orion IV, and several other worlds before relocating to Dantooine, which had a connection with the great Jedi Knights of the past.

Alarmed at the growing opposition, the Emperor initiated Operation Strike Fear to crush Mon Mothma and her followers. However, the Alliance fleet distinguished itself with hard-fought victories, including the capture of the frigate *Priam* and the demolition of the Star Destroyer *Invincible*. More and more planets joined the revolution with each passing day.

The Rebel Alliance had begun.

Less than two years before the Battle of Yavin, the Corellian Treaty was signed—a landmark moment in the history of the revolution. The Corellian Treaty merged the three largest revolutionary groups into a single unified party—the Alliance to Restore the Republic. The document was signed by Bail

PART FOUR

Profiles in History

Galactic history is more than the epic sweep of battles and conquerors, of grand armies and dread discoveries. On its most basic level, history is the story of individual people. Emperor Palpatine and Mon Mothma are so revered and reviled by various segments of the population that they appear as archetypes in the modern consciousness, not as human beings at all. Nevertheless, it is important to remember that even the highest heroes have humble beginnings, and that the actions of a single person can affect billions of lives.

Outcasts and fringe characters are not often given their due in historical memoirs, but their heroism deserves as much note as any Senator, monarch, or admiral. Without the contributions of "scoundrels" such as Han Solo and Lando Calrissian, as well as the youthful heroism of Luke Skywalker, then Princess Leia Organa would have died in Imperial captivity, and the second Death Star would have destroyed the Alliance fleet at Endor. As a service to future historians, we have interviewed these personages, chronicling their elusive early careers to better understand what made them into the heroes they are today.

HAN SOLO

Han Solo never knew his parents. His earliest memory was of being lost and alone on Corellia, until a venal con man named Garris Shrike took the abandoned child under his wing. Solo spent his youth aboard the ancient troopship *Trader's Luck* as a member of Shrike's well-organized "trading clan," a group who earned their keep through begging, pickpocketing, and grand larceny. If the children failed, they were beaten to near death. The only bright spot in Han's early life was a kindly female Wookiee named Dewlanna, who worked for Shrike as a cook and acted as the human boy's surrogate mother. She taught Han to speak and understand Shyriiwook.

Han desperately wanted to learn more about his parents, but that door remained closed to him. The only "Solo" relative he located was his cousin Thrackan Sal-Solo. After an unpleasant encounter, Sal-Solo disappeared from sight, and eventually rose to a leadership position with an anti-alien organization called the Human League. More than three de-

cades would pass before Sal-Solo tormented the New Republic during the Corellian insurrection.

Over the years, Han Solo became an expert thief and street fighter. His skill at piloting swoop racers earned plenty of prize money for Shrike, and his mastery of alien languages served him well when *Trader's Luck* traveled from system to system on moneymaking scams. At seventeen, Han was captured by law enforcement officials and forced to fight in the Regional Sector Four's All-Human Free-for-All on Jubilar. He won the contest by defeating four much larger opponents, but Shrike mercilessly beat him for insubordination when he returned to *Trader's Luck*.

YLESIA
10 B.B.Y.

At nineteen, Han escaped from *Trader's Luck* by stowing away in a robotic cargo freighter. The freighter deposited its passenger on Ylesia, a tropical world located

Han Solo, newly-commissioned Imperial officer
[Art by Mark Chiarello]

and their t'landa Til underlings. Though the pay was good, the attentions of a beautiful woman shook Solo from his complacency. He fell in love with Pilgrim 921, also known as Bria Tharen, and vowed to rescue her from slavery. During the escape, Han and Bria destroyed the primary glitterstim factory and plundered the t'landa Til High Priest's priceless art collection. They fled Ylesia aboard a stolen yacht, after staging a daring rope-ladder rescue of a Togorian prisoner from a neighboring colony.

THE ACADEMY
10–5 B.B.Y.

The Besadii Hutts placed a bounty on Han Solo's head, but they knew him only under the alias of "Vyyk Drago." Han planned to sell the Ylesian loot and enroll in the Imperial Academy to start a new life as a naval officer. He suffered a devastating blow when a suspicious Imperial Bank manager placed a freeze on his account—and another when Bria Tharen left him.

within the lawless borders of Hutt space. Though Ylesia advertised itself to the galaxy as a religious retreat, it was actually a brutal spice-processing planet controlled by the Besadii Hutt crime family. Weak-minded converts, attracted by the empty promises of a pseudo-religion, were shipped to Ylesia and put to work toiling in the glitterstim and ryll factories.

Han Solo ended up piloting spice cargoes for the Hutts

Bankrupt and despairing, Han scraped together his last few credits to obtain a forged set of ID papers and have his retinas surgically altered. Since the Besadii clan was looking for him under an alias, he used his true identity on an application to the Imperial Academy. His final night before enrollment was spoiled by an ugly figure from the past—Garris Shrike, who had been lured by

Chewbacca
[Art by Mark Chiarello]

Vyyk Drago was dead.

Free and clear for the first time in his life, Cadet Solo boarded a troop transport for Carida, the most respected military academy in the Empire. Over the next four years, Han proved to be extremely talented, but not a model Imperial student. During one infamous exercise, he landed a malfunctioning U-33 orbital loadlifter with suicidal flair, earning himself the nickname "Slick" from Lieutenant Badure, his piloting instructor. In another incident, Han's classmate Mako Spince destroyed Carida's mascot moon with a gram of antimatter. Despite the misadventures, Han graduated at the top of his class, beating out Cadet Soontir Fel for the title of valedictorian.

Graduation was followed by eight months of commissioned service in the Imperial Navy. A promising career in the Corellian sector fleet was cut short when Han rescued a Wookiee slave from ill treatment at the hands of a superior officer. This earned him a dishonorable discharge, which prevented Han from obtaining any civilian piloting job. However, the Wookiee—Chewbacca—swore a life debt to Han and promised to follow him everywhere. Han initially tried to discourage Chewie, but gradually realized that a two-and-a-half-meter, fanged Wookiee wasn't a bad thing to have at one's side during cantina brawls. With no hope of lawful employment, Han and Chewbacca headed into Hutt space to work for the criminal syndicates.

the Hutt bounty. Unlike the other bounty hunters on the trail, Shrike was the only person in the galaxy who knew Han's alias. Fortunately, a rival bounty hunter shot Shrike down, and Han killed the second man in a brutal bare-knuckled brawl. He then switched clothes and ID and shot the corpse in the face—destroying all possibility of forensic identification. As far as the Besadii Hutts would know,

THE LIFE OF A SMUGGLER
5–2 B.B.Y.

Hutt politics seethed with intrigue. On Nal Hutta, the two most powerful clans—Besadii, headed by Aruk and his offspring Durga, and Desilijic, led by Jiliac and his nephew Jabba—vied for dominance. The Besadii clan controlled the spice operation on Ylesia, but Desilijic possessed important holdings on Tatooine and elsewhere. Their discreet maneuverings would inevitably be replaced by deadly conflict.

On Nar Shaddaa, the Smugglers' Moon, Han Solo and Chewbacca were introduced to illicit Hutt activities by Mako Spince, Han's old friend from the Academy. As the months passed, the new partners met dozens of offbeat individuals, such as Shug Ninx, Salla Zend, and Xaverri. They visited hideaways and hellholes like Smuggler's Run and Kessel, and Han learned how to fly the dangerous Kessel Run cargo route by skirting the Maw black-hole cluster. Han's piloting skills caught the attention of Jabba the Hutt, and soon Han was making regular smuggling runs for the Desilijic clan.

Rubbing elbows with high-level Hutts was a risky game, especially since Han still had a price on his head from the rival Besadii clan. On Ylesia, the colony's High Priest uncovered astonishing evidence that Vyyk Drago—reported dead five years earlier—had resurfaced under the name "Han Solo." The galaxy's best bounty hunter was hired to bring in Solo's hide.

Boba Fett tracked Han to Nar Shaddaa, but his capture was spoiled with an impromptu rescue by a charming stranger: Lando Calrissian, pilot of a banged-up YT-1300 freighter called *Millennium Falcon,* which he had won in a recent sabacc game. Han taught his rescuer the basics of flying, and Calrissian soon headed off in the *Falcon* for the Rafa system and some adventuring of his own.

Han began working as a magician's assistant on Xaverri's six-month illusionist tour. Upon his return, he purchased a shoddy, cut-rate SoroSuub Starmite, which he christened the *Bria,* after his lost love Bria Tharen.

Sudden scrutiny from the Empire brought normal life on Nar Shaddaa to a screeching halt. Moff Sarn Shild proclaimed that the Hutts' lawless territory would greatly benefit from stricter Imperial control. As a public relations stunt, Shild was authorized to blockade Nal Hutta and turn the Smugglers' Moon into molten slag.

The Hutts responded in typical fashion—they sent a messenger to Shild's offices in an attempt to bribe him. When the Moff refused to bend, the Hutts shifted their attentions to Admiral Greelanx, the officer in charge of executing the assault. Greelanx proved to be considerably more accommodating, agreeing to sell his battle plan. The Hutts organized a defense and placed their ships in precise locations dictated by the admiral's plan, hoping to inflict enough damage on the Imperial fleet to force a strategic withdrawal.

The scheme worked perfectly. The Battle of Nar Shaddaa was a localized conflict involving no ship larger than a Dreadnaught, and today is considered little more than a historical footnote. But for the desperate smugglers who banded together to protect their adopted home from annihilation, it was a life-or-death struggle against staggering odds. Though he did not realize it at the time, Han Solo was pitted against his former Academy classmate Soontir Fel, who was then serving as captain of the Dreadnaught *Pride of the Senate.* The battle came to a premature end when one of Greelanx's three Dreadnaughts was destroyed. Unable to justify further losses, the admiral retreated into hyperspace.

After distinguishing himself in the Battle of Nar Shaddaa, Han Solo lost the *Bria* in a mishap. To raise funds for a new starship, Han entered the annual championship sabacc tournament, held that year in Cloud City's Yarith Bespin casino. Lando Calrissian, freshly returned from his adventures in the ThonBoka, was one of Han's many opponents. The roster of players steadily dwindled, until the two men faced each other alone across a card-strewn table. Han took the final hand, winning the sabacc championship and earning his pick of any vessel on Calrissian's used-starship lot. Han chose *Millennium Falcon.*

Celebrating the acquisition of their new ship, Han and Chewbacca visited Kashyyyk, the Wookiee homeworld, where Chewbacca was married in a formal ceremony to his love Mallatobuck. Han became involved in a serious relationship with fellow smuggler Salla Zend, but, spooked by commitment phobia, he abandoned Zend and fled Hutt space entirely, heading out with Chewbacca for the Corporate Sector in the hope of striking it rich.

Corporate Sector Blues
2–1 B.B.Y.

The semi-independent Corporate Sector Authority was, in many ways, worse than the Empire. The ruling CSA cared little for ideology and ruthlessly rolled over individuals who stood in the way of pure profit. Prior to Han's arrival, the CSA completed construction on the Stars' End prison complex located on the desolate rock Mytus VII. Dissidents, agitators, smugglers, and other troublemakers were quietly rounded up and imprisoned in stasis cells.

Han accepted small-time smuggling commissions for Big Bunji and Ploovo Two-For-One, but he also fell in with a covert team of independent dissidents investigating the recent disappearances. Team members included Bollux, a labor droid, and Blue Max, a positronic processor hidden in Bollux's chest cavity. When Chewbacca was captured, Han became more determined than ever to scuttle the CSA's top-secret prison. Posing as a troupe of entertainers, Han and his team landed on the airless planetoid and were escorted to the dagger-shaped prison tower.

On Han's orders, Blue Max triggered an overload in the prison's reactor core. As the team tried to free their friends and escape, Stars' End's power plant exploded—much more than the simple distraction Han had hoped for. The blast, contained by the prison's anticoncussion field, was funneled downward against the surface of the planet. With negligible gravity and no atmospheric friction, the entire tower rocketed into near orbit.

The structure reached the top of its arc and fell back to-ward the rocky face of Mytus VII. It was a race against time as the *Falcon* docked against the tower so that Chewbacca and other prisoners could be rescued, and then detached just as Stars' End smashed back into the surface. According to unconfirmed reports, the CSA salvaged the molecularly bonded structure and erected it on a different world, a rumor that soured later negotiations between the New Republic and the Corporate Sector Authority.

Han and Chewbacca continued their association with Bollux and Blue Max. They inspired the "Cult of Varn" on the arid planet Kamar by showing the holofeature *Varn, World of Water* to the desert-dwelling native insectoids. When Han replaced the bland documentary with a toe-tapping musical comedy, the water-worshiping Kamarians angrily chased away the false prophet and his great flying chariot. Over the last twenty years, Varn cultists have established evangelical religious orders on Mon Calamari, Bengat, and Varn itself, much to the consternation of the locals.

Heading back to the Corporate Sector, Han Solo was promised ten thousand credits to make a pickup on Lur. When he learned that the pickup consisted of slaves, he turned the tables on the slavers and freed their captives. Han stubbornly insisted that *somebody* still owed him ten thousand credits, and he doggedly followed the slavers' trail to Bonadan, where Fiolla, an assistant auditor-general of the CSA, enlisted Han's help. When the slavers tried to jump them, Han hopped aboard a swoopbike and used the racing skills that Garris Shrike had taught him to throw off pursuit.

The next link in the slaving chain was the planet Ammuud. Han and Fiolla booked passage aboard a luxury liner, while Chewbacca and the droids took the *Falcon* along with the CSA territorial manager, Odumin. Odumin was working to crack the slaving ring on his own and had an agent already in place on Ammuud: the legendary gunman Gallandro. After Han and Gallandro wound up facing each other over a duel, the ruling clan of Ammuud turned over all records they had relating to the slaving ring and its operations. Han and Fiolla fought against the vengeful slavers, and were rescued by the timely arrival of a CSA *Victory*-class Star Destroyer.

Territorial Manager Odumin, while grateful to the two smugglers for their help, fully intended to prosecute them to the fullest extent of the law for their numerous violations of the CSA legal code. With a fast maneuver, Han managed to take both Odumin and Fiolla hostage; then he successfully negotiated his unconditional release—and managed to have his ten thousand credits thrown in to boot.

Destitute in the Tion
1–0 B.B.Y.

All CSA naval patrols now received holographs of *Millennium Falcon* and orders to "destroy on sight." Realizing that their days in the Corporate Sector were over, Han, Chewbacca, and the droids Bollux and Blue Max hopped through the Outer Rim for months, squandering their ten thousand credits on repairs, celebrations, and far-fetched, disastrous schemes. Bankrupt, they eventually ended up in the backwater Tion Hegemony, working as starship mechanics for Grigmin's Traveling Airshow.

Han parlayed this embarrassing vocation into a slightly better job running cargo for the University of Rudrig. While there, he bumped into his old friend "Trooper" Badure, formerly a respected piloting instructor on Carida but now a desperate fortune hunter looking for the fabled lost ship *Queen of Ranroon*. Built during the glory days of Xim the Despot, *Queen of Ranroon* had once hauled the plunder of a thousand conquered worlds. Xim had constructed a vault on Dellalt to house the treasure, but, according to legend, the ship had vanished, along with all her wealth.

Accompanied by Badure and Skynx, a multilegged Ruurian academic, Han landed on primitive Dellalt. The *Falcon* was promptly stolen by rivals of Badure's, who left it on the opposite side of a mountain range. With no other ships available for hire on the uncivilized world, they were forced to head over the mountains on foot. During one fight for survival, Han was slashed across the chin with a primitive

hunting knife. The wound never healed properly, and left a scar that is noticeable to this day.

Marching through the snowy highlands, they were captured by a strange cult called the Survivors. The in-bred, backwards descendants of *Queen of Ranroon*'s honor guard, the Survivors had existed on Dellalt for over a thousand generations, maintaining Xim the Despot's war droid army in their secure mountain keep. Han and the others escaped the Survivors and located *Millennium Falcon* at a contract-labor mining camp. The fast-gun mercenary Gallandro, pining for a rematch with Han after Ammuud, was waiting for him.

Before either party could make a move, the war droids of Xim marched into the clearing, rank on rank. Despite their antiquity, the droids followed their orders and razed the camp with ruthless efficiency. Bollux and Blue Max saved the day by transmitting a rhythmic frequency to the automation army as it paraded over a rickety suspension bridge. The signal caused the droids to march in a pounding lockstep. Beneath their shaking, vibrating footfalls, the bridge bounced, swayed—and collapsed.

Gallandro, one of the few survivors, claimed that he would forget his enmity with Han in exchange for a full share of Xim's treasure. The *Falcon*'s quad guns made short work of the vault gates. When Han discovered the hidden treasure chambers beneath empty decoy chambers, Gallandro showed his true, traitorous stripes. In a one-on-one blaster duel, Gallandro outdrew Han and incapacitated the Corellian with a blaster wound to the shoulder. He then strode down the vault corridor to burn down the fleeing Skynx, but the multilegged Ruurian tricked the gunman into a lethal no-weapons zone. Dozens of laser bolts fried Gallandro to cinders. It was the end of the gunman's legendary career, though he was survived by his infant daughter Anja on the colony world of Anobis. Anja Gallandro would cause new problems in Han Solo's life more than a quarter century in the future.

Han didn't even catch a lucky break on Xim the Despot's treasure. Instead of the priceless jewels Han had expected, he found only kiirium and mytag crystals—valuable war matériel in Xim's day, but worthless in the modern era. Skynx stayed behind on Dellalt to translate and catalog the vault's many historical artifacts, and Bollux and Blue Max remained with the Ruurian rather than accompany Han and Chewbacca back to Hutt space.

Skynx eventually became the lead researcher on the Dellalt Project, as it came to be known in archaeological circles. After ten years of study, Skynx succumbed to the life cycle of his species and metamorphosed into a mindless chroma-wing, but his offspring Amisus grew up to become the leader of the Unified Ruurian Colonies. Amisus pledged the Ruurians' loyalty to Grand Admiral Thrawn during the Hand of Thrawn incident fifteen years after the Battle of Endor.

RETURN TO YLESIA
0 B.B.Y., months before the Battle of Yavin

The devious intrigues of the Hutts had not remained static during Han's absence. Two years earlier, the Desilijic clan had surreptitiously poisoned Aruk the Hutt, ancient leader of the Besadii clan. In that time, Aruk's offspring

Durga had assumed control of Besadii with under-the-table help from Prince Xizor and the Black Sun criminal syndicate. When Durga uncovered the truth about his father's death, he slithered over to the Desilijic palace and challenged clan leader Jiliac to single combat under the Old Law . The two Hutts crashed into each other with their mammoth bodies, swinging their tails as massive bludgeons. After an exhausting contest, Durga emerged victorious.

The death of Jiliac made Jabba the ruler of the Desilijic clan. Jabba immediately began to implement a scheme that would devastate the Besadii clan by eliminating their primary source of income—the spice-processing facilities on Ylesia. To do this, Jabba contacted Han Solo's ex-love Bria Tharen.

Over the past decade, Tharen had become an undercover operative in the growing resistance movement opposed to Emperor Palpatine. She had helped lay the groundwork for Mon Mothma's orchestration of the Corellian Treaty, which merged various dissident groups into a unified Rebel Alliance. Jabba agreed to help Tharen fund a full-scale Ylesian assault that would destroy the spice factories and leave the Besadii with nothing. The Rebels would then be free to sell the spice on the open market to fund their growing insurgency.

On Nar Shaddaa, Han Solo and Bria Tharen fell in love all over again. Accompanied by Lando Calrissian, Han agreed to join in the Ylesian assault with his fellow smugglers for half of the spice profits. While Jabba's assassins killed the Ylesian priests, the smugglers and Rebels assaulted the colonies on foot. Casualties were high, but before long the invaders had eliminated all opposition, and secured the spice factories. In the aftermath, however, Commander Tharen and the Rebel troops double-crossed their smuggler allies and took all the spice for themselves.

The betrayal was a double blow for Han. He and Tharen parted on the worst of terms, and Han's comrades assumed he'd been in on the whole operation from the beginning.

Han soon caught up with Bria again, this time as part of a Hutt-sponsored, galaxywide treasure hunt for the Yavin Vassilika statue. His competitors included the bounty hunters Bossk, Dengar, Zuckuss, 4-LOM, Boba Fett, and an inexperienced Greedo (who won the respect of his peers only at his own funeral, following a deadly confrontation with Han weeks later). After surviving treacherous turnabouts from his rivals, Han saw Bria take possession of the Vassilika on Yavin 4. Once again, she took the prize for the Rebel Alliance and left him with nothing. Lando Calrissian proclaimed that he never wanted to see Han's face again as long as he lived.

THE LAST SPICE RUN
0 B.B.Y., immediately prior to the Battle of Yavin

Hurt and dejected, Han and Chewbacca agreed to make a Kessel Run for Jabba on their way back to Nar Shaddaa. While pursued by Imperial customs vessels that had been tipped off by the spice supplier Moruth Doole, *Millennium Falcon* skimmed closer to the Maw black-hole cluster than anyone had thought possible. The result was a new distance record of less than twelve parsecs. Unfortunately, Han was forced to dump his load of spice to avoid detection; the loss of such a valuable shipment angered Jabba greatly.

Since none of his former friends would loan money to a man they considered a traitor, Han was forced to go to Tatooine in the hope of finding enough credits to pay

The galaxy's most notorious bounty hunters assemble for the funeral of Greedo. [ART BY JOHN VAN FLEET]

off Jabba. There, a bounty hunter from the past made an unexpected reappearance. Boba Fett wasn't interested in Han's head this time—instead, he wished only to relay a message. Fett had once crossed paths with Bria Tharen and had agreed to notify the woman's father in the event of her death. Fett's sources had confirmed Tharen's demise as a member of the Rebel Alliance's Operation Skyhook on Toprawa, which had relayed the Death Star plans. Han passed on the information to Tharen's surviving family.

With his first love dead, one chapter of Han Solo's life closed forever. But a new one was about to begin. The Corellian smuggler strode into the smoky darkness of the Mos Eisley cantina for a fateful rendezvous with two local desert dwellers who needed passage to Alderaan.

LANDO CALRISSIAN

Unlike most reluctant heroes, Lando Calrissian is extremely forthcoming with details about his early entrepreneurial career. Unfortunately, every one of the stories is more outlandish than the last, and few agree. As a result, Calrissian is a riddle. One can only guess at the environment that spawned this ambitious man and the forces that shaped him into a charming gambler who always places his biggest bet on the underdog.

Luckily, Lando entered a high-profile career phase in his late twenties, allowing his stories to be verified through independent eyewitnesses, historical accounts, and interviews with contemporaries such as Han Solo. Approximately four years prior to the Battle of Yavin, Lando was already separating fools from their money as a professional sabacc gambler and con artist. Lando lost quite often, but when he won, he won big. His profits were enough to indulge his tastes in clothing, fine cuisine, and members of the opposite sex.

He hopped around the galaxy in style aboard luxurious pleasure liners such as *Star of Empire,* and so when he won a dilapidated Corellian freighter, *Millennium Falcon,* from a sabacc player on Bespin who couldn't cover his debt, Lando had mixed feelings. It would be an expensive and time-consuming process to learn how to fly, but having his own mode of transportation would come in handy whenever he needed to make a quick getaway. Besides, the ship could always be sold for ready cash if funds ran low.

But first he needed to learn the art of piloting, so Lando Calrissian hired a tutor—Han Solo, a smuggler, a fair sabacc player, and one of the best star jockeys in all of Hutt space. He caught up with Han at just the right time. The bounty hunter Boba Fett had Han at gunpoint, but Lando intercepted the pair and turned the tables on Fett. He injected the bounty hunter with an obedience drug and ordered him to fly off to the Rim of the galaxy. A grateful Han offered to teach Lando how to pilot, at no charge.

THE SHARU AWAKEN
4 B.B.Y.

Lando was a quick study, but learning to single-pilot a freighter was a tricky proposition. He was still an abysmal aviator when he decided to pack up and leave Hutt space for someplace—anyplace—else. Boba Fett would be back looking for revenge, and Nar Shaddaa was not an easy place for a con man to find gullible marks. His next stop was the wealthy asteroid field in the Oseon system, stuck in the outback Centrality region. Normally the Oseon was a gambler's paradise, but Lando had poor luck at the tables. From a pretentious academic, he did win ownership of a droid, which remained in storage on Rafa IV.

Every planet in the Rafa system was covered with colossal plastic pyramids built by the ancient Sharu. At the time of Calrissian's visit, the Sharu were considered a long-vanished aboriginal species; their impregnable pyramids had never been opened or explored. The present natives of the system were referred to as the Toka, or "Broken People." To all appearances the Toka were primitive and

this monumental event, making him a hero to legions of archaeologists and anthropologists.

Initially, though, the gambler had no intentions in the Rafa system beyond picking up his newly won droid. The robot turned out to be a strange, starfish-shaped construction named Vuffi Raa, boasting five detachable limbs and a perky personality; Lando sensed there was more to this unusual droid than he could see.

When Lando was arrested on trumped-up charges issued by the colonial governor, he and his new droid were forcibly enlisted in the hunt for the Mindharp on behalf of Rokur Gepta, the Sorcerer of Tund. The mysterious gray-cloaked wizard was a disciple of ancient Sith teachings, eager to get his hands on the artifact for his own purposes.

On Rafa V, Lando and Vuffi Raa unlocked the largest Sharu pyramid with a transdimensional key. There, they discovered the Mindharp—a strange object that constantly changed form as it shifted through dimensions—and removed it from its eons-old place of rest.

Rafa IV's colonial governor greedily took the Mindharp, sentencing the gambler to a lifetime sentence of hard labor in a penal colony. Vuffi Raa freed Lando, but the planet then began to rock with violent quakes and tremors. The colonial governor had activated the Mindharp, and the artifact's subharmonic emanations stimulated a complete reversal of the social order throughout the entire planetary system. The pyramids crumbled, and bizarre new cities emerged from the dust. Intelligence and memories were restored to the primitive Toka, making them into the legendary Sharu once again.

For weeks the Rafa system was completely blockaded, and when the inexplicable interdiction field suddenly vanished, the first visitors beheld an utterly changed society. The new cities were frighteningly alien, and the Sharu appeared to care little for the concerns of "lesser" sentients. Many of the human cities had been damaged beyond

Lando Calrissian scouts his new acquisition, the Millennium Falcon
[Art by John Van Fleet]

simpleminded, and they were exploited by the human colonists as cheap slave labor.

As Lando eventually discovered, the ancient Sharu had been threatened by an unimaginably powerful alien entity. To ensure their own survival, the Sharu went underground—hiding their cities beneath the plastic pyramids and using crystalline "life-orchards" to temporarily drain their intelligence. Then they spread rumors of a fabulous treasure—the Mindharp of Sharu. When another civilization was advanced enough to reactivate the Mindharp, the Sharu would know that it was safe to come out of hiding. In the course of his adventures, Lando Calrissian was responsible for triggering

repair in the quakes, and the surviving colonists chose not to remain behind in a place where they were the objects of scorn. Trade with the Rafa system dried up virtually overnight.

On the other hand, the event was a boon to scientists, who descended on Rafa in droves. While the Sharu did not shoo the researchers away, neither did they cooperate. Detailed information on Sharu history and technology is still an elusive unknown. Apparently, Emperor Palpatine felt threatened enough by the Sharu to post a permanent picket on the system's outer fringes, though he never made a military move against the advanced race. The New Republic largely ignored the Sharu, with the exception of a five-hundred-member, government-funded research team staffed by the Obroan Institute.

THE BATTLE OF NAR SHADDAA
3 B.B.Y.

Calrissian and Vuffi Raa fled the Rafa system mere hours after the Mindharp's activation, escaping to the safety of hyperspace with a full cargo of rare "life crystals" in the *Falcon's* hold. When worn around the neck, life crystals were rumored to increase a person's life span. Lando possessed the last load of life crystals before the Sharu locked down all trade—which meant that he could set his own price. The gambler cleared nearly a quarter of a million credits on the crystals.

He returned to Nar Shaddaa and, with a portion of his credits, purchased a used-starship lot from a dissatisfied Duros salesman. But running the business was more difficult and expensive than he had anticipated; despite the able assistance of Vuffi Raa, Lando was considering cutting his losses—when the Empire invaded the system. Along with hundreds of other smugglers, Lando took to the sky and successfully blunted the Imperial offensive in the Battle of Nar Shaddaa. Vuffi Raa piloted *Millennium Falcon* through the blaster barrages like a born maestro.

But the Battle of Nar Shaddaa signaled the end of the used-starship lot. Lando, feeling a sense of obligation to his fellow outlaws, donated his entire inventory for the space skirmish. When the dust cleared, less than a tenth of his stock remained spaceworthy. Privately, Lando sold his old friend Roa 90 percent ownership in the lot at a considerable loss, then puzzled over how to salvage his once promising career.

In six months, Cloud City's Yarith Bespin casino would be hosting the regional sabacc championships—the perfect opportunity for Lando to recoup his losses. Unfortunately, the entry fee was ten thousand credits. After paying off his creditors, Lando didn't even have a tenth that amount. Discouraged, he decided to return to the Centrality with Vuffi Raa.

There, Calrissian used the *Falcon* for its original cargo-hauling purpose, but he was a washout as an interstellar trader. Tariffs, import fees, and sales licenses sucked his credit account dry. Thus, when he received an invitation to play sabacc in the Oseon system, Lando jumped at the chance.

BACK TO THE OSEON
3 B.B.Y.

Calrissian and Vuffi Raa arrived just in time for the annual Flamewind. For three weeks each year, stellar flares interact with ionized vapors to create a stunning visual feast in brilliant pulsing hues of green, yellow, blue, orange, and every color between. The Oseon asteroid belts are infamous playgrounds for the wealthy and powerful, but things get even more decadent during the Flamewind: since it is impossible to navigate during the event, guests are stuck in the system until the breathtaking light show subsides.

Lando was apprehended by the administrator senior of the Oseon system and forced to participate in a dangerous drug bust. The trillionaire industrialist Bohhuah Mutdah, drug addict and sole owner of Asteroid 5792, had made some powerful enemies in the upper echelons of the Imperial law enforcement community. The administrator was authorized to arrest him in a sting operation. Posing as Mutdah's drug dealer, Lando ferried two drug enforcement agents to Asteroid 5792, through the heart of the Flamewind. As Lando made the drug exchange, the two agents burst in to place Mutdah under arrest. Ten seconds later, both agents were dead.

As Lando looked on in astonishment, Mutdah set down

his blaster and began to shimmer and fold in a mind-bending display. The disguise melted away, revealing a familiar figure—Rokur Gepta, the Sorcerer of Tund, whom Lando had outwitted with the Mindharp of Sharu.

In hindsight, the fact that Gepta took the time to insinuate himself into this affair is remarkable, given that his only motive was a deep-seated hatred of Lando Calrissian. Gepta blamed the rogue gambler for the loss of the Sharu artifact, and he was spiteful enough to carry a grudge across light-years. He also enjoyed an amicable relationship with Emperor Palpatine, who had given the Sorcerer a decommissioned Republic cruiser and granted him near-total autonomy within the confines of the Centrality. Gepta could command Imperial naval units and call in TIE bomber air strikes on recalcitrant worlds. It is a testament to Lando's notoriety that this power was completely subverted toward making the gambler's life miserable.

Lando was saved from Rokur Gepta when a squadron of starfighters bearing Renatasian markings appeared outside the asteroid's canopy, lasers blazing. The transparisteel dome shattered, and Lando reached his ship through the swirling air and debris. The *Falcon* escaped just as the Renatasians hurled a towed Dreadnaught engine straight into the asteroid, destroying it utterly.

The timely intervention was a lucky coincidence—the starfighters had not been gunning for either Lando or Rokur Gepta, but rather for the harmless but mysterious droid Vuffi Raa. In 13 B.B.Y., Renatasia, one of many "lost" human colonies founded by ancient Grizmallt settlers, had been rediscovered in a seldom-visited pocket of the Centrality. Obeying his programming, Vuffi Raa had landed on Renatasia and paved the way for an Imperial takeover. A group of hand-picked natives had commandeered twelve aging starfighters and vowed to kill the "Butcher of Renatasia."

Lando Calrissian, while sympathetic to the Renatasians' motives, was unwilling to help them annihilate his closest friend. He left them behind in the Oseon. The Renatasians soon teamed up with Rokur Gepta, who had escaped the destruction of Asteroid 5792, and continued their search for Vuffi Raa.

FORTUNE WON, FORTUNE LOST
3 B.B.Y.

The aftermath of the Mutdah drug bust was the most fortuitous turn of fortune Lando Calrissian had *ever* experienced. During the chaos of his escape, Lando lifted the case containing Mutdah's drug payment. In one day, he went from insolvency to being a millionaire twenty times over.

Like all things with Lando, though, it didn't last. He deposited the money in small lump sums across numerous bank accounts to reduce suspicion and the risk of a financial audit. Fifty thousand credits—more than enough to cover the sabacc tournament entry fee—went into the bank first, and was then electronically transferred to another numbered account on Aargau. Lando then departed in *Millennium Falcon* for Dela, the Centrality's financial hub, to deposit the rest of his money. Through sheer dumb luck, he arrived at Dela during the middle of a pirate attack by Drea Renthal's gang. Renthal, the infamous "pirate queen," possessed one of the largest freebooter fleets in the galaxy and had fought against the Imperials in the Battle of Nar Shaddaa.

The *Falcon* was captured and boarded. When the pirate raiders discovered the astonishing sum stashed in Mutdah's lockbox, Lando was brought before Renthal. The queen was an attractive woman, and Lando turned his charm up to maximum wattage in the hope of convincing her to leave him at least a token portion of the cash. He failed, but it was not the last time Lando and Renthal would cross paths.

TO SAVE THE THONBOKA
3–2.5 B.B.Y.

With the sabacc tournament mere months away, Lando and Vuffi Raa made a new friend—Lehesu of the Oswaft. The Oswaft, an extremely reclusive species of gigantic vacuum breathers who resemble a cross between a Corellian sea ray and an Arkanian jellyfish, can instinctively make natural hyperspace jumps.

The Centrality had known of the Oswafts' existence for generations, but the aliens did not come to the attention of the Emperor until just before Lando's debacle at Dela.

Mistrustful of an intelligent species that could traverse hyperspace at will, Palpatine issued orders to exterminate the Oswaft. Five hundred capital ships blockaded the "mouth" of the creatures' home, a sack-shaped nebula known as the StarCave or the ThonBoka. All *Carrack*-class cruisers were modified to emit electrical charges to contaminate the interstellar plankton that drifted inside the nebula. With their sole source of nutrients poisoned, the Oswaft began to starve.

Lehesu's desperate pleas spurred Lando and Vuffi Raa to action. *Millennium Falcon* ran the Imperial blockade, and Lando met with the besieged Oswaft elders—each colossal creature nearly a kilometer in diameter. As the Oswaft had no conception of warfare, Lando was forced to improvise a plan of survival. The alien defenders synthesized Oswaft-shaped excretions through their pores, so that the Imperial gunners shot at false targets and inflicted friendly fire on their own ships. Also, many Oswaft "shouted" at the warships in their information-dense language; their powerful voice-streams were sufficient to destroy many enemy vessels.

The fighting abruptly ceased when a vengeful Rokur Gepta arrived in his battleship and ordered the fleet to stand down. He delivered a startlingly bitter ultimatum: he would fight Lando Calrissian, one on one, in the zero-gravity vacuum between the ships. If Lando refused, he would fire an electromagnetic torpedo and lethally irradiate everything in the nebula.

The holographic log recorder aboard the Star Destroyer *Eminence* recorded the single combat, much to the gratitude of future historians. Zipped up in spacesuits, Lando and the Sorcerer of Tund faced off in the middle of the watching fleet. They shot at one another while maneuvering for position with jet packs. One of Lando's wild shots caught Gepta in the ankle. With a shriek, the Sorcerer's form withered and disappeared.

It is unknown whether Emperor Palpatine was aware that Rokur Gepta was actually a Croke, a tiny snail-like creature from the Unknown Regions. The Emperor had long been interested in the Sorcerers of Tund, since their religious teachings were based on an archaic interpretation of original Sith doctrine. Gepta had used his Croke powers of illusion to infiltrate that secret society, co-opt its Sith teachings, and then annihilate it—Tund is now

an uninhabited, irradiated wasteland, and the death of Gepta marked an end to the Sorcerers of Tund.

The Imperial fleet responded to Gepta's demise with a hail of laserfire. Immediately, a booming cry burst across all comm channels: *"Cease fire or be destroyed!"* Thousands of gargantuan, fifty-kilometer-wide metallic spheres suddenly surrounded the armada on all sides. The new arrivals were self-aware droids, hailing from deep in the Unknown Regions. They had come for Vuffi Raa, their "child."

Vuffi Raa had been constructed by the mechanical beings for the purpose of recording new experiences throughout the galaxy. Now that his purpose had been fulfilled, Vuffi Raa departed with his progenitors. The Imperial fleet quietly withdrew when confronted with this unknown variable and never returned to complete their mission of Oswaft genocide.

The massive, mysterious droids disappeared into the vastness of the Unknown Regions, and have not reappeared since—or have they? Numerous eyewitness reports of massive objects roughly matching the droids' appearance were later compiled from all over the New Republic, including a hundred-thousand-person mass sighting during the Priole Danna festival on Lamuir IV.

ENTREPRENEURISM
2.5–0 B.B.Y.

Lando was sorry to see his companion go, but he had learned a great deal about starship piloting through the strange droid's tutelage. Furthermore, the grateful Oswaft had given him a full cargo hold of precious gemstones as a generous farewell gift. He invested the gemstones into a berubium mine in the Borgo asteroid belt, and then lost the fortune again when the mine proved to be worthless. Once again down to nothing, Lando withdrew the fifty thousand credits from his numbered account and waited for the sabacc tournament.

Two things made the waiting easier. The first was his old used-spaceship lot on Nar Shaddaa. Lando picked up the pieces of the struggling business and hired several new managers. The second was Drea Renthal, the pirate queen. Though he had good reason to carry a grudge against her, Lando realized that he and Renthal shared a similar outlook on life. Against all odds, the two became an item—at least for a few weeks.

The sabacc tournament on Cloud City was a crushing disappointment for Lando, however. The gambler made it to the final championship round and found himself facing his old friend Han Solo—a fair sabacc player, but far from a master of the game. When the final chip-cards were played, though, Solo had won an impressive stack of credits and sole ownership of Lando's ship, *Millennium Falcon.*

After the match, Lando was so impoverished that he was forced to swallow his pride and ask Solo for a fifteen-hundred-credit loan. Over the next year he turned the small sum into hundreds of thousands of credits by gambling with the galaxy's high rollers. He also carried out several masterful con jobs against the Imperials, including a scam on Pesmenben IV similar to the berubium mine that had previously ruined him.

Lando's second run-in with Boba Fett occurred aboard a luxury liner, where Fett had come to capture Rebel Alliance Commander Bria Tharen. He picked up Lando for use as an expendable hostage, but fortunately, a chance attack by Drea Renthal's star pirates saved both their lives. Renthal put up a substantial sum to buy Lando's and Bria's freedom.

Bria Tharen eventually joined forces with the Desilijic Hutts to coordinate a massive attack on the spice-processing planet Ylesia. Lando Calrissian participated in the assault, fighting alongside Han Solo. But when the combined Rebel–smuggler armies had wiped out all resistance, Bria Tharen swindled her allies. The Rebels departed with all the spice, leaving the smugglers with nothing.

Lando, like many others, blamed Solo for the double cross. A few days later, Lando briefly crossed paths with Han again, when both men became pawns in a Hutt wager involving the priceless Yavin Vassilika statue. Watching Bria Tharen claim the Vassilika on behalf of the Rebellion only embittered Lando further. He *knew* that Han must have had something to do with the swindle. When Solo came to Calrissian to ask for a loan to pay off Jabba the Hutt, Calrissian threw him against the wall and declared their friendship to be a thing of the past.

"THE RESPECTABLE ONE"
0–3 A.B.Y.

The Rebels won the Battle of Yavin not long afterward, but Lando Calrissian was busy with larger and larger escapades, including his single-handed decimation of the Norulac pirates in the notorious Battle of Taanab. He briefly investigated Hologram Fun World as a possible investment opportunity and got caught up in the Imperials' Project Starscream.

Lando's greatest coup, however, was in a sabacc game held in the Trest casino on Bespin. His opponent was Dominic Raynor, Cloud City's Baron Administrator. By the time Raynor folded his cards in frustration, Lando had won the title of Baron Administrator—and all the power that went with it.

To his credit, Lando took his new political assignment very seriously. He charmed the citizenry of Cloud City and won over the Exex business administration board. He established an excellent working relationship with the city's computer coordinator, a cyborg named Lobot. He staved off the advances of the Mining Guild and deflected the attention of the Empire, allowing business to continue as usual despite the growing Rebellion. He hired a squadron of commando-pilots to protect the city from pirate raids. When the droid EV-9D9 went psychotic and dismantled a quarter of the city's droid population, he salvaged the situation and enacted new security procedures. He increased net Tibanna-mining profits by more than 35 percent and turned Cloud City into a stable, prosperous center of industry. Millions of citizens looked to him for their well-being.

Which is why the arrival of twin intruders—Han Solo and Darth Vader—along with a third unwelcome interloper, Boba Fett, threw Lando Calrissian into a moral quandary. He balanced the life of Solo against the welfare of an entire city, and found his friend wanting. But Lando was not so foolish that he would keep on playing when the Empire had stacked the deck.

Fortunately for the fate of the galaxy, the gambler made the right decision in the end.

The Skywalker twins emerged from one of the galaxy's most turbulent periods to reverse a generation of injustice and genocide. They were destined for great things from the moment of their birth. Though their early lives are not as colorful as those of Han Solo or Lando Calrissian, Luke Skywalker and Leia Organa have arguably influenced modern history more than any other duo.

Luke Skywalker, Jedi Master, brought the Jedi order back from extinction and presided over a new generation of Force-strong galactic guardians. Leia Organa, the second Chief of State of the New Republic, helped overthrow the Empire and shepherded the civilized galaxy through some of its bleakest years.

The lineage of the Skywalker twins is, quite simply, epic. Their father was Anakin Skywalker, one of the most powerful Jedi Knights in history, whose dark actions under the name Darth Vader nearly brought an end to that order. Their mother was Queen Amidala, elected monarch of Naboo. The two grew up in different foster homes on opposite sides of the civilized galaxy.

Both infants were amazingly strong in the Force. Because Emperor Palpatine feared rival Force users so much, he had overseen the Jedi Purge, and Obi-Wan Kenobi and Yoda helped hide the newborns, both from the Emperor and from their own father. In the care of others, the twins would develop into finely honed weapons that could

eventually be turned against the Emperor.

Kenobi placed Luke with Owen and Beru Lars, hardworking moisture farmers on the sun-seared planet of Tatooine. Owen and Beru told their neighbors that they gave the baby the name *Skywalker* after Owen's stepmother Shmi, whom he had loved. Yoda and Obi-Wan soon learned that Vader had survived the fiery confrontation on Mustafar, but they decided to rely on the fact that since the planet held such

Luke Skywalker
[Art by Mark Chiarello]

Princess Leia Organa
[ART BY MARK CHIARELLO]

Raised on the pacifist planet Alderaan by Senator Bail Prestor Organa, Leia lived a life of privilege and responsibility. House Organa was the royal family of Alderaan, and Leia was accorded all the prerogatives due a Princess. Like her mother, Leia became a confident, poised young woman and a quick political thinker. In the ruling city of Aldera, Leia studied diplomacy, government, and languages, and played in the palace corridors with her best friend, Winter. Senator Organa often brought his adopted daughter on trips to other worlds, including Coruscant, and attended to her physical development by hiring weapons master Giles Durane to instruct Leia in the arts of self-defense and marksmanship. While still in her teens, Leia became the youngest representative ever elected to the Imperial Senate.

The general public did not learn of Luke and Leia's sinister lineage until years after the Battle of Endor. In fact, due to their having been raised apart, the two siblings did not even realize they were brother and sister until four years after Leia's rescue from the Death Star battle station. In the wake of the revelation regarding Darth Vader's ancestry, some partisan politicians accused Leia Organa of following in her father's footsteps. However, most citizens have been surprisingly conciliatory toward the offspring of Vader, holding the view that children should not be punished for the transgressions of their parents. The good that Luke and Leia have accomplished over the decades weighs heavier than any shadow legacy.

painful memories for Anakin following Shmi's death, Vader could never again set foot there. The Larses were low-profile isolationists, and Kenobi remained behind on Tatooine as added insurance. From his sparse hermitage in the Jundland Wastes, "Old Ben" Kenobi hid from Emperor Palpatine and simultaneously watched over young Luke, waiting for the day when the Force would provide a sign and fulfill a destiny.

Leia's upbringing was the polar opposite of her brother's.

PART FIVE

The Galactic Civil War

ARMED REBELLION BEGINS

THE DEATH STAR'S COMPLETION
3-0 B.B.Y.

The Death Star project continued despite scattered efforts at sabotage. The massive skeleton of the battle station moved from location to location in continual response to intelligence leaks. As the years stretched on, doubts emerged as to the viability of its planet-shattering superlaser—the Death Star's entire reason for being.

Wilhuff Tarkin, who secretly harbored his own doubts, decided to create a proof-of-concept model. In the exact center of the Maw black-hole cluster near Kessel lay a hidden island of gravitational stability. Tarkin chose this place, the universe's own fortress, as the site for his own top-secret weapons installation.

Construction slaves and droid-controlled equipment hauled a cluster of small asteroids inside and joined them together. Buildings and vacuum facilities were erected, laboratories stocked, and personnel assigned permanently—their records indicated that they had died in the line of duty. Next, Tarkin gathered the best researchers from across the Empire. Some of these came willingly, such as the great Dr. Ohran Keldor, and the driven and partially insane weapons designer Umak Leth. Other captive scientists were snatched unsuspecting, including Qwi Xux, an Omwati female. She was the only survivor of a large group of Omwati students put through rigorous tests by Tarkin himself.

The austere research station, Maw Installation, was run by the Twi'lek administrator Tol Sivron and guarded by four Star Destroyers under the command of Daala, Tarkin's former lover. Upon giving her this assignment, Tarkin had increased her rank to admiral. Daala remained isolated, never questioning her orders; her job was to ensure that the scientists in the research station continued to work without interruption.

The Maw Installation scientists refined the original plans of Raith Sienar and Bevel Lemelisk, discovering flaws in the Geonosis blueprints that were still being carried out in the current construction. Lemelisk himself worked on the Maw project under Tarkin's orders. Finally, Tarkin—now carrying the rank of Grand Moff—returned to the Emperor with a revised recommendation. Pleased, the Emperor approved the plans for a prototype to test the concept.

Inside Maw Installation, work crews of Wookiee slaves assembled a scaled-down version of the core superlaser mounted inside a stripped-down superstructure, an armillary sphere similar to the skeleton of the final design. When the superlaser proved effective, construction restarted on the stalled Death Star, in orbit around the penitentiary planet Despayre in the Horuz system.

Bevel Lemelisk received the title of chief engineer, and Darth Vader became an unofficial, and often unwelcome, supervisor. The labor force again consisted largely of Wookiee slaves, as well as exiles from the Despayre prison. Grand Moff Tarkin hoped to use the Death Star to enforce his Tarkin Doctrine throughout the Outer Rim territories, which he now controlled. The key precept of Tarkin's philosophy was

"Rule through the fear of force, rather than by force itself." The Grand Moff's personal slave, the Mon Calamari called Ackbar, took careful notes on both the superweapon and Imperial military strategy, waiting for the opportunity to escape back to his people.

Despite the intense security surrounding the project, shortages and sabotage continued to plague the construction site. When Tarkin and his engineer began to lose control of the schedule, Darth Vader came to Despayre and executed several workers and supervisors in order to encourage greater attention to detail. Soon thereafter, the Death Star was back on track.

Darth Vader's grim methods of discipline inspired rebellion within the ranks. Shortly before the Battle of Yavin, several Moffs, including Grand Moff Trachta, banded together and arranged for the assassinations of both Vader and Emperor Palpatine. Trachta's stormtroopers planted a bomb on the Emperor's shuttle and tried to kill Vader aboard his Star Destroyer, but both attempts failed. The treacherous Moffs all met with appropriately lethal ends.

Just after the completion of the battle station, but before it could be tested, a Rebel assassination attempt nearly took Grand Moff Tarkin's life. Tarkin avoided death, but his Mon Calamari slave Ackbar escaped to the Rebel Alliance. Ackbar recruited several of his people and aided the Rebellion, directing such victories as the Battle of Turkana aboard a Mon Calamari star cruiser.

The Rebel Alliance received fresh confirmation of the Death Star project from an informant on Ralltiir; the information was later verified by the Empire's own Lord Tion. Knowing that the Alliance's only chance lay in obtaining a copy of the station's blueprints and analyzing them for vulnerabilities, Bail Organa and Mon Mothma set up multiple plans for the capture operation. Toprawan rebels, in a raid on a space convoy, stole most of the technical information before it could be transferred to the Imperial Information Center. On Danuta, an untested Alliance agent named Kyle Katarn broke into an Imperial facility and made off with another set of plans. When combined, the two readouts formed a complete schematic of the Death Star from pole to pole.

The Rebel cell on Toprawa now had complete data, but Imperial Intelligence had learned of the leak. Star Destroyers blockaded the Toprawa system while stormtroopers moved in to crush the Rebels and recover the plans. The Alliance's only hope lay in a risky in-system data transmission. Princess Leia Organa, adopted daughter of Bail Organa and heir to the legacy of Anakin Skywalker, arrived in the Toprawa system under cover of diplomatic immunity. Her consular ship *Tantive IV,* commanded by Captain Antilles, intercepted the Death Star plans and immediately jumped to hyperspace. The Rebels on Toprawa—led by Commander Bria Tharen and Red Hand Squadron—were killed shortly after Leia's receipt of their transmission.

With the Empire's ultimate weapon compromised, Darth Vader pursued the fleeing Princess in the Imperial Star Destroyer *Devastator.* He vowed to retrieve the stolen information at any cost.

PREPARATIONS FOR BATTLE
0 B.B.Y.

Just before the Toprawan capture of the Death Star plans, Mon Mothma grew alarmed at the number of Imperial Intelligence agents digging for any Rebel activity. She wisely instructed Jan Dodonna—now a Rebel Alliance general in charge of the Dantooine headquarters—to move his operations to the Massassi ruins on the jungle moon of Yavin 4.

Mon Mothma's suspicions were proven correct when the Dantooine Rebels discovered an Imperial tracking device in a cargo shipment. General Dodonna stripped and abandoned the base and moved all personnel to the Yavin system. There, he and his troops waited for battle.

Several months earlier, as an inevitable outgrowth of the Corellian Treaty, Mon Mothma had issued a strongly worded Declaration of Rebellion against Palpatine and his policies. In response to this widely disseminated Declaration, the Emperor formally disbanded the Imperial Senate, sweeping away the final vestiges of the Republic. Palpatine placed regional governors, ruthless Grand Moffs like Tarkin, in direct control over the oversectors.

If it hadn't been apparent before, it was blindingly obvious now: the conflict between Rebellion and Empire could never be settled through political means. The Rebel Alliance prepared for full-scale war.

THE CAPTURE OF PRINCESS LEIA
0 B.B.Y.

Leia Organa disseminated much of the propaganda that helped to bind the Alliance together. Because of her outgoing nature, she traveled from world to world on well-publicized "mercy missions," which were often a cover for her Rebel activities. Darth Vader and the Emperor suspected Organa's involvement, but could not prove it.

Leia had been the perfect agent to intercept the Death Star plans from the Toprawan rebels. She immediately set course for Tatooine, where she hoped to recruit Obi-Wan Kenobi and bring him and the blueprints to Bail Organa on Alderaan. If the Death Star became operational, the Empire could use the battle station to launch an unparalleled reign of terror across the galaxy.

Vader's Star Destroyer *Devastator* caught up with *Tantive IV* near Tatooine. In the ensuing firefight, Leia managed to plant the Death Star readouts inside R2-D2. The little droid escaped the battle in a tiny life pod and, along with his counterpart C-3PO, landed on Tatooine. R2 attempted to deliver Leia's urgent message to Obi-Wan Kenobi, who was still living in a hovel at the edge of the planet's desert wasteland.

Captain Antilles of *Tantive IV* died at the hands of Darth Vader. Leia was brought as a prisoner to Grand Moff Tarkin's newly completed Death Star. She resisted Vader's rigorous interrogations in order to conceal the location of the new Rebel headquarters on Yavin 4. Tarkin, anxious to test his Death Star and to reinforce the Emperor's iron grip, found

General Jan Dodonna
[ART BY MARK CHIARELLO]

another way to coerce her: he threatened to destroy Leia's peaceful homeworld unless she divulged the information he demanded.

Knowing full well the capabilities of the superweapon, and Tarkin's own prior record of ruthlessness, Leia understood that he was not bluffing. Reluctantly, she announced the location of the Dantooine base, hoping that it had already been abandoned as planned. Tarkin, however, needed to make Alderaan a brutal example for the Rebels and the entire galaxy.

In the darkest act of the Galactic Civil War, the Death Star destroyed Alderaan and its billions of inhabitants. Bail Organa numbered among the dead. Leia Organa was returned to her detention block and scheduled for execution.

A New Hope
0 B.B.Y.

At the same time, seemingly insignificant events unfolded on the desert world of Tatooine to set the stage for the Emperor's downfall. R2-D2 and C-3PO were captured by Jawa traders and sold to an out-of-the-way moisture farm, which happened to be the same homestead where Anakin Skywalker's son, Luke, had been raised since infancy. While cleaning his new droids, Luke accidentally discovered the holographic message encoded by his sister, Leia. Not knowing of their brother–sister relationship, but recognizing that the "Obi-Wan Kenobi" in her recording might be the local hermit Ben Kenobi, Luke resolved to pass on the droids to Old Ben.

R2-D2 went searching for Kenobi on his own, and Luke survived a brush with Tusken Raiders in order to retrieve him. When they finally encountered Kenobi and replayed the message, Obi-Wan agreed to break his long exile and escort the Death Star plans to Bail Organa on Alderaan. Obi-Wan believed that the Force was guiding Luke toward a larger destiny, which was what he and Yoda had hoped for when they agreed to raise Anakin Skywalker's children in secret. In Luke's absence, Owen and Beru Lars had been killed and their homestead razed by Imperial stormtroopers, and this revelation only seemed to confirm the presence of a guiding hand. Luke, of course, had no choice but to go along on the Alderaan mission, and Obi-Wan resolved to begin the formal training that would turn Luke into a fitting opponent for the Emperor.

In Tatooine's Mos Eisley spaceport, Obi-Wan commissioned the smuggling duo of Han Solo and Chewbacca to take them to Alderaan. As the Imperial net tightened around the escaped droids, Han Solo's ship, *Millennium Falcon,* blasted away from Tatooine and slipped through a Star Destroyer blockade. En route to Alderaan, Obi-Wan showed Luke the basics of lightsaber combat and the notion that using the Force was a matter of instincts, not intellect. As Obi-Wan had hoped, Luke possessed an astonishing natural talent, indicating that he had inherited the bloodline of the Chosen One.

When *Millennium Falcon* arrived in the Alderaan system, they found only a spinning asteroid cloud. The entire planet had been destroyed by the Death Star, and they became the battle station's next target. Swallowed up by one of the Death Star's tractor beams, Luke and Han disguised themselves as stormtroopers and seized the docking bay's control room. Obi-Wan headed off alone to shut down the tractor beam controls. When Luke learned that Princess Leia was being held prisoner on the battle station, he convinced Han to help spring her by appealing to the Corellian's boundless sense of greed. In an unorthodox rescue that took them through the guts of the Death Star's garbage system, the group escaped the detention block and headed back for their rendezvous point.

Obi-Wan Kenobi sabotaged the tractor beam generator that would have prevented the *Falcon* from fleeing. But before he could return to the docking bay, Obi-Wan encountered his nemesis and former friend, Darth Vader. In a refined, classical duel, far different from the punishing battle that they had engaged in on Mustafar, Master and Padawan parried with lightsabers and words. Obi-Wan called Anakin "Darth," an indication that Kenobi saw little in the black armor that reminded him of the boy who had once been a surrogate son. Luke, Princess Leia, and the rest returned to the *Falcon,* ready to fight their way out, and Obi-Wan realized he could accomplish more with sacrifice than combat. Remembering the teachings of Qui-Gon Jinn, who had maintained his spirit form after entering the netherworld, Obi-Wan Kenobi let Vader cut him down. The *Falcon's* passengers used the opportunity to flee the station.

Bearing the precious Death Star plans, the *Falcon* blasted through a TIE fighter picket line and jumped to hyperspace, emerging at the new Rebel base on Yavin 4. Han Solo realized too late that the Imperials had placed a tracer on his ship. General Dodonna and his team of experts frantically studied the blueprints to find a flaw, even as the Death Star arrived in the Yavin system to destroy the Rebel base.

The Rebels had only one chance. If a small ship were to fly into a surface trench and launch a proton torpedo into a tiny thermal exhaust port, the torpedo could reach the hypermatter core and annihilate the battle station in a catastrophic chain reaction.

As the Death Star orbited into a firing position to destroy the jungle moon, swarms of Rebel X-wings and Y-wings attacked like stinging insects. Many Rebels died in the Battle of Yavin, but one pilot—Luke Skywalker, using his newfound skills with the Force—scored a direct hit. The Death Star exploded, killing Grand Moff Tarkin and eliminating the Empire's ultimate weapon that had taken nearly twenty years to build. It was an enormous victory for the Rebel Alliance.

IMPACT AND CONSEQUENCES
0–0.5 A.B.Y.

In his modified TIE fighter, Darth Vader escaped the destruction of the Death Star. Alone in space and calling on the power of the dark side of the Force, he limped to a nearby Imperial outpost on Vaal.

During the battle, he had sensed that the pilot who destroyed the station had shown unusual strength in the Force. Already suspecting the pilot's possible heritage, Vader chose not to report back to Palpatine in person. Instead, the Dark Lord spent many weeks on a private mission, running down hints about the newest Rebel hero. A Rebel deserter named Tyler Lucian promised to reveal the truth of the pilot's identity, but he committed suicide on Centares before either Vader

or the bounty hunter Valance could extract a confession. Through the torture of another informant, Vader finally got the confirmation he sought—the Death Star's destroyer was Luke Skywalker, Vader's own son.

Back on Coruscant, the Emperor was greatly displeased with the design flaw that had allowed the Rebels to annihilate his Death Star. He summoned Bevel Lemelisk, the

Obi-Wan "Ben" Kenobi
[ART BY MARK CHIARELLO]

original designer of the superweapon, and executed him in the most horrific manner possible. But the genius and imagination of such a brilliant man as Lemelisk would not be wasted by the Emperor. Resurrected through dark alchemy in a cloned body, vividly remembering the agony of his own execution, Lemelisk had no choice but to work even harder on a second Death Star design.

Some questioned the Emperor's wisdom in building a second Death Star, but the superweapon *worked,* as the destruction of Alderaan had proved. No one in the Empire could simply scrap such an expensive creation when a flaw like a carelessly uncovered thermal exhaust port could so easily be rectified.

Vader and the Emperor briefly focused their attentions away from the Rebels and onto the Bounty Hunters' Guild, at the urging of Prince Xizor, the criminal godfather of the Black Sun syndicate. Palpatine approved Xizor's plan to eliminate the guild, over Vader's objections. Boba Fett, now the most notorious bounty hunter in the galaxy, was hired to be the agent of the guild's destruction. In a bloody conflict known as the Bounty Hunter Wars, Fett succeeded in fragmenting the organization into innumerable splinter groups and free agents. Over the next few years, Vader frequently employed these rogue bounty hunters for his own purposes.

REBEL TRAP
0–0.5 A.B.Y.

Immediately after celebrating their victory, the Alliance prepared to abandon their base on Yavin 4. The destruction of the Death Star had been a miracle, and the Rebels knew that they wouldn't stand a chance against the full Imperial armada. Much of the Rebel fleet, including a group of huge Mon Calamari cruisers commanded by Ackbar, as well as refugee vessels containing the government-in-exile led by Mon Mothma, had not been present at Yavin, and were scattered across space to form a mobile task force. General Dodonna orchestrated the Yavin base's evacuation.

The blockade had been ordered by Darth Vader, who did not want the base ground into dust—at least not yet. At the starship yards of Fondor, the first Super Star Destroyer, christened *Executor,* was nearing completion. It was to be Vader's new flagship, carrying as much military might as an entire fleet of smaller ships. As payback for his humiliation at the Death Star, Vader wanted to use the *Executor* as his personal sword of vengeance against the Rebel insurgents.

Han Solo and Chewbacca had left almost immediately, before the implementation of the blockade, hoping to pay off Jabba the Hutt with the reward that they had received from the Rebellion. They had a few adventures on their own, including an encounter with a Sith monster on Aduba III, but events soon conspired to put them back into the Alliance's service. Han also lost his reward money, thanks to the larcenous pirate Crimson Jack. None of Han's subsequent attempts to erase his debt would meet with success.

Luke Skywalker and Leia Organa proved adept at using small ships to slip through the blockade. Hooking back up with Han Solo, the group ran into trouble on the Wheel casino station, but continued to vex Darth Vader, bringing the permeability of the Yavin barricade to light. During the early weeks following the Death Star's destruction, responsibility for the blockade had fallen to the House of Tagge, one of the most influential merchant families in the Empire. The Tagges—brothers Silas, Orman, and Ulric, and sister Domina—were fierce rivals of Vader's, and hoped to gain the Emperor's favor at the Dark Lord's expense. The Tagge presence in the Yavin system collapsed after Luke Skywalker destroyed their base, which had been comprised of a giant turbine suspended in the clouds of Yavin Prime. Admiral Griff, Darth Vader's direct agent, then assumed control of the blockade, directing his efforts from the nearby Jovan Station.

Other high-ranking Imperials derided Vader's choice of military strategy, viewing the *Executor*'s construction as little more than grandstanding in light of the ineffective blockade. Several admirals secretly plotted to sabotage Vader's Super Star Destroyer as it lay in Fondor's shipbuilding docks.

TIE bombers harass the Rebel base on Yavin 4 during the Imperial blockade. [Art by Tommy Lee Edwards]

Admiral Griff, pretending to have turned traitor, provided key information about the *Executor*'s construction to the Rebel Alliance. Luke Skywalker ran the blockade and infiltrated the construction yards at Fondor, but Griff's "treachery" was a ruse, and Skywalker barely escaped. Luke had done little damage, but managed to return to the Rebels with a great deal of information on the huge battleship.

Not long after, while returning from a different mission, Skywalker eluded Imperial pursuit by plunging his ship into the slipstream of a passing hypercomet in an isolated system. Following the comet's trajectory along an asteroid-filled orbit, Skywalker crashed on a forgotten, frozen planet named Hoth. There, he encountered an exiled Imperial governor who had made a primitive home in the ice fields. Skywalker killed the treacherous governor in self-defense, and then reported to the Alliance, suggesting Hoth as a possible location for their next headquarters stronghold.

The Rebellion desperately needed to relocate, and fast—if the *Executor* managed to wipe out the Yavin base, they would lose their emerging nucleus of top star pilots. Luke Skywalker had teamed with Wedge Antilles, a fellow veteran of the Death Star battle, to form a group of X-wing fliers that would ultimately become Rogue Squadron. The existence of the Rogues helped offset the loss that the Alliance had suffered on the same day as the Battle of Yavin, when several starfighter squadrons were lost in the Battle of Ord Biniir.

Darth Vader
[ART BY MARK CHIARELLO]

IMPERIAL COUNTERSTRIKE
0.5–2 A.B.Y.

The blockade situation began to enrage local fleet commanders, who impressed upon Vader the need for a quick and decisive strike. Consequently, the *Executor*'s construction was stepped up. General Dodonna grew concerned—while small ships like the *Falcon* could run the blockade, larger vessels would surely be captured. Dodonna contacted Mon Mothma and Admiral Ackbar aboard the Alliance fleet and arranged for a diversionary assault.

The Empire's attack finally came, six months after the Battle of Yavin. While Ackbar staged a feint in the Vallusk Cluster to draw off most Imperial forces, the mighty *Executor* arrived to decimate the Yavin base. Dodonna scrambled all of the base's fighters and transports, but stubbornly refused to evacuate until the others were away. The old general set off a series of concussion charges that wiped out an entire squadron of attacking TIE bombers. Dodonna was believed killed in the explosion, but in reality he was taken, critically wounded, to the dark Imperial prison *Lusankya*.

The evacuating Rebels rendezvoused with the main Alliance fleet, intending to establish a new base on icy Hoth. Instead, they were forced to put their plans on hold until they could replenish their equipment stores, medical supplies, and foodstuffs. In a dangerous gamble, the Alliance negotiated with Imperial Overlord Ghorin of the Greater Plooriod Cluster for several shipments of badly needed grain, but then turned the tables on Ghorin when they discovered the grain was poisoned.

Alliance agent Kyle Katarn, who had helped capture the Death Star plans, was pressed into service again when Mon Mothma learned of the Empire's Dark Trooper Project, launched to create mechanized super stormtroopers. Katarn scuttled the operation by destroying the Dark Troopers' spacegoing construction site, and also rescued Crix Madine from an Imperial prison. Madine was an elite Imperial—the ex-leader of the Storm Commandos—who had decided to defect to the Rebels after being forced to release an incurable plague on the planet Dentaal.

En route to the Alliance, Madine was nearly recaptured by the Empire during a layover on Corellia, but was rescued by the pilots of the newly formed Rogue Squadron. Mon Mothma welcomed Madine into the Rebel Alliance and made him a general. Madine would work closely with Rogue Squadron for several years.

The stress took its toll on Rebel leadership. Bail Organa had been killed in the destruction of Alderaan, leaving Mon Mothma and Garm Bel Iblis as the highest-ranking Alliance representatives. The two rarely saw eye-to-eye, and when Mon Mothma ordered an attack on Milvayne that Bel Iblis viewed as suicidal, he took his loyal forces and seceded from the Rebellion. His private army would score many independent victories over the next nine years.

The loss of Bel Iblis was offset when the Bothan politician Borsk Fey'lya and his sizable faction joined the Alliance. Fey'lya had been impressed by the Rebel victory at Yavin and made the move not for ideological reasons, but to gain more status and power.

Leia Organa met up with a survivor of the old Jedi Order after her vessel was shot down above the planet Krant. Echuu Shen-Jon, the general who had led the Republic's effort to recover its Decimators during the Clone Wars, still lived on Krant, serving out a sentence of exile for his brush with the dark side of the Force. Echuu helped Leia destroy a Jedi artifact known as the Vor'Na'Tu before dying under the blade of Darth Vader, yet another Jedi casualty attributable to the Dark Lord.

Approximately one year after the Battle of Yavin, Leia learned that a top-secret list containing names of Rebel sympathizers who were embedded within the Imperial government had been left in a place that was accessible to the Empire. Leia tasked two agents—Dusque Mistflier and Finn Darktrin—with the responsibility of capturing the data holocron from the ruins of a Jedi temple on Dantooine. Though the pair recovered the item, Darktrin revealed himself as an Imperial agent and attempted to transmit the file's contents to Darth Vader. Luckily for the Rebellion's leaders, the data stream was incomplete, protecting the identities of most of their top contacts.

The Rebellion staged a series of guerrilla-style strikes against the Empire over the next year, including the Ram's Head mission, which demolished four Star Destroyers in dry dock. But the Alliance fleet remained scattered and on the run as it searched for another central base. The jungle planet Thila was briefly used, but abandoned when it was suggested that the Empire would expect the Rebels to move to another jungle world like Yavin 4. Alliance engineering teams went to a number of possible worlds to begin excavation, including

Borsk Fey'lya
[Art by Mark Chiarello]

Hoth, but Mon Mothma wanted to keep her options open.

The Imperials, too, sent out fleets to search space for the hiding places of their enemies, launching thousands of automated probe droids. But the sheer number of uncharted settlements and smuggler encampments created hundreds of false alarms.

CIRCARPOUS JOINS THE RESISTANCE
2 A.B.Y.

As the business hub of the Expansion Region, Circarpous IV was home to many of the galaxy's financial leaders. Disgusted by the astronomical tariffs and self-destructive spending so common in Palpatine's Empire, these ruling financiers agreed to covertly fund the Rebel Alliance, pending a face-to-face meeting with Leia Organa.

Organa and her protocol droid traveled to the rendezvous on Circarpous IV, escorted by Luke Skywalker. An engine malfunction caused both Alliance ships to crash on Circarpous V—a drenched, strategically worthless swamp planet known locally as Mimban—where the Empire had established an illegal dolovite mine. Leia and Luke became prisoners of the mining colony's governor. Darth Vader headed for the system as soon as he received word about their capture, but by the time he arrived on Mimban the two Rebels had escaped.

Vader caught up with his quarry at the vine-encrusted Temple of Pomojema, deep in the swamps of Mimban. The temple held the fabled Kaiburr Crystal, a luminous shard capable of magnifying the Force a thousandfold. Luke Skywalker took up his lightsaber and faced Vader in a one-on-one duel.

It is interesting to note that Skywalker, still an untrained Jedi, held his own against his much more experienced opponent. Possibly, the Kaiburr Crystal provided an edge, but Luke later admitted that the spirit of Obi-Wan Kenobi appeared to have inhabited his body, guiding his actions as a puppeteer directs a marionette. Obi-Wan's energy drove Luke to sever the Dark Lord's sword arm in a furious drive, but the effort seemed to exhaust Luke's intangible benefactor. Darth Vader shrugged off his injury, and only Vader's chance misstep into a crumbling well allowed Luke and Leia to escape.

When they rejoined the Alliance fleet, Leia notified the Circarpousians of the Imperial mine on Mimban. Outraged by the subterfuge, the Circarpous business underground went ahead with the plans to open a covert supply line to the Rebels. The flow of credits was a critical factor in strengthening the Alliance military, and resulted in the purchase of a KDY Planet Defender ion cannon for installation at their next base.

The recovered Kaiburr Crystal did not perform to ex-

Darth Vader confronts Luke Skywalker in the jungles of Mimban.
[Art by Tommy Lee Edwards]

pectations. Mimban, like Nam Chorios and Dathomir, appeared to be a planet with a biosphere that magnified the Force. Luke discovered that the power of the Kaiburr Crystal decreased in direct proportion to its distance from Mimban and, more specifically, from the Temple of Pomojema itself.

Little more than a curiosity, the trinket remained in Luke's possession for years. Eventually he used it as a teaching aid and even experimented by installing it as a focusing crystal in a lightsaber. He found the resulting blade to be remarkably strong and energy-efficient.

Home in the Ice
2–3 A.B.Y.

Mon Mothma eventually agreed to establish the new Rebel command headquarters on the frozen world of Hoth. Alliance engineers completed the work that had been started months earlier, constructing an installation that took advantage of the climate. "Echo Base" was commanded by General Carlist Rieekan, a survivor of Alderaan who had watched his own world destroyed by the Death Star. Princess Leia Organa also took up residence in the ice tunnels, choosing safety over physical comfort.

The Rebels made every effort to keep their headquarters a secret, minimizing the number of ship arrivals and departures. Han Solo had several run-ins with bounty hunters while offworld on Ord Mantell, but none of the mercenaries learned the location of Echo Base.

Meanwhile, Mon Mothma continued to gather forces at the main Rebel fleet, preparing for another strike. Before she could take action, the Alliance suffered a stunning defeat in the Battle of Derra IV. A badly needed supply convoy and its starfighter escort were blasted to bits in an attack executed by Darth Vader himself. The death of the squadron's flight leader elevated Luke Skywalker to the rank of commander, but nothing could replace the loss of the critical munitions shipment.

It had been years since their major victory on Yavin, and the Empire continued to hound them. It was a dark time for the Rebellion.

THE BATTLE OF HOTH
3 A.B.Y.

One of the Imperial probe droids dispersed to search for the Rebel headquarters picked up faint transmissions in the Hoth system. Upon inspecting the planet, the probot discovered evidence of a military installation and sent a signal to Darth Vader's flagship. Vader deployed his personal Star Destroyer fleet, the Death Squadron, to attack the base.

General Rieekan's team discovered the probot but could not silence it before it broadcast their location. Rieekan realized that Hoth was sure to be the target of an Imperial attack. Having seen firsthand the destruction of Alderaan, he ordered an immediate evacuation. It would be a desperate race.

Vader's fleet arrived before the first transport could be launched, but a surprise blast from the Rebel's new ion cannon cleared an escape corridor for the Alliance ship. While Imperial AT-AT walkers hammered the base at ground level, Rebel snowspeeders harried them in a losing battle. Many defenders sacrificed themselves to buy time for the remaining forces to get away. Echo Base fell after a great loss of life on both sides. Just as Vader strode into the ruined command center, Leia Organa and C-3PO escaped with Han Solo and Chewbacca in *Millennium Falcon*.

Vader launched his fleet into full pursuit. At the time, though he understood Luke Skywalker was his son, he did not suspect that Leia Organa was his daughter. Nevertheless, Leia was a powerful figure in the Rebellion, and Luke was known to never stray too far from his friends in the *Falcon*, so capturing the vessel became a priority for Vader. Han Solo proved a remarkable pilot, eluding pursuit by flying directly through the heart of the Hoth asteroid belt, but faulty equipment prevented his ship from jumping to hyperspace.

To assist in the hunt, Vader called in a rogue's gallery of bounty hunters, most of them independent agents after the destruction of the Bounty Hunters' Guild. Among the hunters was Boba Fett, who had known Vader during the Clone Wars, back when he was Anakin Skywalker. In recent years, the two had established a working relationship and professional rivalry. Before the Battle of Yavin, Fett had recovered the severed head of an Icarii prophetess on the Dark Lord's behalf, a contest in which each player had exhibited his full depth of skill.

Believing that *Millennium Falcon* had escaped Imperial capture, Han Solo limped across the Ison Corridor with a patched-together backup hyperdrive to reach the gas world of Bespin. On Cloud City, he met up again with Lando Calrissian, former owner of the *Falcon* and now a respectable businessman. Though they had had their disagreements in the past, most notably over the aftermath of Ylesia, Han still considered Lando a friend and requested his assistance in getting repairs for his ship.

Unknown to Han or his passengers, Boba Fett had tracked the *Falcon* to Cloud City and betrayed the ship's location to Vader. Darth Vader coerced Lando into setting a trap for Han and Leia, and the two Rebel fugitives became prisoners in Cloud City's detention cells. Vader ordered the torture of Han Solo and Chewbacca, to no apparent purpose. In truth, he meant to stir the Force with the agony of Luke Skywalker's friends, and lure his true prize to Cloud City.

A NEW JEDI
3 A.B.Y.

After flying a snowspeeder alongside Wedge Antilles during the Battle of Hoth, Luke escaped the ice planet to follow a vision he had received from Obi-Wan Kenobi. Days earlier, while lost in a Hoth blizzard and bleeding from a wampa attack, Luke had been told to go to the Dagobah system and learn from a Jedi Master named Yoda. Luke flew his X-wing to the coordinates laid out by R2-D2, crashlanding his starfighter in a swampy bog.

AT-ATs overrun Rebel trenches in the Battle of Hoth.
[ART BY TOMMY LEE EDWARDS]

and discouraging days testing himself in the Force, attempting to meet the strange and seemingly impossible challenges that Yoda gave him. He learned to face his fears and to trust his instincts.

As he opened his mind and explored his Jedi abilities, Luke saw another vision: Han Solo and Leia Organa held in brutal captivity on Bespin. He could no longer focus on his training with the knowledge that his friends were in pain. Luke ignored the dire warnings of Yoda and the spirit of Obi-Wan Kenobi, both of whom told him it was a trap. He boarded his X-wing and followed his heart to Cloud City, just as Darth Vader had hoped.

Now finished with Han Solo, Vader had the smuggler frozen in a block of carbonite and delivered to Boba Fett. Vader intended to use the same freezing process on Luke, in order to capture the novice Jedi. Fett left Cloud City with the preserved Solo in *Slave I*, heading for Tatooine and Jabba the Hutt, who still had a price on Solo's head for unpaid debts.

Jedi Master Yoda
[ART BY MARK CHIARELLO]

Luke could not believe that the unassuming and gnomish creature who greeted him could possibly be a great warrior. Yoda, who had always believed that the Force would one day guide the offspring of Anakin Skywalker to him, had been waiting for this moment for more than two decades. He agreed to train the doubting youth in the ways of the Jedi, and to forge him into a weapon that could at last destroy the Sith. Yoda warned his pupil that upcoming decisions would be difficult, and that he must be strong. Luke spent many long

After Vader's trap was sprung, Lando had a change of heart. His guards freed Leia, Chewbacca, and C-3PO, and the four of them tried and failed to rescue Han. Knowing the Empire would heap retribution on Cloud City and its people, Lando called for an evacuation. In the resulting chaos, their small group escaped aboard *Millennium Falcon*.

Luke made it to Cloud City, but could not rescue any of his friends. Instead, Vader herded him into the carbonite chamber. Luke and Vader fought one another in a clash of lightsabers, and their angry duel spilled over onto a platform overlooking Cloud City's wind core. Darth Vader mercilessly hacked off Luke's right hand.

Vader then revealed the terrible secret that he was Luke's father. He beseeched his son to join him in overthrowing the Emperor and ruling the galaxy together. Reeling from physical and emotional pain, Luke instead stepped into the seemingly bottomless core shaft. He slipped into an airshaft that dumped him out through Cloud City's ventral side, where he desperately clung to a weather vane. *Millennium Falcon* picked him up and fled the system, its hyperdrive repaired. The *Falcon* soon rendezvoused with the remainder of the Alliance fleet.

It had been a devastating defeat for the Rebellion. The base on Hoth was destroyed, Han Solo had been lost, Luke Skywalker had discovered the truth of his dark past, and the scattered fleet seemed to have no chance of victory over the Empire.

IMPERIAL INTRIGUE
3–3.5 A.B.Y.

Against all odds, the Alliance pressed on. Mon Mothma heard rumors of a second, even larger Death Star under construction around the Sanctuary Moon of Endor. Gathering concrete information on the battle station became a top priority.

The Empire continued to implement grand schemes, including the *Tarkin* superweapon and the Phantom TIE project. The *Tarkin*, a scaled-down version of the Death Star similar in principle to the one created inside Maw Installation, was capable of shattering worlds. Grand Admiral Batch had been tasked by the Emperor with developing a working cloaking device, and he used the *Tarkin* to demolish the burned-out planet Aeten II—blasting loose millions of rare stygium crystals. Boasting stygium invisibility screens, Batch's "Phantom TIEs" would have proved invincible in dogfights had Rebel saboteurs not scuttled the project. The *Tarkin* suffered a similar fate, blowing itself apart when Leia Organa and a small team infiltrated the station and disrupted its workings. Years later, one of Grand Admi-

ral Batch's discarded cloaking designs (which suffered from the flaw of not letting its users see *out*) would be used during Grand Admiral Thrawn's military campaign.

Darth Vader employed a subtle stratagem to get closer to the Rebels, and to Luke Skywalker in particular. Shira Brie, one of Palpatine's elite Emperor's Hands, became an undercover agent within the Alliance starfighter corps. Luke respected her as a squadron mate and soon grew close to her as a romantic interest, but during a heated space battle he shot her down—the Force having told him that the pilot of the other ship was an enemy. Shira survived the ordeal, and Vader rebuilt her body with cybernetic parts. Shira Brie became the Dark Lady Lumiya, disciple of the Sith.

These months also saw the long-awaited return of the Mandalorians. Leia Organa visited the Mandalorian homeworld during the search for Han Solo's carbonized body and encountered Mandalorian Supercommandos Fenn Shysa and Tobbi Dala, who had been keeping a low profile since the Clone Wars. Tobbi Dala died in a fight against Imperial slavers, but Fenn Shysa rallied several of his Mandalorian warriors to aid the Rebel Alliance.

PRINCE XIZOR AND BLACK SUN
3.5 A.B.Y.

The unstable political situation fostered by the Rebellion caused certain parties to cast their eyes on the Imperial throne. One was Xizor, a reptilian prince from Falleen and the head of Black Sun, the Empire's largest criminal syndicate. Xizor had masterminded the Bounty Hunter Wars a few years earlier and was now said to be the third most powerful person in the galaxy, behind Palpatine and Vader. Xizor decided to increase his rank by eliminating Vader, his longtime rival.

Prince Xizor was one of the few who knew of the blood ties between Darth Vader and Luke Skywalker. Palpatine wanted Skywalker alive in order to turn him to the dark side of the Force, and had entrusted Vader with the task of capturing the boy unharmed. To make Vader look incompetent in the eyes of the Emperor, Xizor decided that he wanted Skywalker *dead*.

Black Sun criminal operatives began hatching assassina-

Arden Lyn and Grand Admiral Zaarin
[ART BY MARK CHIARELLO]

lives was high. They then brought the freighter's computer core to the nearby planet Kothlis, where a crack team of data slicers decrypted the blueprints and construction schedules. Though the Rebels congratulated themselves on their victory, it was later learned that Palpatine had allowed the freighter to be captured in order to lure the Alliance fleet into a trap at Endor.

On Kothlis, bounty hunters captured Luke Skywalker; fortunately, the Imperial computer core was spirited away by Bothan technicians and eventually made its way into the hands of Mon Mothma. As Vader rushed to Kothlis to collect his son, Luke managed to escape.

On Coruscant, Leia Organa and Chewbacca disguised themselves as bounty hunters to gain access to Prince Xizor's opulent fortress. At first, the Falleen crimelord was polite and gracious toward his guests, but then he imprisoned Leia. Chewbacca escaped, as part of Xizor's master plan: the Wookiee would notify Skywalker, and when Skywalker arrived, he would be killed.

Luke and his companions came to Organa's rescue. They broke into Xizor's castle, found the Princess, and then set off a time-delay thermal detonator to cover their escape. When Xizor realized he had less than five minutes before the thermal detonator destroyed his fortress, he fled to his orbiting skyhook, *Falleen's Fist.* The resulting implosion of Xizor's castle left a gaping hole in the Coruscant cityscape.

Aboard *Falleen's Fist,* Xizor ordered his personal navy to destroy the escaping *Millennium Falcon.* Han Solo's ship fought valiantly, although it was quickly overwhelmed. But then the entire group was overtaken by a vast flotilla of Imperial warships led by the Super Star Destroyer *Executor.* The *Executor* and its TIE squadrons, however, ignored the *Falcon* and opened fire on Xizor's vessels instead.

Darth Vader, never a subtle or patient man, had been driven over the edge by Xizor's brazen attempt to eliminate Skywalker. The Dark Lord delivered an ultimatum: if Xizor

tion plots against Skywalker, who was busy tracking down Boba Fett and the carbonized body of Han Solo. Distressed by this latest turn of events, Leia Organa ironically turned to Black Sun, hoping the syndicate's underground spy network could uncover the identity of the assassins.

Luke returned to Tatooine, where he constructed a new lightsaber to replace the weapon he had lost on Cloud City. When he received a message from the Bothan homeworld of Bothawui, Luke Skywalker and the smuggler Dash Rendar went there to assist in the capture of the Imperial freighter *Suprosa,* which was carrying plans for the Empire's second Death Star.

Luke and a squadron of Bothan pilots intercepted the Imperial freighter and disabled it, though the cost in Bothan

did not immediately recall his navy and surrender himself into Imperial custody, the *Executor* would destroy his skyhook. Xizor refused to respond, and Vader's gunners blasted *Falleen's Fist* into flaming debris.

Xizor's death created a power vacuum within Black Sun. His second in command, the human replica droid known as Guri, dropped out of sight, and Xizor's various lieutenants began squabbling. The body count climbed as the struggles escalated into open warfare.

While Vader was preoccupied with Black Sun, one of the Emperor's Grand Admirals finalized his plans for a daring, but ultimately doomed, coup d'état. Immediately after Xizor's death, Grand Admiral Zaarin attacked Vader's fleet in the Ottega system, and captured the Emperor's private shuttlecraft at Coruscant. To catch Palpatine unaware, Zaarin enlisted the assistance of Arden Lyn, one of the Emperor's Hands. The coup failed thanks to the appearance of loyal Imperial forces, and Zaarin soon died in a confrontation with Grand Admiral Thrawn. Palpatine later took revenge on the twenty-five-thousand-year old Lyn, killing her at last.

The computer core captured aboard the *Suprosa* revealed the existence of a second Death Star at Endor, but the Rebellion wanted to confirm the data. Rebel spy Tay Vanis had supposedly captured similar information, but had not been heard from for weeks. Luke Skywalker, Leia

Prince Xizor, head of Black Sun.
[Art by Mark Chiarello]

Organa, and Lando Calrissian ran down clues to Tay Vanis's whereabouts, discovering that he was now a broken man, the victim of Imperial torture.

ALLIANCE TRIUMPHANT

THE REBELLION REGROUPS
4 A.B.Y.

Learning that Han Solo's carbonite slab now hung inside Jabba the Hutt's palace, Luke Skywalker helped organize a complex and desperate plan to free his friend. Leia Organa and Lando Calrissian gained entry to the palace in disguise, Chewbacca masqueraded as a prisoner, C-3PO and R2-D2 were given to Jabba as gifts, and Luke Skywalker simply walked in the front door. All Luke's preparations seemed to fall apart when the group was discovered and sentenced to die in the Great Pit of Carkoon, but the rookie Jedi Knight decimated the Hutt's entourage with ease. Leia strangled Jabba, leading to the collapse of the Desilijic crime family.

Admiral Ackbar
[Art by Mark Chiarello]

decrypted computer core from Kothlis, containing the details of the second Death Star's construction site around the green moon of Endor. As Mon Mothma and Admiral Ackbar planned their attack, another piece of data galvanized them even more: Emperor Palpatine himself would be at the station on an inspection tour. If they could strike quickly and succeed in destroying the new battle station, they would eradicate the Empire's superweapon, as well as the evil despot himself.

THE BATTLE OF ENDOR
4 A.B.Y.

After gathering in the Sullust system and executing a feint attack, Rebel commandos slipped through the Imperial security net around Endor. A team led by Leia Organa, Luke Skywalker, and Han Solo (newly promoted to general) crept through Endor's dense forest in an effort to destroy the shield generator that was protecting the Death Star's orbital construction site. Unfortunately, the team encountered numerous difficulties, first when a squad of Imperial speeder bike scouts threatened to expose their location, and again when Endor's native Ewoks mistook the Rebels for invaders and nearly roasted them in a cooking fire.

Luke felt conflicted by his dual role as a Jedi and as Anakin Skywalker's son, and voluntarily gave himself up to the local Imperial commander. He became a prisoner aboard the Death Star, Luke's words of compassion failing to penetrate the shell that Darth Vader had constructed around his own emotions. As the Rebel Alliance's attack fleet swept through hyperspace to strike at the Death Star, the shield generator continued to protect their target.

In the Death Star's throne room, Vader presented Luke Skywalker to Emperor Palpatine. When the Rebel fleet arrived in the Endor system and launched its assault, Luke learned of the web of deceit that had been spun by Palpatine

Leia, Lando, and a thawed Han Solo rejoined the Rebel fleet in preparation for a major strike against the Empire. Luke Skywalker returned to Dagobah to continue his training under Yoda. When he arrived, however, he found the nine-hundred-year-old Jedi Master near death. Yoda said his farewells, and at last confirmed the truth that Darth Vader was indeed Luke's father. The spirit of Obi-Wan Kenobi revealed another startling fact, telling Luke that Princess Leia Organa was his sister. Obi-Wan urged him to destroy Vader, calling the Dark Lord "more machine than man," but Luke couldn't entertain the thought of killing the man who had once been Anakin Skywalker, his father. Reeling from the information and from the death of Yoda, Luke returned to the fleet.

On the Rebel flagship out in open space, Alliance leader Mon Mothma addressed the troop leaders and explained the Rebellion's latest plan. Bothan spies had delivered the

The Super Star Destroyer Executor collides with the second Death Star during the Battle of Endor. [Art by Tommy Lee Edwards]

himself—the whole thing was a trap. An enormous Imperial battle fleet, led by the Super Star Destroyer *Executor,* emerged from the far side of Endor and began hammering the Alliance armada. Luke appealed to the lost sentiments of his father, trying to touch Vader's heart and turn him back to the light side of the Force. Darth Vader remained unconvinced.

The Rebel forces continued to be decimated, both by the Imperial fleet and by the Death Star's operational superlaser, which targeted capital ships and blasted them to powder. Lando Calrissian, leading the starfighter attack in *Millennium Falcon,* encouraged Admiral Ackbar to press the attack against the enemy battleships at point-blank range. Lando's move was risky, but it was the only tactic that could buy time until the team on the ground brought down the Death Star's shield projector.

The Emperor goaded Luke into snatching up his lightsaber, and father and son battled one another in a rematch of the duel they had fought on Cloud City. During the struggle, Vader's resolve began to flicker as he saw the good in his son. Through the Force, he also read in Luke's thoughts and learned of the existence of his daughter, the second of Padmé's twins. When Vader speculated that his daughter might make for a fitting dark side apprentice, a frantic Luke unleashed his pent-up rage. His fury gave him the strength to severely wound his father and cut off Vader's sword hand. Seeing Skywalker's raw emotion, the Emperor applauded, pleased to see him take the first steps toward the dark side.

But Luke surprised Palpatine by surrendering, refusing to continue the fight that would have resulted in his father's death and made him the Emperor's new Sith apprentice. A livid Palpatine then used his own dark powers to attack, searing Luke with blasts of blue lightning. As he watched the agony of his son and the Emperor's glee, Vader finally broke the hold of evil that had suffocated him for so long. Vader grabbed the energy-seething Palpatine and hurled him into the Death Star reactor shaft, where the evil leader was disintegrated. The shock waves of dark power mortally wounded Vader. Luke Skywalker could do nothing for his dying father, the terrible enemy who had saved him in the end.

On the surface of Endor, General Solo's mission had gone critically off course when stormtroopers and AT-ST scout walkers had ambushed the Rebel strike against the shield generator bunker. The Rebellion might have perished there had it not been for the Ewoks, who sprang from the forest to assail the Imperials with slings, arrows, and log traps. Han Solo planted explosive charges inside the bunker, and the giant projector dish vanished in a riot of fire. The energy shield surrounding the Death Star sputtered and died.

Rebel starfighters led by Lando Calrissian and Wedge Antilles raced into the Death Star's superstructure to drop a warhead directly into the central reactor core and trigger a chain reaction similar to the one that had destroyed the Death Star at Yavin. Outside, Admiral Ackbar's fleet continued the battle against enemy commander Admiral Piett's Star Destroyers. Rebel pilot Arvel Crynyd, his doomed A-wing disintegrating, steered his fighter into the bridge of Piett's flagship, the *Executor.* The grand Super Star Destroyer crashed into the hull of the Death Star and was completely annihilated. Lando and Wedge dropped their charge in the battle station's reactor and raced back out to space, one step ahead of the detonation wave.

Luke Skywalker dragged his dying father to a shuttle bay, but Vader died before they could escape. Skywalker took the black-clad body with him as he flew away, seconds before the Death Star detonated.

All around the galaxy, freedom-loving citizens celebrated the end of the New Order and the death of Emperor Palpatine. Though the Empire was far from vanquished, the Battle of Endor signified a crucial and decisive victory for the Rebellion.

At last, a New Republic could be born.

THE TRUCE AT BAKURA
4 A.B.Y.

After the remaining Imperial fleet's retreat from Endor, the Rebel Alliance had no time to savor their victory. The following day, an Imperial drone ship arrived at the site of the Death Star's cooling wreckage, with a message addressed to Emperor Palpatine. "Bakura is under attack from an alien invasion force from outside your domain. We have lost half our defense force and all outersystem out-

posts. Urgent, repeat urgent, send stormtroopers."

Mon Mothma gathered a small task force to go to the remote planet's defense. Luke Skywalker, still suffering from his injuries at the hands of the Emperor, received a visit from the Force spirit of Obi-Wan Kenobi. Kenobi urged his former protégé to attend to the Bakura matter personally, and Luke agreed to lead five Corellian gunships, one corvette, and *Millennium Falcon* to Bakura, at the edge of known space.

Bakura's peril came at the hands of the Ssi-ruuk, a species of warm-blooded saurians who had embarked on a campaign of conquest. Their "entechment" technology could transfer a human prisoner's life-energy into the circuits of a battle droid, giving the Ssi-ruuk a cheap and expendable fighting force. If they succeeded in enteching the population of Bakura, the Ssi-ruuk would have enough mechanical warriors to pose a threat to the entire galaxy.

The beleaguered Imperials of Bakura welcomed the small Alliance fleet. Eager to discuss a formal truce, Leia Organa met with Imperial Governor Wilek Nereus in the capital city of Salis D'aar. Governor Nereus, along with Prime Minister Yeorg Captison and his beautiful niece Gaeriel Captison, listened to the Alliance's offer. Nereus agreed to a cease-fire. With a handshake, the first-ever truce between Rebel and Imperial forces took effect.

Later that evening, Leia Organa received a visitation by an unwelcome presence—the spirit-form of Anakin Skywalker, her true father. The man who was once Darth Vader begged his daughter for her forgiveness. Leia, who had learned of her parentage only days earlier, was unable to forget the fact that Vader had tortured her aboard the Death Star and blasted her homeworld of Alderaan into cinders. The apparition vanished, and did not appear to his daughter again.

On board the mighty flagship *Shriwirr*, the Ssi-ruuk's Admiral Ivpikkis readied his battle droids for a single, overwhelming assault against Bakura. One of Ivpikkis's subor-

Ssi-ruuk armies run riot over a Bakuran plaza.
[ART BY TOMMY LEE EDWARDS]

dinates owned a brainwashed human "pet" who had been raised by the Ssi-ruuk since he was a young boy. This human collaborator, Dev Sibwarra, sensed the presence of Luke Skywalker through the Force and alerted his masters. The Ssi-ruuk hoped this powerful Jedi would be capable of entenching victims from great distances, sucking their life-energies from afar. Sibwarra secretly contacted Governor Nereus with an offer. If the governor would turn over Skywalker, the Ssi-ruuvi fleet would leave Bakura in peace.

Nereus was far too shrewd to take the aliens at their word, but he saw a devious way to eliminate *both* threats—Skywalker and the Ssi-ruuk—with a single thrust. He placed three Olabrian trichoid egg pods into Skywalker's food. The bloodsucking, highly contagious larvae would hatch in Skywalker's body once he was safely aboard the Ssi-ruuik flagship, killing him in gruesome fashion and infecting the aliens with a lethal parasite to which they had no natural immunity.

Nereus felt confident of victory, and arrested Leia Organa on charges of sedition. Many of Bakura's citizens saw the action as a clear abuse of authority, and rioting broke out in Salis D'aar.

Luke, captured by the Ssi-ruuk, was hooked into the *Shriwirr*'s entenchment rig. Dev Sibwarra, impressed by the Jedi's heroism, shrugged off his masters' brainwashing and helped Luke escape. Ivpikkis and the Ssi-ruuvi crew escaped the *Shriwirr* in life pods.

In orbit above Bakura, the Rebel and Imperial fleets formed a united front against the invaders, shelling the Ssi-ruuvi armada. In order to live and fight on, the saurians began a full retreat. Every Ssi-ruuvi vessel (except for the abandoned flagship *Shriwirr*) vanished into hyperspace toward the Unknown Regions.

But Nereus turned traitor yet again. With the Ssi-ruuk gone, he ordered his fleet to open fire on their ostensible allies. The Rebel flagship and many other ships were destroyed by Nereus's treachery. The surviving Rebel fighters were caught in a bottleneck with no hope of escape. General Solo grimly lined up a suicidal "carom shot" in which the *Falcon* would ram a small Imperial patrol craft, ricocheting the patrol craft into the Imperial command ship's main generator. Success meant escape for the Rebel fleet, but death for everyone aboard the *Falcon*.

The enemy craft, however, broke formation to strike at the *Shriwirr*. The *Falcon* aborted its carom shot, and instead rescued Luke Skywalker and Dev Sibwarra from the damaged *Shriwirr*. Luke had already sensed the presence of the Olabrian larval parasites in his bronchial tubes and used the Force to eliminate the threat.

The Rebel fleet rallied from near disaster. Commander Pter Thanas, leader of the Imperial defense force, surrendered. On Bakura, Governor Nereus was captured by resistance fighters, and killed in a mishap not long afterward.

It was a welcome victory. Prime Minister Captison assumed control of Bakura and joined the Rebels' fledgling Alliance of Free Planets. Commander Thanas oversaw the Imperial withdrawal from Bakura and then defected, agreeing to lead the Bakuran home defense force. Senator Gaeriel Captison had grown quite close to Luke Skywalker over the course of the incident, but she loved her homeworld even more. Gaeriel married Commander Thanas, and was eventually elected Prime Minister of Bakura. One of her first actions was to commission new, powerful defensive warships in case the Ssi-ruuk should ever return.

Despite all the medical attention Luke Skywalker could provide, Dev Sibwarra succumbed to injuries sustained during the battle aboard the *Shriwirr*. But Luke vowed to find more Force-sensitive candidates and eventually restore the order of Jedi Knights.

Onward to Ssi-ruuvi Space
4–5 A.B.Y.

A footnote to the Ssi-ruuvi incident, the invasion of Ssi-ruuvi space stretched on for a year and involved a dozen Nebulon-B frigates and smaller vessels accompanying the refitted Ssi-ruuvi flagship. This latter vessel had since been renamed *Sibwarra*, but its crew commonly called it the *Flutie*—a derisive nickname for the Ssi-ruuk, derived from their musical speech patterns.

Life aboard the *Sibwarra* was exceedingly odd. Throughout their tour of duty, the crew struggled with the ship's baffling onboard equipment. Several crewers were injured or killed by the confusing alien devices.

The Empire declined to join in on the attack. It was quite a surprise, then, when the *Sibwarra* arrived at the Ssi-ruuvi star cluster and discovered a half-beaten foe. The Chiss, striking from deep in the Unknown Regions, had already attacked the Ssi-ruuvi Imperium on the opposite front. It is believed that Grand Admiral Thrawn, newly returned to the Unknown Regions following his defeat of Grand Admiral Zaarin, had orchestrated the attack, combining his Imperial warships with renegade Chiss craft in what he was already calling his "Empire of the Hand."

The *Sibwarra* strike force engaged Admiral Ivpikkis of the Ssi-ruuvi fleet as they battled their way to Lwhekk, the Ssi-ruuvi homeworld. Eventually the two sides reached a standstill. Satisfied that the Ssi-ruuvi could not mount another invasion, Mon Mothma ordered the Alliance vessels to fall back and assist in the liberation of Clak'dor VII.

In the aftermath of the defeat, a Ssi-ruu called the Keeramak, whose multicolored scales were believed to be a sign of his near divinity, helped rally the P'w'eck slave species and overthrow what was left of the Ssi-ruuvi social order.

PART SIX

Birth of the New Republic

While Leia Organa, Han Solo, and Luke Skywalker defended Bakura from the Ssi-ruuk, Mon Mothma made preparations to establish a new galactic government. Clearly, it could take years, even decades, to eradicate the Empire, but the victory at Endor was a symbolic starting point for marking a new era.

THE ALLIANCE OF FREE PLANETS
4 A.B.Y.

Within days of the Battle of Endor, the Rebel Alliance became the Alliance of Free Planets, an interim stage until the details of the government could be worked out. Already, key star systems, including the Fondor shipyards in the Tapani sector, were announcing their defections from Imperial rule. From a temporary headquarters on Endor, the new government—which had just closed the books on the Ssi-ruuvi incident—suddenly had to deal with an invasion from a different quarter.

The Nagai, chalk-skinned humanoids who specialized in emotionless cruelty, launched an assault on the galactic southern quadrant. Believed to hail from one of the dwarf galaxies that orbit tightly around the known galaxy, the Nagai had allied with Shira Brie, now the Dark Lady Lumiya, to crush the fledgling government in its infancy. The Nagai forced the Alliance from its Endor base and attacked worlds from Iskalon to Zeltros.

The Nagai invasion ended as quickly as it began. The Tofs, a robust, boastful species from the same dwarf galaxy and the traditional enemies of the Nagai, followed their prey to the new killing grounds. In a final confrontation on Saijo, the Alliance wound up fighting alongside the Nagai to force a surrender from the Tof crown prince. The Nagai survivors returned home. Lumiya fled the battle and retreated to the ancient Sith worlds, where she trained her first apprentice, Flint, and later the Royal Guardsman Carnor Jax.

Dark Lady Lumiya, formerly known as Shira Brie.
[ART BY MARK CHIARELLO]

DECLARATION OF A NEW REPUBLIC
4 A.B.Y.

One month after the formation of the Alliance of Free Planets, Mon Mothma formally issued the "Declaration of a New Republic" on the public HoloNet channels. Though the Battle of Endor is viewed as the beginning of the New Republic era, Mon Mothma's pronouncement marked the official establishment of the true government. The document was signed by Mon Mothma, Leia Organa, Borsk Fey'lya, and Admiral Ackbar, as well as officials from Corellia, Duro, Kashyyyk, Sullust, and Elom. Under the New Republic's first charter, these nine individuals comprised the New Republic Provisional Council. Mon Mothma was elected Chief Councilor.

For several months, the New Republic made no large-scale military invasions into Imperial territory. Instead, they consolidated their holdings and won over hundreds of planets through diplomacy. News of the Emperor's death caused countless worlds to join the New Republic's fold, most of them in the Rim territories. Captain Wedge Antilles and the X-wing pilots of Rogue Squadron acted as scouts, escorts, and negotiators during this period.

Disappointingly, a promising opportunity to bolster the New Republic Fleet fell apart when Kuat Drive Yards (KDY), the Empire's leading shipbuilder, failed to switch allegiances. During the Battle of Endor, KDY's former CEO had committed suicide and destroyed a portion of the Kuat shipyards rather than see his independent corporation nationalized by the Empire. The New Republic hoped that his successor would be an ally, but she quickly repaired the damaged dry docks and cozied up to Sate Pestage, the new Imperial leader.

IMPERIAL FRAGMENTATION
4–4.5 A.B.Y.

One reason the New Republic saw no need for an immediate strike against the Empire was that the Empire was doing a fine job of tearing itself apart.

Without Palpatine's commanding presence, the Imperial war machine seemed unfocused. After the destruction of the second Death Star, the Imperial fleet had continued to fight for four hours under the command of Grand Admiral Teshik—but were systematically beaten back by their numerically inferior foe. When Rebel forces disabled Teshik's ship, Captain Gilad Pellaeon of the Star Destroyer *Chimaera* ordered the fleet to retreat and regroup at Annaj, where the first signs of stress began to show.

Admiral Harrsk, commander of one task force within the Endor fleet, saw the death of the Emperor as a great opportunity, and was unwilling to take orders from Pellaeon, a mere captain. Harrsk took his segment of the fleet and jumped to the restricted Deep Core at the very center of the galaxy. There, among the secure Imperial safeworlds, Harrsk began building up his own pocket empire.

Though Harrsk was the Empire's first breakaway warlord, he wouldn't be the last. The Empire had long rewarded ambition over cooperation—only cruel and intimidating leaders, such as Palpatine and Vader, had kept their subordinates in line. Suddenly, post-Endor, everyone wanted to rule the Empire, or at least create their own kingdoms. More than any other factor, warlordism was responsible for the decline of the Empire.

Many other warlords broke away in the first few months. Admiral Teradoc followed Harrsk's lead and established a miniature empire in the Mid Rim just days after Endor. Admiral Gaen Drommel became the dictator of his home sector using the Super Star Destroyer *Guardian*. Grand Moff Ardus Kaine, Tarkin's successor, walled off a large chunk of the Outer Rim Territories and dubbed it the Pentastar Alignment. "Superior General" Delvardus laid claim to most of the worlds near the Rimma Trade Route, until battles forced him into the Deep Core. Grand Admirals Grunger and Pitta locked themselves into a struggle over the Corellian sector. Admiral Zsinj, ruler of the Quelii sector, would later prove to be one of the New Republic's most formidable foes.

To add to the confusion, Palpatine had not been truly destroyed at Endor. As with Obi-Wan Kenobi, the Emperor's spirit-form had survived when his body died. Palpatine's life-essence made a tortuous journey to his hidden throneworld of Byss in the Deep Core, where it inhabited the body of a fresh young clone. Palpatine's clone began to consolidate his own forces, though it would be years before he made his presence known to the galaxy.

It was obvious that Sate Pestage, the Emperor's former Grand Vizier and the man responsible for keeping the Empire intact, was failing miserably. Pestage had been cunning enough to assume the Imperial throne upon learning of his master's death. But the Grand Vizier lacked the charisma and influence to lead the Empire, and he had a host of enemies within the Imperial Palace. Pestage's chief rivals were Palpatine's former advisory staff, who had formed a tribunal known as the Ruling Circle. As they schemed to overthrow the new Emperor, Pestage plotted to keep the Ruling Circle in check. Ysanne Isard, head of Imperial Intelligence, acted as a neutral intermediary between the two parties.

Neither faction realized Isard's true goal until it was too late. Isard was secretly pitting each side against the other so she could rise from their ashes and rule as Empress.

BLACK NEBULA
4–4.5 A.B.Y.

The Black Sun criminal syndicate could not recover from the death of its leader, Prince Xizor. The various lieutenants, or vigos, began to fight over what remained. One of Black Sun's lesser operatives, a Jeodu named Dequc, tried to revive the organization under the name Black Nebula, with himself as its head. Palpatine had ordered Dequc eliminated; mere days before Endor, Mara Jade, one of the Emperor's Hands, had executed him on Svivren. Mara later learned that the victim on Svivren had been a decoy. Dequc continued to expand Black Nebula in the post-Palpatine Empire, until Mara tracked him down and killed him on Qiaxx several months later.

Ysanne Isard and Sate Pestage discuss who will inherit the Emperor's throne. [ART BY TOMMY LEE EDWARDS]

At the same time, Savan, Prince Xizor's niece, attempted to piece together the remaining factions of Black Sun. The key to Savan's plot was the human replica droid known as Guri, who had formerly been Xizor's second in command and knew all the syndicate's secrets. Savan located Guri on Hurd's Moon, where she was undergoing synaptic rewiring to erase her memory and her assassin droid programming.

Councilor Leia Organa and generals Han Solo and Lando Calrissian also journeyed to Hurd's Moon, attempting to prevent the rise of another destructive criminal empire. After a shootout, they took Savan into custody. Guri, her criminal programming purged, was allowed to go free.

Black Nebula crumbled without Dequc, and Xizor's vigos murdered each other in an internecine bloodbath. Black Sun was dead, and it would remain defunct until the New Republic inadvertently resurrected the syndicate during the liberation of Coruscant three years later.

ISARD'S ASCENSION
4.5–5 A.B.Y.

Ysanne Isard's conspiracy began to bear fruit when the New Republic threatened Brentaal, a wealthy and influential Core world not far from Ralltiir, which had fallen to the New Republic only days before. As the New Republic military geared up for an all-out assault from their base on nearby Recopia, Sate Pestage vowed that Brentaal would not fall.

Under Isard's advice, Pestage allowed the incompetent Admiral Isoto to defend Brentaal. Baron Soontir Fel and the legendary 181st Imperial fighter wing did what they could, but Isoto's bumblings allowed the New Republic to capture the world. During the final battle, Baron Fel was taken prisoner by the New Republic. Fel would later fly with the X-wing pilots of Rogue Squadron, until his disappearance into the Unknown Regions.

To all appearances, Pestage had been responsible for the loss of Brentaal, and the Ruling Circle screamed for his head. Knowing that Isard had sold him out, Pestage

Mara Jade, former Imperial assassin.
[ART BY JOHN VAN FLEET]

made preparations to defect.

On Axxila, Pestage held a secret meeting with Councilor Leia Organa to discuss the terms of his surrender. In exchange for leaving Coruscant undefended against a New Republic assault, he asked for twenty-five planets that he could rule as he pleased. Realizing that Coruscant was the key to the war effort, Leia agreed to Pestage's offer, despite her misgivings. Isard learned of the Axxila talks and informed the Ruling Circle of Pestage's treachery. An order was issued for his arrest, and the Ruling Circle set itself up as the new governing power in the Empire.

Sate Pestage fled to Ciutric, but was apprehended by the local Imperial governor. Though the Axxila deal was obviously dead, the New Republic felt it had to take action. If Pestage were rescued by the New Republic, it would serve as an example to other high-ranking Imperials and encourage further defections. Rogue Squadron and a commando team were sent to Ciutric to retrieve Pestage.

The rescue operation failed. Pestage was murdered by Imperial Admiral Krennel, who then seized Pestage's personal territory—the Ciutric Hegemony—and set himself up as the Empire's latest breakaway warlord. On Coruscant, Ysanne Isard ruthlessly exterminated the Ruling Circle and assumed the throne in their place. Isard would succeed where the others had failed, holding the crumbling Empire together for more than two years.

Eight months after the Battle of Endor, Admiral Ackbar and the New Republic Fleet made another aggressive push into Imperial territory. Ackbar defeated Grand Admiral Syn at Kashyyyk and scored other victories in the Mid and Inner Rims. Concerned that the campaign might presage a siege of Coruscant, Isard recalled hundreds of Star Destroyers to defend the capital planet and other key Core Worlds.

One of the Imperial armadas that received the order was the Black Sword Command in the Koornacht Cluster, a little-known patch of territory at the fringes of the Deep Core. As the Black Fleet prepared to evacuate the central shipbuilding planet of N'zoth, the shipyards' Yevethan dockworkers erupted in a shocking uprising. Led by underground commando Nil Spaar, the Yevetha murdered thousands of Imperials, captured hundreds more, and seized every Star Destroyer in the Black Fleet armada—including the Super Star Destroyer *Intimidator*.

The Yevetha covered up the incident. The New Republic never heard a word about it, and Isard—operating on inaccurate intelligence data—believed that the Black Fleet had perished in a debacle at Cal-Seti, several sectors over. The Koornacht Cluster would remain a closed-border curiosity until the frantic events of the Black Fleet Crisis, twelve years in the future.

General Skywalker challenges Lord Shadowspawn's troops on Mindor.
[Art by Tommy Lee Edwards]

One year after the Emperor's death, the Central Committee of Grand Moffs decided to increase their own power base by moving against Isard. They proclaimed their own candidate—Trioculus, a former Kessel slave lord—as Imperial leader, and attempted to rally the fleet behind him, eliminating such possible rivals as Grand Admiral Takel. Some followed their lead, but the bulk of the fleet, including Captain Pellaeon of the Star Destroyer *Chimaera*, remained loyal to Isard.

The New Republic moved against the Grand Moffs under the auspices of the Senate Planetary Intelligence Network (SPIN), a newly formed analysis and infiltration task force. Isard, meanwhile, freed Jabba the Hutt's father, Zorba, from

prison and sent him into the fray as her unwitting agent. Zorba seized Cloud City from Lando Calrissian, who had only recently rescued the city from the clutches of the Empire. In the end, the matter was settled without a fleet battle. Trioculus, Zorba, and a shadowy group of mystics called the Prophets of the Dark Side wiped each other out in an internal struggle. Those Grand Moffs who had been involved in the conspiracy were executed, and Isard's position at the head of the Empire was more secure than ever.

Several months later, Ysanne Isard was instrumental in foiling a New Republic espionage mission to Coruscant. Pilot Tycho Celchu, a member of Rogue Squadron, took a TIE fighter that had been captured during the truce at Bakura and infiltrated the Imperial capital. Isard, however, uncovered the spy and imprisoned him in the hellish prison known only as *Lusankya.* Celchu eventually escaped to the New Republic, but was viewed with suspicion by many, who suspected that he had been brainwashed into becoming a sleeper agent.

GENERAL SKYWALKER
5–5.5 A.B.Y.

Throughout the Trioculus affair, the New Republic was engaged in a protracted military campaign for possession of Milagro, a world at a key hyperspace junction.

The Empire was prepared to lay waste to Milagro rather than allow the Rebels access to its manufacturing facilities. Following three months of exhausting clashes between AT-AT walkers and the New Republic Army, the defeated Imperials slagged the planet's surface with a withering orbital bombardment, then fled.

The New Republic remained in the system, using the Dreadnaught *New Hope* as an orbital HQ. Soon after the disbanding of SPIN, a damaged Imperial Star Destroyer leapt into the Milagro system, hoping to effect repairs. Instead, they stumbled into a brawl with the *New Hope.* General Solo led the fighter attack, while Mon Mothma coordinated the battle from the bridge of *New Hope.* Finally, Luke Skywalker's superior X-wing tactics forced the Imperials' surrender. The captured Star Destroyer was renamed *Crynyd* in honor of the A-wing pilot whose self-sacrifice at the Battle of Endor took down the Super Star Destroyer *Executor.* For his heroism at Milagro, Commander Skywalker was at last promoted to the rank of general.

General Skywalker was quickly saddled with the responsibilities of command, a burden he loathed. Ever since his experience at Bakura, Skywalker had grown less interested in military conquest and more interested in the spiritual understanding of the Force. Skywalker's views were reinforced when he witnessed the heroic deeds of Kyle Katarn—a Force-sensitive individual who, five years earlier, had helped recover the Death Star plans and sabotaged the Empire's Dark Trooper program. Now Katarn was realizing his own potential as a Jedi.

Several of the Emperor's Dark Side Adepts, led by the Dark Jedi Jerec, had attracted corporate backers to form a warlord cabal. Their influence was limited, but Jerec had discovered the Valley of the Jedi on Ruusan, where the spirits of the Brotherhood of Darkness and Army of Light had been trapped in limbo for a thousand years. Jerec planned to use the valley's power to topple Isard and rule a vast new Empire. Katarn single-handedly defeated Jerec and his minions before the Dark Jedi's grandiose plans could come to fruition.

Skywalker, impressed, offered to train Katarn as a Jedi apprentice, but the other man declined. Soon afterward, the New Republic became bogged down in a brutal military campaign in the Inner Rim. Skywalker led his troops onto the battlefields of Mindor, digging out entrenched pockets of Imperial resistance. Stormtroopers, under the command of Lord Shadowspawn, fought to the last man. Though Fenn Shysa and his new Mandalorian Protectors helped deliver the deciding blow against Shadowspawn, Skywalker grew dismayed at the bloodshed and unnecessary loss of life.

Less than six months after receiving his general's commission, Luke Skywalker resigned from the New Republic military.

The Last Grand Admiral?
6 A.B.Y.

Emperor Palpatine frequently rewarded his most capable servants with grandiose titles, further encouraging the notorious Imperial culture of greed and ambition. The best stormtroopers were molded into Royal Guards, and there were rumors that the best Royal Guards became Imperial Sovereign Protectors on Byss. Initially, the highest possible rank in the Imperial Navy was admiral, until two years before the Battle of Yavin, when Palpatine created the elite rank of Grand Admiral. There could never be more than twelve Grand Admirals at one time.

The twelve Grand Admirals, easily recognizable by their stark white uniforms and braided gold epaulets, were the best of the best—unparalleled geniuses at military strategy. Only Admiral Ackbar could be considered their equal in the New Republic Navy. In the aftermath of Endor, had the surviving Grand Admirals united against their common enemy, the New Republic could have been wiped out while still in its infancy.

Fortunately, that threat never materialized. The first Grand Admiral to fall was Zaarin, whose coup d'état had ended in disaster just before Endor. Grand Admiral Declann perished with the second Death Star. Grand Admiral Teshik, captured at Endor, was executed by the New Republic. Grand Admiral Syn was outfought by Ackbar during the liberation of Kashyyyk, his flagship vaporized. Grand Admirals Grunger and Pitta turned warlord and annihilated each other in a bitter and ultimately futile fight for control of the Corellian sector. Grand Admiral Takel was executed by Trioculus, while the Central Committee of Grand Moffs did away with Grand Admiral Tigellinus for perceived disloyalty. The fanatical Grand Admiral Il-Raz committed suicide by plunging his flagship into the heart of the Denarii Nova, shortly before the events that eliminated Grand Admiral Makati. Grand Admiral Batch was assassinated by his second in command, who then took the ships in Batch's task force and joined Warlord Harrsk in the Deep Core.

Grand Admiral Grant, the so-called last Grand Admiral, defected to the New Republic on the condition that he be granted immunity from prosecution for war crimes and allowed to retire on Rathalay. The defection took place two years after Endor. The New Republic closed the books on the Emperor's Grand Admirals, believing that they had finally all been accounted for.

No one realized that one Grand Admiral remained at large, possibly the most dangerous of all. Blue-skinned Thrawn, the "thirteenth Grand Admiral," had been promoted by Palpatine in a secret ceremony following the treason of Grand Admiral Zaarin. Soon afterward, Thrawn had been sent to the Unknown Regions to continue his exploration near Chiss space, accounting for the New Republic's oversight. Years would pass before Thrawn's return, when the New Republic would once again learn to fear the title of Grand Admiral.

THE BATTLE FOR CORUSCANT
6.5–7 A.B.Y.

Two and a half years after the birth of the New Republic, the Empire was still the galaxy's dominant government. Despite the rise of rogue warlords, Imperials held a majority of settled planets and had a stranglehold on the important Core Worlds. Without an aggressive military push, the New Republic would never bring about an end to the Galactic Civil War.

The most effective way to destroy the Empire would be to capture Coruscant, the universal symbol of governmental power and authority. The New Republic began seizing planets in Imperial territory as "stepping-stones" to a strike at Coruscant. As part of the mobilization, Wedge Antilles was recalled from a propaganda tour and restored to active duty. Antilles's legendary X-wing unit, Rogue Squadron, was reformed with a roster of new pilots.

The New Republic captured Borleias, in the Colonies region, after two costly attacks. Borleias was perfectly situated as a forward base for a Coruscant assault. Admiral Ackbar, however, knew that the capital's defensive energy shield would negate any orbital bombardment. Before any attack could begin, Coruscant's shield must fall.

Antilles and Rogue Squadron were sent undercover into Imperial City to sabotage the planet's shield generator. At the same time, sixteen of the galaxy's worst criminals were freed from the spice mines of Kessel and let loose on Coruscant, in the hope that they would foster chaos. The latter decision was unusual for the New Republic, and opposed by many members of the Ruling Council, who were proven correct in the end. The freed criminals, led by Y'ull Acib, resurrected the defunct Black Sun criminal cartel, which would plague the New Republic in later years.

Rogue Squadron's operatives gambled that if they could condense a large amount of water vapor and create a massive storm, they could knock out Coruscant's shields with lightning strikes. The Rogues commandeered a forty-story construction droid to take them to a command building, and then took remote control of one of the planet's orbiting solar mirrors. The tightly focused light beam from the mirror flash-boiled one of Imperial City's artificial reservoirs. The steam cloud coalesced into an angry cloudburst, and soon the shields collapsed.

With Coruscant vulnerable, Ackbar leapt into the system with a full armada. The battle was intense, but victory came surprisingly easily—Ysanne Isard had kept only a handful

of Star Destroyers to defend the capital. Ackbar wiped out all resistance, and at last Coruscant was in the hands of the New Republic.

THE KRYTOS VIRUS
7–7.5 A.B.Y.

When the New Republic secured the Imperial Palace, they discovered that Isard had vanished. Worse, she had left behind a sick and dying world.

After years of work on an isolated biological research asteroid, Isard's chief scientist, Evir Derricote, had engineered an artificial plague—the Krytos virus. Within days of transmission, Krytos turned healthy flesh into a bloody soup. Isard had seeded Coruscant's water reservoirs with the plague before the Rebels arrival, and millions of citizens had already contracted the disease. However, Derricote had carefully tailored the Krytos virus to affect only specific nonhuman species—Sullustans, Gamorreans, and others. The fact that Coruscant's human population was immune drove a wedge between the New Republic's member species.

The Krytos plague spoiled the New Republic's triumph and made it look ineffectual and weak. Thus, governing the civilian population of Coruscant was nearly impossible. Furthermore, Mon Mothma was forced to spend millions of credits on voluminous amounts of bacta to treat the infected and research a vaccine—credits that the near-bankrupt government didn't have.

Diverting the public's attention during this difficult time was the trial of Tycho Celchu. Celchu, a member of Rogue Squadron, had been arrested for treason and the murder of his fellow pilot Corran Horn immediately following the liberation of Coruscant. No one had forgotten that two years earlier, Celchu had been captured on an undercover mission and incarcerated in the Empire's *Lusankya* prison. Prosecuting attorneys at his trial claimed Celchu had been operating as a brainwashed Imperial agent ever since.

Victorious troopers raise the New Republic banner on Coruscant.
[ART BY TOMMY LEE EDWARDS]

The truth was even more shocking—not only was Celchu innocent, but Corran Horn was alive. Horn had been secretly captured by Isard and himself imprisoned in *Lusankya,* where he was forced to undergo regular torture and indoctrination sessions. His only relief came in conversation with his fellow prisoners, one of whom was the famed Alliance leader Jan Dodonna, who had been captured during the evacuation of Yavin 4 seven years earlier.

Horn escaped, forcing Isard to abandon her hiding place. As the members of Rogue Squadron flew a mission above Imperial City, a panicked call suddenly came from the Manarai Mountain district. Antilles saw a massive object rising from the subterranean depths, obliterating vast tracts of homes and businesses as it came to the surface—a Super Star Destroyer that answered to the name *Lusankya.* Despite the efforts of Rogue Squadron to stop it, the *Lusankya* tore a gaping hole out of Imperial City's heart, killing millions in its effort to free itself. It then vanished into hyperspace.

The presence of Corran Horn, alive, cleared Celchu of the murder charge. Luke Skywalker investigated Horn's background and discovered that the pilot was actually the grandson of the great Jedi Nejaa Halcyon, who had fought with honor at Praesitlyn during the Clone Wars. Horn refused Skywalker's offer to train him as a Jedi, but he reconsidered his decision years later.

New Republic scientists developed a cure for the Krytos virus by mixing bacta with the spice ryll kor. The resulting vaccine, rylca, was administered to Coruscant's alien population and prevented further loss of life.

THE BACTA WAR
7.5 A.B.Y.

Ysanne Isard fled Coruscant aboard the *Lusankya* and quickly acted to hold her power base. At Thyferra, the bacta-manufacturing planet, she supported a coup and was elected Head of State by the victorious faction. The New Republic was unhappy with the development, but it was against their principles to depose a duly elected planetary leader. Since the Thyferran government refused to move against Isard, Antilles and Rogue Squadron resigned from the New Republic Fleet. As civilians, they answered to no one, and were free to move against Isard on their own.

But the bacta planet was defended by four capital ships: the *Lusankya,* two Imperial Star Destroyers, and a Victory Star Destroyer. A direct, frontal assault would be a quick way to commit suicide. Instead, Antilles flitted around like a Sacorrian grain fly—stinging Isard, then retreating to a safe distance before she could swat back. The Rogues occupied an abandoned space station near Yag'Dhul as a base of operations, and hired smuggler Booster Terrik to manage the station. Terrik obtained weapons from the smuggling kingpin

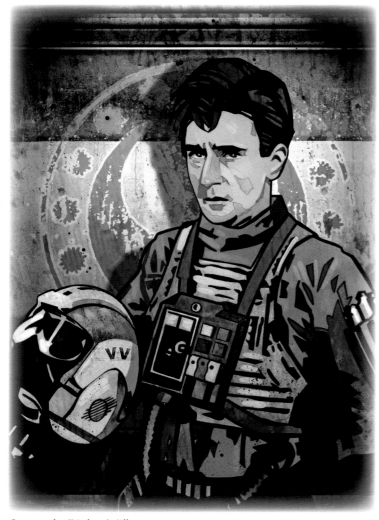

Commander Wedge Antilles
[Art by John Van Fleet]

Talon Karrde, and Rogue Squadron began harassing Isard's bacta convoys.

Rogue Squadron destroyed one capital ship in a fight near the rubble of the Alderaan Graveyard, and convinced the captain of another ship to defect. With half of her defensive force suddenly gone, Isard ordered the *Lusankya* and her remaining Star Destroyer to blast the Rogues' Yag'Dhul space station into atoms.

Antilles and the other Rogues seized the opportunity and jumped into hyperspace to attack the now undefended Thyferra. At Yag'Dhul, the *Lusankya* closed to firing range, but the space station suddenly locked on to the Super Star Destroyer with more than three hundred proton torpedoes. Knowing that no vessel's shields could withstand such a volley, the *Lusankya* fled to Thyferra, and the remaining outgunned Star Destroyer surrendered.

It was all a bluff perpetuated by Antilles. The Yag'Dhul space station didn't have *any* torpedoes, just three hundred targeting locks. The torpedoes were aboard the small armada of freighters and X-wings heading for Thyferra.

At the bacta planet, the Rogues and the *Lusankya* both emerged from hyperspace and fell upon one another with a vengeance. More than eighty proton torpedoes impacted against the Super Star Destroyer, collapsing its shields and ripping its guts open. When Booster Terrik arrived aboard the newly captured Star Destroyer and joined the fight, the ailing *Lusankya* surrendered. The *Lusankya* was towed to a secret shipyard for extensive repairs. Sadly, Jan Dodonna and the rest of the prisoners had been transferred off the ship weeks earlier. Their rescue would happen another day.

Ysanne Isard was smart enough to know when she was beaten, and attempted to escape Thyferra. Her shuttle was destroyed while trying to make the jump to hyperspace, and Isard was believed killed. Isard, however, had engineered the incident to cover her tracks. She spent the following years putting herself back together mentally, and would plague the New Republic again in the wake of the Thrawn incident.

Antilles and Rogue Squadron were welcomed back as heroes. After much wrangling, New Republic Intelligence allowed Booster Terrik to keep his captured Star Destroyer, which he renamed the *Errant Venture.* The ship became a movable trading bazaar, famous for eclectic merchandise.

In the aftermath of the Bacta War, the New Republic captured another Star Destroyer, the *Tyrant,* from an underdefended Imperial fueling outpost. This ship had been a member of Vader's Death Squadron and had assisted in the decimation of Echo Base on Hoth. Impressed by the symbolism, Councilor Organa renamed the vessel *Rebel Dream* and made it her personal flagship.

THE HUNT FOR ZSINJ
7.5–8 A.B.Y.

The New Republic had been right about one thing: controlling Coruscant was the key to the Galactic Civil War. As soon as Isard lost control of the capital world, the fragmentation of the Empire grew more severe as officers lost faith in their leaders. A coalition of Moffs and Imperial advisers replaced Isard, but found their power slipping away in favor of warlords like Zsinj.

Zsinj was now the most powerful Imperial warlord, having gained many new officers, ships, and planets during the post-Isard defections. He was also arrogant enough to fight his war on two fronts, both against the New Republic and against his former comrades in the Empire, whom he viewed as weak-willed and ineffectual. Furthermore, he possessed the mighty Super Star Destroyer *Iron Fist,* which could take on an entire armada by itself. The New Republic made the liberation of Zsinj's dominion a top priority and put together a task force under the command of General Solo to hunt down the warlord. The task force departed on its mission just prior to the events of the Bacta War.

Aboard the Mon Calamari flagship *Mon Remonda,* Solo probed the borders of Zsinj-controlled territory and witnessed firsthand the horrors that the warlord perpetrated on worlds that resisted his will. Solo was supplemented by the best military units the New Republic had to offer, including the legendary Rogue Squadron—but another group of X-wing pilots would provide the key to toppling Warlord Zsinj.

Commander Wedge Antilles, following his reinstatement in the New Republic military, chose not to join *Mon Remonda.* Instead, Antilles assembled a new group of pilots, dubbed Wraith Squadron, composed of commandos, snipers, spies, and infiltrators to whom piloting a starfighter was of only secondary importance. Soon after their formation, the Wraiths captured a Corellian corvette belonging to Zsinj and decided to pose as the corvette's crew. The ruse allowed them to infiltrate Zsinj's fleet and learn of an ambush planned against the New Republic on Ession in the Corporate Sector. The Battle of Ession was a victory for the New Republic, which demolished one of Zsinj's Star Destroyers and bombed a key manufacturing plant into oblivion.

The subterfuge with the captured corvette would not work a second time, so the commandos of Wraith Squadron changed tactics. They posed as a pirate band in order to work their way into Zsinj's loose organization of freelance raiders. The warlord hired the disguised Wraiths as mercenaries for his strike on the vast shipbuilding facilities in the Kuat system. Kuat Drive Yards, still allied with the Empire, had nearly completed a new Super Star Destroyer. Zsinj planned to steal the colossal vessel and pair it with *Iron Fist* to deliver a double hammer blow to his enemies. New Republic saboteurs foiled Zsinj's plans by destroying both of the new vessel's topside shield generator domes, and *Mon Remonda* blasted the unprotected warship to scrap. *Iron Fist* escaped into hyperspace.

Solo headed back out to hunt down Zsinj. The warlord, however, had a more devious plot afoot. Several of Zsinj's pet scientists had developed a method of rapid, forced brainwashing that could turn even the most placid citizen into a raving murderer, and the technique was tailored to work only with specific species—Twi'leks, Gotals, Sullustans, and others. Much as Ysanne Isard had attempted to do with the "aliens only" Krytos virus, Zsinj preyed on the suspicions and resentment that many species felt toward humans. "Project Minefield," as it was known in Zsinj's organization, resulted in hundreds of deaths, including several high-profile assassination attempts. A brainwashed Twi'lek tried to kill Ackbar, while Mon Mothma's loyal Gotal bodyguard suddenly turned on her, but died before he could injure the Chief Councilor. Aboard *Mon Remonda,* a Twi'lek A-wing pilot shot out the bridge viewport and nearly killed Han Solo through explosive decompression. New Republic Intelligence cracked the pattern behind the attacks and shut down Project Minefield before it could cause further havoc.

In an unprecedented move, the New Republic formed a loose alliance with the Empire to wipe out Zsinj. The Imperial fleet had its own anti-Zsinj task force, led by Admiral Rogriss. A New Republic representative held a secret meeting with Rogriss aboard his flagship, and the two sides hammered out an uneasy agreement—each side would exchange all intelligence data it had gathered on Zsinj's organization, no strings attached. The Empire and the New Republic now viewed Zsinj as their common foe.

Growing frustrated at the length of the campaign and the paucity of his victories, Han Solo authorized a number of lures to draw out Zsinj and force a confrontation. Since the warlord increasingly regarded the conflict as a personal showdown between himself and Solo, a mock-up of *Millennium Falcon* was constructed and flown to worlds deep in Zsinj's territory. This vessel was later fitted with a bomb and used to destroy an enemy Dreadnaught.

Zsinj, however, did not take the bait. He realized the Imperial–Republic collaboration was crippling his ability to hold his kingdom together, and devised a secret stratagem of survival. Since his enemies seemed fixated on the destruction of *Iron Fist,* Zsinj resolved to give them the illusion of what they craved. His agents gathered up the wreckage of the Super Star Destroyer ruined at Kuat and pieced it back together in a hodgepodge of structural beams and hull plates. On the bow of the makeshift vessel they printed the words IRON FIST, then waited for the warlord's orders.

Solo and Rogriss collaborated on an assault in the Va-haba asteroid belt that severely damaged the real *Iron Fist.* The wounded Super Star Destroyer jumped to the nearby system of Selaggis, but Solo followed with his full fleet, intent on blasting Zsinj into vapor. As *Mon Remonda* closed to firing range, the crippled *Iron Fist* disappeared into a black cube of nothingness.

Warlord Zsinj had obtained an orbital nightcloak—a string of satellites that absorb all visible light. By deploying the nightcloak in a cube pattern, he had created a small hideaway that his enemy's sensors couldn't penetrate. The decoy Star Destroyer was already in position inside the nightcloak, and Zsinj triggered its destruction. Then *Iron Fist* jumped to hyperspace.

When the nightcloak collapsed, Solo saw the wreckage of a Super Star Destroyer that clearly bore the markings of *Iron Fist.* Confident that Zsinj's fleet had been crippled beyond recovery, Solo ordered a triumphant return to Coruscant.

THE HAPANS AND THE DATHOMIR NIGHTSISTERS
8 A.B.Y.

General Han Solo and *Mon Remonda* returned to Coruscant after their seeming victory over Warlord Zsinj. The arduous, five-month campaign had exhausted everyone in the task force, and Han planned to put his crew in for some much-needed downtime. When he arrived at the capital world, however, he was startled to see dozens of saucer-shaped Battle Dragons in orbit. The mysterious Hapans had made a social call.

Any description of the Hapes Consortium requires superlatives—it is the most powerful, wealthy, cultured, and standoffish political federation in its region of space. Three thousand years earlier, the Hapan Queen Mother had sealed the borders of the star cluster, and as Hapes developed in isolation behind the Transitory Mists, legends of its fantastic riches continued to grow.

Several months earlier, Councilor Leia Organa's diplomatic visit to the sixty-three Hapan worlds had convinced the Queen Mother Ta'a Chume to consider the possibility of a union with the New Republic. The Hapan honor fleet

circling Coruscant was a remarkable sight, the first time in millennia that the reclusive society had made significant outside contact.

In Coruscant's Grand Reception Hall the Hapan delegation presented Councilor Organa with many extravagant gifts, including several Imperial Star Destroyers captured by the Hapans during recent border skirmishes. But the final gift was the biggest surprise of all. Prince Isolder, the Queen Mother's son and heir, presented himself to Leia as a marriage suitor.

Leia was shocked, but politically savvy enough to realize the benefits of an arranged marriage between two political factions. Knowing that the Hapan navy and treasury could help greatly in ending the Galactic Civil War, Mon Mothma urged her friend to accept Isolder's offer.

General Solo, however, grew deeply jealous of the attention showered on his longtime love interest. Hoping to secure Leia's affection, he won a habitable planet, Dathomir, worth 2.4 billion credits, in an outrageously high-stakes sabacc game. Han hoped the planet could house the homeless refugees of Alderaan. Unfortunately, Dathomir was deep in the heart of Zsinj's territory. Disappointed that his gamble had failed and desperate to get Leia's attention, Solo impulsively resigned his general's commission and kidnapped her.

Millennium Falcon emerged from hyperspace near the blue-green world of Dathomir. There, Solo discovered that Zsinj had built an orbital stardock above the planet, where the Super Star Destroyer *Iron Fist* was undergoing reconstruction. The *Falcon* fell under attack and barely managed to touch down on Dathomir's forested surface.

The group headed off on foot through the woods, but they were soon intercepted by a patrol of female warriors belonging to the Singing Mountain Clan. These Witches of Dathomir rode trained rancors and could cast "magic spells" by tapping into the Force. They were the descendents of

The Nightsisters—Sith witches of Dathomir
[Art by Tommy Lee Edwards]

143

Warlord Zsinj
[Art by John Van Fleet]

Isolder of Hapes on a rescue mission to Dathomir. The two men discovered the rusting wreck of the *Chu'unthor* and met Teneniel Djo, a beautiful witch of the Singing Mountain Clan. She reunited them with Han and Leia.

But their problems were far from over. The Nightsister clan launched an attack on the Singing Mountain Clan in an effort to steal the *Falcon.* The Nightsisters wielded dark side powers, and had an army of Imperial slaves at their disposal. Eight years earlier, the Emperor had constructed a prison on Dathomir, but when he'd learned of the Nightsisters, he had destroyed all of the prison's starships from orbit—better to lose a prison than to let rival Force users loose upon the galaxy. The Nightsisters were desperate to escape their planet, and directed their prison army in a fierce but ultimately futile attack on the Singing Mountain stronghold.

THE DEATH OF ZSINJ
8 A.B.Y.

Warlord Zsinj was well aware of the existence of the Nightsisters and the depth of their power. He opened negotiations with Gethzerion, leader of the Nightsisters, and delivered an ultimatum. Gethzerion would give him Han Solo, or he would activate his orbital nightcloak—the light-absorbing device used at the Battle of Selaggis. A full array of nightcloak satellites in position around Dathomir would turn the planet into an ice ball within days.

When he learned that the Nightsisters' attack on the Singing Mountain Clan had failed, Zsinj activated the nightcloak to encourage Gethzerion's immediate compliance. The skies grew dark and the temperature plunged as the shrewd Witch made her counteroffer. Gethzerion agreed to provide Han Solo, but also asked for a ship to escape her dying planet. Zsinj agreed to send two ves-

Allya, the fallen Jedi Knight who had been exiled to the planet more than six centuries in the past, and they had been largely ignored since Quinlan Vos's investigation into the Infinity Gate incident prior to the Clone Wars.

Luke Skywalker, meanwhile, had been scouring the galaxy for lost secrets of the Jedi Order. On Toola he discovered data cards telling the story of Master Yoda's efforts to recover the Jedi training ship *Chu'unthor* from Dathomir. Skywalker returned to Coruscant and learned of his sister's kidnapping; before long he had agreed to team up with Prince

sels—an armed craft for transporting Solo, and a defense-less, stripped-down model for the Nightsisters to use as they pleased.

Han Solo was brought to the Imperial prison, where Zsinj's twin shuttles were landing. Gethzerion turned trai-tor, killing all the Imperial guards—including Zsinj's longtime aide, General Melvar—with a crushing blow of Force energy. Solo was saved from certain death by the timely arrival of the *Falcon,* but Gethzerion and her followers escaped on the armed shuttle. Two of the warlord's Star Destroyers inter-cepted the Nightsisters just outside the planet's atmosphere. After a brief but withering crossfire, all that remained of the shuttle was a cloud of glowing metal.

The Nightsisters were gone, but Zsinj's fleet still barri-caded Dathomir. *Millennium Falcon* knocked out the orbital nightcloak, and the full battle fleet of the Hapes Consortium arrived to take on *Iron Fist* and dozens of Zsinj's smaller war-ships. During the chaos, Solo flew the *Falcon* straight at the bridge of *Iron Fist* and released a pair of concussion missiles at point-blank range. Warlord Zsinj was vaporized in an in-stant. The Battle of Dathomir was over.

In the aftermath, Singing Mountain Clan Mother Augw-ynne united the Witch clans of Dathomir and petitioned for planetary membership in the New Republic. Luke Skywalker was given a box filled with log recorder disks from the *Chu'unthor* wreckage, which would prove invaluable when he established the Jedi academy three years later.

Prince Isolder of Hapes had fallen madly in love with Teneniel Djo of the Singing Mountain Clan, an arrangement that outraged Queen Mother Ta'a Chume. Nevertheless, Isolder soon married Djo, making her the heir apparent to the throne of the Hapes Consortium. Isolder and Djo soon had a daughter, Tenel Ka, who proved to be very strong in the Force.

The adventure on Dathomir had resulted in Han Solo and Leia Organa growing even closer to each other, and they agreed to be married upon their return to Coruscant. The wedding was held in the Alderaanian consulate building on Coruscant, attended by hundreds of friends and dignitaries,

and watched on holovid by billions across the galaxy. The two honeymooned on the scenic Corphelion asteroid resort.

PICKING UP THE PIECES
8.5 A.B.Y.

With such a promising start, the prospect of full cooperation between the Hapes Consortium and the New Republic had a disappointing denouement. Prince Isolder had vowed to join the New Republic after the Dathomir incident, a pledge that did not sit well with the Hapan Royal Court and the individual planetary potentates. Queen Mother Ta'a Chume was only too willing to bend to the court's will in the interest of preserving internal stability. Hapes promised to commit their full Battle Dragon armada "in due time." Mon Mothma's hoped-for strategic alliance never materialized.

The sudden implosion of Warlord Zsinj's domain em-boldened the Imperial fleet. The coalition of advisers that had supplanted Isard had worked just as furiously as the New Republic in an effort to eliminate Zsinj. Now that that goal had been achieved, Admiral Rogriss and other fleet commanders moved to seize the newly liberated territory, all pretense of former partnership abandoned.

One benefit of the Hapan incident was the New Republic's acquisition of the several new Star Destroyers presented to Leia Organa during the Coruscant reception. These warships, added to the Star Destroyers that the New Republic had already captured, gave the fleet some formidable muscle. Admiral Ackbar led the New Republic ships to the Outer Rim to fight over the scraps of Zsinj's empire.

Ackbar and Rogriss ran directly into a *third* fleet—that of Warlord Teradoc, the self-appointed High Admiral of the Mid Rim. The New Republic Star Destroyers were thrown into the worst of the fighting, and consequently took the brunt of the punishment. Most of the Hapan ships, as well as the Star Destroyer *Crynyd,* were destroyed. The *Emancipator* and *Liberator* suffered severe damage and were recalled to un-dergo extensive repairs at the Hast shipyards. At the Battle of

Storinal, Princess Leia's flagship *Rebel Dream* was mercilessly shelled by the Imperial Star Destroyer *Peremptory* and recaptured by the Empire, its crew of thirty-seven thousand taken prisoner. Luckily, Organa Solo was on Coruscant at the time of the incident.

But for every hit the New Republic took, they gave it back to the Empire threefold. Admiral Rogriss lost the majority of the engagements. Bloodied, Rogriss ordered a retreat. Warlord Teradoc, whose hit-and-run strikes had made him an exasperating gadfly, also scurried back to his own territory. Admiral Ackbar charged into the region and fortified his newest gains.

The New Republic at last captured Kuat, giving access to the system's unparalleled shipbuilding docks, though damage to the yards was so extensive that new construction was delayed indefinitely. Unfortunately, the Kuat Drive Yards design team escaped to the Deep Core aboard the half-completed warship *Eclipse.* But with the seizure of Kuat and its subsidiary systems, the New Republic now controlled three-quarters of the settled galaxy.

During the relentless battles, the Republic and Empire had both suffered grave fleet losses. The construction and acquisition of new warships became a top priority for both sides.

RETURN TO TATOOINE
8.5 A.B.Y.

As Han and Leia settled into their marriage, the question of children reverberated among the HoloNet news outlets. Would two of the Rebel Alliance's greatest heroes give rise to a new generation of champions? For Leia, the answer was emphatically no. All too aware of the legacy of her biological father, a part of her saw too much risk in continuing the bloodline.

Although the Force spirit of Anakin Skywalker had appeared to Leia during the truce at Bakura, she still knew almost nothing about the man whose genes she carried. Leia got the chance to connect with the forgotten branch of the Skywalker family tree on a visit to Tatooine. Auction-

Han Solo and Leia Organa Solo gain clues to the past in Tatooine's Tusken Raider "ghost oasis." [ART BY TOMMY LEE EDWARDS]

eers in the city of Mos Espa had announced the impending sale of the Alderaanian moss-painting *Killik Twilight,* which depicted the insectile species that had inhabited Alderaan before human colonization. Leia was one of the few who knew that the lost masterpiece concealed an encrypted Shadowcast key containing codes once in use by the Rebel Alliance. If the Imperials bought the painting at auction and decrypted its contents, it could imperil dozens of New Republic deep-cover operations.

Arriving at Tatooine in *Millennium Falcon,* Han and Leia tried to bid on the *Killik Twilight,* but couldn't match the sum offered by Commander Quenton of the Star Destroyer *Chimaera.* Determined to destroy the painting rather than let the enemy take possession, Leia tried to incinerate it with a grenade. One of the attendees, a local man named Kitster Banai, saved the painting and fled on a swoopbike.

In their efforts to recover the *Killik Twilight,* Leia and Han met many people who had known Anakin Skywalker when he was only a nine-year-old slave and a gifted Podracer. Kitster Banai had been one such associate. Others willing to share their stories included the Rodian trader Wald (now running Watto's junk shop in Mos Espa) and the younger sister of Beru Whitesun, the woman who had raised Luke as his "Aunt Beru," and been present when Anakin Skywalker had buried his mother, Shmi. At the moisture farm where Luke had grown up, the new owners, the Darklighters, welcomed Leia and gave her a video diary that had once belonged to Shmi. Watching Shmi narrate the entries, Leia became acquainted with her grandmother, and learned what had transpired in the ten years between Anakin joining the Jedi and Shmi's death at the hands of Tusken Raiders.

Leia and Han—intermittently assisted by a trio of furry Squib con artists—caught up with Kitster and the *Killik Twilight* at a sacred Tusken oasis. It was here that Anakin Skywalker had slaughtered an entire village in retaliation for the torture and murder of his mother. Through the Force,

Leia could sense the pain, rage, and blood that permeated the sand as a psychic stain. The Sand People would have sacrificed Kitster Banai to the vicious "ghost" they believed still haunted the oasis, but Han and Leia rescued him and escaped offworld. The *Killik Twilight*, its Shadowcast key destroyed, ended up in the greedy paws of the Squibs.

Although the crimes of Vader were unforgivable, Leia's time on Tatooine had given her an understanding of the choices that had led Anakin Skywalker down the path of evil and, in his final moments, allowed him a last shot at redemption. No longer worried that her children might carry a dark mark of destiny, Leia made plans with Han to start a family. Soon afterward, she learned that she was pregnant—with twins.

PART SEVEN

Empire Resurgent

The Imperial dominion had been reduced to a mere quarter of what Palpatine had once called his own, most of it in outlying sectors along the Rim. The surviving Moffs were forced to fight the Republic on one front, while simultaneously keeping their beloved Empire from splitting into ideological factions under squabbling warlords.

Since Imperial forces had suffered decisive defeats at Endor and Coruscant, overconfident New Republic prognosticators predicted the imminent end to all Imperial resistance—but the wheels of the Empire continued to turn, even in secret. The next two years very nearly saw the death of the New Republic.

The Depredations of Grand Admiral Thrawn
9 A.B.Y.

The ailing Empire needed a miracle. It got one when a brilliant military commander emerged from the Unknown Regions—Thrawn, the last of the Emperor's Grand Admirals, who had been in isolation since before the Battle of Endor. Upon his return, Grand Admiral Thrawn picked the Imperial Star Destroyer *Chimaera* as his flagship, making Captain Pellaeon his de facto second in command. This further elevated Pellaeon in the eyes of the Moffs.

For six months, Thrawn reorganized the fleet and executed strategic raids along the Republic–Imperial border. It had been Thrawn who had led the efforts to recover the *Killik Twilight* from Tatooine. While these incursions were not sufficient to panic the New Republic, they deeply impressed the Moffs, governors, and other political leaders. Thrawn was effectively handed the reins of the Empire.

Thrawn consolidated loyal Imperial forces and marginalized warlord fiefdoms such as Admiral Krennel's domain and Grand Moff Kaine's Pentastar Alignment. Before long, he made his first overt strike against the New Republic, capturing key information from the library world of Obroa-skai. Analysis of the data led him to Wayland, site of the Emperor's secret Mount Tantiss storehouse. On Wayland, Thrawn collected three items that would soon devastate the New Republic.

The first was a functional cloaking device, an offshoot of the Project Vorknkx research conducted before the Emperor's demise. The second was an array of Spaarti cloning cylinders stored deep in the bowels of Mount Tantiss—technology that the Emperor had adapted for his own uses in the Deep Core. The third item was the mad Jedi Joruus C'baoth, apparently a clone of the Jorus C'baoth who had led the Outbound Flight mission. C'baoth had been stranded on Wayland for years and had gone completely insane. Grand Admiral Thrawn, protected by the Force-blocking abilities of ysalamiri lizards, secured C'baoth's cooperation by promising him that he could deliver Luke Skywalker and Leia Organa Solo, as well as Leia's unborn twins. The lunatic Jedi Master wanted to mold them into his evil, twisted apprentices.

Joruus C'baoth held up his end of the bargain, Force-linking the ships of Thrawn's fleet into a supernatural fighting force. Grand Admiral Thrawn was determined to fulfill his part of the deal. Twice, he dispatched teams of Noghri death

Grand Admiral Thrawn, with an ysalamiri, plots the defeat of the New Republic from the bridge of the Chimaera. [Art by Tommy Lee Edwards]

commandos to kidnap Luke Skywalker and Leia Organa Solo, but both attempts failed.

Thrawn activated the cloning complex and produced thousands of clone soldiers; he also sent a Spaarti cylinder to his secret base on Nirauan in the Unknown Regions to produce a clone of himself. The use of Force-blocking ysalamiri allowed him to grow clones in mere days, instead of the years that the process had taken during the Clone Wars. However, though he had an endless supply of loyal vat-grown troopers, he did not have the military infrastructure to outfit and transport them to the battlefield. In the aftermath of the post-Zsinj campaign, both the Empire and New Republic were desperate for starships.

Thrawn developed a novel way to restock his fleet and simultaneously rob the New Republic of much of its own. Mole miners, compact burrowing vehicles, could drill through a starship's hull. The Grand Admiral planned to steal dozens of mole miners, then use them to dispatch armed boarding parties onto every New Republic warship stationed at the Sluis Van shipyards.

Unfortunately for the galaxy's unluckiest entrepreneur, Thrawn chose the planet Nkllon for his mole miner raid. Lando Calrissian had invested millions of credits into the construction of Nomad City, a mobile mining complex that remained on the cool shadow side of the planet throughout Nkllon's ninety-day rotation. Nomad City had just begun to turn a profit when one of Thrawn's Star Destroyers arrived, stealing fifty-one of the expensive mole miners.

After the calamity, Calrissian accompanied Han Solo to Myrkr, the base of operations for smuggling kingpin Talon Karrde. Solo hoped to convince Karrde to ship cargo for the New Republic. Neither man realized, however, that Talon Karrde had a very familiar figure locked up in a storage silo.

Several days prior, Luke Skywalker's X-wing had been yanked out of hyperspace by an Interdictor cruiser and severely damaged by Thrawn's flagship. When Skywalker was picked up by Karrde's personal freighter, the smuggling chief remembered the sizable Imperial bounty on his captive's head and imprisoned Luke at his base.

Shortly after the arrival of Solo and Calrissian, Luke es-caped and stole a Skipray blastboat, but Mara Jade, Karrde's second in command, pursued in a second blastboat. The high-speed chase ended when the two ships collided and crashed, and Luke and Mara were forced to hike through Myrkr's dense forest for three days. Mara revealed that she had once been an Emperor's Hand in the service of Palpatine, and since Luke was indirectly responsible for the Emperor's death, she had vowed to kill him. But Mara put aside her homicidal impulses until they reached Hyllyard City at the edge of the forest, where Karrde's men rescued them from an Imperial scout patrol. Karrde's actions placed him squarely on the side of the New Republic.

Luke, Lando, and Han Solo departed Myrkr and headed for Sluis Van. Coincidentally, they arrived just as Grand Admiral Thrawn unleashed his fleet on the shipyards, using his new cloaking device to increase the element of surprise. Commander Wedge Antilles and Rogue Squadron fought against the enemy starfighters, but Lando realized that his stolen Nkllon mole miners had drilled into the docked vessels. Once inside, commando teams leapt out and seized control of the bridges. Within minutes, dozens of hijacked capital ships pulled out of their berths and headed toward a hyperspace jump point on the fringe of the system. Lando transmitted a master control code that reactivated all the mole miners simultaneously. The machines began to drill again, grinding through the navigation and propulsion controls. Thrawn was forced to retreat without his prize.

THE NOGHRI SWITCH SIDES
9 A.B.Y.

Leia Organa Solo had sat out the Battle of Sluis Van on the Wookiee homeworld of Kashyyyk, in order to protect herself from Thrawn's Noghri kidnapping teams. The Noghri attacked a third time, but the Wookiees took one of them captive. From this solider, Khabarakh, Leia learned that the Noghri revered Darth Vader for his help in restoring their homeworld of Honoghr after its poisoning during the Clone Wars. The Noghri had served Vader, and later Thrawn, as death commandos. What the Noghri did not realize was that the Imperial restoration teams had deliberately *kept* Honoghr in a state of ruin, thus ensuring that the Noghri remained in the Empire's thrall indefinitely.

As the daughter of Darth Vader, Leia suspected she might be able to bring the aliens around through diplomacy. Bringing Chewbacca and C-3PO, she traveled with the captured Noghri, and surveyed Honoghr's endless plains of scorched grass. Before long, Leia uncovered the Empire's trickery and demonstrated the proof to a square filled with angry Noghri, dramatically winning them over to her side.

Immediately, word was sent to all Noghri death commandos out on missions for the Empire. They either secretly abandoned their assignments and returned to Honoghr, or attempted to sabotage the Empire's aims before being killed. News of the Imperial treachery even reached the Star Destroyer *Chimaera,* where the Noghri warrior Rukh worked as Grand Admiral Thrawn's bodyguard. Rukh chose to bide his time, waiting for the appropriate moment to take revenge on the deceivers of his people.

THE KATANA FLEET AND THE CLONE TROOPERS
9 A.B.Y.

Thrawn's machinations were not limited to military maneuvers; he also manipulated financial records and banking transactions to make it appear that Admiral Ackbar, the commander of the New Republic fleet, was guilty of treason. At the urging of the Bothan Councilor Borsk Fey'lya, Ackbar was placed under house arrest until the matter could be resolved.

Solo and Calrissian decided to investigate, and they ended up encountering three vintage Dreadnaughts under the command of General Garm Bel Iblis. In the nine years since he had quit the Rebel Alliance, the legendary Corellian Senator had built up a private army. His hit-and-run strikes against the Empire were successful, but limited in scope. His stubborn pride, and simmering anger toward Mon Mothma, had prevented Bel Iblis from joining the New Republic.

Bel Iblis's Dreadnaughts came from the *Katana* fleet. The two hundred *Katana* Dreadnaughts had been the object of countless "lost treasure" hunts for generations, but now, with both sides in the Galactic Civil War desperately in need of warships, the acquisition of the lost armada could easily tip the scales. While Bel Iblis did not know the location of the fleet, he had a contact who did; unfortunately, before Solo and Calrissian could meet with him, Grand Admiral Thrawn apprehended the man.

Fortunately, the smuggling chief Talon Karrde also had discovered the location of the *Katana* fleet. The New Republic hastily threw together a strike team and arrived at the point in space where the forgotten Dreadnaughts had been drifting battle broke out as Luke Skywalker and Han Solo boarded the

Smuggling kingpin Talon Karrde
[ART BY JOHN VAN FLEET]

flagship *Katana*. Unexpected reinforcements—General Garm Bel Iblis and his Dreadnaughts, along with members of Talon Karrde's smuggling organization—briefly bolstered the New Republic, but the Imperials called in their own reserves.

Aboard the flagship, Han Solo remembered that the *Katana* fleet had been primarily slave-rigged. The slave controls in the *Katana*'s bridge allowed Solo to reactivate one of the idle Dreadnaughts and remote-steer it straight into the nose of the Star Destroyer *Peremptory*. Both ships exploded in a spectacular fireball, and Thrawn's Imperials fled.

The New Republic's victory was dampened by two pieces of sobering news. Out of the original two hundred Dreadnaughts, only fifteen remained—the others were already in Imperial hands. The second grim reality came to light after examining the bodies of the dead stormtroopers aboard the *Katana*. Each corpse shared the same face.

In the five years since the Empire's defeat at Endor, the cloning technology that had once produced legions of stormtroopers had vanished, made useless by dwindling resources or destroyed outright in accordance with Emperor Palpatine's posthumous orders. The surviving clone stormtroopers perished through attrition, and, for years prior to the Thrawn incident, the stormtrooper corps had been composed almost exclusively of conscripts and recruits. The idea that Grand Admiral Thrawn had resurrected this lost science terrified the New Republic, particularly the news that he had found a way to grow fresh clones in a matter of days. Mon Mothma and the others envisioned a new round of Clone Wars, this time with Coruscant on the losing side, and made the uncovering of Thrawn's cloning complex their top priority.

Admiral Ackbar was reinstated as fleet commander, the financial scandal having been revealed as an Imperial setup. On Coruscant, Leia Organa Solo gave birth to twins, a boy and a girl—Jacen and Jaina—who were to join the new generation of Jedi Knights.

Because she had been an Emperor's Hand, Mara Jade had known many of Palpatine's secrets—including the location of the Mount Tantiss cloning facility on Wayland. Mara led Luke Skywalker, Han Solo, Chewbacca, Lando Calrissian, and their

droids to Wayland to destroy Thrawn's ready-made soldier factory. Upon reaching Mount Tantiss, Luke and Mara headed for the Emperor's throne room. Waiting for them on the throne, like an arachnid at the center of its web, was Joruus C'baoth.

The demented Jedi Master was easily a match for both Skywalker and Jade combined. While he toyed with them, he unleashed a shocking surprise: C'baoth had grown a special clone from Skywalker's own genetic material, taken from the hand Luke had lost at Cloud City. The mindless drone, Luuke Skywalker, was his exact duplicate.

The clone had a lightsaber as well—the blue-bladed saber that had once belonged to Anakin Skywalker, a weapon that had been considered lost since the tragic events in Cloud City. The doubles squared off in a frenzied duel. Though she had often expressed her desire to murder the man who had brought about the Emperor's death, Mara Jade ended the combat by killing the Luuke clone. C'baoth, in a fit of rage, collapsed the chamber's ceiling, but Mara skewered him cleanly through the torso.

Deep in the lower levels, Lando Calrissian and Chewbacca sabotaged the central equipment column of the cloning complex, triggering an irreversible overload spiral. The infiltration team escaped just as Mount Tantiss exploded spectacularly.

The laboratory's destruction meant the loss of priceless artworks and historical artifacts stored in the Emperor's private vaults. It also seemed to bury forever all evidence of Bothan involvement in the devastation of Caamas, much to Councilor Borsk Fey'lya's relief. More than a decade would pass before a data card plucked from the rubble would stir up old animosities and touch off a galaxywide search for the Caamas Document.

THRAWN'S FALL
9 A.B.Y.

Grand Admiral Thrawn seemed infallible in his military strategy. While the Emperor had used cloaking devices for the straightforward purpose of disguising warcraft (as in the experimental "Phantom TIE" project), Thrawn relished devising ingenious, nonstandard uses for the invisibility screen. One ruse was to cloak a number of cruisers and slip them beneath a planet's energy shield. When an attacking

Star Destroyer fired at the shield, its lasers dissipated harmlessly. But the cloaked cruisers waiting beneath the shield at precise, predetermined locations would fire their own lasers simultaneously, creating the illusion that the Star Destroyer's lasers could punch through energy barriers. This trick worked so well that dozens of planets surrendered to the Empire without a fight.

Thrawn also used cloaking technology to create an innovative siege weapon. After fitting twenty-two asteroids with cloaking devices, Thrawn's Star Destroyers carried them to Coruscant, then dumped the invisible asteroids into close planetary orbit. The New Republic couldn't risk dropping Coruscant's energy shield lest one of the asteroids impact the heavily populated surface. Until they could find a way to eliminate the unseen obstacles, Coruscant was thoroughly blockaded.

Following this incident, Ackbar planned a retaliatory raid that would severely damage Thrawn's shipbuilding capability, as well as simultaneously net them a sophisticated gravfield detector that could pinpoint the asteroids' mass shadows. Thrawn learned of the raid, and was waiting for the New Republic armada when it emerged from hyperspace at Bilbringi.

Commander Wedge Antilles and Rogue Squadron led the fighter attack, while Ackbar launched withering cannonades from his capital ships. Talon Karrde's smuggling associates executed quick hit-and-fade strikes against the Imperial defense platforms, forcing Thrawn to split his forces. Nevertheless, it seemed only a matter of time before the Imperial noose drew tight.

The New Republic was handed a victory through chance. Thrawn's Noghri bodyguard Rukh, burning with anger toward the Empire ever since Leia Organa Solo's revelations on Honoghr, fatally stabbed his master through the heart. Rukh fled the scene and tried to reach a shuttlecraft, but was intercepted and executed by a stormtrooper squad under the command of Major Grodin Tierce.

Captain Pellaeon took command of the beleaguered Imperial fleet, but was smart enough to realize that he had no hope of winning the battle. Pellaeon ordered a full retreat, to live and fight again another day.

The Imperial fleet regrouped near the Unknown Regions while Pellaeon assessed the situation. Thrawn had captured an astonishing amount of territory, nearly doubling the size of the Empire, but it had been held together by his authority alone. Without a similarly charismatic leader, the union would splinter yet again. Pellaeon, while respected, was not such a leader. The Empire again reverted to warlordism, and the New Republic began recapturing its lost territory, planet by planet.

THE RETURN OF ISARD
9–10 A.B.Y.

While the New Republic reveled in the victory, ominous developments bubbled just beneath the surface. On Byss, in the Deep Core, Emperor Palpatine's spirit had finally recuperated from its difficult transition into a new clone body. Palpatine knew the New Republic had little interest in the Deep Core, since hyperlanes into the starchoked region were practically nonexistent. Protected from prying eyes, the resurrected Emperor secretly began contacting specific fleet commanders, warlords, and Moffs. Those who pledged fealty to their former master were rewarded; those who resisted were slaughtered. The secret Imperial war fleet swelled in size as new ships arrived daily.

The Deep Core warlords, particularly Harrsk and Delvardus, were among the first to join Palpatine's cause. Ysanne Isard also learned of the Emperor's return. Isard, who had been lying low since her "death" at Thyferra, was terrified of being executed for losing Coruscant to the enemy, and devised a strategy to win a place of honor for herself in Palpatine's new Empire. Her peace offering would be the Super Star Destroyer *Lusankya*, undergoing reconstruction in a New Republic dry dock.

New Republic forces were amazed at the ease with which they swept up small pieces of the Empire, as if the Imperial fleet had gone into hiding. The New Republic Provisional Council made its next goal the liberation of the Ciutric Hegemony, a region dominated by Imperial Admiral Krennel. According to New Republic Intelligence, the prisoners who had once suffered aboard the *Lusankya* were likely to be found within the borders of the Ciutric Hegemony. The New Republic leadership placed a high priority on recovering the *Lusankya* inmates, particularly General Jan Dodonna, Rebel hero of the Battle of Yavin.

A raid by Rogue Squadron ended in failure, but surprisingly, the Rogues were rescued by TIE defender pilots in the service of Ysanne Isard. Isard met with her old enemies and explained that she had as much stake in bringing down Krennel as they did—the warlord had betrayed her years

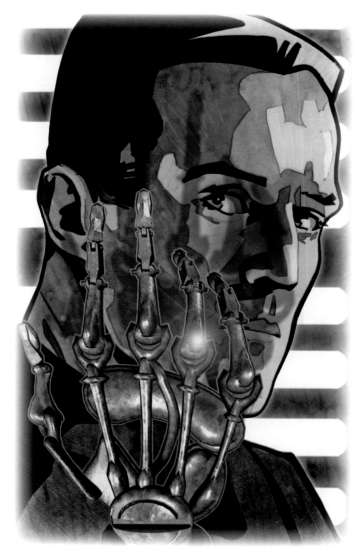

Admiral Delak Krennel
[ART BY JOHN VAN FLEET]

before, and had stolen the *Lusankya* prisoners from under her nose. Worse, Krennel was in league with a clone of Isard, grown through unknown means years before Grand Admiral Thrawn had activated the Mount Tantiss cloning facility. In exchange for the destruction of her clone and the humiliation of Krennel, Isard agreed to assist Rogue Squadron members in their mission.

The Rogues posed as TIE pilots hoping to defect to Krennel's empire, while a New Republic commando team prepared to spring Dodonna and the other prisoners. Admiral Ackbar also commanded a substantial force of New Republic capital ships and support craft, drawn from the defenses around the Bilbringi Shipyards. All three groups coordinated their actions in a single, unified assault on Krennel's heavily defended throneworld of Ciutric.

Isard did not participate in the mission; instead, she treacherously struck the weakened defenses of the shipyards containing the *Lusankya.* Isard's handpicked infiltration team quickly seized the Super Star Destroyer's bridge and prepared to steer the monstrous vessel toward the nearest hyperspace jump point. Isard's treachery had not taken New Republic Intelligence entirely by surprise, though. Agent Iella Wessiri had prepared for a possible hijack and already had a team in place to prevent the theft. In a confrontation inside Isard's former quarters, Wessiri shot and killed the deranged Imperial. The *Lusankya* was recovered immediately afterward.

The attack on Krennel's base succeeded. The admiral and the Isard clone both died. The *Lusankya* prisoners were rescued and brought back to the New Republic for disease treatment and psychological evaluations. General Dodonna, however, adamantly refused all testing and insisted on an immediate meeting with Mon Mothma to discuss the current state of the Galactic Civil War. Dodonna formed a body of aged advisers called the Gray Cadre, which included such luminaries as Adar Tallon and Vanden Willard, and reassumed the role of senior military adviser as if he had never been gone.

Krennel's dominion crumbled without his leadership,

and the New Republic Navy pushed farther forward. In only a short time since the death of Thrawn, the Empire had lost nearly all of its recently won territory. Tasting victory, the New Republic Fleet advanced outward into the Imperially held sections of the Rim, leaving Coruscant and the Core Worlds relatively unprotected. Which was exactly how Emperor Palpatine wanted it.

THE RESURRECTION OF EMPEROR PALPATINE
10 A.B.Y.

In the six years following the Emperor's death at Endor, the New Republic had established itself as a governing force as well as a military power. But without the thousands of Jedi Knights who formed the backbone of the Old Republic, the political confederation remained a precarious one. At no point was that deficiency more obvious than during Palpatine's ghastly return—a nightmarish year of horror, calamity, and ruin.

Immediately after the defeat of Admiral Krennel, the Imperial fleet commanders joined with surviving members of the Emperor's ruling council, a development no one had predicted. The unified Imperial force launched from the Deep Core with stunning violence, surprising the New Republic, whose own fleet was hopelessly out of position in the Rim. Within days, the Imperials had conquered several key systems, forcing Mon Mothma to consider a last-ditch plan for the defense of Coruscant itself. She didn't get the chance.

An Imperial armada began a merciless bombardment of Coruscant's energy shield, waiting for the shield to buckle and break. Rather than see the civilian population decimated, Mon Mothma evacuated the capital world. Ralltiir, Chandrila, Esseles, and other key Core Worlds soon fell to the Imperials, and the leaders of the beleaguered New Republic returned to guerrilla fighting to battle their old enemy.

The resurrected Palpatine had done a better job of reuniting the Imperial factions than anyone before him, including Thrawn—only the Emperor could rule the Empire. Surviving warlords such as Harrsk, Delvardus, and Teradoc swore obedience to the same master and fought under the same banner, and even forces that did not yet know of Palpatine's return (such as the mainline Imperial forces under Pellaeon) fought alongside the warlords. The New Republic remained unaware of the identity of the mastermind behind the sudden unification.

Then suddenly, everything appeared to fall apart. Now that Coruscant was theirs, the factions of the Empire fell upon each other like nek battle dogs in a civil war to grasp control. The brief but bloody struggle, known as the Imperial Mutiny, involved the ruling council, the Moffs, the fleet, the Inquisitorius, COMPNOR, and the Imperial Security Bureau, each trying to claim the whole sabacc pot at the expense of the others. The New Republic seized this chance to create confusion among the feuding Imperials, using two captured Star Destroyers to conduct hit-and-run sorties into the war zones. Longtime Alliance hero Wedge Antilles was promoted to general, while other old warriors, including Han Solo and Lando Calrissian, reactivated their commissions and returned to the military. In one such raid over the battleground of Coruscant, the Alliance Star Destroyer *Liberator*, commanded by Luke Skywalker, Wedge Antilles, and Lando Calrissian, crashed into the planet's surface. Leia Organa Solo and her husband led a mission to rescue their comrades.

Taking *Millennium Falcon* into the heart of the battle zone, they found Antilles and Calrissian barricaded in and fighting for their lives. Then, with a swirl of Force, Jedi Luke Skywalker strode into the fray and single-handedly defeated an AT-AT walker. Luke had sensed an evil power reaching out to him, and warned his companions to stay back. A Force storm opened a hole in space, dragging Luke and R2-D2 into it.

Luke became a prisoner on Byss at the heart of the Deep Core. Eager to meet his captor, Luke learned that the dark side nexus he had sensed was none other than the cloned reincarnation of Emperor Palpatine himself. The Emperor, who had been unable to fully implement Darth Plagueis's teachings and cheat death through the Force, had settled for a lesser solution that required cloning technology to create host bodies.

Palpatine was allowing the Imperial Mutiny to rage on, considering it the culling of the weak from his forces, while he prepared his own attack on the water world of Mon Cala-mari. Luke believed the only way he could ultimately defeat Palpatine was to use the Emperor's own knowledge of the dark side against him. Believing that he could destroy the dark side from within, Luke agreed to join Palpatine as the Emperor's new apprentice.

The government-in-exile of the New Republic had established a secret "Pinnacle Base" on the isolated moon of Da Soocha V at the heart of Hutt space. Here, Ackbar and Dodonna discussed the ongoing assault against Mon Calamari, which involved new superweapons called World Devastators. Designed by Umak Leth, one of the engineers involved with the Death Star project, these weapons consumed everything in their path, feeding automated manufacturing plants that then spewed out war machines. The combined military might of the ragtag New Republic rushed out to fight the World Devastators, and suffered terrible losses. The Alliance Star Destroyer *Emancipator* crashed into the resource-hungry Maw and became scrap.

Sensing that Luke had slipped into terrible danger, Leia set out to rescue her brother, despite being pregnant with her third child. Leia and Han first made a stop at the Smugglers' Moon of Nar Shaddaa. They hooked up with Solo's former girlfriend, Salla Zend, and an old smuggling buddy, Shug Ninx. Leia also came across a decrepit crone named Vima-Da-Boda, who had once been a Jedi.

Leia and Han won their way to Byss aboard Salla Zend's freighter, which was licensed to haul military cargo to the Deep Core. Once in port, Leia used the Force to guide them to the citadel where her brother reigned as the Emperor's protégé, but then they became Imperial captives. The Emperor visited Leia in her cell, revealing that he knew of Luke's plans to trick him, but was confident that he would win in the end. Playing on her emotions, Palpatine also said that his aging body would soon burn out from the dark forces he wielded—and that he wanted to shift his consciousness into

Rebel commandos lead an amphibious assault on the reborn Emperor's World Devastators. [Art by Tommy Lee Edwards]

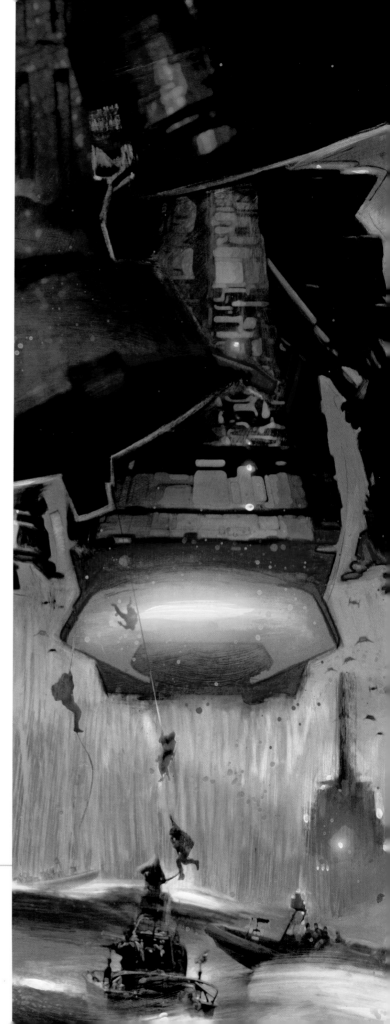

the new baby that Leia carried in her womb. Revolted, Leia attacked the Emperor and escaped.

Salla Zend helped rescue them, but Luke claimed he had more work to do on Byss. He had, however, already loaded the override codes for the World Devastators into R2's memory circuits. New Republic forces used the data to complete their victory at Mon Calamari.

Before the decrepit Palpatine could use his sorcery to switch into one of his new clones, a grim Luke Skywalker marched into the laboratory chamber and smashed tank after tank. But Palpatine succeeded in transferring his consciousness to one of the last remaining clones, a strong and agile fifteen-year-old. Filled with dark side power, the reborn Emperor engaged Skywalker in a ferocious lightsaber duel—and forced the Jedi Knight into submission.

Broken and lost, Skywalker accompanied the victorious Emperor in his enormous flagship *Eclipse* to the New Republic stronghold on Pinnacle Base. There, the Emperor issued an ultimatum—he would destroy all the Rebels, unless the pregnant Leia Organa Solo agreed to come aboard his ship.

Leia boarded the *Eclipse*, but defied the Emperor and tried to bring Luke back to the light side. Her efforts allowed Luke to break the hold of evil, and they both turned against Palpatine. The desperate Emperor summoned up a huge Force storm, but he could no longer control what he had unleashed. As brother and sister fled, the conflagration consumed the gigantic black ship and, presumably, all that remained of the Emperor.

OPERATION SHADOW HAND
10 A.B.Y.

The Rebel triumph was to be short-lived. Palpatine had anticipated even this worst-case scenario and had hidden another of his clones in a secret location on Byss. His loyal forces already had a plan—Operation Shadow Hand—designed to subjugate the galaxy in a series of unstoppable assaults. Palpatine's military executor, Sedriss, led the operation, assisted by seven of the Emperor's most skilled Dark Side Adepts, a group he called his "Dark Jedi."

Executor Sedriss consolidated the forces remaining in the newly subjugated Core and Colonies regions. First, he targeted the weapons factories on Balmorra, which had turned against Imperial domination. But when Sedriss attacked the weapons world, massive new combat droids rebuffed his forces.

Upon returning to Byss, Sedriss found that two of the Emperor's Dark Side Adepts had turned traitor and completed destroying the clone laboratory, so they could control the Empire themselves without worrying about Palpatine's return. Fiercely loyal even in his master's absence, Sedriss killed the saboteurs and turned at last to see the Emperor reborn, in his only remaining clone body. Rewarded for his faith, Sedriss received the mission to track down Luke Skywalker and bring him back to the Emperor—alive.

Palpatine's traitorous adepts had not been working alone. Carnor Jax, one of the Emperor's crimson-armored Royal Guardsmen, had secretly trained in the Force under the Dark Lady Lumiya and had paid the Byss clonemaster to damage the genetic structure of all Palpatine's clones, knowing it would trigger a premature aging cycle and a quick death for the resurrected Emperor. Jax escaped Sedriss's notice, and quietly waited for his own chance to ascend the throne.

Meanwhile, Luke traveled to the abandoned space city of Nespis VIII, where he found Kam Solusar, a hard-bitten survivor of Darth Vader's Jedi Purge. Initially angry and reclusive, Solusar faced Skywalker in an ancient and risky Jedi game called lightsider. After Skywalker bested him, Solusar agreed to join the Jedi. Skywalker and Solusar proceeded to the ruined library world of Ossus, which had been obliterated by the Cron Cluster explosion during the Sith War. Amid the blasted rubble on Ossus, Skywalker and Kam Solusar found a group of primitive shamans, the Ysanna, who exhibited a weak and untrained ability to use the Force.

Before the two could complete their search for information, Executor Sedriss tracked them down. The Jedi and Ysanna warriors drove back the Imperial shock troops. Desperate, Sedriss took a young Ysanna woman, Jem, as a hostage, and backed up against a twisted tree. When the tree began to move, it revealed itself as Master Ood Bnar, who had clung to life since the firestorm had swept Ossus millennia ago. Ood destroyed both himself and Sedriss in a final confrontation.

Beneath the ruins of the dead Jedi, Luke uncovered a precious stockpile of ancient lightsabers. Taking this discovery as an omen, Luke allowed two of the young Ysanna—Jem and her brother Rayf—to accompany him and Solusar. Also intent on finding other Jedi Knights, Leia Organa Solo went to the underworld of Nar Shaddaa and tracked down the fallen Jedi Vima-Da-Boda, despite the intervention of Boba Fett. Along the way they also found another Jedi warrior, Empatojayos Brand, who had lost much of his body during an earlier battle with Darth Vader.

In the previous few months, Palpatine's weapons designer Umak Leth had completed a terrible new armament, the Galaxy Gun. In orbit around Byss, this weapon could fire hyperspace projectiles to any part of the galaxy and destroy any target. Palpatine launched the first projectile toward Pinnacle Base, hoping to destroy the Rebels with a single blow.

The projectile annihilated the hidden moon just as Luke returned from Ossus. The Rebel base exploded, but Mon Mothma and the core of the resistance had evacuated in time. The Emperor continued to launch his deadly projectiles, destroying unruly worlds and bringing the resistance to its knees. Within a short time, Palpatine had regained key territories in the Inner and Outer Rim. The future of the New Republic looked bleak.

Luke and his companions went to the secret world of New Alderaan, where the Solo twins Jacen and Jaina had been taken for protection. But the Emperor's commando forces struck there, too, killing Jem Ysanna. The survivors fled to the derelict space city of Nespis VIII, where Leia gave birth to her third child, named Anakin after her father.

When he discovered the location of the latest Rebel hideout, the Emperor launched yet another projectile from the Galaxy Gun. The surviving New Republic forces barely escaped before the ancient space city exploded. The ragged remnants of the cowed Alliance scattered across the galaxy, fleeing in separate small groups.

PALPATINE VANQUISHED
11 A.B.Y.

Though Palpatine seemed to be winning his war of conquest, his final cloned body had begun to fail him, aging at a rapid rate and eaten from the inside by the sabotage of Carnor Jax. He tried to clone other bodies so that he could resurrect himself again, but Jax's manipulations had tainted even the genetic source material. Palpatine's scientists and physicians could offer no solutions.

Attempting to find an answer, Palpatine journeyed to the Sith tomb world of Korriban, where the spirits of fallen dark lords informed him that he needed to find a Jedi body. They told him where to locate the newborn Anakin Solo, a child powerfully strong in the Force.

The Emperor brought his latest flagship, *Eclipse II,* to Onderon, where the Solos had taken their three children. While New Republic defenders attacked the Imperial juggernaut in orbit, Luke Skywalker and his Jedi companions sought out Palpatine himself. During the space battle, Lando Calrissian infiltrated the flagship and, using R2-D2's computer specialization, sabotaged the hyperdrive engines. *Eclipse II* took off into hyperspace, toward coordinates set to match the location of Umak Leth's Galaxy Gun. The out-of-control Imperial flagship crashed into the huge weapon, destroying both in a titanic collision. The Galaxy Gun's final projectile, pulled by the gravity of Byss itself, turned the central world of the Deep Core into space debris.

A final battle was fought on the surface of Onderon. Very sick and barely able to walk in his festering body, Palpatine demanded Anakin Solo as the new repository for his spirit. Luke Skywalker and the other Jedi joined the battle. Rayf Ysanna and Empatojayos Brand were both mortally wounded in the confrontation. Luke tried to take Palpatine alive—but Han Solo shot the old man with his blaster.

As the Emperor fell toward death yet again, he attempted to send his spirit into the baby Anakin—but Empatojayos

Brand intercepted the dark essence. Clasping himself to the light, Brand held the Emperor's presence within his body as they both succumbed to death.

With all of his clones destroyed, Emperor Palpatine was finally defeated. Without orders, the confused Imperial fleet went into retreat, abandoning Coruscant and other Core planets. Mon Mothma spread the news that the New Republic had once again regained control. To cement the victory, the leaders reestablished their capital on devastated Coruscant.

This fresh start allowed them to establish a new system of government. The Provisional Council and position of Chief Councilor had worked effectively in the past, but that system was now viewed as the government that had lost Coruscant to Palpatine. A new, more powerful single leader was desired, as well as a more clearly defined governmental hierarchy. Mon Mothma was elected Chief of State and President of the Senate. Leia Organa Solo was elected her second in command, the Minister of State.

JAX, KANOS, AND THE INTERIM COUNCIL
11 A.B.Y.

The Empire forged by Thrawn and expanded by Palpatine's clones collapsed at last, its death presided over by a former Royal Guardsman named Carnor Jax. Palpatine's scarlet-robed bodyguards had been trained on the harsh planet Yinchorr to show unswerving loyalty, but Jax's dreams of power had overcome his devotion. Jax had arranged for the insidious sabotage of Palpatine's clones, a shortsighted and selfish move. When the last clone finally succumbed on Onderon, the Empire was left without the iron ruler who had conceived and guided it. Jax, though, preferred to rule over a dying Empire than to serve in a thriving one.

The speed with which the Empire crumbled after Palpatine's final death was amazing, surpassing the mass confusion that had occurred following the Battle of Endor. Jax manipulated the creation of a thirteen-member Interim Council to succeed Palpatine, with himself a senior member.

Powerful alien leaders—including a Devaronian, a Whiphid, a Givin, and a Defel—were granted membership in the Interim Council, a remarkable move for the historically anti-alien Empire. Carnor Jax felt that alien strength might give new life to the dying Imperial military. Unfortunately, it was too little, too late.

Many fleets refused to follow the dictates of the council. Admiral Harrsk returned to his power base in the Deep Core and other warlords followed suit, realizing that the protected Deep Core offered an opportunity for them to regroup and plan their next course of action.

Carnor Jax and the Interim Council held the Empire proper, a narrow band stretching from the Outer Rim to the Colonies. But even this would not remain intact. The last of the Emperor's Royal Guardsmen, Kir Kanos, was everything Jax was not in terms of loyalty and devotion. Kanos had learned of Jax's culpability in Palpatine's death, and had survived the Jax-ordered massacre of the remaining Royal Guards on Yinchorr. Kir Kanos vowed to track down his former comrade-in-arms and execute him as a traitor.

On Phaeda, an Imperial holding in the Outer Rim, Jax's Star Destroyers attempted to capture Kanos, but he escaped to Yinchorr. Jax followed, leaving one of his ships at Phaeda, where it was surprised by General Wedge Antilles and the New Republic Super Star Destroyer *Lusankya*. After years of time-consuming repairs, the *Lusankya* had finally been launched in the wake of Operation Shadow Hand, and was still such a secret that many Imperials were unaware of its existence. Antilles, aided by Rogue Squadron, captured Jax's Star Destroyer and liberated Phaeda.

At Yinchorr, Kir Kanos used a booby-trapped assault bomber to annihilate Jax's flagship. On the surface of the barren world, Kanos and Jax faced off inside the abandoned Royal Guard training compound, a place of dark memories for both. On an elevated platform suspended above a bottomless pit, Kanos killed his rival, then vowed to avenge his master further by destroying every member of the sham Interim Council.

While Kanos began moving against his enemies, another

group was also trying to sabotage the council—the criminal organization Black Sun. The syndicate arranged to have several of the council members replaced with clones. After several assassinations had already thinned out the ranks of the council, the ranking member, Xandel Carivus, decided to disband the organization and rule alone as the new Emperor. Carivus was operating on the instructions of Nom Anor, an advance agent for the extra-galactic Yuuzhan Vong who was careful to keep his true allegiances a secret.

Carivus's actions angered Baron D'Asta, a pro-Imperial business leader who controlled the largest privately owned fleet in the galaxy. Baron D'Asta's fleet attacked the council headquarters on Ord Cantrell, forcing "Emperor" Carivus to sue for peace. In a confrontation on the planet's surface, Kir

Kanos executed the spurious Emperor.

With the Interim Council gone and most of the Imperial fleet disappearing into the Deep Core to form warlord allegiances, die-hard Imperial planets like the Academy world Carida were left with no significant defensive forces. Carida and many other worlds throughout the former Imperial jurisdiction drew in upon themselves, fortifying their planetary defenses to make any New Republic invasion difficult and costly. The New Republic chose to leave most of these "fortress worlds" alone, hoping that a lack of trade would eventually force them to open up their borders.

Pellaeon, now a vice admiral, reluctantly joined in with the Deep Core warlords as well. The Star Destroyer *Chimaera* had been severely damaged and abandoned in the capture of Duro during Operation Shadow Hand; many of Pellaeon's most loyal and skilled officers had been killed. Lacking his core power base and his flagship, Pellaeon cast his lot with High Admiral Teradoc, who had lost his Mid Rim holdings, but now carved out a kingdom in the Deep Core. Teradoc possessed the largest intact military, and Pellaeon felt that this would provide a safe haven for his surviving fleet until the post-Palpatine confusion could be sorted out. Teradoc placed Pellaeon in charge of his Crimson Command, a huge flotilla of red-hulled *Victory*-class Star Destroyers.

Immediately following the resurrected Emperor's brutal assaults, the New Republic had ordered a sweeping new warship development program—the "New Class." During the days of the Rebellion, most of the Rebel warships were secondhand Corellian models, captured Imperial craft, or heavily modified noncombat vessels (such as Mon Calamari cruisers, originally built as pleasure liners). The ease with which Palpatine's clone was able to rout the New Republic fleet highlighted the need to replace these aging and outdated craft with dedicated combat vessels.

The New Class consisted of eight basic designs—the *Agave*-class picket ship, the *Warrior*-class gunship, the *Sacheen*-class light escort, the *Hajen*-class fleet tender, the *Majestic*-class heavy cruiser, the *Defender*-class assault carrier, the *Endurance*-class fleet carrier, and the *Nebula*-class New Republic Star Destroyer. The first finished ship of the New Class was the *Sacheen*, but it would be years before all eight designs were engineered and manufactured.

PART EIGHT

The Return of the Jedi Knights

SKYWALKER'S JEDI ACADEMY
11 A.B.Y.

After the final defeat of the resurrected Emperor, the New Republic understood the need to consolidate its political hold on the worlds of the New Republic. Luke Skywalker spoke before Mon Mothma and the Senate on the oratory floor of the former Imperial Palace. He voiced his dream to re-create the Jedi Knights, a beacon of hope in the old times, once nearly wiped out by Palpatine.

Though his own training had not been completed by Obi-Wan Kenobi or Yoda, Luke asked permission from the Chief of State to train others in the use of the Force. He knew that his sister Leia, her three children, Kam Solusar, the Witches of Dathomir, Kyle Katarn, and Mara Jade had all exhibited an aptitude for the Force. Surely, there must be others across the galaxy who showed similar, latent abilities.

Luke went to the volcanic planet Eol Sha, where he found a fiery-tempered leader named Gantoris. Next, he tracked down the cloud prospector Streen, living as a hermit in an abandoned floating city on Bespin. Later, he found Tionne, a woman with only a minor talent in the Force, but a great interest in the history of the Jedi.

He located other candidates, including the clone Dorsk 81, the warrior woman Kirana Ti from Dathomir, and Corran Horn from Rogue Squadron. New Republic Commander Kyle Katarn also joined the first batch of students, having spent the previous year battling Palpatine's Imperials and investigating a Sith temple on Dromund Kaas with Mara Jade, where he nearly fell to the dark side. Luke chose the abandoned Rebel base on Yavin 4 for his "praxeum," a place for

the learning of action. In the temple ruins left by the ancient Massassi, Luke began to instruct his candidates in the ways of the Force.

MAW INSTALLATION
11 A.B.Y.

In an attempt to open a diplomatic dialogue with the glitterstim spice miners of Kessel, General Han Solo and Chewbacca visited the planet in *Millennium Falcon*. Since the fall of the Empire, freed inmates from Kessel's Imperial correctional facility had been running the operations; Solo hoped to convince the planet to join the New Republic.

Moruth Doole, a fat Rybet who had set himself up as Kessel's planetary governor, took Han and his Wookiee copilot prisoner. Doole sent his two captives to work in the spice mines, where they met fellow prisoner Kyp Durron. The young man had a strong affinity for the Force, having been trained by Vima-Da-Boda during her stay in the mines. Durron helped the two escape from Kessel, under hot pursuit by Doole's space navy.

In a desperate move, their vessel plunged into the navigational nightmare of the Maw black-hole cluster, where enormous gravity wells made a maze of hyperspace paths. Only Kyp's intuitive use of the Force allowed them to reach the gravitational stability at the center—a site that housed Maw Installation, Grand Moff Tarkin's secret weapons research facility. The skeleton of the Empire's prototype Death

Luke Skywalker and several members of his starting class at the Yavin 4 Jedi academy. [ART BY TOMMY LEE EDWARDS]

Star still orbited the asteroid laboratories, guarded by four Imperial Star Destroyers under the command of Tarkin's former lover, Admiral Daala.

Han Solo and his companions found themselves captured again, this time by an Imperial commander who had no inkling that the war was over and the Emperor dead. Admiral Daala refused to believe what her new captives told her. In prison, Han met Qwi Xux, a brilliant Omwati scientist who had helped develop the Death Star's workings along with Bevel Lemelisk and Umak Leth. Qwi Xux had recently developed an even deadlier weapon—the Sun Crusher—that could set up a supernova chain reaction in the core of a star.

Eventually, Han convinced Qwi Xux to turn against the Imperials and help them escape. Together, they stole the Sun Crusher and headed out of the black-hole cluster, protected from Daala's Star Destroyers by the vessel's quantum armor.

The Sun Crusher streaked out of the Maw cluster, running right into Moruth Doole's space navy. Doole's fleet collided with Daala's four Star Destroyers in a titanic and unexpected space battle, which destroyed one of Daala's vessels and most of the Kessel warships. Now unleashed from her confinement, Daala decided to make up for lost time. With her three Star Destroyers, she vowed to fight a guerrilla war against the New Republic.

POLITICAL TROUBLES
11 A.B.Y.

During a seemingly minor spat at a Coruscant diplomatic reception, Ambassador Furgan from the Imperial Academy world of Carida hurled his drink in Mon Mothma's face. It wasn't clear until later that Furgan had contaminated Mon Mothma with a slow-acting, specially tailored toxin that debilitated the Chief of State. As Mon Mothma grew gravely ill from the poison, rumors spread that she was dying.

A short time earlier, on a diplomatic mission to Vortex, Admiral Ackbar had made a piloting error and crashed into the Cathedral of Winds, killing hundreds of Vors. In disgrace, Ackbar had resigned from his duties and retired to his watery homeworld of Mon Calamari. Leia Organa Solo went to Mon

Calamari to talk to the retired admiral, hoping to convince him to return to his post in light of Mon Mothma's illness.

Admiral Daala's Star Destroyers began to prey on star systems, causing death and devastation. The renegade Imperial fleet struck Mon Calamari during Leia Organa Solo's search for Ackbar, bombarding the planet's floating cities from orbit. Ackbar was forced to take charge to defend his people, destroying another of Daala's Star Destroyers.

The ordeal had given a reticent Ackbar his catharsis, but he refused to return to Coruscant. His main duty was on his homeworld, helping his people rebuild. He would not take the place of the Chief of State, though Mon Mothma grew weaker every day.

EXAR KUN'S REVENGE
11 A.B.Y.

The continuing threats to the New Republic reinforced Luke Skywalker's need to reestablish the Jedi Knights. The training of candidates on Yavin 4 was, however, a process of trial and error. Kyp Durron joined the Jedi trainees, though Luke found a disturbing shadow in Kyp's personality.

Gantoris soon began to receive guidance from a grim spirit that haunted his dreams. Gantoris built his own lightsaber and challenged Master Skywalker to a duel. That night, Gantoris was found burned to a crisp, consumed by a black fire within himself.

Kyp Durron proved to be a phenomenal student who rapidly surpassed the other trainees. In the privacy of his quarters, Kyp encountered the same presence that had corrupted Gantoris: the spirit of Exar Kun, the long-dead Dark Lord of the Sith. Trapped within the Massassi temples for four thousand years, Exar Kun had been awakened by the new Jedi and their explorations of the Force. Restricted to his ethereal form, Kun increased Kyp's hatred of the Empire, brainwashing him to believe that he was the best hope for the salvation of the New Republic. Kyp took it upon himself to wipe out Admiral Daala's renegade fleet. Still manipulated by Exar Kun, Durron stole a ship and flew off alone.

The New Republic Senate had agreed to destroy the Sun

Crusher superweapon that they had recovered from Maw Installation. Their plan called for someone to deposit the quantum-armored ship in the high-pressure heart of the gas giant Yavin. Wedge Antilles and Qwi Xux sent the Sun Crusher into the swirling maelstrom, leaving Qwi as the only person alive with knowledge of the Sun Crusher's workings. But Kyp Durron tracked down Xux on Ithor, using his newfound dark side powers to wipe clean the weapons knowledge from her memory.

Now set on his course of action, Kyp returned to Yavin 4. Standing alone atop the academy's Great Temple, he summoned the Sun Crusher from the mists of Yavin. Luke Skywalker confronted him in a titanic duel of Jedi powers, but the spirit of Exar Kun joined with Kyp to overwhelm Master Skywalker, leaving him for dead. The Jedi students found their Master's motionless body, showing no breathing, no heartbeat, and no response.

Fleeing the scene, Kyp Durron piloted the Sun Crusher to the Cauldron Nebula, where Admiral Daala's fleet had hidden inside an ocean of coalescing gas. When Kyp triggered the superweapon, a cluster of stars went supernova, obliterating the third ship from Daala's original quartet of Star Destroyers. Kyp then reached Carida, the stormtrooper training center represented by Ambassador Furgan. Kyp issued an ultimatum: renounce the Empire or face complete destruction. When the planetary defenses mobilized instead of capitulating, Durron fired at Carida's sun, starting a chain reaction. The sun exploded, and its shock wave wiped out every living thing in the system. Ambassador Furgan escaped the destruction but was later killed in an abortive attempt to kidnap the youngest Solo child, Anakin, on the isolated world of Anoth.

At the Jedi academy, Luke Skywalker remained trapped in stasis for a month, neither dead nor alive. In fact, Luke had been freed from his body and was aware of his surroundings, though no one else could see him. Exar Kun's malevolent spirit possessed other Jedi students in failed at-

Admiral Daala
[Art by John Van Fleet]

tempts to destroy Skywalker's physical form.

Once the true nature of Exar Kun's existence became known to the trainees, Skywalker's students pooled their newfound powers. In a final battle, fighting alongside the spirit-forms of Luke Skywalker and even the long-dead Jedi Master Vodo Siosk-Baas, the students vanquished Exar Kun for all time. Luke Skywalker returned to full health.

Kyle Katarn left the academy after the Exar Kun incident. His brush with the dark side on Dromund Kaas still fresh in his mind, he set aside his lightsaber and allowed his Force skills to atrophy. He would advise Luke in a military capacity only, until the Desann incident nearly two years later.

THE RECAPTURE OF MAW INSTALLATION
11 A.B.Y.

Han Solo and Lando Calrissian tracked down Kyp Durron, urging him to cease his Sun Crusher rampage. Kyp attempted to destroy *Millennium Falcon*, but at the peak of his fury, the anger faded from him. The manipulative spirit of Exar Kun had been destroyed.

Realizing the magnitude of what he had done, he surrendered and agreed to return to Coruscant. After a hearing in which many voices were raised in opposition, an ailing Mon Mothma wielded her veto power. "You have the blood of billions on your hands, Jedi Knight, but I am not the one to judge you. Go to Yavin Four. Let the Jedi Master decide your punishment."

A repentant Kyp Durron asked Master Skywalker how he could find forgiveness. Luke announced that the Sun Crusher needed to be utterly obliterated, and that Kyp Durron must do it himself as an act of contrition. Together, they would go to the Maw cluster and plunge the superweapon into one of the black-hole singularities.

The New Republic assembled a force to return to Maw Installation, to liberate and take control of the weapons outpost. Joining the troops were Chewbacca, who wished to free the remaining Wookiee slaves at the research facility, and ex-researcher Qwi Xux. The occupation force picked its way through the black-hole cluster. Upon seeing the arrival of his enemies, the flustered Maw administrator Tol Sivron commandeered the Death Star prototype and escaped.

New Republic soldiers scoured through the unfinished work of Installation scientists, taking what they could. Before the New Republic forces could secure the station, a battered Star Destroyer appeared inside the Maw—the sole remaining ship of Daala's guardian fleet. Admiral Daala intended to take back Maw Installation, or die in the attempt.

Unlike Grand Admiral Thrawn, throughout her reign of terror Daala had never claimed to be a great military leader or strategist. She had no interest in ruling the Empire or governing conquered worlds—she knew that she couldn't win. Like a nek battle dog, she was willing to attempt even

suicidal plans. With all her remaining weapons, she fired upon the Installation as the occupation soldiers scrambled to protect themselves.

At the same time, Tol Sivron took the Death Star prototype out of the black-hole cluster to the adjacent Kessel system. He used the battle station's superlaser to wipe out some of the massed New Republic battleships, as well as to destroy Kessel's moon. Unbeknownst to Tol Sivron, Han Solo had managed to hide *Millennium Falcon* inside the Death Star's tangled superstructure. With Lando Calrissian and Mara Jade, Han sabotaged the Death Star's superlaser before Sivron could fire on Maw Installation.

Kyp Durron and Luke Skywalker arrived at the Maw cluster on their mission to destroy the Sun Crusher. Wanting to make up for the destruction he had caused, Kyp flew the Sun Crusher, leading the prototype Death Star in a moog-and-rancor game through the gravitational quicksand of the black-hole cluster. The Sun Crusher and the Death Star both plunged into the event horizon of a black hole, and both craft fell to their doom—though Kyp escaped the gravitational pull inside a tiny message pod.

Chewbacca led the offensive against Daala's remaining Star Destroyer. As the occupation force evacuated the Installation, Daala came in on a suicide run, firing on the facility's main power reactor. It exploded in a blinding flash, presumably destroying the Imperial ship, but Daala used the blinded sensors to make good her escape to the Deep Core territory of the major Imperial warlords.

On Coruscant, Mon Mothma's condition had grown progressively worse. In an unlikely gambit, the Force-strong Mon Calamari ambassador Cilghal worked for hours at Mon Mothma's deathbed. Focusing her powers, Cilghal was able to remove the insidious poison one molecule at a time. Though healed, Mon Mothma did not wish to continue as Chief of State, and nominated Leia Organa Solo as her successor.

Soon ratified by a popular vote, Leia assumed her role as leader of the New Republic. General Carlist Rieekan took up Leia Organa Solo's former post as Minister of State. Admiral Ackbar had regained his confidence as a military leader and offered his assistance to the new Chief of State. After years of turmoil, the New Republic looked forward to a time of recovery.

THE EMPEROR'S HAND AND THE SENEX LORDS
12 A.B.Y.

Following Admiral Daala's defeat and the destruction of the Sun Crusher, nearly a full year elapsed with few overt conflicts. Corran Horn, one of the Jedi trainees who had helped defeat the spirit of Exar Kun, left the academy in the middle of the Daala conflict to rescue his wife from Leonia Tavira, a pirate leader and former Imperial who coordinated her destructive raids from her flagship Star Destroyer *Invidious.* Over several months, Horn infiltrated the "Invid" pirates, where he fell afoul of Tavira's Jedi advisers. The presence of new Jedi intrigued Master Skywalker, and he teamed up with Horn on a successful rescue mission to Tavira's headquarters. The strange, reclusive Jedi sect called themselves the Jensaarai, and they traced their origin back several decades to the tutelage of Nikkos Tyris, an Anzati Dark Jedi. Despite their evil influence, the Jensaarai were not sinister, and Skywalker resolved to continue studying their unique approach to the Force.

Centralized Imperial authority had collapsed utterly. The warlords in the Deep Core engaged in open warfare among one another, entire battle fleets clashing amid the dense backdrop of stars. The New Republic adopted a wait-and-see attitude, hoping that the Imperials would eventually burn themselves out.

One warlord, Admiral Harrsk, began shuttling troops out of the Deep Core and amassing a force in the Atravis sector in the Outer Rim, where he was supported by several Imperial fortress worlds. While New Republic Intelligence kept a close eye on this development, they completely missed the ominous stirrings in the Senex and Juvex sectors of the Mid Rim.

Both the Senex and Juvex sectors are ancient aristocracies ruled by a multitude of houses. Emperor Palpatine kept only a token military force in the region, and the New Republic had no success in persuading the Senex Lords to take a more active role in galactic affairs. Their arrogance and sense of noblesse oblige prompted the Senex Lords to forge an alliance with Roganda Ismaren. The woman did not have a blue-blooded pedigree, but she answered to the title by which Palpatine had called her—Emperor's Hand.

Palpatine, of course, had employed many Hands. Arden Lyn had been among the first, and Mara Jade was arguably the best. Others had included Maarek Stele, Sarcev Quest, Blackhole, and Roganda Ismaren. Following the death of her Master, Roganda had gone to ground on the sleepy world of Belsavis. As the years passed, she trained her son Irek in the ways of the Force.

Irek was rumored to be the offspring of Palpatine himself, and had been implanted with a subelectronic converter allowing him to control any machine with a mere thought. Roganda also located a long-dormant Imperial battlemoon—*Eye of Palpatine*—and ordered her son to call the distant ship to Belsavis. The *Eye* was her bargaining chip with the Senex and Juvex Lords, and they had no choice but to listen.

Chief of State Leia Organa Solo made a goodwill visit to the Ceremony of the Great Meet on Ithor. A wild-eyed psychotic shattered the festivities, raving about "the children of the Jedi." Research into the subject revealed that Force-strong children had lived on Belsavis during the dark times, following the establishment of the Empire. Under cover of a diplomatic visit, Leia, Han, Chewbacca, and R2-D2 headed there to investigate, learning that eighteen years prior to the Battle of Yavin, dozens of Jedi younglings had been sheltered on Belsavis by Plett, a Ho'Din Jedi Master. The Emperor had sent the battlemoon to destroy them, but when *Eye of Palpatine* miraculously failed to arrive and carry out its assigned massacre of the settlement, Plett and the children had fled to parts unknown.

In Belsavis's Plawal rift domed city, Leia ran into Roganda Ismaren, whom she recognized from Palpatine's court. Roganda stunned Leia and took her prisoner, locking her in a room near the lip of the rift dome. Leia learned the details of the Ismaren plot, including *Eye of Palpatine,* the Senex and Juvex financial backers, and Irek's ability to scramble the electronics of attacking New Republic fighter craft. But when *Eye of Palpatine* finally emerged from hyperspace in the Belsavis system, Irek Ismaren found that he could no longer control it. Without guidance, the ship reverted to its original mission of complete planetary annihilation.

By the time things had settled down, the Ismarens had vanished to seek asylum within the Senex sector, and they eventually made their way to a laboratory on Coruscant, where Roganda subjected her son to further experiments. Irek Ismaren would not reemerge until the new Jedi order era.

EYE OF PALPATINE
12 A.B.Y.

The colossal, asteroid-shaped *Eye of Palpatine* had been constructed in an era when Palpatine had still found it necessary to hide the extent of his cruelty. His abominable action of wiping out every inhabitant in the Plawal rift—most of them children—would have caused untold outrage in the Senate had it become known. Instead, Palpatine had diverted governmental funds to construct the *Eye,* and ordered the ship's contingent of stormtroopers to await pickup on scattered worlds throughout the Outer Rim.

Luckily, Palpatine's plan never came to fruition. Thanks to the sabotage efforts of the Jedi Knights Geith and Callista, *Eye of Palpatine* had remained dormant in the Moonflower Nebula. The inhabitants of Belsavis escaped, and the waiting stormtroopers grew old and died. The *Eye* slept for thirty years until Roganda Ismaren found it. While Irek Ismaren used his subelectronic converter to summon the ship, Jedi Master Luke Skywalker boarded the *Eye* in the Moonflower Nebula and was inadvertently carried along for the ride.

Two of Luke's Jedi students—Cray Mingla and Nichos Marr—accompanied him. Both had recently joined the Yavin 4 praxeum: Mingla was a brilliant computer programmer and showed much promise as a Jedi, but her lover Nichos Marr had been diagnosed with fatal Quannot's syndrome. In order to preserve Marr's

life, Mingla had transferred his consciousness into the body of an amazingly life-like droid. She had hoped to parallel the Ssi-ruuvi "entenchment" method of harnessing life-energy, but instead it appeared that she had accomplished little more than programming a droid with a false set of memories.

Trapped aboard the *Eye,* Luke and Cray Mingla were forcibly brainwashed by the ship's automated indoctrination equipment. Skywalker had the strength of mind to overcome the imprinting, but the other prisoners did not. *Eye of Palpatine* had attempted to fulfill its programming by picking up its stormtrooper contingent—but after three decades, the *Eye* had settled for whatever warm bodies it found in the appropriate places.

Callista
[ART BY JOHN VAN FLEET]

Two tribes of Gamorreans engaged in a full-scale clan war aboard the automated vessel. Talz, Kitonaks, Tusken Raiders, Affytechans, and other aliens aimlessly roamed the halls, waiting for orders. Jawas began ripping out wires, and a tribe of Tusken Raiders nearly killed Luke. While Luke pondered how to destroy the battlemoon before it could wipe out all life in the Plawal rift, a Jawa gave him a strange object they had found on board: a lightsaber.

Luke soon discovered that the saber's owner, Callista, had transferred her life-essence into the *Eye*'s central computer during her sabotage mission thirty years prior. Though they could communicate only through a computer screen, Skywalker soon realized that Callista—someone whose strength in the Force was as great as his own—was a woman with whom he could spend the rest of his life. The decision to destroy the *Eye* now meant that he would have to destroy Callista as well.

As time ran out, Luke managed to get the aliens loaded aboard escape shuttles. He steeled himself to trigger the *Eye*'s self-destruct, but Cray Mingla unexpectedly dropped him to the floor with a stun blast. Luke woke up on one of the fleeing lifeboats just in time to see *Eye of Palpatine* explode with a soundless roar.

During recovery operations above Belsavis, a team of workers discovered a life pod containing Cray's hibernating body. But the woman who opened Cray's eyes was *not* Cray Mingla. In the *Eye*'s final moments, Cray had voluntarily left her body and allowed Callista to step inside, using the same form of Jedi spirit transference that had allowed Emperor Palpatine to inhabit a succession of fresh clones.

An unexpected side effect of the transfer was Callista's sudden inability to touch the Force. For the moment, though, Luke and Callista were together in body as well as spirit.

The Darksaber Threat
12 A.B.Y.

By this time, several of the Jedi had built their own lightsabers and become Knights of the Republic. New Jedi student Dorsk 81, an alien clone from Khomm, accom-panied Kyp Durron on a mission to Khomm. The planet lay at the fringes of the Deep Core, and Kyp wanted to check in on the current activities of the Imperial warlords.

Inside the Deep Core, Admiral Daala had been trying to unify the squabbling warlords into a full-fledged attack force. Not until she allied herself with Vice Admiral Pellaeon—Thrawn's former second in command—did she make any headway. Prepared to do anything necessary in the name of the Empire, Daala murdered thirteen of the strongest Imperial warlords, including Harrsk, Teradoc, Yzu, and Delvardus, and gathered their forces under her own banner. Before his death, Superior General Delvardus had constructed a Super Star Destroyer, *Night Hammer,* which Daala took as her own flagship. Aware of the battles that she would have to fight against the Jedi Knights, she renamed it *Knight Hammer.* Finally, having learned from mistakes of her first depredations, Daala coordinated her massive space fleet and prepared to launch against the New Republic.

At the same time, the Besadii Hutt clan—which had grown to dominate all the other Hutt clans over the previous decade—and the reborn Black Sun criminal syndicate had embarked upon a scheme of their own. The leader of both groups, Durga the Hutt, had established a secret construction base in the Hoth asteroid belt. Armed with the blueprints to the original Death Star and the expertise of engineer Bevel Lemelisk, Durga intended to build his very own superweapon.

The weapon, code-named Darksaber, was a bare-bones version of the Death Star's planet-destroying superlaser, similar in principle to the Empire's experimental *Tarkin* battle station. Small, simian taurill composed the construction force, using their hive mind to work as a single entity. But the taurill were easily distracted, and the Darksaber Project was beset by hundreds of small, but potentially catastrophic, design errors. Once the taurill had finished the Darksaber, Durga planned to extort protection money from star systems wherever he went.

Suspicious of Durga's activities, Chief of State Leia Or-

gana Solo arranged a diplomatic visit to the central Hutt world of Nal Hutta. A two-pronged military fleet accompanied her (ostensibly engaged in "war gaming exercises"), commanded by General Wedge Antilles and Admiral Ackbar. General Crix Madine, New Republic chief of covert operations, also slipped onto Nal Hutta. He used his espionage skills to plant a tracker beacon on Durga's ship.

Madine soon uncovered the Hutt hideout in the Hoth system. With a group of handpicked commandos, Madine went into the asteroid field to infiltrate the industrial assembly, and the team breached the Darksaber laser housing. Before he could sabotage the works, Madine became a prisoner; his team members died trying to buy his escape. Madine sent out an alarm via an implanted transmitter as the guards hauled off him to face Durga the Hutt.

On the command bridge, Durga ordered his crew to power up the Darksaber. Then, as a christening for his new weapon, Durga ordered the execution of General Crix Madine, who died a hero to the New Republic.

As the Darksaber lumbered into motion, military fleets arrived in the asteroid field in response to Madine's distress signal. Wedge Antilles issued an ultimatum to Durga. Bevel Lemelisk was appalled to see his Hutt boss push the engines to maximum and warm up the superlaser. Sensing disaster, Lemelisk slipped away and jumped ship in a small shuttle. Durga, arrogant and confident, flew the Darksaber into a danger zone of colliding asteroids. He intended to use his superlaser to blast a path through the rubble, but the weapon fizzled without igniting even a spark. Asteroids obliterated the Darksaber weapon and Durga the Hutt in a shattering space collision.

Bevel Lemelisk's shuttle was intercepted by New Republic forces. Later, Lemelisk was incarcerated on Orinackra—ironically, a prison where General Madine himself had once been held—and tried for his crimes of genocide. He became one of the few Imperial criminals to receive the death penalty. The sentence was carried out four years later, and Lemelisk's only comment was "At least make sure you do it right this time."

ADMIRAL DAALA RETURNS
12 A.B.Y.

In the Deep Core, Admiral Daala served as the spokesperson for the reunited Imperial forces. She had caused a dramatic attitude shift in the Imperial military by allowing aliens and women to participate; previously, with the exception of Carnor Jax's Interim Council, they had been largely excluded because of Palpatine's prejudice. In closed consultations, Daala and Pellaeon chose their first strike—they would attack the Jedi academy on Yavin 4. This was a battle they could certainly win, Daala concluded, and it would cost them few casualties and minimum damage.

During these preparations, Kyp Durron and Dorsk 81 had infiltrated the Deep Core. Upon learning of Daala's plans, the two Jedi spies fled, sounding the alarm. Vice Admiral Pellaeon arrived at Yavin 4 with a vanguard fleet of twelve Star Destroyers. The Imperial ships sent down assault forces, armored scout walkers, and ground assault machinery, with orders to crush the Jedi training center to dust. Only hours behind the vanguard force, Daala followed in her Super Star Destroyer, the *Knight Hammer*.

Luke Skywalker, occupied elsewhere with Callista, was not on hand to lead his trainees, but the Jedi candidates defended their academy using everything they had learned of the Force. Durron, Dorsk 81, Kam Solusar, Tionne, Kirana Ti, Streen, Kyle Katarn, and others fought against the Empire's forces. But in the face of such massive military strength, they had no chance. Gathered for a last stand at the stronghold of the Great Temple, Dorsk 81 suggested combining all the Force abilities of the Jedi into a single dramatic effort. He cited

Yoda's famous adage, "Size matters not," and suggested that they could strike directly against the Imperial battleships.

The Jedi channeled their unified push through the conduit of Dorsk 81—a blast strong enough to shove Pellaeon's entire Star Destroyer fleet to the fringes of the Yavin system. The surge of power was too great for Dorsk 81's physical body, and he died, incinerated from within. When Admiral Daala arrived in her *Knight Hammer* for the second wave of the assault, she could not find Pellaeon or his ships. She bitterly launched a renewed attack on the small green moon, blasting the jungles from orbit.

The *Millennium Falcon* arrived during the fighting, carrying Luke Skywalker, Callista, Han Solo, Chewbacca, and Leia Organa Solo. Luke and Callista landed to assist the Jedi trainees against the ground attacks. Callista had been unable to reconnect with the Force following her ordeal on *Eye of Palpatine*, but chose to fight in other ways. Stealing an Imperial ship, she piloted it alone to *Knight Hammer* and planted explosive charges near the rear engine bank.

As Callista had hoped, the exploding charges set off a chain reaction that ripped out *Knight Hammer*'s engine chambers. Within moments, the Super Star Destroyer, with no engines and no guidance control, plunged toward the gas giant Yavin. Daala ordered an immediate evacuation and rushed to the executive command pods to make her own escape. Callista confronted her there, her lightsaber drawn.

At last Callista sensed the potential for using the Force again, but her anger only allowed her to feel the cold tendrils of the dark side. Daala tricked her, however, blasting Callista with a stunner and fleeing as the gas giant Yavin dragged *Knight Hammer* down forever.

Luke later learned that Callista had managed to climb aboard one of the last escape pods and make her way to safety, but after her brush with the dark side, she swore not to return to him until she learned how to control her anger. Luke would not see Callista again for nearly a year.

At the far edge of the Yavin system, Pellaeon had regrouped his damaged Star Destroyers and retrieved as many of *Knight Hammer*'s escape pods as possible, including Ad-

miral Daala's. Once again, Daala's grand plans had fallen to rubble. She relinquished full command of all Imperial forces to Pellaeon in the hopes that he could lead the Empire better than she had. This transfer of power had enormous implications for the eventual settlement of hostilities between Imperial and Republic forces, seven years later.

At the Jedi academy, Luke Skywalker and his students mourned the passing of Dorsk 81. Within months, however, Dorsk 81's clone successor, Dorsk 82, had arrived from Khomm to pick up where his predecessor had left off. On his first official mission, Dorsk 82 teamed with Kyp Durron to investigate the mining planet Corbos. They ran across two monstrous Leviathans, still alive after the devastation of Corbos during the Hundred-Year Darkness, and freed dozens of trapped spirits.

DESANN'S REBORN
12 A.B.Y.

Now working as a New Republic–affiliated mercenary, Kyle Katarn no longer felt a connection to the Force. Late in the year, he accepted Mon Mothma's request to investigate the activities of Galak Fyyar, an Imperial admiral who had allied himself with an ex-Jedi student named Desann. Prior to the *Eye of Palpatine* incident, Desann had killed a fellow Jedi trainee and fled Yavin 4. Now the reptilian Chistori had used Sith alchemy and artusian crystals to artificially imbue a legion of followers with the Force.

After reenergizing himself with a trip to Ruusan's Valley of the Jedi, Katarn proved to be more than a match for Desann's "Reborn" warriors. With help from Luke Skywalker and Lando Calrissian, Katarn defeated Admiral Fyyar and destroyed Desann's flagship *Doomgiver* in the skies above Yavin 4. In a lightsaber duel on the jungle moon's surface, Katarn killed the power-mad Chistori. This time, Kyle Katarn agreed to stay on as an academy instructor and permanent

Luke Skywalker's Jedi academy students take down a Juggernaut.
[ART BY TOMMY LEE EDWARDS]

member of Luke's emerging order of Jedi Knights.

THE EMPIRE REGROUPS
12–13 A.B.Y.

Thanks to Daala's unification efforts, the Empire was stable, though still only a shadow of its former self. If anyone could restore the Empire, or at least slow its inexorable decline, Pellaeon appeared to be the one.

Daala had already pulled all the warlord fleets out of the Deep Core, so Pellaeon abandoned that region as a staging area. The Outer Rim and Mid Rim offered much more favorable opportunities for harassing New Republic shipping. These systems also had more resources, better-traveled hyperspace lanes, and hundreds of thousands of worlds ripe for conquest. Pellaeon hooked up with the existing Imperial fortress worlds, and used his considerable fleet to carve out a well-defined territory for the Empire stretching from Wild Space to the Mid Rim, with a few scattered holdings in the other regions of the galaxy.

The Moffs of the former Imperial fortress worlds threw support behind their new commander, donating carefully hoarded stores of munitions and war matériel. The most impressive acquisition was the Super Star Destroyer *Reaper*. The colossal vessel had once been the flagship of Grand Moff Ardus Kaine's mini Empire, the Pentastar Alignment, before Kaine's death during Operation Shadow Hand. Pellaeon absorbed the remnants of the Pentastar Alignment and made the *Reaper* his personal command vessel.

Six months after Daala relinquished her command, Pellaeon made an aggressive lunge at the New Republic by seizing the small planet Orinda. By the time General Antilles mounted a counterattack, Pellaeon had already captured six neighboring systems. In a monthlong campaign, the New Republic pushed Pellaeon back, but suffered a grave defeat in the Battle of Orinda. There, the *Reaper* destroyed most of Antilles's starfighters by annihilating the fleet carrier *Endurance*. Rogue Squadron, stationed aboard the *Lusankya*, covered the fleet's retreat. The New Republic chose to leave Orinda in Imperial hands, and instead fortified the surrounding systems.

Admiral Daala had no role in Pellaeon's effort. She had voluntarily withdrawn from the Empire and was now the president of an independent settlers' group on Pedducis Chorios. Daala remained disgusted by the overall composition of the Empire—various pockets were still under the sway of petty governors and greedy Moffs. One such pocket was the Antemeridian sector under the rule of Moff Getelles.

MISSION TO ADUMAR
13 A.B.Y.

The New Republic saw the remote planet of Adumar as a way to threaten the Empire on two fronts. Located on the fringe of Wild Space, Adumar was maniacally militaristic, possessing a rigid duel-oriented culture and a worshipful reverence toward starfighter pilots. The first side to bring it into their fold would gain a military powerhouse.

Adumari culture eschewed diplomats in favor of military heroes. Consequently, General Wedge Antilles was sent to the city of Cartann to negotiate with the leadership. His ambassadorial counterpart on the Imperial side, Turr Phennir, had assumed command of the legendary Imperial 181st fighter wing following Baron Fel's defection to the New Republic years before. Antilles witnessed firsthand the locals' love of bloodsport and their ritualized death duels. Appalled by the unnecessary loss of life, Antilles made his feelings known, prompting the Cartann monarchy to lean toward an alliance with the Empire.

Unlike most civilized planets, Adumar did not possess a single worldwide government. Though Cartann's nation was the most powerful, dozens of smaller states existed. Representatives of the other nations contacted Antilles, who agreed to lead their combined militaries in a major offensive that broke Cartann's rule. Adumar reverted to a coalition government with representatives from every nation. After

due deliberation, the planet agreed to join the New Republic.

THE DEATH SEED PLAGUE
13 A.B.Y.

One month after the Battle of Orinda, eight months after the destruction of *Knight Hammer*, Chief of State Organa Solo and a small fleet traveled to the backwater Meridian sector, which ran up against the Antemeridian sector and was thus situated directly on the contentious Republic–Imperial border. Organa Solo was there to meet with Seti Ashgad of Nam Chorios, who had requested New Republic intervention on his planet. Ashgad claimed to be the son of the original Seti Ashgad, who had been exiled to Nam Chorios by Chancellor Palpatine during the Clone Wars.

Seven hundred years earlier, Nam Chorios had been a prison colony. The prisoners' descendants had grown into a tough, independent group called the Oldtimers, who were in direct conflict with the more recent colonists, the Newcomers. Ashgad asked that Organa Solo force the Oldtimers to open up their planet to outside trade, but this request was only a stalling tactic. Aboard Leia's ship, Ashgad's synthdroid bodyguards released thousands of squirming droch beetles that carried the Death Seed plague. Ashgad knocked Leia out

The pilots of Rogue Squadron:
Derek "Hobbie" Klivian,
Wedge Antilles, Wes Janson, and
Tycho Celchu
[ART BY MARK CHIARELLO]

and had spent the past eight months tracking her down. He arrived on Nam Chorios,
and Seti Ashgad's men destroyed the Bleak
Point gun station. Without the anti-orbital
cannon in place, Ashgad would escape the
planet and join Moff Getelles's fleet.

Luke and Leia rushed back to Ashgad's
fortress. While Luke pursued Ashgad's
vessel, Leia faced off against Beldorian.
Beldorian, at nine meters, was staggeringly
large even for a Hutt, and possessed none
of the corpulent rolls that immobilized lazy
Hutts like Jabba. All muscle and fire, he slithered toward
Leia like a snake, but a long, swift side cut with her lightsaber messily ended the career of Beldorian the Splendid.

In the atmosphere, Luke used the Force to convince the
crystals of Nam Chorios of the danger the galaxy would face
if Ashgad's plan succeeded. As Ashgad's ship neared a Star
Destroyer, several of Moff Getelles's needle fighters—pow-
ered by Chorian crystals—suddenly broke formation and
destroyed the craft.

In the Battle of Nam Chorios, Getelles's fleet battled a
makeshift armada thrown together by Han Solo and Lando
Calrissian, as well as Admiral Daala, fighting on the New Republic's side. Daala had nothing but contempt for an Imperial who would ally himself with a schemer and a madman
like Ashgad. Commanding her own warships, she defeated
Getelles in the name of Imperial honor.

In the aftermath, Skywalker completed negotiations with
the Chorian crystal mind. It agreed to send hundreds of crystals offplanet to destroy every plague-carrying droch in the
Meridian sector, in exchange for the eventual return of every
crystal that had been installed in a Loronar product. The
New Republic forced Loronar to comply with the decree, and

and brought her to his fortress on Nam Chorios.

Leia soon learned that the man who captured her was
the *original* Ashgad, kept young and vital through stomach-turning "renewal treatments" administered by Dzym, a
grossly mutated humanoid droch beetle. Ashgad had allied
with Moff Getelles of the Antemeridian sector, who hoped to
cripple the Meridian sector through the spread of the Death
Seed. The Moff's sector navy would then invade, armed with
automated "needle fighters" from the Loronar Corporation.
Loronar's CEO had pledged to arm the plotters in return for
the rights to strip-mine Nam Chorios's minerals. The crystals
of Nam Chorios were more than just programmable matrices
for synthdroids or needle fighters. They were intelligent, sili-
con-based life-forms.

Leia escaped Ashgad's fortress, crossing paths with the
Hutt Beldorian the Splendid, a former Jedi Knight who had
been living on the world for centuries. Leia fled across the
rocky wasteland to the planetary gun station at Bleak Point,
where she saw a familiar face among the Oldtimer settlers:
her brother's lost love, Callista.

Luke Skywalker had been devastated by Callista's decision to abandon him following the *Knight Hammer* incident,

also canceled a government contract for *Strike*-class cruisers. The move nearly sent Loronar into bankruptcy.

Luke Skywalker's reunion with Callista was bittersweet. Luke had slowly come to realize that his life lay along a different path than his lover's. They did not even exchange words—merely a warm look and a wave, and then Luke boarded a shuttle and left Callista behind.

Back on Coruscant, Leia had to accept more elaborate security precautions. She was assigned a pair of bodyguards, whom she nicknamed "the Sniffer" and "the Shooter." Also during the Nam Chorios crisis, Minister of State Rieekan had been incapacitated by poison. One of the culprits, Senator Q-Varx, was arrested and tried for treason. Rieekan's recovery was the only thing that saved Q-Varx from a death sentence, though Rieekan chose not to return to his former post. Mokka Falanthas became Minister of State in his stead.

The New Republic pressed its advantage and entered Moff Getelles's Antemeridian sector with two full fleets. Getelles was powerless to stop them, and the sector (along with a huge chunk of neighboring space) became New Republic territory. Admiral Pellaeon, initially preoccupied with a protracted campaign against Adumar, eventually stopped his enemy from advancing into the heart of the Empire, though the effort cost him the Super Star Destroyer *Reaper*.

Admiral Daala's history following the battle was the most curious of all. While surveying the combat wreckage on Nam Chorios, Daala caught sight of Ashgad's pilot, Liegeus Vorn. Vorn had once had a romance with Daala, and the two rekindled their connection and departed for Pedducis Chorios. The couple then dropped out of sight for nearly a year, during which time Daala reclaimed a leadership position with the new warlords of the Deep Core. Successors to Harrsk, Delvardus, and the others now held power within the Deep Core kingdoms, and while warlords such as Foga Brill and Moff Tethys lacked military muscle, they made up for it in base cruelty. Still trying to impose order, Daala united the squabbling factions to make preparations for a unified strike against the New Republic.

PART NINE

Uprisings and Insurgencies

Following the previous year's crisis in the Meridian sector, the New Republic settled into a period of relative stability. Luke's new Jedi Knights now served as active peacekeepers and powerful symbols of the restored Republic. Chief of State Organa Solo marked the occasion by embarking on a peaceful tour of remote member worlds with her three children. Tragically, the tour indicated just how fragile that peace actually was. The "Empire Reborn" was the first of several localized movements that would cause substantial regional troubles over the next four years.

THE EMPIRE REBORN MOVEMENT
14 A.B.Y.

As Organa Solo visited the provincial planet Munto Codru, her children were kidnapped while at play. Chairman Iyon tried to reassure the Chief of State by speculating that the incident was a "coup abduction"—in Codru-Ji society, children of royal birth were routinely kidnapped and ransomed by rival political factions. The truth was much more complicated.

The children had been kidnapped by Lord Hethrir, a near-human Firrerreo. During the Empire's reign, Hethrir and his mate, Rillao, had been trained by Darth Vader in the ways of the Dark Jedi. Palpatine was so impressed with Hethrir's abilities that he promoted him to Procurator of Justice—an unprecedented appointment for a nonhuman in the New Order. The Procurator of Justice was responsible for carrying out Imperial death sentences against both individuals and entire worlds. As

a sign of his loyalty, Hethrir condemned his own homeworld, Firrerre, to death. But the position was so shadowy that the Rebel Alliance was never able to uncover the Procurator's name. Hethrir lost his power and position in the aftermath of

Hethrir, leader of the Empire Reborn, contemplates grand schemes.
[ART BY JOHN VAN FLEET]

Endor. He fled to the Outer Rim aboard an artificial planetoid given to him by the Emperor, and began attracting wealthy backers to fund his fledgling "Empire Reborn" movement.

His skills with the dark side of the Force, while minor compared to those of Vader or Palpatine, were enough to win over any doubters. Hethrir's core financing came through the sale of slaves. While serving as Procurator, he had dispatched dozens of passenger freighters into deep space, each loaded with prisoners kept in suspended animation. Since he was the only one who knew the location of the freighters, Hethrir could visit them whenever funds were running low, and select potential slaves at his leisure.

At the time of their kidnapping, Jacen and Jaina Solo were five, Anakin only three and a half. Hethrir locked them in individual rooms aboard his worldcraft and placed them under the control of older, uniformed proctors. It was Hethrir's hope that all the captive children would be purchased by his wealthy sponsors.

Hethrir had also forged an alliance with an enigmatic being called Waru on the floating bazaar of Crseih Station. He planned to sacrifice the Force-strong Anakin Solo to Waru in exchange for the creature's help.

Back on Munto Codru, the Chief of State took immediate action to rescue her children, breaking all protocols. She told no one of her intentions—she simply dropped out of sight. Minister of State Falanthas stepped in to keep the government running smoothly. A curious public was told that Organa Solo had fallen ill, and the truth did not become known until months after the actual incident.

Organa Solo, accompanied by Chewbacca, followed the kidnappers' trail in her personal yacht *Alderaan*. Eventually, she crossed paths with Rillao, Hethrir's proud ex-mate. Rillao pointed them on the trail of Crseih Station.

On the way, Organa Solo stumbled across Hethrir's worldcraft. After ensuring the safety of everyone on the tiny planetoid, Organa Solo loaded her other two children aboard the *Alderaan* and raced for Crseih Station to save Anakin's life.

THE POWER OF WARU
14 A.B.Y.

Hethrir's sudden decision to kidnap the children of the Chief of State was shockingly brash. But Hethrir would not have taken such action without feeling confident about his payoff—specifically, the extra-dimensional anomaly called Waru.

During the height of the Empire, Crseih Station been an Imperial research center where Hethrir had authorized

New Republic agent Kyle Katarn
[ART BY JOHN VAN FLEET]

experiments that tested the limits of realspace, hyperspace, and the theoretical realm of otherspace. In the sinkholes near a black hole and a crystallizing white dwarf star, Hethrir's scientists breached the walls between dimensions and brought into existence a massive slab of meat covered with shining golden scales. Though this entity, Waru, lacked discernible sensory organs, it was highly intelligent and could communicate in a deep resonating voice. Waru could heal any disease and could open up other beings to the limits of the Force, but it also consumed life-essences to gain enough power to return to its own dimension.

Waru had gained fame as a healer, curing the sick at the Altar of Waru. Luke Skywalker and Han Solo investigated the goings-on at Crseih, running across Han's old flame Xaverri, who had helped Han's smugglers seventeen years earlier at the Battle of Nar Shaddaa. Before long, Hethrir arrived with a retinue of wealthy supporters, bearing Anakin Solo for a sacrifice. In exchange for Anakin's life-essence, Hethrir hoped that Waru would bestow omnipotent Force powers upon him.

Han, Luke, and Leia rescued Anakin, but Luke let himself be drawn inside Waru's golden essence. He nearly fell into the dark vortex that led to Waru's home dimension, but broke the seductive spell and swam away from the swirling mass. An enraged Waru consumed Hethrir instead, and both of them vanished from the known universe.

Outside Crseih Station, the white dwarf star had reached the final stages of compression into an unstable quantum crystal. The heroes helped fire up Crseih's long-dormant hyperdrive to escape the catastrophic fragmentation of the crystal star. The movable space bazaar arrived at Munto Codru and then relocated to the neighboring Pakuuni system, where it remained.

The most tangible benefit of the Empire Reborn incident was the acquisition of Hethrir's worldcraft. This astonishing structure—a movable planetoid with a forested surface and a blue sky—was scoured by teams of researchers including Death Star designer Bevel Lemelisk (before his execution). The New Republic had no interest in replicating the ridiculously expensive design, but gained insights into engineering and energy management issues, which aided the rollout of the "New Class" warship program.

The eight new starship designs of the New Class had been commissioned following the victory over the resurrected Emperor. The last of the ships, the *Nebula*-class New Republic Star Destroyer, was christened eleven years after Endor. One year later, enough of the New Class had been produced at the Kuat yards to make an entire armada, the New Republic's Fifth Fleet. Some Senators began to question the Chief of State, even going so far as to compare the Fifth Fleet to the sweeping military expansions of Emperor Palpatine.

Later the same year—three years after the defeat of Exar Kun's spirit on Yavin 4—Luke Skywalker's academy students endured another brush with the ancient Sith. Trainee Jaden Korr, who had studied under Kyle Katarn, uncovered traces of a new Sith cult. Inside Vjun's Bast Castle, Jaden Korr confronted fellow student Rosh Penin, who had fallen to the dark side under the cult's influence.

In their efforts to root out the Sith cult, Jaden Korr and Kyle Katarn learned that the spirit of long-dead Sith Lord Marka Ragnos had survived for five millennia in the tombs of Korriban, and was largely responsible for this latest dark side outbreak. Jaden Korr's heroics brought an end to the crisis, as well as pride to his teacher.

THE BLACK FLEET CRISIS
16–17 A.B.Y.

The Black Fleet Crisis had its genesis eight months after the Battle of Endor, during the Imperial Black Sword Command's retreat from the Koornacht Cluster. Yevethan dockworkers at N'zoth rose up, murdered their captors, and seized the Black Fleet armada for themselves. Over the next twelve years, the Yevetha learned to operate their captured warships, including the Super Star Destroyer *Intimidator*. Nil Spaar, chief commando behind the uprising, became the leader of the Yevetha and head of the Duskhan League, a political federation of pure Yevethan colony worlds.

Twelve years after the fall of the Empire, the New Republic was in a tranquil state of relative peace. Other than Hethrir's kidnapping of the Solo children, the galaxy had experienced no serious crisis since the power struggle in the Meridian sector. Leia Organa Solo engaged in a series of peaceable talks with Nil Spaar. Admiral Hiram Drayson, head of a covert New Republic intelligence agency, suspected Spaar was hiding something, and arranged for an unarmed scout ship to make a reconnaissance run deep into the Koornacht Cluster. The ship was promptly blown to bits. Spaar seized upon the incident as proof of Organa Solo's "warmongering," and milked the tragedy for all it was worth to a citizenry weary of war. Several member worlds went so far as to submit articles of withdrawal from the New Republic.

It was the perfect time for the Yevetha to make their move. In a series of lightning raids, they used stolen Black Fleet warships to strike at all non-Yevethan colonies within the Koornacht Cluster. To the Yevetha, this act of genocide was merely the extermination of "alien vermin." They proudly labeled their bloody crusade the Great Purge.

Leia faced a political disaster. Unlike the high-profile strikes of Thrawn and Daala, the Yevetha's Great Purge failed to agitate the electorate. Koornacht was too isolated—most citizens were unwilling to risk New Republic lives to defend worlds they'd never visited. Leia delivered an ultimatum to Nil Spaar, ordering the Yevethan leader to surrender the planets he had seized through immoral force. Spaar called her bluff.

At the cluster colony world Doornik-319, the Yevethan fleet and the Republic armada clashed. But as K-wing bombers lined up for strafing runs against enemy thrustships, the Yevetha broadcast a signal across all wavelengths—the pleading cries of recently seized hostages who begged for Republic restraint lest they be killed along with their captors. Enough K-wings hesitated, and the carefully planned attack runs failed. The New Republic retreated in shameful defeat.

Nil Spaar of the Yevetha rallies his people while thrustships launch behind him. [ART BY TOMMY LEE EDWARDS]

Leia Organa Solo wasn't willing to back down. Several recon flights revealed that every warship in the "lost" Black Fleet was now in the hands of the Duskhan League, including the Super Star Destroyer, now rechristened *Pride of Yevetha*. Han Solo, given the temporary rank of commodore, was placed in charge of a massive New Republic force sent to patrol the cluster's borders. On his way to take command, Han's shuttle was yanked from hyperspace and captured. Han was taken as a prize to N'zoth and brought before a gloating Nil Spaar.

With her husband a prisoner of Nil Spaar, some believed that Leia might risk the lives of New Republic soldiers in an ill-advised attempt to free him. Many Senators thought she should be replaced with someone "less involved" and started drafting a recall petition. Leia continued the fight, ordering an attack that demolished the Yevetha's Black Nine shipyards. Nil Spaar was livid. He transmitted a private hologram to the Chief of State in which he savagely beat and kicked a trussed-up Han Solo for an excruciating twenty minutes. Only three words were spoken throughout the whole stomach-turning display: "Leave Koornacht now."

By revealing his naked cruelty, the hologram was the worst tactical mistake Spaar could have made. With righteous fire in her heart, the Chief of State addressed the Senate regarding the petition of no confidence. She calmly announced that, mere hours before, the New Republic had declared war on the Duskhan League.

Several Wookiees, including Chewbacca and his young son, organized a rescue of Han Solo, exhibiting typical Wookiee subtlety by charging at *Pride of Yevetha* with all guns blazing. *Millennium Falcon* attached itself to the Super Star Destroyer and cut through its hull, allowing Chewbacca and his son to rescue Han Solo from his cell.

With Spaar's bargaining chip eliminated, it was time for a decisive strike against the Duskhan League. The New Republic fleet leapt into the heart of the Koornacht Cluster and squared off against the enemy. The clash grew into a savage brawl, but the Republic received an unexpected gift from a surprising source.

Every ship in the Black Fleet was partially crewed by Imperial prisoners of war, captured years earlier during the shipyard uprising at N'zoth. While the Imperials had no love for the Rebels, they despised their Yevethan captors even more. The human captives activated a hidden slave circuit web that they had installed piecemeal in the Black Fleet's control boards over the previous decade. The Imperials stopped the warships dead, brought them about, and jumped every last Star Destroyer in the direction of Byss in the Deep Core. Nil Spaar, aboard the *Pride of Yevetha,* disappeared along with them.

Many Yevethan thrustships remained, but the battle was essentially over. Even so, the Yevetha fought to the bitter end. The Battle of N'zoth was a victory, but a costly one.

When the Black Fleet finally arrived at Byss, it found a scorched asteroid field expanding in Byss's orbit after the planet's destruction by the Galaxy Gun. Within a month, the vast majority of the Black Fleet had accepted the reality of their situation and defected to the New Republic. Four *Victory*-class Star Destroyers hooked up with Daala's warlords in the Deep Core, and two of the most advanced Star Destroyers, as well as the experimental weapons test bed *EX-F*, chose to join Admiral Pellaeon's shrinking Empire in the Outer Rim. *Pride of Yevetha* vanished entirely. The Super Star Destroyer was discovered four years later, drifting near the Unknown Regions and damaged beyond repair.

Master Skywalker and the Fallanassi
16–17 A.B.Y.

The resolution to the Black Fleet Crisis would not have been possible without the intervention of a mysterious group of women known as the Fallanassi. The members of this reclusive religious order practiced pacifism and followed the "White Current." Similar to the Witches of Dathomir or the disciples of Ta-Ree, the Fallanassi used the White Current in much the same way that Jedi Knights manipulate the Force. As Luke Skywalker has said, "The Force is a river from which many can drink, and the training of the Jedi is not the only cup which can catch it."

Just prior to the crisis, Luke had been visited by Akanah Norand Pell, a member of the Fallanassi. As a child, Akanah had been forced to leave her people and was embarking on a search to pick up their trail. To secure Luke's help, she told him that his mother, "Nashira," had once been a Fallanassi herself. Everything about Akanah's story turned out to be counterfeit, including the name *Nashira,* but at the time Luke was unaware of the identity of his true mother, Padmé Amidala.

The trail of the Fallanassi led to J't'p'tan in the heart of the Koornacht Cluster. There, the Fallanassi had hidden from the Yevetha by projecting the illusion of a bombed-out ruin over their thriving temple settlement.

Luke convinced the Fallanassi to lend assistance to the New Republic by creating an illusory "phantom fleet" at the Battle of N'zoth. The phantom fleet did not frighten the Yevetha, but it did split their fire and allow the New Republic to take out the thrustship armada with fewer casualties than expected. Following the battle, the Fallanassi departed on their private starliner and remained out of public view for nearly two decades, until Jacen Solo ran into them during the events of the Killik expansion.

The Teljkon Vagabond
16–17 A.B.Y.

Lando Calrissian spent his time during the Black Fleet Crisis chasing a "ghost ship" code-named the Teljkon vagabond. Lando and Lobot, accompanied by R2-D2 and C-3PO, spent weeks trapped aboard the vagabond before discovering that the organic vessel had been built by the Qella species, just prior to a catastrophic ice age that had befallen their homeworld. The vagabond was a "tool kit" for melting a frozen planet. Beneath the kilometer-thick ice, thousands of Qella lay in hibernation, waiting for the thaw.

The vagabond took up position in orbit and began melting the ice. It eventually completed its work in the middle of the Yuuzhan Vong invasion, when no New Republic scientists could be spared to oversee the reveal. When an overdue team finally arrived at the planet, the Qella and their strange starship had vanished. The Teljkon vagabond still ranks as one of the most significant archaeological discoveries of the past century, alongside the Corellian repulsors, the cities of the Sharu, and the Jedi library on Ossus.

Uprising at Almania
17 A.B.Y.

The Black Fleet Crisis had serious repercussions for galactic peace. The Yevetha were an isolated and numerically insignificant foe, yet they had caused the New Republic more grief than anyone since Admiral Daala. Other groups, including the remnants of Pellaeon's Empire and the Deep Core warlords, began to reconsider armed conflict against their old foe. To add more fuel to the fire, the Senate passed a measure allowing former Imperial officials to hold elective office.

The measure's most vocal opponents predicted that admitting unrepentant Imperial loyalists into the Senate would cause the government to dissolve into partisan gridlock. The ex-Imperial Senators delighted in opposing Organa Solo at every turn. On the fifty-first day of the new term, when Organa Solo stepped into the Senate Hall to address the body, a tremendous explosion knocked her off her feet.

The Chief of State survived with minor injuries, while dozens of Senators died instantly. Senate Hall was a ruin, closed off to visitors as construction began on its replacement, the Grand Convocation Chamber.

The bombing had been executed by Brakiss, a former Imperial spy who, years before, had unsuccessfully tried to infiltrate Luke Skywalker's Jedi academy on Yavin 4. Brakiss was in league with Dolph, a fallen Jedi trainee. Dolph had abandoned his training in order to fight the despotic Je'har regime on remote Almania. He rose to prominence among the resistance, assuming the name Kueller and hiding his identity behind a formfitting death's-head mask. Over several years, Kueller employed dark side skills to exterminate the Je'har and become Almania's undisputed leader.

Brakiss had fled the Jedi academy when Skywalker had forced Brakiss to confront the darkness in his soul. Kueller had helped put him back together, and Brakiss served the powerful man out of gratitude and fear. For two years, Brakiss had been the sole operator of the Telti droid factories, and had secretly rigged his droids with explosive detonators. This was Kueller's secret weapon—unexpected, unseen, and completely devastating.

In addition to the Senate bombing, Kueller used rigged droids to obliterate the populations of Pydyr and Auyemesh, two of the three inhabited moons orbiting Almania. Despite the fact that Almania had never been a member of the New Republic, many pro-Imperial observers dubbed this struggle between mismatched opponents "the new Rebellion."

Luke Skywalker investigated Brakiss's droid-manufactur-ing plant on Telti and set out for Almania. Luke's sabotaged X-wing fighter exploded, however, and he became a captive of Kueller's, imprisoned on Almania to serve as bait for his headstrong Jedi sister.

Back on Coruscant, Leia presided over the political equivalent of a ticking thermal detonator. The opposition Senators now held a majority, and a petition of no confidence—the second in less than two years—was entered into the record. When Kueller threatened to kill Luke unless Leia turned the reins of the New Republic over to him, Leia resigned her position as Chief of State. This nullified the no-confidence vote and freed her to go after Kueller on her own. Mon Mothma returned to lead the New Republic in a temporary role, until new elections could be held.

Mon Mothma sent a small fleet under the command of General Wedge Antilles to provide firepower for the rescue mission. Leia Organa Solo left for Almania in her personal ship, accompanied by Antilles in a Mon Calamari star cruiser and a number of smaller warships.

When they arrived in the Almania system, three *Victory*-class Star Destroyers rose from the planet, unleashing scores of deadly TIE fighters. Antilles streaked into pitched battle with Kueller's armada, while Organa Solo slipped through the fighter screen and landed on Almania's surface. General Antilles soon realized the reason for the enemy ships' oddly precise maneuvers—they were crewed entirely by droids.

Brakiss (foreground) and Kueller
[ART BY JOHN VAN FLEET]

With this knowledge, Wedge exploited the tactical flaws of artificial intelligence and crippled the Star Destroyers with turbolaser hits.

On Almania, Leia rescued her brother, but found Kueller standing between them and freedom. Kueller ignited his energy blade and joined battle with Luke, who realized that his aggression was only making Kueller stronger. Recognizing the Master–student parallels with Kenobi and Vader's showdown aboard the Death Star, Skywalker prepared to sacrifice his own life. If Kueller struck him down, he would return in spirit-form and guide Leia to victory.

But as Luke raised his lightsaber in a passive salute, a native thernbee animal—carrying Force-repelling ysalamiri in its belly—nullified Kueller's Force advantage. In a blind rage, Kueller pulled out a master detonator that could trigger the explosion of every droid manufactured on Telti. Before anyone could stop him, he stabbed his finger on the button.

Light-years away, on Telti, C-3PO and R2-D2 had infiltrated Brakiss's droid factories and, with help from the mechanic Cole Fardreamer and an army of astromechs, had broken into the control room. Jacking into a computer terminal, R2 intercepted Kueller's master control signal and deactivated the remote detonators at the last instant.

Leia had no way of knowing whether Kueller's bombs had been discharged, so she took the quickest possible route to prevent further trickery. Drawing a blaster, she shot Kueller cleanly in the head. Was her deed—a violent killing committed in anger—an act born from the dark side? At that moment, she didn't care.

Leia, Luke, and Wedge Antilles returned to Coruscant as heroes. Mon Mothma gladly stepped down, and Leia returned to her former position, which was ratified without dissent. The Chief of State addressed the congress in the temporary Senate Hall, vowing to make this new term one of unity and strength.

In the wake of his failure on Telti, Brakiss fled the droid-manufacturing moon. He disappeared for several years, and was later discovered serving as a neutral intermediary between the warlords of the Deep Core. Eventually Brakiss rose to a leadership position with the Second Imperium, a group that caused significant headaches for the New Republic during the later years of Imperial–Republic peace. He founded a training center for dark Jedi, the Shadow Academy, with the intention of creating evil Force warriors for the continuing battle.

IMPERIAL SKIRMISHES
17–18 A.B.Y.

Hot on the heels of the Almanian uprising, both the Deep Core warlords and Pellaeon's Empire attempted to reclaim some formerly held sectors. They gambled that the New Republic wouldn't put a full effort behind stopping them, for fear of inspiring another public relations debacle like the Yevethan conflict at Doornik-319. They were mistaken.

The New Republic added the Super Star Destroyer *Guardian,* captured during the previous year from the rogue Imperial Admiral Drommel, to the third fleet, then sent both the Third and Fifth fleets out to engage Pellaeon in several major brawls. The most notable were the Battle of Champala and the Battle of Anx Minor. In the latter climactic conflict, Admiral Ackbar scored a last-minute victory by focusing a hail of concentrated fire on the engines of the experimental vessel *EX-F* (also known as *Glory of Yevetha*). The ship exploded, igniting its volatile antimatter reservoir and annihilating six nearby Star Destroyers. When the dust from the conflicts finally settled, Pellaeon's Empire had been pushed back into a mere eight sectors of a strategically barren section in the Outer Rim.

The Deep Core warlords fought on the opposite edge of space, but did not present a unified front. Therefore, they crumpled under a series of deadly perimeter assaults from the Republic's Fourth Fleet. In one of the final assaults, General Bel Iblis attempted to capture Admiral Daala in a pincer move with a pair of CC-7700 gravity-well frigates. In a shocking move, Daala's lead frigate rammed one of the CC-7700s, destroying it, and eliminating its projected mass shadow.

Admiral Gilad Pellaeon
[Art by John Van Fleet]

The Corellian Insurrection
18 A.B.Y.

During the lull, Chief of State Leia Organa Solo visited a major trade conference on Corellia. The system itself contained five inhabited planets—Corellia, Drall, Selonia, and the double worlds of Talus and Tralus—which had been transported into their orbits by an unknown pre-Republic power. As the home of major conglomerates including Corellian Engineering and the birthplace of famous Republic heroes such as Han Solo and Wedge Antilles, the Corellian sector was respected throughout the galaxy.

In the post-Palpatine era, however, the sector had surrounded itself in airtight isolation. The ruling Corellian diktat vanished, and the sector became inward looking and inward thinking. Lucrative trade routes dried up, and businesses relocated elsewhere. The New Republic installed a Frozian named Micamberlecto as Corellia's governor-general, but he was little more than a figurehead attempting to control a discontented populace. The Chief of State hoped this trade conference would be the first step in bringing the sector more fully into the fold.

Lando Calrissian, meanwhile, had decided to turn over regular operation of the Kessel mines to Nien Nunb, his Sullustan copilot during the destruction of the second Death Star at Endor. Calrissian invested his funds in an underground housing project on Coruscant called Dometown, but when that didn't satisfy the gambler's yearning for a quick score, he decided on the easiest and oldest method of getting rich quickly—marrying into money. Lando and Luke embarked on an outlandish "wife hunt," which unexpectedly bore fruit when Lando met Tendra Risant on the Corellian sector world of Sacorria. Both men found themselves expelled from Sacorria, however, when they offended the planet's repressive government, the Triad.

Neither Luke nor Lando realized that the masterminds of an imminent Corellian insurrection were lying right under their noses. The Triad of Sacorria had orchestrated a plot to

Daala's badly damaged flagship then vanished into hyperspace, and has not been encountered since. New Republic Intelligence was tempted to declare Daala killed in action, but it had learned from past experience never to presume an enemy's death—especially not hers.

The New Republic's enemies were in retreat, their navies spent. No further galactic conflicts loomed on the immediate horizon. Ackbar took advantage of the temporary respite to order most warships into dry dock for repairs and upgrades. Those fleet vessels not affected by the recall were put to work patrolling the borders of the Empire and the Deep Core.

break away from the New Republic and have the Corellian sector recognized as an independent state. The key to their scheme was Centerpoint Station, a pre-Republic space depot located between the twin worlds of Talus and Tralus. Millions of citizens lived inside the alien artifact, both in its labyrinthine corridors and along the spherical walls of its hollow interior. After more than thirty thousand years, the Triad had at last uncovered Centerpoint's purpose.

As a massive hyperspace tractor-repulsor, Centerpoint Station had been used by alien architects to pull the Corellian planets through hyperspace. Vast repulsor chambers buried beneath the crust of each world then nudged the planets into stable orbits around the star Corell. The Triad realized that Centerpoint, and the individual planetary repulsors, could be turned into superweapons. They backed various insurgent groups on each planet—the Human League on Corellia, the Overden on Selonia, and the Drallists on Drall—and ordered them to find their respective planetary repulsors, thus preventing the devices from being used against the Triad. They also learned how to make Centerpoint Station fire hyperspace repulsor bursts and trigger supernovas in distant stars. Finally, the Triad used Centerpoint to generate an interdiction field that encompassed the entire star system, making hyperspace travel impossible within its sphere of influence. With Chief of State Organa Solo trapped by the interdiction field, and a supernova countdown as their non-negotiable ultimatum, the Triad planned to create a breakaway "mini Empire" with themselves at the head.

Unfortunately for them, the Triad made a fatal mistake by approaching Thrackan Sal-Solo, the treacherous leader of Corellia's anti-alien Human League. When Leia arrived at the trade conference, the Triad triggered the interdiction field. Sal-Solo, however, double-crossed his masters and also activated Centerpoint's jamming field, preventing the Triad from negotiating with the Chief of State. Sal-Solo declared himself diktat, figuring that he could grab most of the Corellian system for himself before the Triad could move against him.

What was supposed to have been a quiet trade conference had turned into a catastrophe. The Chief of State was held captive by Human League troops. Chewbacca and the three Solo children, along with their Drallish tutor Ebrihim, had escaped Corellia on *Millennium Falcon*, but were trapped in-system by the interdiction field. Han Solo had been captured by Thrackan Sal-Solo, and in the underground head-

every intention of turning their closely guarded prize over to the current Imperial leadership on Bastion.

Admiral Voss Parck—a longtime associate of Thrawn's from the Empire's early days—operated the stronghold, along with many blue-skinned, red-eyed Chiss. They had been waiting on Nirauan for a decade, for Thrawn had always promised his followers that if he should ever be killed, he would come back to them in ten years' time. Parck, Baron Soontir Fel, and other former Imperials now lived in the Un-known Regions, where they worked alongside Chiss soldiers in a kingdom called the Empire of the Hand. Their realm did not answer to either the Empire or the Chiss Ascendancy.

Skywalker and Jade realized that they couldn't allow Parck to contact Bastion. The two Jedi escaped the castle, and Mara used the beckon call installed aboard *Jade's Fire* to rouse her cherished ship and guide it directly into the Hand of Thrawn's docking bay, destroying every craft on the launching pad.

But that was not enough, and they both knew it. Luke and Mara returned to the enemy citadel, this time arriving at a series of chambers far beneath the structure's foundation. There, in a room so protected that not even Parck knew of it, they found a Spaarti cloning cylinder. And floating inside the cylinder was a fully grown clone of Grand Admiral Thrawn.

Their difficult moral choice—to execute a helpless being or to stand aside and allow a new Thrawn to possibly re-subjugate the galaxy—was decided for them. The room's automated defensive systems focused hot blasterfire on the intruders, weakening the chamber's rock wall. With an angry gurgle, thousands of gallons of icy lake water flooded the room and drowned the Thrawn clone before it could be born. Luke and Mara escaped, waterlogged but very much alive.

Over the past decade, Luke and Mara had progressed from enemies to friends to fellow Jedi. But their experiences on Nirauan marked a turning point in their relationship. They both realized that no two people in the universe were

A clone of Grand Admiral Thrawn nears completion in the fortress on Nirauan. [ART BY TOMMY LEE EDWARDS]

so perfectly matched in ability and in attitude, in strength and in spirit. Though they didn't always see eye-to-eye, their differences complemented one another perfectly, meshing together peak-to-valley in a hold that was far stronger than either standing alone. Luke Skywalker proposed marriage. Mara Jade accepted.

The two lovers left Nirauan behind in a stolen alien starship and headed back to the New Republic with a copy of the Caamas Document gleaned from Thrawn's personal library.

THE MARRIAGE OF LUKE AND MARA
19 A.B.Y.

Symbolically, the union of Luke Skywalker and Mara Jade held even more value than the signing of the peace treaty. The marriage of the Rebel Alliance's iconic hero to the woman who had once been Emperor Palpatine's top assassin drew attention from all corners of the galaxy, including the embittered residents of the shrunken Empire, now called the "Imperial Remnant" on New Republic maps.

To those who had once claimed near-total dominion over known space, their territory, no matter how small, would always be known as the Empire. On snowy Dolis 3, a band of Imperial partisans viewed the looming nuptials with contempt. Believing the event to be more proof that the Empire had been watered down like weak caf, the loyalists made plans to slip into Coruscant and sabotage the ceremony.

One of their number claimed to be a former Royal Guardsman, and though his experience was likely a mere boast, his attempt to kill Mara Jade during her dress fitting gave a murderous edge to the plot. The other Imperials focused on infiltrating the event site and hiring a gang of swoopbikers to harass the wedding guests.

Despite the scheming, the wedding went off with minimum mayhem. Following Luke's raucous bachelor party in Coruscant's lower levels, the happy couple joined together in a private Jedi ceremony officiated by Kam Solusar in the renovated Jedi Temple. The public ceremony, held in Coruscant's Reflection Gardens, remained peaceful thanks to extra muscle provided by Booster Terrik and others, who kept the swoopbikers at bay. When the final Imperial plotter crashed the ceremony and threatened to release a crippling computer virus, Luke persuaded him to give himself up and join the party. With that quiet denouncement, a generation of hostilities suddenly seemed as dead as Palpatine himself. Weeks later, Lando Calrissian wed Tendra Risant, the woman he had met during the events of the Corellian insurrection.

After his wedding, Luke Skywalker decided to alter the instruction schedule of his Yavin academy, devoting more time to the training of younger pupils. Some of the more advanced trainees left Yavin 4 to engage in one-on-one Master–apprentice relationships throughout the galaxy. Tionne took over many of the historical chores, enriching the legacy of the Jedi Knights. Mara Jade insisted that she was no teacher and spent little time on the jungle moon, even when her husband returned to the praxeum to address his students.

PART ELEVEN

Generations of Jedi Knights

The armistice brought about by the Pellaeon–Gavrisom treaty was a durable peace. Three long, quiet years passed, blissfully uninterrupted by Imperial schemes, mad Jedi, local brushfires, or unexpected alien invasions.

After more than a decade of labor, Luke Skywalker had many successes in his Jedi praxeum on Yavin 4. He had found many new trainees, some human and some exotic. However, because Skywalker was frequently called away on his own adventures and also to spend time with Mara Jade, one of his first trainees—the scholar and minstrel Tionne—took over Luke's duties. Interplanetary squabbles and trade conflicts were as much a constant as always. At the urging of her friends in the government, Leia Organa Solo ran again for the post of New Republic Chief of State, and was elected back into that office in 21 A.B.Y. Organa Solo's three children, the twins Jacen and Jaina and her younger son Anakin, all had a strong talent in the Force. The three youths spent much time at the Jedi academy.

THE GOLDEN GLOBE AND KENOBI'S LIGHTSABER
22 A.B.Y.

Though there had been a few lessons in historic Jedi Holocrons regarding the training of extremely young children, Luke Skywalker was unaware of any specific rule for the age at which a talented person could begin to learn the ways of the Force. Anakin Solo came to the Jedi academy when he was midway through his eleventh year. Different from his outgoing twin siblings, Anakin was studious and reserved, often a loner. He liked puzzles, mysteries, mental challenges, and brainteasers. On Yavin 4 he

befriended a young girl named Tahiri Veila, who had grown up with the Tusken Raiders of Tatooine, keeping her face fully bandaged and breathing through metal filters until discovered by the Jedi instructor Tionne.

Anakin and Tahiri crossed the nearby jungle river to the Palace of the Woolamander, a crumbling ruin abandoned ages before. Both young trainees had been drawn there by identical dreams. As they explored the dim ruins, they broke into a sealed chamber that contained a glowing sphere of golden light. Curled up at its base lay a mysterious furry creature, deep in sleep; it had large eyes, floppy ears, and simian features. The furry being identified himself as Ikrit, a Kushiban Jedi Master who had come to the jungle moon to study the Massassi temples four centuries earlier. He had discovered the golden globe, but could not break its curse, and he had been hibernating ever since.

After journeying to the nearby moon of Yavin 8, they learned that the golden globe contained the trapped spirits of young Massassi victims of Exar Kun's experimentations. Anakin and Tahiri broke past the barricades erected long before by Exar Kun, and freed the trapped Massassi spirits. When the two emerged, they found Luke Skywalker waiting for them, standing beside Ikrit.

Anakin remained troubled by dreams of himself as a Dark Jedi, by his heritage as the grandson—and original namesake—of Darth Vader. When Leia Organa Solo was pregnant with Anakin, the resurrected Emperor had touched her and tried to take over the unborn child. To be sure that he didn't have the potential for evil inside him, young Anakin asked if he could go to the cave on Dagobah, as Luke Skywalker had done, and face himself.

Before arrangements could be made, a stowaway teenager was found on one of the supply ships to the Jedi academy. The young man, Uldir Lochett, begged Skywalker to train him as a Jedi—though when tested, Uldir showed no Force potential whatsoever. When Anakin, Tahiri, and Ikrit traveled to Dagobah, Uldir stowed away again and fell into trouble with some swamp creatures. The group finally reached the cave where Skywalker had faced his own dark side during his training with Yoda; there, Anakin faced down the manifestations of his own doubts and fears and emerged with confidence.

Back on Yavin 4, the Jedi historian Tionne had learned that Darth Vader had saved Obi-Wan Kenobi's lightsaber after their fight aboard the Death Star. It had been sent to Vader's stronghold, Bast Castle, on Vjun. Tionne, Ikrit, Anakin, Tahiri, and Uldir made the journey to Vjun, but as soon as they had retrieved the artifact, a group of mercenaries and pirates stormed into the room. Their leader, Orloc, claimed to be a Mage with great powers. In a brief confrontation, Orloc tempted Uldir, promising the powerless boy that Orloc could grant him all the Jedi skills that Uldir wished. But Tionne, Ikrit, and the others rescued him and retrieved the lightsaber, as well as a Holocron filled with Jedi knowledge.

Uldir remained obsessed with what the Mage had told him. He stole both artifacts and a ship and fled to find Orloc. Anakin, Tahiri, Tionne, and Ikrit pursued him to an ancient ghost city in space, Exis Station, where Tionne herself had met Luke Skywalker in her search for relics. There, Mage Orloc had set up his base and taken Uldir as a new recruit. Orloc actually had no Force talent himself, but used high-tech gimmicks to fool others with demonstrations of "power."

In a battle of Force versus fake technomagic, Uldir saw true Jedi power in action. He helped to defeat Orloc and left Exis Station with the Holocron and Kenobi's lightsaber. The students returned to the Jedi academy, knowing they still had much to learn—and many years yet in which to do so.

THE RETURN OF OUTBOUND FLIGHT
22 A.B.Y.

The Outbound Flight Project had been one of the curiosities of the Old Republic, nearly forgotten in the rush of the Clone Wars and the Jedi Purge that followed. Certainly, no one had expected to hear from the Outbound Flight Dreadnaughts after their disappearance a half century earlier. Luke Skywalker and Mara Jade believed that Grand Admiral Thrawn had destroyed the vessels during his early career as a Chiss military renegade.

Now, however, Luke and Mara received word that their assumptions about Outbound Flight may have been faulty. Through Admiral Parck at Nirauan's Hand of Thrawn base, the two Jedi learned that the Chiss had located the remains of the Outbound Flight vessels in an inaccessible pocket of the Unknown Regions known as the Redoubt. As official representatives of the New Republic, Luke and Mara boarded the Chiss Diplomatic Vessel *Chaf Envoy* for the long journey into the heart of the Redoubt.

The ship's other passengers appeared to be evenly split between politicians and pilgrims. Aristocra Formbi, the head Chiss aboard *Chaf Envoy,* welcomed guests that included Commander Chak Fel (one of the sons of Baron Soontir Fel) of the Empire of the Hand; Dean Jinzler of the New Republic, who wanted to see Outbound Flight to honor his Jedi sister; and a mass of timid Geroons who wished to pay their respects to the Outbound Flight Jedi who had freed them from their "Vagaari enslavers."

Eventually reaching a planetoid inside the Redoubt, the passengers of *Chaf Envoy* discovered that, while the Outbound Flight Dreadnaughts still hung together in their original hexagonal-linked configuration, only the topmost Dreadnaught protruded above the loose shale that passed for a surface on the irradiated world. Within the junk-strewn corridors of the vessel, they soon made two shocking discoveries: a band of crash survivors had established a colony and

The final resting place of the Outbound Flight Project.
[ART BY TOMMY LEE EDWARDS]

remained alive for the last five decades, and the Geroon penitents were not the innocents they had claimed to be. Rather, the Geroon *were* the Vagaari slavers, come to take revenge on the Chiss for defeating them long ago.

As Vagaari troopers fanned out to assume control of the Outbound Flight complex, Luke and Mara worked with Commander Fel's stormtroopers and several of the colonists to minimize the bedlam. Most of the Vagaari packed aboard the uppermost Dreadnaught, freed it from its sister ships with explosive charges, and escaped into space. Pursuit seemed impossible until one of the colonists revealed the existence of a mothballed starfighter. Luke and Mara activated the craft, caught up to the Dreadnaught, and eliminated the threat posed by the Vagaari renegades.

In the aftermath, Aristocra Formbi revealed that the Chiss had known the nature of the Geroon/Vagaari ruse all along. Since the Chiss had a moral principle against making first strikes, Formbi had hoped the Vagaari would take advantage of the Outbound Flight bait and make an aggressive move. Now that they had, war had been declared between the Chiss Ascendancy and the Vagaari.

Dean Jinzler found closure, realizing that his sister had done everything she could to protect Outbound Flight, and had died with honor during Thrawn's attack. The Outbound Flight colonists left the Redoubt, the only home they'd known for decades. Most of them began new lives in the Empire of the Hand.

The Shadow Academy and the Second Imperium
23 A.B.Y.

The Solo twins—Jacen with his quirky sense of humor and rapport with animals, and Jaina with her aptitude for mechanics—became two of the most talented of the new generation of Jedi Knights. Together with their companions Tenel Ka, warrior daughter of Prince Isolder of Hapes and Teneniel Djo of Dathomir, and Lowbacca, the Wookiee nephew of Chewbacca, they fought for the New Republic with as much bravery as the legendary Jedi Knights of old.

During a training exercise in the jungles of Yavin 4, the young Jedi Knights discovered the wreckage of a TIE fighter—an Imperial ship that had crashed there years before, during the Rebel battle against the first Death Star. The Jedi Knights were unaware that the original pilot, a grizzled old man named Qorl, had survived the crash and had been eking out a living in the wilderness. Qorl forced the Jedi students to complete the final repairs so that he could flee the jungle moon, and then flew off to rejoin the Empire . . . wherever he could find it.

Months later, as the Jedi continued their training, Jacen, Jaina, and Lowbacca accompanied Lando Calrissian to his new Corusca gem mining facility, *GemDiver Station,* in the atmosphere of the gas giant Yavin. While Calrissian showed them his operations, the station came under attack by a frightening black-clad woman, Tamith Kai, one of the Nightsisters of Dathomir. Jacen, Jaina, and Lowbacca were stunned and taken prisoner.

They awoke aboard the Shadow Academy, a cloaked space station that acted as a dark counterpart to Skywalker's Jedi academy. Brakiss, the former academy student who had assisted in the Almanian Uprising six years earlier, now headed the Shadow Academy on behalf of the Second Imperium, a radical Imperial group that did not recognize the "sham" peace accords signed by Pellaeon. The Nightsister Tamith Kai, along with the former TIE pilot Qorl, planned to use Jacen, Jaina, and Lowbacca as recruits for Imperial brainwashing.

The captives resisted all attempts to convert them to the dark side. They escaped, with some surprising assistance from the troubled TIE pilot Qorl.

Returning to Coruscant to spend time with Han Solo and Leia Organa Solo, the young Jedi Knights recovered from their ordeals. They explored the lower levels of the huge planetary city with Zekk, an orphaned street urchin the twins had known for years. Soon, however, Zekk—along with the members of the Lost Ones street gang—became a new recruit for the Shadow Academy.

Aboard the Shadow Academy, Brakiss showed Zekk how

Republic military forces. The Shadow Academy vanished into hyperspace, once again foiling pursuit.

With the known threat of the Shadow Academy and the Second Imperium, Luke Skywalker decided that his students must build their own lightsabers. When finished, the students trained against remotes and then each other—but in a tragic accident during a sparring match against Jacen Solo, Tenel Ka lost her arm when her weapon failed.

Recuperating, Tenel Ka went home to be pampered on the wealthy world of Hapes, home of her father, Isolder. She refused to be fitted with an artificial arm. While on Hapes, Tenel Ka and her Jedi friends foiled an assassination attempt designed to overthrow Tenel Ka's grandmother Ta'a Chume.

Agents of the Second Imperium struck next on Kashyyyk, with the intention of raiding New Republic stores of powerful new computer units. Zekk led the Imperial commando team. Jacen, Jaina, Tenel Ka, and Lowbacca defeated most of the Imperial troops, and Jaina faced off against her former friend Zekk in the deep jungle. Zekk could not bring himself to hurt her, but he warned her to stay away from Yavin 4.

On the Shadow Academy itself, Brakiss had learned the astonishing news that Emperor Palpatine himself was coming to the cloaked station. Brought aboard in a giant isolation tank on repulsorlifts, "Palpatine" gave no explanations as to how he had survived the destruction of all his clones years earlier. The Emperor's red-armored Royal Guards, who blocked all of Brakiss's inquiries, were former stormtroopers promoted to guardsman status during Admiral Daala's rule, as a symbolic display of power.

Jacen Solo and Tenel Ka
[Art by John Van Fleet]

to tap into unsuspected Jedi potential. Suddenly, Zekk found himself in control of great powers he had never dreamed of—and became an easy mark for Imperial brainwashing. He turned into one of the most exceptional of the new Dark Jedi.

Jacen, Jaina, and their friends discovered that Zekk had been taken captive—and that the Imperial station was secretly in orbit around Coruscant itself. Using giant solar mirrors in space, they burned out the Shadow Academy's cloaking systems and exposed the station to rallying New

(The last true Royal Guard had been Kir Kanos; Major Tierce had been a simple clone.)

On Yavin 4, the young Jedi Knights braced for an attack by the Shadow Academy. Imperial assault teams dropped to the surface: TIE fighters, stormtroopers, and swarms of Dark Jedi Knights led by Zekk and the Nightsister Tamith Kai. Tenel Ka sabotaged Tamith Kai's floating battle platform and the structure crashed into the river, killing the Nightsister.

When the tides of battle turned against him, Brakiss demanded to see the Emperor. Two Imperial guards blocked his way, but Brakiss cut them down with his lightsaber, then chopped through the door of Palpatine's isolation chamber. Inside, he found a third guard working a bank of controls, computer screens, and hologrammic generators, maintaining the illusion that Palpatine had returned to lead the Second Imperium. The last guard escaped before using the override controls to trigger the Shadow Academy's self-destruct systems. The giant station turned into a fireball.

On Yavin 4, an Imperial soldier planted a bomb inside the Great Temple, but Zekk prevented the Jedi from entering, saving all their lives. He was a broken young man now, realizing what damage he had caused and how he had betrayed his friends. The bomb's explosion destroyed much of the Great Temple.

The Second Imperium had been quashed in a single major confrontation, the Shadow Academy destroyed, and the remaining Imperials and Dark Jedi taken prisoner. Qorl, the castaway TIE pilot, returned to his former life in the jungle.

The Diversity Alliance

23–24 A.B.Y.

Skywalker's trainees set to work rebuilding the academy. While Zekk recovered from his injuries, he was haunted by nightmares stemming from his deep involvement with the dark side. Zekk never wanted to use the Force again. He left Yavin 4 in search of his home, in search of peace, and eventually decided to use his talents to become a bounty hunter.

During the repairs, Han Solo arrived with a grim message for Jedi student Raynar Thul, a prince of the surviving highborn family that had escaped Alderaan. Raynar's father, Bornan Thul, a wealthy merchant and shipping magnate, had disappeared while en route to an important trade meeting with the Twi'lek Nolaa Tarkona, leader of the radical Diversity Alliance, an "aliens first" political movement.

Nolaa Tarkona was the embittered half sister of the dancing girl Oola whom Jabba the Hutt had fed to his pet rancor. By being both vicious and skillful, Nolaa had succeeded in becoming the first female leader of her race. She held many charismatic and enthusiastic rallies, whipping up support for her all-alien Diversity Alliance, whose ultimate goal was to punish humans for the horrors of the Empire and past excesses. From the Twi'lek world of Ryloth, she offered a huge reward for Thul, and most especially for the mysterious cargo he carried.

Ailyn Vel, believed to be the daughter of bounty hunter Boba Fett, assumed the identity of her renowned father and took up the Thul bounty. The Fett impersonator tried to capture the Solo children near the remains of Alderaan, but Zekk drove the bounty hunter off. Jaina tried to convince Zekk to come back with them, but now he was even more determined to make his own life. Later he, too, decided to search for Bornan Thul.

Hoping to track down Thul themselves, the young Jedi Knights searched the man's last known locations, from ancient ruined worlds to the droid factories of Mechis III. They found a female Wookiee named Raaba who had joined the Diversity Alliance. Raaba recruited Lowbacca to leave his friends and come with her to Ryloth, so that he could learn more about the antihuman organization.

On Thul's trail, Zekk learned that Thul had stumbled upon the location of a secret asteroid laboratory that held stockpiles of horrific plagues. This research center had been the scientific headquarters of the Imperial scientist Evir Derricote, who had unleashed the devastating Krytos plague in the early days of the New Republic. Though Derricote was long dead, his legacy of disease and death remained sealed on the asteroid. In her political fervor, Nolaa Tarkona wanted to exterminate humanity, and needed Thul so that she could uncover the Emperor's plague storehouse.

Terrorist acts against humans escalated, including several assassination attempts. The young Jedi Knights journeyed to Ryloth to bring Lowbacca back, and barely escaped from a sentence of slavery in the ryll spice caverns. Master Skywalker requested an inspection tour be sent to Ryloth, and Nolaa Tarkona frantically covered her tracks.

The Fett impersonator had also succeeded in tracking down the location of the plague storehouse and, per contract, reported it to the Diversity Alliance. Nolaa Tarkona set off with her forces to obtain the Emperor's human-killing pestilence. Zekk and his Jedi friends set to work planting explosive charges throughout the asteroid depot in a race against time.

Summoned by the young Jedi Knights, the New Republic emergency fleet arrived, led by Han Solo. The fleet engaged the Diversity Alliance ships in orbit, while commandos below set off explosions to wreck the Imperial weapons depot. Bornan Thul sealed himself inside the central containment chamber that held the disease solution, trapped with Nolaa Tarkona. When they fired upon him, the plague cylinders cracked. Thul died, hoping he had succeeded in denying the Diversity Alliance access to the bioweapon. Nolaa Tarkona escaped, but didn't realize that she had been infected by one of the alternate strains of Derricote's plagues. She died alone in quarantine on an asteroid not long afterward.

Jaina Solo and Zekk
[Art by John Van Fleet]

THE RETURN OF BLACK SUN
24 A.B.Y.

Finally, after confronting his dark past, Zekk agreed to stay at the Jedi praxeum to learn to control his anger. Zekk later won the Blockade Runners Derby at Ord Mantell, a classic race judged by Han Solo, one of its previous champions. Czethros, a race sponsor, had once been an enemy of Solo's, but now claimed to be a respectable businessman.

A mysterious young woman, Anja, helped Han drive off some chameleon creatures in the hangar bay. Anja had her own lightsaber, but no Jedi training, relying instead on doses of spice to enhance her senses. She revealed that she was the daughter of Gallandro, the gunslinger whom Han Solo had battled in his early smuggling days. Anja, who believed that Han had murdered her father, had vowed revenge.

Anja worked for Czethros, who was in reality a leader of the Black Sun criminal organization. Black Sun had kept a low profile for years, but continued to work behind the scenes, infiltrating agents into positions of political and economic power throughout the New Republic. Czethros had addicted Anja to spice in order to keep her under his thumb.

Han promised to show Anja his good side by helping in the civil war that had ravaged Anja's planet Anobis for so long. When *Millennium Falcon* arrived on Anobis, Solo met with the two factions and brokered an uneasy peace. Anja began to wonder if her hatred might have been misplaced. She agreed to join Jacen, Jaina, and the others back at the Jedi academy to see what she could learn from Master Skywalker.

Lando Calrissian, who still owned *GemDiver Station* around Yavin, had repurchased a controlling interest in the spice mines of Kessel several years earlier with dividends from a mining operation on Varn. He had invested the profits in his new commercial venture, SkyCenter Galleria, an amusement park on Cloud City. He and his business partner Cojahn wanted the Solo twins and their friends to be "test subjects" for the new attraction.

When they arrived at Cloud City, Calrissian learned that his partner Cojahn was dead. The Jedi investigated, and discovered that Czethros had tried to extort cooperation from Cojahn in order to control the casinos for Black Sun. When Cojahn refused, Czethros had murdered him.

New Republic investigation teams searched the galaxy for Czethros, but he had gone to ground, hoping to set in motion the final stage of his plot for a government takeover. But Anja realized that without Czethros around, she had no supplier for the spice that fed her addiction. Desperate, she slipped away from the academy, stole Zekk's ship, and flew off to retrieve a spice stash hidden under the polar ice cap of Mon Calamari.

The Sullustan Nien Nunb, Calrissian's longtime manager of the Kessel mines, barely survived an "accident" in the carbon-freezing sections of the processing facility. Black Sun had infiltrated even here, and Nien Nunb felt he was in great danger. His own workers were turning against him.

Jaina and Lowbacca agreed to help Nien Nunb on Kessel, while Jacen, Zekk, and Tenel Ka raced off to Mon Calamari to catch up with Anja. At the floating resort city of Crystal Reef, they confronted her as she tried to lease a mini sub to explore the ice cap. By now Anja had admitted her addiction to spice, and she meant to get her revenge on Czethros by destroying his Mon Calamari stockpile.

The Jedi trainees followed her to the ice cap, where she destroyed the drug stash. During their escape through the ice from a sea creature, the Jedi used healing techniques to free Anja of her chemical addiction to spice—though she would have to deal with the mental part herself.

On Kessel, Czethros had landed with an army of mercenaries. Black Sun took over the planet's spice mines. Nien Nunb became a prisoner, but Jaina and Lowbacca hid in the tunnels and learned that Black Sun had established infiltrators in the government, in the military, and on numerous allied planets and industrial stations. From his new HQ on Kessel, Czethros planned to send a signal that would call them to arms.

However, Czethros did not count on the sabotage work of Jaina and Lowbacca, who destroyed the transmitter before Black Sun could send its signal. They also freed the prisoners in the spice mines and drove back the mercenaries who had taken over Kessel. Rather than allow himself to be captured, Czethros fell into a vat of carbonite. Later, Chief of State Leia Organa Solo supervised his unthawing and interrogation and uncovered the names of the Black Sun infiltrators who remained.

After their numerous successes, Master Luke Skywalker declared that his group of young trainees could now consider themselves full Jedi Knights—a new generation of defenders for the New Republic.

PART TWELVE

The New Jedi Order

It was a time for transitions. Mon Mothma, the Rebellion's guiding spirit, died peacefully in her sleep. Borsk Fey'lya, also a longtime member of the Rebellion, but about as different from Mon Mothma as it was possible to be, ascended to the office of Chief of State after Leia's voluntary retirement, despite several dark scandals in his past.

Luke Skywalker's new Jedi order found itself at a crossroads. Since the dawn of the Jedi, tension had existed between the meditative Jedi consulars and the more militaristic Jedi guardians. Now, with the first true peace the galaxy had known in decades, Luke's Jedi showed signs of philosophical fracture.

Luke, dividing his time between Coruscant and Yavin 4, considered reestablishing the concept of a ruling Jedi council. Other, more proactive Jedi Knights followed the lead of Kyp Durron and found new targets for their aggression. Durron and his former apprentice Miko Reglia formed a freelance starfighter squadron called the Dozen-and-Two Avengers to harass smugglers in the Outer Rim. Jaina Solo found herself increasingly attracted to Kyp's aggressive faction; Anakin Solo remained loyal to his Uncle Luke. Jacen Solo found himself wondering if he could follow the Force without having to pick sides.

Mara Jade, now a Jedi Master, supported her husband's efforts to keep the Jedi order focused, but grew weaker and weaker, victim of a mysterious ailment she had contracted during a diplomatic meeting on Monor II, a meeting at which professional firebrand Nom Anor had been present. Years before, Anor had manipulated Carnor Jax's Interim Council; now he was stirring up trouble between the planets of Rhommamool and Osarian. Soon, Anor would drop his façade and reveal his true identity as an advance agent.

Nom Anor, and Mara's disease, were harbingers of a much greater threat. All of the galaxy's major powers—the New Republic, the Empire, the Hutts, and the Chiss—would soon be pushed to the brink of extinction by invaders from outside.

THE INVASION BEGINS
25 A.B.Y.

The Yuuzhan Vong came from another galaxy. In their legends, they had once fought against a machine-based civilization that solidified their hatred of high technology. The Yuuzhan Vong had developed a society in which everything was grown, cloned, or otherwise bioengineered, from handcuffs to worldships the size of moons. Their love for organic grafting extended to themselves, and ritual mutilation and the replacement of body parts came to signify veneration of the gods.

The gods of the Yuuzhan Vong, who all stood beneath Yun-Yuuzhan the Creator, were closely aligned with their rigid caste system. Yun-Yammka the Slayer was the patron god of warriors. Yun-Harla the Trickster was often associated with priests. Yun-Ne'Shel the Modeler was invoked by shapers, the members of the bioengineering caste. Members of the intendant and worker castes could call any god their own, including Yun-Txiin and Yun-Q'aah, the Lovers. Yun-Shuno the Pardoner was the patron god of the Shamed Ones—those Yuuzhan Vong from every caste whose bodies had rejected biological implants of rank. Curiously, all

Yuuzhan Vong seemed to be unable to use, or even register within, the universal energy field of the Force.

The Yuuzhan Vong had embarked on a nomadic lifestyle following the ancient Cremlevian War, in which Supreme Overlord Yo'gand defeated Warmaster Steng by dropping a moon on his encampment. With many of their colony planets destroyed, including their homeworld of Yuuzhan'tar, their warrior society continued its program of aggressive religious fanaticism. After thousands of years, they had bled dry their home galaxy. The Yuuzhan Vong eventually found themselves aboard a fleet of worldships, wandering the void between galaxies in search of a new home.

Our galaxy was first scouted long ago, first by Yuuzhan Vong–engineered slivilith creatures and, starting during the Clone Wars, by advance bands of scouts and political infiltrators. At 29 B.B.Y., Supreme Overlord Quoreal, leader of the worldship fleet, received word of his scouts' encounter with the living planet Zonama Sekot. Quoreal recognized that Zonama Sekot held some connection to his home galaxy, but didn't realize it was actually a seed of Yuuzhan'tar, grown to full size after the destruction of its "parent" world. Nevertheless, Quoreal believed the legends that said such a planet could bring about the end of his species, and declared that the Yuuzhan Vong would leave this galaxy in peace and continue their wanderings.

The news made Quoreal suddenly unpopular, and a rival named Shimrra chose that moment to usurp the throne. Shimrra covered up the evidence of Zonama Sekot's existence. He distracted his people with the announcement that the gods had declared this galaxy to be the rightful home of the Yuuzhan Vong—once it had been purified of infidels. Now the time had come to strike.

The first invasion ship breached the galactic disk in the northern fringe, far from any major population centers. The vessel, easily mistaken for an asteroid or comet, carried legions of Yuuzhan Vong warriors belonging to the advance force known as the Praetorite Vong.

Two embedded Yuuzhan Vong infiltrators helped prepare the way for the Praetorite Vong. On Belkadan, site of a New Republic research outpost, agent Yomin Carr killed most of the outpost's staff and released a plague into the atmosphere that would reshape the planet into a biofactory. On Rhommamool, Nom Anor had touched off war between that planet and its sister world, Osarian. Both actions helped distract the New Republic long enough for the Praetorite Vong worldship to reach the ice world Helska 4 and unload its "war coordinator"—a colossal, tentacled brain known as a yammosk.

Several scientists from the Belkadan outpost had been offplanet at the time of Yomin Carr's sabotage. They stumbled across the new Yuuzhan Vong headquarters at Helska, as did the Dozen-and-Two Avengers under Kyp Durron's command. The Yuuzhan Vong's acid-secreting grutchin insects made short work of both groups. Only Kyp Durron escaped. The Yuuzhan Vong captured the scientist Danni Quee and Kyp's Jedi lieutenant Miko Reglia.

Pieces of the puzzle started to come together when Luke and Mara arrived at ruined Belkadan. Defeating an enraged Yomin Carr and witnessing the speed of the planet's environmental reprogramming, they realized the face of their enemy and the breathtaking extent of their foes' biology-based powers.

THE DEATH OF CHEWBACCA
25 A.B.Y.

Altering the atmosphere of a planet paled next to what the Yuuzhan Vong did then, at the Outer Rim world of Sernpidal. Using the tactic they called "Yo'gand's Core," the Yuuzhan Vong used a gravity-altering dovin basal creature to pull the planet's moon Dobido down to a shattering collision. Han Solo, Anakin Solo, and Chewbacca, all present on Sernpidal during a supply run for Lando Calrissian, did all they could to save the doomed world, but not even the Force could slow the moon once it had slipped into a terminal orbit.

Loading *Millennium Falcon* with refugees as Dobido loomed overhead, Chewbacca paused to help Anakin, who

Chewbacca dies a hero's death on Sernpidal.
[ART BY TOMMY LEE EDWARDS]

had fallen. Chewie threw Anakin aboard the *Falcon,* but his actions had cost him precious seconds. Anakin believed that the *Falcon* and its passengers would not survive if they remained in the area to make a pickup for Chewbacca, and he rocketed the ship away from Sernpidal at full speed. Han, watching from the boarding ramp, saw Chewbacca receding in the distance, his fists raised in defiance at the sinking moon as the atmosphere superheated around him.

After the Sernpidal atrocity, the Yuuzhan Vong could no longer operate in secret. The warships of the Praetorite Vong attacked Dubrillion—site of Lando Calrissian's latest moneymaking venture—and massed for more assaults. Borsk Fey'lya and the New Republic leaders on Coruscant remained skeptical of the threat. The only battleship Leia could recruit for a counterattack on the Yuuzhan Vong forward base was the Star Destroyer *Rejuvenator.*

This inadequate force moved against the Yuuzhan Vong at Helska 4 and failed spectacularly, victim of the New Republic's ignorance of the enemy's technology. Though Jacen Solo rescued Danni Quee from imprisonment, the Yuuzhan Vong yammosk coordinated a swarm of coralskipper starfighters, who used their shield-stripping dovin basals to annihilate the *Rejuvenator.* Jedi Knight Miko Reglia also died during the fighting.

The crushed New Republic forces withdrew, but returned for a second Battle of Helska 4. This time, they came with a small fleet of umbrella-shaped shieldships. Using the shieldships to accelerate the plant's natural evaporation, they froze the world and killed the real threat—the yammosk embedded under the ice. The entire planet of Helska shattered under the strain.

The victory at Helska provided some breathing room. Two months passed while the main Yuuzhan Vong force assembled its own invasion fleet. On Coruscant, Borsk Fey'lya claimed the lull was proof that no threat was imminent. Some elements of the New Republic military, including Bothan Admiral Kre'fey of the assault carrier *Ralroost* and Colonel Gavin Darklighter of Rogue Squadron, knew better. They risked insubordination and court-martial by remaining on high alert.

The death of Chewbacca had deep repercussions for the Solo family. Han sank into a deep depression, blaming Lando for sending him on the Sernpidal mission and Anakin for choosing to fly away when he did. Leia found herself unable to connect with her husband. Anakin, wondering if he'd done the right thing, recommitted himself to the fight against the Yuuzhan Vong. C-3PO and R2-D2 used the time to compile an oral history of Chewbacca from those who had known him best. Among those interviewed was Chewie's father Attichitcuk, who sighed, "No father should ever outlive his own son."

DANTOOINE ONSLAUGHT
25.2 A.B.Y.

On Yavin 4, Luke Skywalker assembled all his Jedi Knights for a council of war. Though Kyp Durron ached for a bloodier role, most Jedi departed on scouting missions to ascertain the extent of the danger.

Corran Horn and Ganner Rhysode went to sand-swept Bimmiel in the Outer Rim, where an archaeological team had uncovered the remains of a Yuuzhan Vong warrior, mummified after fifty years in the desert. They discovered that the Yuuzhan Vong had already beat them to Bimmiel, and Corran and Ganner enlisted the planet's native slashrats to help them wipe out the enemy's slave colony. Yuuzhan Vong commander Shedao Shai arrived in the aftermath of the battle, and saw that the hated *Jeedai* Knights had disturbed the body of his ancestor Mongei Shai. Enraged, he vowed to kill Corran Horn and taste his blood.

Luke and Jacen arrived at Belkadan, discovering that the Yuuzhan Vong–terraformed planet now served as a "farm" for growing new coralskipper starfighters. The slaves toiling in the jungle fields remained docile due to chunks of surge-coral implanted in their faces. Jacen recklessly tried to rescue them and became a prisoner himself, but Luke fought for Jacen's freedom and both Jedi escaped Belkadan.

Mara Jade and Anakin Solo traveled to Dantooine, where Mara hoped to halt the progress of her disease in the un-

Corran Horn battles Shedao Shai for the fate of Ithor.
[ART BY TOMMY LEE EDWARDS]

spoiled expanses of the gentle grasslands. Yet the Yuuzhan Vong invaders had already reached Dantooine, and what should have been a peaceful convalescence turned into a gritty struggle to stay alive.

As it turned out, Mara and Anakin soon had plenty of company. Lando Calrissian had decided to evacuate the citizens of Dubrillion before the Yuuzhan Vong could finish the job they'd begun two months prior. Thousands of Dubrillion refugees arrived on Dantooine, and the Yuuzhan Vong soon followed.

The Battle of Dantooine began as a slaughter. The Yuuzhan Vong used the opportunity to test new ground tactics against their prey, unveiling beetle-like crawlers and throngs of reptilian Chazrach slaves from their home galaxy. The Jedi staged delaying actions, allowing most of the surviv-

ing refugees to pack up and head for space, where Rogue Squadron (including its newest member, Jaina Solo) and Admiral Kre'fey of the *Ralroost* helped them escape to hyperspace. Dantooine remained in the hands of the enemy.

The Ruin of Ithor
25.3 A.B.Y.

Commander Shedao Shai hadn't forgotten his vow to kill Corran Horn. During this, the first phase of the invasion, Shai had been tasked with paving the way for the arrival of the Yuuzhan Vong's warmaster, Tsavong Lah. No fan of Lah's, Shai hoped to consolidate his own power by eliminating the hated *Jeedai*.

New Republic Senator Elegos A'Kla, under a flag of am-

bassadorial truce, met with Shedao Shai at the new Yuuzhan Vong headquarters on Dubrillion. At first amused by the weakling Caamasi, Commander Shai eventually grew tired of A'Kla and murdered him. Knowing that A'Kla and Corran Horn had been friends, Shai believed he could use the act as a challenge to Horn's honor.

Corran Horn had been busy with a mission to Yuuzhan Vong–occupied Garqi, where his forces rescued several slaves and accidentally discovered a critical secret—the pollen of the bafforr tree reacted violently with the vonduun crab armor worn by all Yuuzhan Vong warriors. Bafforr trees were native to Ithor, the unspoiled homeworld of the "Hammerhead" Ithorian pacifists. Ithor had unwittingly become a target in the war.

Forces began to gather above Ithor. Admiral Pellaeon of the Empire arrived to lend a hand. A squadron of enigmatic Chiss aliens from the Unknown Regions also made an appearance, led by Jagged Fel, the eighteen-year-old son of Baron Soontir Fel and Syal Antilles (the sister of Wedge Antilles). Anakin Solo also showed up, fresh from an adventure where he had helped stop two rogue Jedi from reactivating old Imperial superweapons for use against the Yuuzhan Vong.

Shedao Shai dispatched a shuttle to Ithor. It contained the bejeweled skeleton of Elegos A'Kla, bearing a message to Corran Horn explaining that *this* was the proper way to venerate the dead. Shortly after, Shai's cruiser, *Legacy of Torment*, arrived at Ithor, its holds filled with murderous warriors.

The Yuuzhan Vong combatants attacked the floating herd ship *Tafanda Bay* and Ithor's virgin surface, until Corran Horn forestalled further attacks with an appeal to Shai's pride. According to the terms of Horn's challenge, if he defeated Shai in a one-on-one duel, the Yuuzhan Vong would leave Ithor alone. If he lost, Shai would win back the body of his ancestor Mongei Shai.

Corran won the duel, killing Shedao Shai. But Shai's second in command refused to honor the terms of the pact, loosing bioweapons that turned the rain forests of Ithor into oozing swamps of black ash. The New Republic managed to destroy *Legacy of Torment,* but the death of Ithor horrified the public.

Many were quick to blame Corran Horn for arranging the duel in the first place. In response, Horn placed himself in exile on his homeworld of Corellia. As anti-Jedi sentiment grew, Borsk Fey'lya gained even more power over the New Republic.

THE PEACE BRIGADE
25.5 A.B.Y.

The Yuuzhan Vong had broken their pact at Ithor, and the aliens apparently felt there was little use in pursuing further treaties. Instead, warships led by Supreme Commander Nas Choka captured a swath of worlds lying in the northern invasion corridor over the next four months, including the library planet Obroa-skai. Choka also sponsored uprisings on Atzerri and other isolated pockets along the galaxy's southeastern face.

This new aggression frightened many groups, which approached the Yuuzhan Vong with their own entreaties. The Hutts proposed an alliance with the Yuuzhan Vong based on information sharing, while a despicable gaggle of humans calling themselves the "Peace Brigade" offered to sell out their fellow citizens in exchange for favorable treatment in the postwar galaxy.

Nom Anor, now working with the priest Harrar, had a new scheme—poisoning the Jedi by infecting them with fatal bo'tous spores. The priestess Elan agreed to pose as a defector. Once she had arranged a meeting with the Jedi, she would exhale the virulent spores that nested in her lungs. Elan was accompanied by her pet, a bird-like alien called Vergere. None of the Yuuzhan Vong realized that Vergere was a Jedi of the old Order, lost after her mission to Zonama Sekot nearly a decade before the Clone Wars.

Chewbacca's family held a belated memorial service for him on Kashyyyk. Han Solo chose that moment to embark on his own quest. Hooking up with Roa, his companion on the caper to pilfer Xim's treasure vaults decades before, Han set off for Ord Mantell, gunning for the Peace Brigade traitors. More old faces resurfaced on Ord Mantell, including the bounty hunter Bossk and Han's old employer Big Bunji, but

Droma
[Art by John Van Fleet]

a Yuuzhan Vong attack force crashed the reunion party. The enemy fleet ravaged Ord Mantell's orbital station and captured thousands, including Roa.

To get his friend back, Han joined forces with Droma, a member of the furry, gypsy-like Ryn species. Aboard the starliner *Queen of Empire,* the two crossed paths with Yuuzhan Vong "defector" Elan and her companion Vergere, just as Peace Brigade raiders attacked the vessel and a Yuuzhan Vong fleet jumped in-system.

Han soon realized that the Yuuzhan Vong acted a bit *too* nonchalant about recapturing their defector. Her ruse revealed, Elan fell victim to her own poison, while Vergere

inexplicably left a vial of her tears with Han before departing. To everyone's surprise, the dosage of Vergere's tears sent Mara Jade's disease into temporary remission.

THE BATTLE OF FONDOR
25.7 A.B.Y.

The Yuuzhan Vong had now moved halfway across the galaxy and had penetrated the Expansion Region. Jedi Knight Wurth Skidder allowed himself to become a prisoner during the Battle of Gyndine, and found himself assigned to a yammosk-nurturing vessel called the *Crèche.* Alongside his fellow prisoner Roa, Skidder toiled at menial tasks designed to stimulate the growing, telepathic brain.

The alliance between the Hutts and the Yuuzhan Vong remained one in name only, as neither side held one atom of trust for the other. The Yuuzhan Vong carefully leaked information to the Hutts concerning their supposed battle plans, and this information soon found its way into the New Republic's possession. Yet another world, lake-dappled Tynna, fell to the Yuuzhan Vong and became a breeding ground for organic communications villips.

Han and Droma, on the hunt for Roa and any sign of Droma's relatives, followed the refugee trail to Ruan, where they met a droid who acted curiously like Bollux, Han's droid companion from his early adventures. Once they realized that Ruan was a dead end, the two followed further clues to the starship yards of Fondor.

Leia Organa Solo had been spending her time in the isolated Hapes Consortium, trying to convince Isolder's people to join the fight. Isolder defeated a political challenger in a combat duel to ensure the Consortium's compliance, and agreed to commit his fleet to the aid of the New Republic. The Hapans' first test would come at Fondor.

Jacen and Anakin Solo, with unwelcome help from Thrackan Sal-Solo, had succeeded in reactivating Centerpoint Station in the Corellian system. The famed "starbuster" had been dormant since the Corellian insurrection, but New Republic Intelligence hoped to use its awesome destructive energies against the enemy. Now, with reports coming in that the Yuuzhan Vong had arrived at Fondor, the time for action had come. Jacen advised against taking rash action, and Anakin hesitated—long enough for Thrackan to seize the controls and fire the superweapon himself.

Centerpoint's poorly aimed energy pulse shot through the Fondor system just as Isolder's Hapan armada began taking up positions. The shaft of white light took out three-quarters of Isolder's fleet and nearly half of the Yuuzhan Vong forces.

Though considered a victory (Thrackan Sal-Solo won election to the post of Corellian governor-general for his part in the incident), the Battle of Fondor cost the New Republic dearly. The Hapan fleet limped on in tatters, Wurth Skidder had died during a rescue attempt on the *Crèche,* and Centerpoint Station switched off again, this time for good.

The Fall of Duro
26 A.B.Y.

Over the following four months, more critical planets fell. The Yuuzhan Vong moved against their former allies in Hutt space, annihilating Nal Hutta and forcing the Hutts from territory that had been theirs for more than twenty-five thousand years. The Yuuzhan Vong attacked Rodia, Druckenwell, Falleen, and Kalarba in an attempt to cut off the Corellian Run. In the assault against Kalarba, the Yuuzhan Vong used a copy of the Sernpidal tactic, drawing in Kalarba's moon Hosk and destroying both spheres. Lieutenant Jaina Solo, flying with Rogue Squadron, suffered injuries that temporarily blinded her. She received a medical leave transfer to the planet Duro, home of the famed pre-Republic spacefarers.

Duro had been chosen as a refugee relocation site for citizens displaced by the invasion. Though Duro's surface had long ago been rendered inhos-

pitable to life, Leia Organa Solo and other New Republic personnel worked to erect atmosph eric shelters and begin long-term terraforming. Despite the Yuuzhan Vong's stab at Fondor, New Republic Intelligence believed the enemy lacked the resources to mount a serious campaign against a major Core world.

But Warmaster Tsavong Lah, second only to Supreme Overlord Shimrra in the Yuuzhan Vong hierarchy, had at last settled in the galaxy. With his arrival, the war had assumed a more belligerent face. The invasion corridor took a sharp right turn toward the galactic center, with Duro squarely in its sights.

Jacen Solo, on Duro with his family to help settle the ref-

Warmaster Tsavong Lah
[Art by John Van Fleet]

ugees, received a Force-induced vision of a galaxy in danger of tilting out of balance. Believing that withdrawal from the Force might mark the path to peace, Jacen began taking on more and more of the trappings of a Jedi hermit. Han and Leia used this time to repair a relationship that had been strained since the death of Chewbacca.

Nom Anor, hoping to make up for his failure with the bo'tous spores, had already set up shop on Duro, using an ooglith masquer disguise to impersonate a Duros scientist. He created a beetle swarm that chewed up the refugee shelters before Mara Jade and Jaina Solo uncovered his identity. Anor eluded capture long enough for Warmaster Tsavong Lah's fleet to arrive, giving the New Republic much bigger things to worry about.

Jacen had been using his time to investigate suspicious dealings of the CorDuro Shipping corporation on one of the many orbital cities that ringed the poisoned world. His discovery that CorDuro had hoped to offer up the refugees as sacrifices in exchange for amnesty came too late to make a difference. Tsavong Lah had only contempt for CorDuro's cowardice, and his warships attacked refugees and orbital cities alike.

On Duro's surface, Yuuzhan Vong warriors captured Leia Organa Solo and brought her before the warmaster. Slashed across the knees when she tried to resist, Leia was rescued by her son Jacen, who abandoned his doubt in this critical moment and opened himself fully to the Force. The telekinetic storm summoned by Jacen picked up everything in the room and sent Tsavong Lah flying out a window.

The Solo family escaped the Battle of Duro, but most combatants did not. Every orbital city save one died in spectacular fashion, pulled to the surface by dovin basals. Warmaster Tsavong Lah now had his foothold in the Core Worlds, and used the occasion to make a galaxywide broadcast. The Yuuzhan Vong invasion would end here, he stated, if the New Republic would surrender its Jedi.

Now viewed with suspicion and greed by a fearful populace, the Jedi had little to cheer. Luke Skywalker, however, found some solace in the news that his wife was expecting a child—a boy. Luke vowed to win peace for the next generation, or die trying.

TREACHERY IN THE SENATE
26.2 A.B.Y.

Han Solo took Leia to a medcenter on Corellia, knowing that she could lose her legs without immediate bacta treatments. But Peace Brigade thugs attacked there, and the newly elected Governor-General Thrackan Sal-Solo made it clear that neither his cousin nor his cousin's wife was welcome in the Corellian system. While finding a new spot to recuperate, Han and Leia ran into a former Jedi student of Luke's named Eelysa, who, along with her maverick Jedi pupils, had formed a rogue starfighter squadron called the Wild Knights.

Leia recovered in time to act against Viqi Shesh, the New Republic Senator from Kuat. Shesh, in response to Tsavong Lah's decree, had sponsored an "appeasement bill" that would outlaw the Jedi order. Leia was nearly killed by mines on her way to Coruscant, but could not prove that Shesh had arranged for her murder. The Senator placed all blame on her aide, and while the appeasement bill went on to defeat, Shesh continued to hold secret talks with Nom Anor. If the New Republic lost the war, a possibility that looked increasingly likely, Shesh wanted to head the collaborationist government.

After fortifying their prize conquest of Duro, the Yuuzhan Vong made an experimental thrust at the Corellian sector, capturing the Nosaurian homeworld of New Plympto. The occupation quickly became a headache, with the Twi'lek Jedi sisters Alema and Numa Rar leading a resistance army of guerrillas. The Yuuzhan Vong ultimately sterilized the troublesome planet, killing nearly seven million.

BIRTH OF THE HERETIC MOVEMENT
26.2 A.B.Y.

Cowed by Tsavong Lah's ultimatum, worlds such as Ando and Devaron began offering up their Jedi protectors to prevent further bloodshed. Dorsk 81 was among the Jedi sacrificed. Witnessing the way such citizens had been so easily turned, Luke Skywalker called for the evacuation

of the Yavin 4 academy, currently home to only the youngest
Jedi initiates. Information kingpin Talon Karrde agreed to assist
in the evacuation, and Anakin
Solo also flew to Yavin 4 to help
his friend Tahiri Veila.

Anakin arrived to find the
base already under siege by the
Peace Brigade. Master Ikrit, the
tiny Kushiban who had advised
Anakin during his own time
at the academy, died in battle
against the brigadiers. Tahiri became a prisoner.

With help from Qorl, the
TIE pilot who lived in Yavin 4's
jungles, Anakin set off to rescue
Tahiri. Fortunately, by this time
Talon Karrde had evacuated the
rest of the academy students,
for the arriving Yuuzhan Vong
forces cared little for what had
come before. The Yuuzhan Vong
obliterated the five-thousand-
year old Massassi temples, erect-
ing damuteks that served as
vivisection laboratories for the
members of the shaper caste.

Luke Skywalker and Mara Jade Skywalker, with newborn baby Ben
[Art by John Van Fleet]

The shapers had already created monstrosities such as the
crab-legged Vagh Rodiek slave species on conquered Rodia.
On Yavin 4, head shaper Mezhan Kwaad and her apprentice
Nen Yim began brainwashing Tahiri, replacing her personality with that of "Riina Kwaad," an identity formed out of
memories copied from Nen Yim's own childhood. Mezhan
Kwaad had a secret she kept carefully guarded from the rank
and file—she had no reverence for the gods. Nen Yim, who
loved only science, shared her heresy.

In the jungle, Anakin encountered Vua Rapuung, a former Yuuzhan Vong warrior now relegated to the caste of
Shamed Ones after a failed bio-implant condemned him to
the lowest possible status in Yuuzhan Vong society. Rapuung
knew that his ex-lover Mezhan Kwaad had engineered his
humiliation, and was willing to fight alongside a *Jeedai* if it
brought him closer to revenge.

Infiltrating the shaper compound, Anakin and Vua
Rapuung fought their way to a shuttle that carried Mezhan

Kwaad, Nen Yim, and Tahiri. In front of hundreds of Yuuzhan Vong, Kwaad revealed her heresy and her part in Vua Rapuung's Shaming, then died at Tahiri's hands.

Rapuung also perished, but a movement had been born. The story of Vua Rapuung, the Shamed One who had earned redemption fighting alongside a Jedi Knight, was endlessly whispered within the ranks of the Shamed Ones. Among this ignored caste of Yuuzhan Vong, the Jedi began to be seen not as enemies, but as saviors.

THE GREAT RIVER
26.5 A.B.Y.

Seeds of change among the Shamed Ones did little to soften the hearts of some New Republic citizens, who now viewed the Jedi as their enemies. Luke Skywalker enlisted many of his most trusted operatives to establish a "Great River"—a secure network by which Jedi could be moved out of hostile areas and into safe houses, including a secure base set up in the Maw cluster near Kessel. Uldir Lochett, the failed Jedi student who had adventured with Anakin Solo years ago, acted as a key link in the Great River. Uldir and his crew crossed paths with a Jedi calling herself Klin-Fa Gi, who led them to Wayland to uncover evidence of a Yuuzhan Vong plot to poison the galaxy's bacta supply. On the bacta planet of Thyferra, Uldir uncovered a Jedi traitor and stopped the scheme before it could trigger a new Bacta War.

THE BATTLE OF YAG'DHUL
26.5 A.B.Y.

Even on Coruscant, the Jedi had become pariahs. Certain members of the Senate issued a warrant for Luke Skywalker's arrest. Jaina decided to take the fight to the *real* enemy, and joined Kyp Durron's vigilante Jedi faction in the Outer Rim. Durron, who knew that the Yuuzhan Vong were building a new worldship from the broken fragments of Sernpidal, deceived Jaina into believing that the construction site housed a new Yuuzhan Vong superweapon. The Jedi squadron attacked and destroyed the worldship, killing thousands of enemy noncombatants. Jaina felt sick over her part in it.

Anakin Solo and the recovering Tahiri, safeguarding the Jedi students aboard Booster Terrik's Star Destroyer *Errant Venture*, decided to join Corran Horn on a supply run to Eriadu. Horn had emerged from his voluntary exile following the debacle at Ithor, and felt confident that his small group would encounter little trouble on Eriadu.

A brush with Peace Brigaders, however, tipped them off that a Yuuzhan Vong invasion of Yag'Dhul was imminent. They rushed to the Givin homeworld to warn the skeletal mathematicians of the danger. During the Battle of Yag'Dhul, the three Jedi faced down Nom Anor, and Anakin and Tahiri shared a tentative kiss while sealed in a storage locker. The advanced ships of the Givin fleet helped beat back the Yuuzhan Vong attackers.

Luke and Mara arrived at *Errant Venture* after their departure from unfriendly Coruscant. There, a disease-weakened Mara went into labor, knowing that the effort would probably kill her. Through the Force, Luke joined minds with his son, using their shared energies to scour every trace of contagion from the cells in Mara's body. Mara and Luke named their newborn baby Ben, in honor of Ben Kenobi.

Elsewhere, the heretical shaper Nen Yim struggled with her punitive assignment to the dying worldship *Baanu Miir*. Soon, aboard the vessel, a master shaper who had spent weeks tormenting Nen Yim revealed himself as Onimi, the misshapen court jester who served at the side of Supreme Overlord Shimrra. It seemed that Shimrra had great need for someone with Nen Yim's scientific talents.

THE DEATH OF ANAKIN SOLO
27 A.B.Y.

By this point the Great River network had moved most Jedi out of harm's way, and Luke Skywalker reestablished a fixed Jedi headquarters, this time on a secret Deep Core planet code-named Eclipse.

The Yuuzhan Vong shaper caste had also kept busy.

Jacen, Jaina, and Anakin Solo face off against a ring of voxyn while infiltrating the worldship at Myrkr. [Art by Tommy Lee Edwards]

Realizing that many Jedi still remained at large, they had fashioned a horde of six-legged monsters called voxyn. Flawless Jedi-killers, the voxyn contained genetic material taken from Myrkr's Force-hunting vornskrs, and used this sensitivity to compensate for their masters' Force blindness. Numa and Alema Rar, the Twi'lek sisters who had led New Plympto's failed resistance, were the first Jedi to battle a voxyn. Numa died, a victim of the creature's razor claws and acid-spitting glands. Alema barely escaped with her life.

This new threat finally united the Jedi order. Kyp Durron and other renegades, including the "Wild Knights" Jedi squadron that had appeared after the Battle of Duro, closed ranks behind Luke Skywalker. To prevent the Yuuzhan Vong from cloning more voxyn, Anakin Solo agreed to lead a strike team behind enemy lines, to destroy the genetic template aboard the worldship *Baanu Rass*, orbiting Myrkr.

Anakin's squad included his brother and sister, along with many of their old academy classmates such as Lowbacca, Tenel Ka, Raynar Thul, and Tahiri. Ganner Rhysode stood out in their ranks as the oldest adult. Despite their youth, the team landed on *Baanu Rass* and systematically fought their way to the heart of the cloning center.

Along the way they liberated two prisoners, Lomi Plo and Welk, who had been captured during the Yuuzhan Vong conquest of Dathomir. Both were disciples of the new Nightsister philosophy taught by Brakiss's now-defunct Second Imperium. True to their nature, they stole a ship and deserted Anakin's group at the earliest opportunity, dragging Raynar with them to face an unknown fate.

Anakin Solo had been widely considered the logical choice to succeed Luke Skywalker as head of the Jedi order. His actions on *Baanu Rass* only deepened his legend. He fought against hordes of enemies without ego or fear, and in the end sacrificed himself so that the other members of his team could live. Cut down by a rain of Yuuzhan Vong amphistaffs while buying time for the others to destroy the queen voxyn, Anakin passed into the Force with a shudder felt halfway across the galaxy.

The death of her younger brother sharpened the edge of Jaina Solo's rage. Now bathing in the violence of the dark side, she burned several Yuuzhan Vong with Force lightning to retrieve Anakin's body. When the fierce fighting separated her from Jacen, she left her twin behind on *Baanu Rass* and escaped with the surviving members of the strike team aboard the Yuuzhan Vong frigate *Ksstar*.

Jacen Solo became a trophy captive. Ever since he had defeated Tsavong Lah on Duro, he had become the most-wanted enemy combatant on the Yuuzhan Vong rolls. Vergere, the former Jedi and current Yuuzhan Vong pet, warned Jacen that his true education was about to begin.

THE FALL OF CORUSCANT
27 A.B.Y.

On Coruscant, Chief of State Borsk Fey'lya had pulled a 180-degree attitude change from his former hostility toward the Jedi. When Nom Anor came to address the Senate, Fey'lya denounced him as a coward and rallied the fractured New Republic. Fey'lya's refusal to negotiate meant that the Yuuzhan Vong would probably execute the hostages whom they held aboard a refugee colony in the Talfaglio system—unless the Jedi got there first.

In a frenzied assault on Talfaglio, Jedi and New Republic forces broke the Yuuzhan Vong cordon and liberated the hostages. Fuming over the effrontery of his opponents, Warmaster Tsavong Lah gave the order to all his warriors to initiate Battle Plan Coruscant. Nearly every vessel in the Yuuzhan Vong fleet assembled into two pincers: one based at Reecee and one at Borleias, and both pointed squarely at the galactic capital.

The New Republic's defense of Coruscant was noble, but futile. No force could stand against the power that Tsavong Lah had assembled. Even Coruscant's planetary shields, the strongest in the galaxy, warped and ruptured when the Yuuzhan Vong hit them with wave after wave of powerless refugee vessels. The tactics of old warhorses like General Rieekan, Garm Bel Iblis, and Lando Calrissian delayed the conquest long enough for many evacuation transports to reach orbit. Ben Skywalker was one of those who escaped the Coruscant battle zone, despite attempts by Viqi Shesh to kill the newborn and curry favor with her new masters.

Borsk Fey'lya made no attempt to leave. He remained in his executive office, watching Yuuzhan Vong landing ships descend on the world that had once been his. When warriors burst in, he demanded to speak to Tsavong Lah face-to-face, but the warmaster could not be drawn into Fey'lya's trap. With a sigh of finality, Fey'lya triggered the proton bomb hidden beneath his desk. Twenty-five thousand Yuuzhan Vong died in a white-hot blast radius that stretched for kilometers.

It is doubtful that the Yuuzhan Vong appreciated the symbolic value of Coruscant's capture, but the galaxy's citizens could feel it in their bones. For years the New Republic and the Empire had fought over Coruscant as a way to give their reigns legitimacy. The latest conquest was more than another tally in the enemy's column. It meant that the Yuuzhan Vong were not just a nightmare that would disappear with the dawn.

Coruscant held a different symbolic meaning for the Yuuzhan Vong. Using a tremendous allocation of resources, they set out to transform the world into a mirror of Yuuzhan'tar, the forgotten home of their ancestors. Dovin basals pulled Coruscant closer to its sun and jump-started a tropical climate. More dovin basals pulverized one of Coruscant's moons, allowing the planet to wear a flat disk of spectacular rings. Green vegetation began to cover gray durasteel, in preparation for the arrival of a seedship that would complete the metamorphosis.

INTRIGUE ON HAPES
27.2 A.B.Y.

Jaina Solo, piloting the Yuuzhan Vong frigate *Ksstar* after her escape from Myrkr, flew the vessel back to where she believed she could find safe harbor. Instead, she emerged in the middle of the battle for Coruscant. Barely escaping intact, she rendezvoused at the Hapes Consortium with her parents, who wished to commiserate over Anakin's death and Jacen's capture. But Jaina's guilt and rage ran too hot. Rather than seek the support of family or friends, she desired only to inflict pain on the Yuuzhan Vong.

Tsavong Lah warranted most of her hatred, but the warmaster remained untouchable. Closer enemies included the priest Harrar and Khalee Lah, the warmaster's son. These two Yuuzhan Vong had tracked the *Ksstar* to Hapes, but Jaina's uncanny ability to elude and confound her enemies elicited comparisons between her and Yun-Harla, the Yuuzhan Vong goddess of trickery.

On Hapes, three personalities circled around Jaina like satellites. The first, Jagged Fel, agreed to fly with Jaina, accompanied by his Chiss wingmate Shawnkyr. Jag believed he might have a future with Jaina, but viewed Kyp Durron as a rival for her attentions.

Kyp had arrived on Hapes shell-shocked, having lost his newest squadron mates during the Battle of Coruscant. Though he and Jaina had parted on bad terms following the raid on the Sernpidal worldship, her recent ordeal with the dark side meant that they had more in common than ever. Jaina spurned her childhood friend Zekk in order to consider Kyp's offer of apprenticeship.

Finally, Ta'a Chume had lost none of her malevolence in the nearly two decades since she had been deposed as Queen Mother of the Hapes Consortium. Teneniel Djo, the current Queen Mother and Isolder's wife, had been rendered nearly comatose by psychic pain when the Hapan fleet had been devastated at the Battle of Fondor. Ta'a Chume wanted a new Queen Mother that she could manipulate, and she set her sights on Jaina to become Isolder's new bride.

Anakin Solo's body at last received a proper Jedi burning on Hapes. While Luke Skywalker, Kyp Durron, Han Solo, Tahiri Veila, and others read a eulogy, the flames of the funeral pyre consigned Anakin's body to ash and his spirit to the Force.

Harrar and Khalee Lah massed their war fleet around Hapes, but Jaina hatched her most devious plan yet. By manipulating the gravitic signatures of vessels within the Yuuzhan Vong fleet, she could trick them into mistaking friend for foe. Her tactic worked brilliantly, with dozens of Yuuzhan

Vong warships destroyed by friendly fire. The Yuuzhan Vong withdrew, earning Jaina even more comparisons to Yun-Harla. In honor of her new status, Jaina gave the *Ksstar* a new name—the *Trickster*.

The palace machinations of Ta'a Chume had become murderous. She arranged for the fatal poisoning of the invalid Teneniel Djo. Tenel Ka, daughter of Teneniel and Jedi veteran of the Myrkr mission, stepped in to restore order by assuming her rightful place as the next Queen Mother of Hapes.

THE STRUGGLE FOR BORLEIAS
27.3 A.B.Y.

The New Republic responded to the loss of Coruscant by striking back while they knew their enemy was overextended. A small task force under the command of General Wedge Antilles reclaimed Borleias from its outgunned Vong occupiers, establishing a foothold on the world that had traditionally been seen as the "stepping-stone to the Core."

The surviving members of the New Republic Advisory Council regrouped on Borleias. One of their number, the Quarren Senator Pwoe, had named himself Fey'lya's successor as Chief of State in absence of a proper vote. No one could yet make a claim to challenge Pwoe, and the Quarren made it clear to General Antilles that no additional forces would be spared to defend Borleias against counterattack. Later, he grudgingly requested that the Super Star Destroyer *Lusankya* bolster Borleias's defensive line, but it became clear that Pwoe was organizing a stalling tactic in order to buy time for a New Republic surrender.

Wedge and the others vowed not to let that happen, advocating a return to the guerrilla tactics of the Rebel Alliance of old. But Warmaster Tsavong Lah, on conquered Coruscant, had already fixed his gaze on Borleias. He entrusted the counterattack to his father, Czulkang Lah, who had once held the title of warmaster and now spent his days as a tactics instructor. Once New Republic forces at Borleias used a "Starlancer" to fire a laser beam through hyperspace and damage Tsavong Lah's worldship at Coruscant, Lah gave the reconquest his highest priority. In truth, the Starlancer had been more of a light show than a true superweapon, but the Yuuzhan Vong retaliatory strike proved to be real enough.

Czulkang Lah's attack on Borleias involved thousands of starfighters and ground assault crawlers. Jaina Solo, leading Twin Suns Squadron, did what she could with assistance from Jagged Fel, but Yuuzhan Vong troops continued to advance on the New Republic base. In desperation, the Super Star Destroyer *Lusankya* responded with a tactic not seen since the days of the Empire—it initiated an orbital bombardment, annihilating every Yuuzhan Vong on the ground and turning several square kilometers of jungle into blackened glass.

BEHIND ENEMY LINES
27.5 A.B.Y.

Luke Skywalker missed out on the fighting, having volunteered to lead a team of infiltrators to enemy-held Coruscant. Accompanied by Mara Jade, Tahiri, Danni Quee, and several members of Wraith Squadron, the team roamed the transformed city-planet while wearing Yuuzhan Vong disguises. From local survivors they learned that, more than twenty years after the death of Vader, a Dark Jedi strode Coruscant once more. The survivors called the marauder "Lord Nyax" after a terrifying figure from Corellian legend.

After days of searching, Luke's team learned the truth behind Nyax. After the *Eye of Palpatine* incident on Belsavis fifteen years prior, Roganda Ismaren and her son Irek Ismaren had come to Coruscant. Roganda had placed her son in a laboratory, where scientists held him in suspended animation, adding muscle and bone mass to his frame and implanting lightsaber blades into his wrists, elbows, and knees. Irek had awoken during the Yuuzhan Vong invasion and, suffering from brain damage, had killed his mother. Now he roamed Coruscant as Lord Nyax, trying to breach a Force wellspring hidden at the site of the old Jedi Temple.

The Super Star Destroyer Lusankya sacrifices itself in the Battle of Borleias. [ART BY TOMMY LEE EDWARDS]

Luke, Mara, and Tahiri faced off against Nyax, who by this time had tapped into the Force repository and could toss debris around in a whirlwind of power. Their combined efforts were enough to fell the Dark Jedi.

Ex-Senator Viqi Shesh also met her end on Coruscant. Far from being named the head of a collaborationist government as she had hoped, Shesh had been marked for death by Warmaster Tsavong Lah. Wraith Squadron foiled her efforts to escape offworld. In the end, Shesh stepped out a window to her death rather than face a life without power.

Warmaster Tsavong Lah had been busy dealing with internal problems, including a plot initiated against him by the shaper caste, who had tainted Lah's recently grafted arm in a manner that would seem to indicate the gods' disfavor. Lah took his revenge by feeding the disloyal shapers to hungry rancors, then turned his attention to Borleias.

His father, Czulkang Lah, organized another onslaught to recapture the world, this time using so much firepower that the New Republic could not hope to win. At first his tactics seemed to work—the New Republic evacuated Borleias, surrendering possession of the planet to the Yuuzhan Vong—but the situation was rapidly reversed. The Super Star Destroyer *Lusankya* rammed Czulkang Lah's worldship, destroying both vessels, while the priest Harrar's efforts to capture Jaina Solo were also met with shameful failure.

IN THE BELLY OF THE BEAST
27–27.9 A.B.Y.

After his capture by Yuuzhan Vong forces on the worldship *Baanu Rass*, Jacen Solo became the victim of unrelenting torment. Shaved bald and locked into a torture rack called the Embrace of Pain, he suffered for unknowable stretches of time while being visited by Vergere, who spoke only in riddles. Though Vergere had once been a Jedi and now lived with the Yuuzhan Vong, it became clear that she answered only to herself. She promised to be Jacen's guide through a painful spiritual journey which she likened to the rebirth of a shadowmoth emerging from its cocoon. The one truth that Jacen could count on, she told him, was that "everything I tell you is a lie."

Nom Anor and Warmaster Tsavong Lah approved of Vergere's actions. Both believed that Jacen could be broken

and made to accept the True Way of Yuuzhan Vong worship and sacrifice.

Jacen spent weeks aboard a seedship, a gigantic repository for Yuuzhan Vong genetic specimens. The seedship nurtured a number of growing dhuryams, telepathic blobs related to the yammosks that were used as battle coordinators. The dhuryam that displayed the most promise would become the "World Brain" to oversee the terraforming of Coruscant. Like children playing with toys, the dhuryams forced slaves into meaningless tasks as they honed their mind-controlling powers.

One of the dhuryams formed a special bond with Jacen, who convinced the developing brain that he was a friend to be trusted. When the seedship arrived at Coruscant, Jacen made his move, slaughtering the competing dhuryams and killing scores of Yuuzhan Vong warriors as the seedship prepared to implant itself on Coruscant.

Vergere knocked Jacen out and arranged for his safe passage out of the seedship. When Jacen awoke on the planet's surface, the vessel had already done its work. Moss now dripped from towers, and rivers roared through right-angled canyons. Beneath the "rainbow bridge" formed by Coruscant's new planetary rings, almost every centimeter of the cityscape wore a thick carpet of vegetation. Only the lower levels remained more or less intact, and down there, frightening examples of wildlife from the Yuuzhan Vong home galaxy hunted the desperate survivors.

Yuuzhan Vong warriors pursued Jacen through the transformed landscape in an effort to recapture him. The chase took Jacen to the former site of the Jedi Temple and into the gullet of a building-sized monster before he arrived at the Solo family apartment, where the spirit of his brother, Anakin, seemingly appeared to him. No longer willing to fight, Jacen allowed Nom Anor to take him prisoner, claiming to have become a convert to the truth of the True Way.

Alone among the Jedi, Ganner Rhysode believed that

Vergere
[ART BY JOHN VAN FLEET]

Jacen had survived the mission to Myrkr. He pursued clues, but wound up a prisoner on Coruscant. Nom Anor proposed that Jacen prove his new faith by killing Ganner at the Well of the World Brain, where the dhuryam nested in a fluid-filled pit at the bottom of the former Galactic Senate's Great Rotunda. In full view of thousands of assembled Yuuzhan Vong, Jacen and Ganner marched to the Well, where Jacen opened his mind to the dhuryam and gave it a special message. Ganner bought time by guarding the building entrance, massacring hundreds of Yuuzhan Vong with a flashing lightsaber and the battle cry, "None shall pass." Ganner eventually perished under the weight of the assault, but earned the respect of the awestruck Yuuzhan Vong.

Jacen escaped Coruscant with Vergere, who shared with her new pupil a radical understanding of the Force. To Vergere and Jacen, the Force had no light side and no dark side—the Force was simply what one made of it. Jacen revealed that his instructions to the World Brain would cause little things to go wrong with the ongoing terraforming. This subtle sabotage might teach the Yuuzhan Vong how to live with compromise.

VICTORY AT EBAQ 9
28 A.B.Y.

The loss of Coruscant, then of Borleias, forced the New Republic Advisory Council to hop back to the water world of Mon Calamari, a planet far from the front lines. Despite Mon Calamari's strategic importance as a military shipyard, it had remained relatively isolated after the severing of the Perlemian Trade Route. For the moment, Mon Calamari provided a welcome opportunity to regroup and formalize a new government.

Senator Pwoe's power grab at Borleias was ignored in favor of new elections. Alderaanian Senator Cal Omas, a friend of the Jedi, received sufficient votes to become the next Chief of State. Omas approved Luke Skywalker's suggestion of a Jedi council composed of both Jedi and "regular" members. Those with seats on the new council included Skywalker, Kyp Durron, and the Barabel Saba Sebatyne, as well as politicians including Omas, the Wookiee Senator Triebakk, and Caamasi Minister of State Releqy A'Kla, the daughter of Elegos A'Kla.

Omas's new position made him a target for Yuuzhan Vong assassins, but New Republic forces were already taking the fight to the enemy. Above occupied Obroa-skai, Jaina Solo worked with Queen Mother Tenel Ka and Jedi General Keyan Farlander to destroy the flagship of Supreme Overlord Shimrra, though Shimrra was not aboard. At Mon Calamari, the arrival of Jacen Solo and Vergere brought cheers from those who had thought Jacen dead at *Baanu Rass.*

Supreme Overlord Shimrra, accompanied by his jester Onimi, had arrived at Coruscant to take a direct hand in the galaxy's subjugation. Chief among Shimrra's concerns were the planet's malfunctioning World Brain and the growing heresy of Jedi worship among the lowly caste of Shamed Ones.

The galaxy's lesser political factions had reacted in wildly differing fashion to the news of Coruscant's fall. The Empire had maintained a policy of noninterference since Ithor, while the Bothans—stirred by the noble death of Borsk Fey'lya—had initiated ar'krai, a condition of genocidal war that would end only when the Yuuzhan Vong had been utterly exterminated. The notion of ar'krai appealed to the black ops Alpha Blue division of New Republic Intelligence. Working in conjunction with Chiss scientists, Alpha Blue had developed a biological weapon keyed to Yuuzhan Vong DNA. If unleashed, this "Alpha Red" virus would exterminate every Yuuzhan Vong and Yuuzhan Vong creation in the galaxy.

Luke Skywalker opposed such indiscriminate slaughter, believing it to be against the will of the Force. The debate was rendered moot, however, when Vergere used the healing properties of her tears to render Alpha Red inert.

Admiral Ackbar, slowed by his advancing years but still sharp of mind, helped the New Republic plan a trap for Warmaster Tsavong Lah. In the Deep Core, where gravitic anomalies warped hyperspace into a near-impassable morass, New Republic forces would set an ambush near the ninth moon of Ebaq, at a former Imperial base called Tarkin's Fang. When the Yuuzhan Vong fleet arrived, the New Republic would blockade the only hyperroute leading into or out of Ebaq and pin the enemy under a blistering crossfire.

The first stage of the Ebaq 9 trap unfolded according to plan. With his fleet in ruins, Tsavong Lah ordered his remaining troops to the surface of the moon to capture the Tarkin's Fang installation. Knowing that at this point he would be unlikely to secure a victory, Lah wished instead to disembowel the *Jeedai* who had caused him so much pain.

Vergere sacrificed her life, thinning the enemy ranks by crashing an A-wing into the vacuum-sealed base. Tsavong Lah survived the explosive decompression, eventually facing

Tahiri Veila
[ART BY JOHN VAN FLEET]

Galactic Federation of Free Alliances. Under a new constitution, the Galactic Alliance incorporated a new federalism that defined the boundaries between the Senate and planetary governments, as well as strengthening the judiciary in order to check the power of the Senate.

More good news came in from the planet Ylesia in Hutt space, where New Republic forces had driven the Yuuzhan Vong away from the Ylesian spice factories. They had also captured Thrackan Sal-Solo, who had been forced by the Yuuzhan Vong to give up his governor-general position in the Corellian system in order to become the head of the Ylesian Peace Brigade.

ACROSS THE STARS
28.2–28.7 A.B.Y.

The Yuuzhan Vong's defeat at Ebaq was intended to result in them pulling inward to consolidate the rest of their hard-won territory. Instead, like krakanas maddened by a blood-boil, they continued to send their surviving warships against new targets. Among the newest worlds to fall were Barab I, Rutan, and Belderone.

The latest attacks—and the sudden loss of Holo-Net communications with scores of worlds—prompted Han and Leia to take *Millennium Falcon* on a mission to reestablish the broken information chain. Tahiri came with them, still haunted by the brainwashing she had received on Yavin 4, and by the Yuuzhan Vong personality of "Riina Kwaad" that tried to take over her dreams.

At their first stop, Galantos, they learned that the native Fia had struck a deal with the Yuuzhan Vong—capitulation in exchange for the elimination of their enemies, the Yevetha. The Yuuzhan Vong, it seemed, had accomplished what the New Republic chose not to do during the Black Fleet Crisis. The Yevetha had been bombed to the point of extinction.

The *Falcon*'s next trip took it to Bakura, where recent events appeared to have ushered in a new age of coopera-

off against Jaina Solo in a one-on-one duel—the warmaster against the so-called Sword of the Jedi. Living up to her reputation as the living incarnation of Yun-Harla, Jaina outmaneuvered Lah and speared her lightsaber through his throat.

The Battle of Ebaq 9 was a rousing success for the New Republic, by far its most significant victory since the start of the war. Many began to believe in the New Republic's ability to turn the tables on its overextended enemy, but Cal Omas disagreed. That is, Omas could not see the *New Republic* winning the war—but a rebuilt, streamlined government might have a fighting chance. He used the current political shake-ups as an opportunity to restructure the New Republic as the

tion between the Bakurans and the P'w'eck Emancipation Movement, a group composed of the Ssi-ruuk's traditional slave species. Unknown to any of the players at hand, the Yuuzhan Vong had already infiltrated Ssi-ruuvi society. Chaos soon enveloped Bakura, with Prime Minister Cundertol revealed as a human replica droid and Malinza Thanas—daughter of Gaeriel Captison and leader of the Freedom revolutionaries—arrested for kidnapping. The various plots collapsed when the Keeramak, the current head of the Ssi-ruuvi Imperium, attempted to claim Bakura for his own, renaming it "Xwhee." But fighting again broke out between the Ssi-ruuk and their P'w'eck slaves, sparing Bakura from enemy conquest.

The *Falcon*'s third mission involved the planet Esfandia. Han's Ryn friend Droma, who had emerged as the head of a Ryn intelligence network, emphasized the importance of maintaining Esfandia's HoloNet relay station, which the Yuuzhan Vong were already threatening to smash. Esfandia was blanketed by a soup-thick atmosphere populated by starfish-like Brrbrlpp, who helped the Galactic Alliance shatter the Yuuzhan Vong strike force. By the conclusion of her adventures, Tahiri had established a balance between her dueling personalities. She now viewed herself as half human, half Yuuzhan Vong.

Military campaigns seemed to be unraveling for the Yuuzhan Vong, and their internal problems were even more severe. Nom Anor had gone underground on Coruscant, afraid of Shimrra's wrath in the wake of the Ebaq 9 disaster. There he had hooked up with Shamed Ones preaching the Jedi heresy that had begun on Yavin 4. Ever willing to exploit any opportunity for power, Nom Anor reinvented himself as "Yu'shaa the Prophet" and attracted thousands of heretic followers to his banner. Shimrra dispatched warriors to crush this newest threat to his rule, but Nom Anor kept abreast of court developments thanks to a spy in Shimrra's confidence.

Nom Anor, as Yu'shaa the Prophet, overlooks the greening of Coruscant. [Art by Tommy Lee Edwards]

INTO THE UNKNOWN REGIONS
28.2–28.8 A.B.Y.

Following the Yuuzhan Vong's defeat at Ebaq 9, Luke Skywalker decided to press the advantage in the face of the enemy's weakness. Before her death, Vergere had told him the story of the living planet Zonama Sekot and how it had repelled a squad of Yuuzhan Vong scouts decades before. Now Luke assembled a small team, including Jacen, Mara, Saba Sebatyne, and Danni Quee, to seek out Zonama Sekot in the Unknown Regions, with the hope that it could help put an end to the war.

Aboard Mara's ship *Jade Shadow*, they made an initial stop at the Empire to obtain maps of the hyperroutes through the Unknown Regions. But they were unprepared for the sight that greeted them at the Imperial capital of Bastion. The Yuuzhan Vong had thoroughly routed the Empire there, forcing Admiral Pellaeon to retreat to Yaga Minor. Recognizing that his enemy's success had been due to surprise only, Pellaeon soon ordered his Star Destroyers to strike back in the Battle of Borosk, snapping the spine of the Yuuzhan Vong fleet.

Luke Skywalker and his companions proceeded into the Unknown Regions, where they established contact with the reclusive Chiss Ascendancy. Baron Soontir Fel and his wife, Syal Antilles, provided familiar faces on the icy capital of Csilla, but rogue elements within the Chiss Expansionary Defense Fleet tried to kill the visitors. After helping to quell the uprising, Jacen scoured the Chiss data library to learn Zonama Sekot's current location—an unknown system called Klasse Ephemora.

Penetrating even deeper into the Unknown Regions, *Jade Shadow*'s crew landed on Zonama Sekot and received a welcome from the Magister, Jabitha. Decades of time and half a galaxy of distance had passed since Jabitha had welcomed Obi-Wan Kenobi and Anakin Skywalker to her world, yet she retained a primal connection to the planet's green consciousness.

The hyperjumps that Zonama Sekot had taken in order to reach the Klasse Ephemora system had scarred the world and killed many of its Ferroan settlers. Several angry Ferroans now kidnapped Jabitha, but the actions of the Jedi in rescuing the Magister convinced Zonama Sekot of the rightness of the visitors' cause.

Luke and his Jedi were not the only ones seeking more information on the living planet. Supreme Overlord Shimrra had always believed that Zonama Sekot would be a threat to his rule. Now, working with master shaper Nen Yim, he developed plagues that could exterminate Sekot's biosphere. Nen Yim, convinced that Shimrra had lost his mind, established a secret alliance with the priest Harrar. When Corran Horn and Tahiri Veila arrived on Coruscant, the two Yuuzhan Vong escaped aboard the Jedi vessel, accompanied by Nom Anor in his guise as Yu'shaa the Prophet. Though none of the five trusted one another, they entered the Unknown Regions and soon reached Zonama Sekot. The Yuuzhan Vong members immediately remarked on how "right" the world felt, and Nom Anor realized that he could gain great power in Shimrra's eyes if he could poison this powerful world.

Corran and Tahiri tried to establish contact with Luke's team. The two groups eventually hooked up, but by then Nom Anor had made his move—bashing in Nen Yim's head with a rock, he stole her collection of tailored plagues. Anor released a virus into Sekot's neural interface, then escaped offworld while the pained planet shuddered with groundquakes. As Anor watched aboard his vessel, Zonama Sekot and its passengers fled into hyperspace.

Back in known space, the Galactic Alliance struggled with a separate problem—the near-total collapse of the HoloNet communications system due to enemy sabotage. During a mission to liberate the Bilbringi Shipyards, General Wedge Antilles found himself unable to contact reinforcements. Han Solo and Leia Organa Solo prevented the battle from becoming a rout by using the *Falcon* as a courier. Most Galactic Alliance troops escaped Bilbringi, but other soldiers, including lifelong military men Pash Cracken and Judder Page, became prisoners of war.

THE DEFENSE OF MON CALAMARI
29 A.B.Y.

Judder Page and Pash Cracken found themselves part of a prisoner camp on occupied Selvaris. The Yuuzhan Vong had never been kind to their captives, yet the news uncovered on Selvaris revealed a true atrocity. On Coruscant, within a few weeks, the Yuuzhan Vong would kill every prisoner in a massive blood sacrifice.

Responsibility for the decision rested at the feet of Supreme Overlord Shimrra, now believed by even his closest advisers to have gone completely mad. Shimrra, reassured by the news of Zonama Sekot's poisoning, had forgiven Nom Anor for his past failures, and made him prefect of Coruscant. Shimrra had also forced his shapers to create a band of monstrous warriors to act as his bodyguards, and dubbed them the Slayers.

While the Supreme Overlord's insanity boded well for an end to the war, the Galactic Alliance couldn't let the prisoner sacrifice go unchallenged. A strike against a Yuuzhan Vong convoy freed many captives, but enemy raiders forced *Millennium Falcon* to retreat to the besieged orbital outpost at Caluula. There, Han Solo received help from the last man he ever expected—Boba Fett, flanked by a new squad of Mandalorian Supercommandos. The armored warriors put the fear of Mandalore into the attacking Yuuzhan Vong, and Han escaped the station with a newfound respect for the veteran hunter.

The Yuuzhan Vong defeat underscored their desperation. With territory slipping out from under their heels and Coruscant's World Brain growing strange things in its imperfect attempts at terraforming, the Yuuzhan Vong desperately needed to amend their situation. Despite the fact that Shimrra had clearly stretched his military forces beyond their capacity, he ordered a titanic assault against the Galactic Alliance provisional capital on Mon Calamari. The Galactic Alliance anticipated this move, and held only half of its forces for Mon Calamari's defense. The other half would launch a strike on Coruscant.

Jaina Solo and hundreds of other pilots fought in the space surrounding Mon Calamari. The Galactic Alliance won the day, thanks in part to the death of a yammosk on nearby Caluula that the Yuuzhan Vong had hoped to use as a battle coordinator. Han, Leia, and Kyp Durron soon discovered that the forbidden Alpha Red plague had killed both the yammosk and a wide swath of Caluula's biosphere. In the year following Vergere's nullification of the original Alpha Red, certain elements of Intelligence had restarted the project and test-released it on Caluula, resulting in two major problems: the virus wasn't as precise as planned and could cross-contaminate non–Yuuzhan Vong life-forms, and an infected Yuuzhan Vong had already escaped Caluula, bound for Coruscant.

THE RECAPTURE OF CORUSCANT
29 A.B.Y.

Zonama Sekot had at last completed its hopscotch journey across the galaxy, and now entered into a close orbit near Coruscant. Millions of Yuuzhan Vong faces looked to the sky and beheld the celestial visitor, as tidal stresses from its proximity buckled the ground beneath their feet. The Shamed Ones who had followed the Jedi religion of the Prophet Yu'shaa believed that this sign could signal their salvation. Shimrra knew it to be his doom.

While the Galactic Alliance and the Empire brawled with Nas Choka's warships in cold vacuum, the Solos and Skywalkers began a ground advance on Shimrra's citadel. The Supreme Overlord sent bioengineered behemoths against his attackers and even set the landscape on fire. The Jedi received aid from a groundswell army of Shamed Ones, who were eager to kill their historical caste oppressors. Nom Anor became an unlikely ally as well, due to his experience as Yu'shaa and his familiarity with the inner workings of Shimrra's operations. Jacen Solo also assisted by reestablishing his link with the World Brain and using the planet itself to ease their passage.

Luke, Jacen, and Jaina at last penetrated the inner sanctum of Shimrra's palace. The Supreme Overlord and his capering jester Onimi sent a phalanx of Slayers against the Jedi trio, only to see their finest warriors struck down. Onimi fled,

pursued by Jaina. Shimrra launched himself at Luke, battering the Jedi with his amphistaff. Luke held him at bay, the Jedi's own lightsaber in one hand and Anakin's in the other. Luke burned through the amphistaff with the twin blades, then closed the tips together like a pair of shears, neatly severing Shimrra's head.

Onimi knocked Jaina unconscious and reached an escape ship. When Jaina regained her senses aboard the getaway vessel, Onimi revealed that he had been the power behind the throne all along. As a former master shaper who had grafted telepathic yammosk brain cells into his own cortex, Onimi was a literal puppet master who could force even Shimrra to do his bidding.

Millennium Falcon caught up with Onimi's fleeing craft, and Jacen came aboard to confront the true mastermind behind the invasion. Reaching deeper into the Force than any known Jedi had ever done, Jacen briefly became a "luminous being" of pure Force energy. The power proved too much for Onimi, who faded into oblivion.

Nom Anor could see the future, and it had no place for him. He had no loyalties to anyone except himself, and was unwilling to live in a galaxy where compromise was a way of life. Anor voluntarily rode Onimi's disintegrating ship back down to Coruscant, where it crashed into the surface.

With the battle lost, many vessels under Supreme Commander Nas Choka's command sacrificed themselves in suicide attacks against Galactic Alliance battleships. Choka, however, saw honor in survival. He ordered his surviving warships to stand down and signaled his willingness to discuss the terms of a Yuuzhan Vong surrender.

During the fighting, the ship from Caluula carrying an infected Yuuzhan Vong had reached Zonama Sekot. Yet Alpha Red, once released, had not withered the boras trees or blackened the grasslands. The planetary consciousness had nullified the virus, and now Sekot called its children home. Yuuzhan Vong who set foot on the planet realized that this world held answers that they had sought their entire lives, answers not to be found within their hierarchy of butcher gods.

Sekot announced the planet's intention to return to the Klasse Ephemora system in the Unknown Regions, taking as many Yuuzhan Vong as were willing to come. Tahiri Veila, Danni Quee, and the Chadra-Fan Jedi healer Tekli agreed to make the journey as well.

Coruscant had been abandoned by the New Republic two years before; now it was reclaimed by the new Galactic Federation of Free Alliances. Cal Omas appointed Admiral Traest Kre'fey as Supreme Commander of the Galactic Alliance military. The government immediately set to work restoring the HoloNet.

The Galactic Alliance moved its provisional capital from Mon Calamari to industrialized Denon in the Inner Rim, until Coruscant could once again be made hospitable. Jacen Solo convinced the World Brain to slowly reverse the terraforming it had wrought, though it was clear to everyone who arrived that the greening of Coruscant would never be truly eliminated.

The time came for farewells. Admiral Ackbar, who had died of advancing age prior to the battle for Coruscant, received a hero's funeral on his homeworld. Jagged Fel returned to Chiss space in the Unknown Regions, though his new position as Chiss liaison to the Galactic Alliance would give him plenty of opportunities to visit Jaina. Jacen Solo left on a personal journey, becoming a Jedi wanderer, not bound by the strictures of his uncle Luke's new Jedi order. Jacen intended to seek out other schools of thought regarding the Force in order to deepen his understanding of the immensity of the unifying Force.

Leia received a gift from Admiral Pellaeon—*Killik Twilight,* the Alderaanian moss-painting Leia had sought on Tatooine two decades prior. Han received his own "gift" in the form of Lowbacca, who, along with Chewie's son Lumpawaroo, had pledged to continue Chewbacca's life debt to Han, whether the Corellian liked it or not.

Luke Skywalker battles Supreme Overlord Shimrra to the death.
[ART BY TOMMY LEE EDWARDS]

THE KILLIK EXPANSION
35–36 A.B.Y.

The galaxy had restructured itself. But as often happens, smoothing out one spot had raised wrinkles in another. The Unknown Regions had been left relatively unscarred by the Yuuzhan Vong advance, leaving some of its more obscure species in an unexpected position to upset the balance of power.

The insectile Killiks had long existed in a private pocket of the Unknown Regions, following their abandonment of Alderaan more than thirty millennia in the past. The Yuuzhan Vong had not disturbed them, but the Killik colony had been stirred into a state of frenzy by the accidental arrival of three of the war's castaways.

In 27 A.B.Y., during the Jedi strike mission against the worldship *Baanu Rass* orbiting Myrkr, the Nightsister-allied Lomi Plo and Welk had fled the battle with Jedi Knight Raynar Thul as their captive. Believed to have become casualties of war, the three had in fact crashed their stolen craft in the heart of Killik space. Like sugar melting in water, the three became absorbed into the Killik collective mind. From Lomi Plo, the Colony learned paranoia, and concealed her in a Dark Nest, where she became their Unseen Queen. From Welk, the Colony acquired his devotion to Lomi Plo; Welk became the phantom-like Night Herald, the Unseen Queen's guardian. From Raynar, the Colony gained an understanding of individual value. Raynar became the "Jedi lord" emissary of all the nests that made up the Killik Colony. As a public figure, Raynar helped conceal the sinister subconscious represented by the Dark Nest.

The influence of these three outsiders led to a Killik population boom. The insects ravaged world after world like a swarm of leafhoppers, eventually bringing them to the border of the Chiss Ascendancy. The territorial dustup between the Chiss and the Killiks now threatened to become a galactic-scale whirlwind.

The first hint of trouble came when the Jedi veterans of

Raynar Thul, spokesbeing for the Killik hive mind
[ART BY TOMMY LEE EDWARDS]

the Myrkr mission, including Jacen and Jaina Solo, received a Force summons from Raynar. Reuniting with their friend in the Unknown Regions, they allowed themselves to be influenced by the Killik hive mind, and began leading missions against the Chiss. Naturally, this didn't sit well with the Chiss, who threatened war against the Galactic Federation of Free Alliances if the attacks continued.

Luke Skywalker killed Welk, the Night Herald, and Leia Organa Solo secured a temporary cease-fire by arranging for the Killiks to move into a cluster of uninhabited planets in the Paradise Nebula. The experience prompted Leia to once again take up the path of the Jedi, a life decision she had been putting off for decades. She selected the Barabel Jedi Saba Sebatyne as her Jedi Master.

The state of détente between the Killiks and the Chiss lasted for a year. But Jacen Solo, the new Jedi order's wandering mystic, received a terrifying vision of an impending Chiss invasion. If the assault came to pass as he had foreseen it, the resulting Killik counterattack would sweep across Chiss space and eventually reach all edges of the galaxy, embroiling every culture in an endless war.

Jacen and several other Jedi, including his sister, rallied to prevent the Chiss from ever launching their first attack. Jaina found herself fighting her former love, Jagged Fel. Alema Rar, the Twi'lek Jedi who had led New Plympto resistance against the Yuuzhan Vong, became the new Night Herald of the Dark Nest. The Galactic Alliance, eager to maintain good relations with the Chiss, sent Commodore Gavin Darklighter and several Star Destroyers to enforce a blockade of Killik space. Tensions escalated when the Killiks hijacked a Star Destroyer. The incident put the Killiks and the Galactic Alliance in a state of war. The experience led Luke to an epiphany. In his efforts to structure a new Jedi order in which everyone felt engaged and important, he had neglected to provide one critical element: leadership with vision. With an eye to the future, Luke hoped to bring a new era of peace to the galaxy, thus upholding the grand legacy of the Force that has continued for over a thousand generations.

Route Key

▬▬▬▬▬	Hydian Way
▬▬▬▬▬	Corellian Trade Spine
▬▬▬▬▬	Rimma Trade Route
▬▬▬▬▬	Corellian Run
▬▬▬▬▬	Perlemian Trade Route

Ilum

Csilla

Klasse Ephemora

Rakata Prime

Unknown Regions

N'zoth

Byss

Abregado

Giju

Fondor

Core Worlds

Ghorman

Kiffex

Colonies

Devaron

Bestine

Inner Rim

Thyferra

Lwhekk

Rattatak

Kooriva

Cerea

Yag 'Dhul

Bakura

Expansion Region

Derra IV

Endor

Kinyen

Vandelhelm

Mid Rim

Nkllon

Lorta

Haruun Kal

Outer Rim

Sullust

Bespin

Tibrin

Malastare

Anoat

Eriadu

Naboo

Hoth

Clak'dor

Mustafar

Sluis Van

Bpfassh

Praesitlyn

Polis Massa

Dagobah

Svivren

Alzoc

Subterrel

Utapau

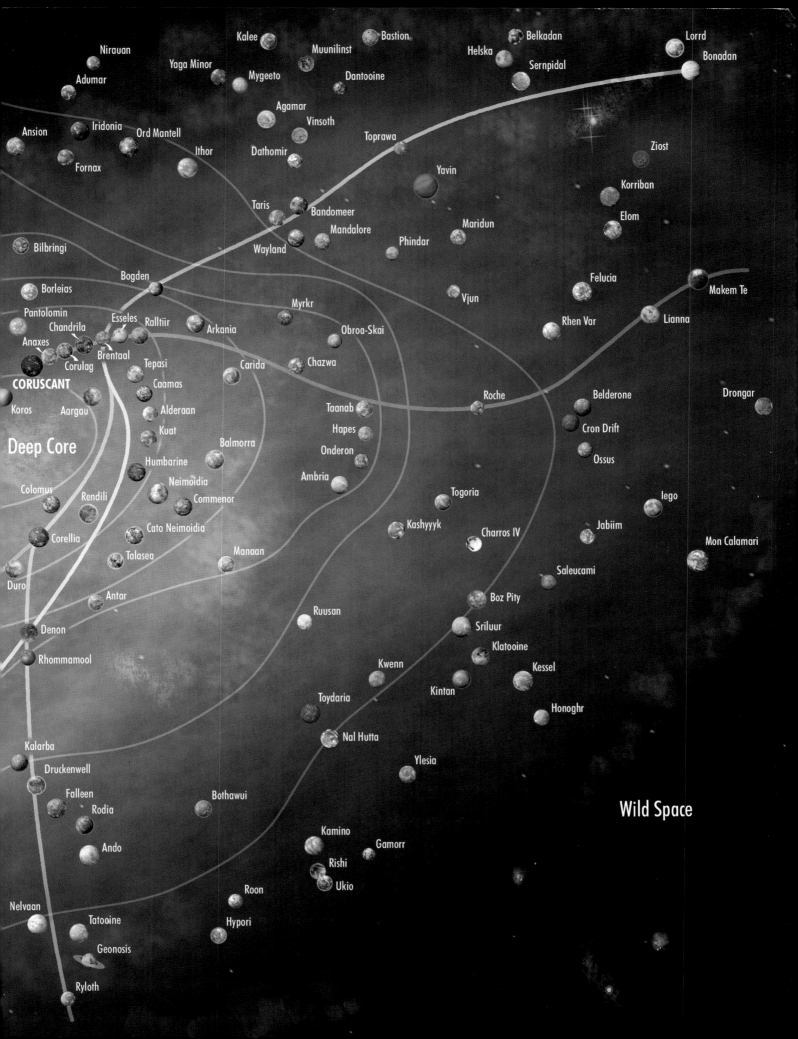

R2-D2 and C-3PO
[ART BY MARK CHIARELLO]

INDEX